Vigil

Vigil: a period of time to keep watch; to keep awake and pray, especially during darkness

A village church faces the reality of spiritual warfare.

Veronica M. Podbury

Faithbuilders Publishing
12 Dukes Court, Bognor Road,
Chichester, PO19 8FX, United Kingdom
www.faithbuilderspublishing.co.uk

ISBN: 978-1-913181-81-9

Formatted by Faithbuilders Publishing
Cover by Esther Kotecha, EKDesign
Printed in the United Kingdom

Contents

Main Characters

Revd James Gilchrist	Vicar of Appleton and Netherton
Anna Gilchrist	James' daughter, recently graduated
Hilda Marshall	Lives in Netherton, eighty-two
Morag McCulloch	Close friend of Hilda
Martin Fielding	Executive officer, Bluebird Design and Construction in Exton Bluebird Design and Construction
Jonah Forman	Master craftsman, twenty-four
John Miller	New Master of the Guild
George Wright	Landlord of The Mason's Arms
Meg Somers	Works part-time at The Mason's Arms
Harold Williams	Senior member of the Guild
Fred and Susan Roland	Senior executive officers at Bluebird Design and Construction
Mia	Owner of Moonstone Crafts
Malcolm and Barbara Morton	Villagers, Netherton
Mike Small and Geoff Crawshaw	Members of the Guild
Rob Beccles and Tim Hallthorpe	Old schoolfriends of Jonah

"Awake and strengthen what remains." (Revelation 3:2)

Chapter One

"What was that?" She stopped to listen, her hands still in the soapy water. Her ears, dulled by age, were straining to pick up an unusual sound – not the wind in the chimney of the cottage as the storm increased, but another sound from deep in the ground. It stirred something in her memory, from childhood years... the sound of the river which ran beneath the streets of the village.

She dried her hands quickly, a sense of foreboding growing in her, then put on her raincoat and stepped outside into the gale. Beneath the wind's roar was the gushing sound of the river deep in the ground, the River Ishka at its most aggressive, forcing its way along beneath the streets of Netherton. At the end of the village, where the river emerged from the ground, an old stone bridge crossed the river giving access by foot to a high outcrop of land on which stood an ancient church; this was where she was heading.

Struggling against the force of the gale, Hilda made her way along the High Street and arrived at the bridge, bracing herself against the wind. She gazed at the torrent of water rushing toward the bridge, crashing against its two stone pillars. The pillars consisted of individual stones, packed tightly together, holding up heavy planks of wood fitted into the pillars and spanning the width of the river. Usually, the surface of the water was well below the wooden planks, but in the half-light of evening she could see the flow of water had risen up and was battering against its structure. How long before the bridge gives way? she wondered.

At that moment, the howling wind increased its power, forcing her backwards. She staggered, then retreated, clutching at gateposts and fences as she retraced her footsteps back to her cottage in the gathering darkness.

All night the storm continued. The electricity supply failed and all the villagers sat in darkness, rain driving against the windows. On the other side of the surging river, the power of the storm was even greater. The wind was howling round the old church of St Brannock, tearing at the roof. The timbers holding it in place creaked as the wind tried to force its way inside. In the stillness of the interior, however, all was quiet and calm. An occasional flash of lightning lit up the stone altar with its simple cross, and the inscription, *I will build my church and the gates of hell shall not prevail against it.* The heavy oak door stood firm against the onslaught of the storm, protecting the sanctuary which had been hallowed by centuries of prayer.

*

At 3.30am, a helicopter flew low over the village, its loudspeaker announcing, "This is the Fire and Rescue Service. Do not try to leave your homes. Flooding is imminent. Stay upstairs for the duration of the storm."

By lunchtime the following day the water in the village streets was already receding and the dark grey clouds had parted, revealing a pale sun. Most of the houses, including Hilda's, had been spared the encroachment of water flowing down off the hillside and out of the overflowing river but some cottages had suffered considerable damage. At one o'clock, she left her cottage and waded through the few inches of water still flowing down the High Street. She returned to the same spot as yesterday during the storm, but today the Ishka and the bridge looked very different. The water was no longer an angry torrent; it had settled into a fast-flowing grey stream contained by the steep river banks, but the centuries-old bridge had been destroyed, blasted apart by the strength of the water. here was no way across.

*

A few hours later, the landlord of the Mason's Arms, the only pub in the village, opened up as usual at six o'clock. He went outside and hung up the wooden board advertising the bar menu of burgers and chips, steak pie and chips, haddock and chips (caught fresh today) and local ales – Bishop's Brew, Ishka Special Ale, Master Mason's Bitter. Nobody ever questioned whether the fish really was caught fresh every day; it was enough for the locals that they got cheap hot bar food and decent beer – they weren't interested in where it had come from.

Before long, the first customers arrived, keen to tell stories of the previous night's drama, and to enjoy the strangeness of wading through the last of the muddy water which had threatened to invade their pub. They stamped their feet in their clumsy wellingtons on the mat by the door, and then continued into the bar, walking much of their mud in with them.

"All right then, George?" Mike Small called out to the landlord as he and his friend took up their regular places on the bar stools. "Yes, pretty much business as usual," replied George, pulling Mike a pint of bitter without needing to ask for his order – he knew what his regulars liked. "The Ishka does this every seventy-five years or so, that's what everyone says."

The other man, Geoff Crawshaw, banged his fist on the bar laughing, "Well, give us a pint of Ishka Special then to celebrate! It didn't come into my cottage anyway."

"Lucky for you, but don't let anyone else hear you celebrating if they've just had their carpets ruined." He nodded in the direction of a small group of tired-looking people coming in through the door. Crawshaw looked over his shoulder at the group, then turned back to watch his beer flowing into the pint glass. "Bet you'll have a lot in this evening, George – with no electricity still, it's much cosier in here."

George Wright nodded. It was true; the Mason's Arms, with its own emergency generator, should pull in plenty of extra trade while much of the village was without power. He tried to avoid sounding too cheerful, "Yes – we'll just have to make the best of it." He moved on quickly to the next customer. "What can I get for you, sir?"

All through the evening, more people arrived at the pub. Some had intended to stay at home, making do with candlelight, but as the evening went on had given in and hurried along to the Mason's to share their troubles with their neighbours.

From early evening, some young men had occupied one of the round tables near the window. Rob Beccles, Tim Hallthorpe and Jonah Forman had been friends since primary school days. All were now in their early twenties, in that period before responsibilities caught up with them. They spent many evenings in the Mason's Arms, drinking beer and playing darts. At half past ten, Jonah, dark-haired and strongly-built, felt a tap on his arm. A sudden waft of perfume hit his nostrils, "Hi there, Jonah." A girl's face appeared at his shoulder, "I suppose it's too late for you to come out to play?" she simpered.

"Go away, Sandy," he pulled his arm away from her grip.

"Come on, Jonah, you've been playing darts with the boys, now it's time to play with the girls."

Rob and Tim howled with laughter, "Go on, Jonah, get in there mate! Don't miss your big chance!" They slapped him on the back, while he reddened with annoyance and grunted at the girl through

9

gritted teeth, "*Go away,* you sound like you're had too much to drink."

Sandy tossed her head and pulled her fake fur jacket tighter round her thin shoulders, "Please yourself, loser!" She flounced away.

"Got your eyes on better than Sandy, then?" persisted Rob. "She's about the best you'll get around here," he sniggered.

"I've got to go anyway," said Jonah, "Got to be in work early. I've got a new commission to get started on."

"A new commission – sounds very grand. You're not getting above being with your old schoolmates, are you?"

Tim joined in sarcastically, "You've got to remember, Rob, he's got his own business – not just an ordinary tradesman like us."

"Come off it," countered Jonah, "Both of you will probably start up your own business soon, won't you?" "Maybe, maybe not. Just so long as we're earning enough beer money, that'll do for us simple folk." The mocking tone sharpened, "For those among us getting more *elevated* tastes, well, who knows what people like that'll get up to next – I wouldn't know, above my league." He laughed and held up his glass, which was almost empty, "Time for another round."

Jonah got up, "See you then." For months now he had been experiencing a sense of impatience with the other young men: he sometimes wondered if his old friends would ever change.

Chapter Two

A day and a night had passed since Monday night's storm. Hilda woke at half past seven as usual, got up and went to the window, pulling the curtain aside to check the weather. It was a fine clear morning. "Thank you, dear Lord, for this lovely morning," she said quietly. "It will help the people with their drying out." She put on her blue woollen dressing gown and sat down on the small chair next to the window, wanting to start the day consciously in God's presence. She committed the new day to him, reading some Bible verses and giving thanks for all her blessings. Then she prayed for the people of Netherton, that they would become aware of their true identity, as people created by God who would only find lasting peace when they turned to him. Finally, she prayed for the old church on the hill, that it would continue to be a beacon of true faith to the area. A quarter of an hour passed quickly, and she went down to the kitchen for breakfast.

At nine o'clock she telephoned her friend to ask her to come for a walk. By half past ten, Hilda and Morag were standing next to the river, looking sadly at the place where the bridge had, until two days ago, linked the village to the small church on the hill on the far side of the water. They watched the grey water of the River Ishka racing past them, impassable.

"I can hardly believe it, Morag; the storm has completely destroyed the old bridge, almost nothing left of it."

"Perhaps it's for the best in the long run; we can't keep trekking up that hill forever, can we?" Morag took a pragmatic approach in all circumstances. Her native city of Edinburgh had left a lasting imprint on her; stoicism mixed with equal amounts of gentility and believing in the "right way" of doing things. Thankfully, she also had a very pleasant sense of humour. Morag looked across the tumbling water to the track which led up to the small church standing on a promontory, looking out over the county.

Hilda's eyes were already fixed on the stone church. She spoke thoughtfully, "So many things are just for a period of time. But this church still has a job to do. It *must* continue to be here, standing up on the hill, watching over this county, and accessible to people, and pilgrims."

"Goodness me, Hilda, you sound very serious!"

"I take it very seriously – I really do." She looked down into the water of the Ishka, "And you, Ishka, will not block the way to this holy place."

Morag was watching her friend, "Are you feeling all right? I think perhaps the shock of it all has got to you. Shall we go back now and sit down with a cup of tea?"

Hilda looked round at her, her eyes bright, "We can certainly have a cup of tea, but as for '*going back and sitting down*', I don't think that's a good idea at all." Hilda smiled quietly, amused at the hidden implication of her words. "Don't worry, I haven't 'lost the plot'! In fact, I think I have just this moment found it!" A bold idea had begun to form in her mind, the determination to resist the destruction of the last few days, and to fight for the continued presence of the pilgrims' church.

They walked back together, passing cottages with various household items still put outside to dry, the muddy tidemark still clearly visible on the exterior cottage walls. Morag paused, "I do hope they'll be all right, the old cottages. How awful to see them like this."

"They'll be fine – they're old, but they're good quality – good for many more years of service yet!" Hilda said emphatically, chuckling at her at her own private joke. Her friend watched her, frowning, wondering for a moment if the trauma of the storm had triggered the onset of senility.

*

Thirty miles away from Netherton, Martin Fielding, twenty-nine years old, slim, stylish and in a hurry, got out of his top-of-the-range Lexus in the car park of Bluebird Design and Construction, already talking on his iPhone, "Tell them to shift their ---!" He was almost shouting, slamming the car door. Then he noticed one of the staff watching him as she locked the door of her car. He turned the phone away from his mouth to speak to her, "Hello, sweetheart, sorry, just a bit stressed this morning!"

The girl smiled at him, "Good morning, Mr Fielding." She hurried towards the door of the building. She always treated him with careful deference, not liking to get too close to him. It was a shame; he had film star good looks, she thought, but something about him scared her. It lay beneath the surface – he had never shouted at her, or even been impatient, but she sensed anger in him beneath the smooth facade.

As the girl disappeared through the main door of the building, Fielding continued the conversation on his phone, his voice rising again, "I won't accept that! Lean on them, let them know there is no point in being awkward. They might as well give in quickly – it'll come to the same thing in the end. Who do they think they are, taking us on, the pathetic -----s!"

Once again Bluebird was seeking to expand its empire by various means, buying pieces of land, taking over smaller companies, sometimes by putting them under so much pressure that they gave in against their own interests, aware that they could not withstand the aggressive methods of the larger company. It was part of Fielding's job description to watch for opportunities to buy any properties standing on land which was likely to have future development potential. Like a bird of prey sitting high up on a tree, he scanned the area, and whenever he caught sight of a victim, would swoop in for the kill, relentlessly pursuing it. Everyone always wanted a good deal, plenty of money on the table. It was his job to drive a hard bargain, ruthlessly applying pressure wherever he could. His boss always called their business method a twin-track approach – carrot and stick – if their target didn't respond quickly to the promise of a carrot, they would find an appropriate stick to beat them with. This was not generally spoken aloud, apart from in the privacy of the company boardroom.

He was still speaking into his phone as he walked into the boardroom, cutting the call short as soon as he saw Arnold Wheeler sitting at the end of the table, ready to chair the meeting. Two more board members arrived: Fred and Susan Roland. Fielding had always resented having a married couple at board level. He knew that they always stuck together, backing each other up, covering for each other's weaknesses. Together they might have been a threat to the boss's absolute dominance of the company except for the total awe in which they held him. The tightness of these relationships left Fielding always feeling like an outsider, outnumbered, second-class, the junior member.

Arnold Wheeler coughed, signifying they were about to start. His voice was rasping – an unattractive Northern accent, impatient, scornful, "Fielding – I want you to update us on progress." Fielding reached for his laptop, flipping open its case, ready to open his presentation which was set up to be projected on to a section of wall.

"No, no, no!" snapped Wheeler. "Just tell us – I don't have time for all the fancy stuff, just give us the facts."

Fielding smiled, glossing over his annoyance. He had spent four hours the previous evening putting together his presentation. He knew when Wheeler was in this mood he would only get three or four minutes at the most to outline latest developments. He started, "We have three possibilities for prime land developments. Firstly, a stretch of privately-owned coastline, it used to belong to a film star; the word on the grapevine is it's coming up for sale. Secondly, a stretch of moorland with a shooting lodge – could be right for development into a high-class recreational facility. Thirdly, a strange one, heard about it from someone at the squash club, the possibility of getting hold of a large section of a country estate, evidently the family haven't lived there for years. It's perfectly positioned within commuting distance of two major business centres, and—"

"Good," cut in Wheeler. "Problems? There are always *problems*." He looked across at Fielding, a mocking expression on his face.

Fielding hesitated, clearing his throat, wrong-footed by his boss's interruption, then tried again, "First option, the coastline; we need to know if we could get planning permission to develop – could be difficult – it's a designated area of outstanding beauty. Road links and access on to the site are very poor... Second possibility, the hunting lodge; it would need a lot of investment and the potential profits would be good, but it could be a long time before we built up the clientele into sufficiently big numbers. Third one, if we got planning permission for building executive mansions – six, seven, eight bedrooms, or even a mixed dwelling housing development, we could capitalise on incredible countryside views etc. within easy reach of cities. Bluebird could make billions—"

"Is that a problem then?" sneered Wheeler. The old man's in a filthy temper this morning, thought Martin, carefully concealing his exasperation at being treated in such a derisory fashion.

"Apologies, Arnold, of course you're right, '*the problem*,' that's what you want to know about." Martin tried to keep the tinge of sarcasm in his voice almost hidden but Wheeler, like a bloodhound, sniffed it out, jerking up his head and fixing his small eyes on him, firing out, "Fielding! Don't try to get smart with me, remember who keeps your bread buttered!" Wheeler's accent became rougher when he was angry.

Yes, remember, thought Martin, itching to say, *It's me who does all the legwork for Bluebird, making deals, arranging backhanders. Without my efforts, there wouldn't be much butter at all.* But Wheeler maintained nobody was indispensable, anyone could be squashed like a fly if they got in his way.

Fielding adopted his most conciliatory expression and continued. "The problem is that the country estate land, assuming the owners are willing to sell, may have restrictions on its use. There is a very old church, built by the landowning family. It is sitting on the most attractive part of the estate, with views across the county."

Wheeler narrowed his eyes, "We could stick a wall round it. No one need know it's there. But then, some sentimental types might actually *like* having an old ruin nearby – it could even increase the value of houses. But then there would probably be Health and Safety restrictions, or some such rubbish. But that aside, this development sounds like it might just be the goose that lays the golden egg. Or a lot of golden eggs even!" He laughed coarsely, pleased at his own joke, and stood up. "Keep looking into it, Fielding – I'm off to the golf club now; just time for nine holes before lunch. Keep up the good work folks. Progress report on this table by Friday morning. Chop, chop!"

Wheeler had already gone through the door before Susan Roland said quietly, with a touch of pique, "And good morning to you too, Arnold, so nice to spend time together."

Fred looked at her, surprised at her boldness, then said, "We'd better sort out some business." He opened his file, stuffed with documents to be discussed. They spent another hour making decisions about mundane matters to do with the day-to-day running of Bluebird Design and Construction. Much of the work was delegated to people lower down the pecking order, but Fred and Susan always liked to keepinvolved at quite a detailed level. Sometimes Fielding felt they knew far more than him about the internal working of the company, but when it came to who held the reins, there was never any doubt that Wheeler was kingpin. Fielding was the member of the team who was expected to fix things, to make things happen, but he was always at arms-length; Fred and Susan had known Arnold since they were young, and they had somehow formed an alliance with him, which Martin knew he could never join.

*

The same morning, in the village of Appleton, two miles away from Netherton, Reverend James Gilchrist unlocked the heavy oak door of St Gregory's. He glanced at his watch, only ten minutes before Morning Communion was due to start. He was late. Strange that there was no sign of anybody about. The same faithful band of church members turned up each time, arriving a few minutes before the service began. This morning all was quiet, only his own footsteps echoed as he walked down the central aisle of the church. Perhaps it was the effect of the storm, people still needing to repair the damage. At St Gregory's there was a congregation of about sixty people, split between the small group who attended the early morning communion services on Sundays and Wednesdays, those who preferred the lively family service at half past ten on Sunday mornings, and those who came to the monthly choral Evensong. There was very little mixing of the different groups apart from special events, but here at St Gregory's this did not cause division, instead there was peaceful co-existence.

James also had responsibility for the neighbouring village of Netherton, which seemed to be living in difficult times. The Anglican church there had a very small elderly congregation. James held services there on Sunday evenings; many years ago, there were morning services too, and a Sunday School, but numbers had steadily dwindled until it hadn't been worth continuing the morning services. All the children had stopped coming, and the few older people left were content with just an evening service. More recently, the parish church council had discussed whether fortnightly services would suffice during the winter in order to save on the heating bills. So far, James had managed to dissuade them from reducing the number of services any further. He pondered the reduction in Christian presence in the locality. The familiar words from the Gospel of Matthew about followers of Jesus Christ ran through his mind: "You are the light of the world. A city located on a hill cannot be hidden. People do not light a lamp and put it under a basket but on a lampstand, and it gives light to all..." The witness of Christians in this area was far from a light to all, raised up for all to see. Thinking about an elevated Christian presence reminded him of the old church outside Netherton, St Brannock's. Certainly it was high up, standing on its hill, looking out over the area. It had a beacon tower too. Someone long ago had thought about this, of the need for the church to be seen, a shining light in the dark landscape.

James looked at his watch – minutes had passed while he was deep in thought. He had finished his preparations to celebrate communion, and was about to continue alone when the heavy latch of the church door made its familiar loud *click!* Two of the regulars hurried in.

"Sorry!" they whispered to him.

No others arrived, so the three of them proceeded through the familiar phrases, using the well-worn service books, with the early morning sun reaching them through the stained-glass windows.

Half an hour later, James was already setting off along the path in the direction of the vicarage. In the vicarage kitchen, his daughter Anna had started to cook breakfast. "In here, Dad! Bacon and eggs nearly ready!"

James inhaled the aroma as he hurried through the hallway, thinking how good it was that Anna was home again for a while. Since his wife died three years ago, he had become resigned to living most of the time in an empty vicarage. It was only during university vacations, when his daughter returned, often bringing friends with her, that some comfort and warmth filled the emptiness of the house again. Now she was spending a year based at home again, having completed her degree in Textiles and Design, while she attempted to set up her own business.

"How did it go, Dad?"

"Oh, fine, not many people there today. Not sure why. Perhaps related to Monday night's storm – people still clearing up."

"I should have come across to swell the numbers. I was awake but just didn't get up quickly enough. Next Wednesday I will."

James cut his bacon up thoughtfully, "Hmm, that would be good, Anna. I just don't want things here to start going downhill like Netherton."

"Netherton's not like here Dad. Different people, different atmosphere."

"Yes, I'm sure you're right." He looked unconvinced.

Anna continued brightly, "I'm going into Exton later. There's a crafts shop there I want to visit – I've looked at their website and they sell all sorts of crafts designed by local artists and designers. I'm going to ask if they would stock some of my designs."

"Sounds promising. Is it a big place?"

"Won't know until I get there. I'll tell you all about it this evening over supper."

The telephone in the hallway rang. James went to answer it while Anna finished her breakfast, putting her father's into a warm oven to

17

keep for him. She could hear his voice, kind and calm, "Of course I'll come. I'm so sorry to hear of your loss.... Yes, I can come at the end of the afternoon, would that be convenient?" She could hear him taking down details; it must be a family who did not come to the church, but had experienced a sudden bereavement, and at that point contacted the local vicar. Always more difficult to meet a family for the first time when they were in sudden shock or distress, she thought, but it gave the church the chance to befriend people at a time of need. It was a shame that afterwards they sometimes associated the church with death and sorrow, and had no further contact, wanting to move on into happier times. Dad's job was not an easy one, she reflected.

Soon after breakfast Anna carried her portfolio of designs out to her small blue car, feeling hopeful. There was little traffic, and in just over half an hour she was driving down Forge Lane in Upper Exton, originally a village but now joined to the large town of Exton. She spotted the shop's sign without difficulty, its black Gothic lettering, "Moonstone Crafts," clearly visible with smaller writing underneath, "Arts for the discerning eye." Sounds interesting, she thought, and parked the car outside the shop. Before going in she paused for a moment to scan the display in the shop window, her heart sinking a little. There was a clutter of Native American wind-catchers, three well-worn Tibetan prayer wheels, some tie-dye scarves, and some crystals hanging from a twisted branch. She had got the impression from the shop's website that it sold original work from local designers, not just hippie-type paraphernalia. A strong smell of incense sticks greeted her as she went through the door. She almost turned around and left straightaway, but a voice stopped her, "May I help you?"

"I was just looking," said Anna, conscious that she had a conspicuous artist's portfolio case under her arm.

"Really?" said the woman behind the counter, "I thought for a moment you had some designs to show me." She pointed towards the portfolio.

"I did... happen... to bring some with me," Anna replied, aware she sounded hesitant, amateurish.

"Good," said the woman pleasantly, "I'm always willing to support local designers and craftspeople."

Anna opened the portfolio case and took out some boards with photographs of her designs and details of the materials used. She watched as the woman leaned over the samples of work, her long dark hair falling forward as she studied them.

"Interesting," said the woman. "How lovely that you use natural products – wool and handmade paper. Natural things have such beauty and... *life-force*, don't they?" She looked up from the photographs and fixed her eyes on Anna with an uncomfortable intensity.

"Yes... thank you." said Anna, feeling strangely under pressure.

The woman's dark eyes were studying Anna intently. Anna's feeling of discomfort increased and she began to close her portfolio just as the woman said, "Do you live nearby?"

"In Appleton, about thirty minutes' drive from here."

"I know the area. I belong to a group of artists and craftspeople that meet in the next village to you. It's very useful for connecting, and mutual support. Actually, you may be interested in coming along. It really helps when you're trying to get established."

"That sounds really good, thank you." Anna was interested in anything which could help to build up her fledgling business.

The woman held out her hand to her, "I'm Mia." She smiled, dark eyes sparkling.

"I'm Anna Gilchrist," said Anna, reaching across the counter to shake hands; she looked down at the cool white hand she was touching; it wore several rings, two inlaid with large, coloured stones and one simply a metal spiral with a small reptile's head, coiling round the ring finger.

Mia was speaking again," I really love the photographs, Anna, I'm sure I could stock some of your designs. If you'd like to come to one of the group meetings, we could talk about terms and conditions."

Anna couldn't believe it could be as simple as this to find a sales outlet for her work, "That's wonderful. I really appreciate it."

"Good. Write down your mobile number and address for me, and I'll pick you up the first time to make it easy for you to get to the place."

"Are you sure you don't mind?"

"Not at all," she replied, passing a notepad and pen across the counter.

Anna wrote down her contact details and returned the pad to Mia. She looked at the address, smiling, then said, "Take one of my little cards – it has my number on it." She put a small decorated card into

Anna's hand. It had the words *Mia at Moonstone Crafts, Beauty and Growth in Body, Mind and Spirit.*

"And I'll see you soon," she said brightly. "It's on Monday evening in Netherton Village Hall. Shall I pick you up just before seven?"

"Yes, thank you." Anna picked up her portfolio and left, feeling excited and a little apprehensive.

She drove back into Appleton feeling pleased with what she had achieved that morning. The sun was shining; she was smiling as she drove past the row of shops on Broad Street and decided to stop and get something special for tonight's supper to celebrate finding her first outlet for selling her designs. She went into the small butcher's shop and looked at the meat displayed. The steaks took looked well-matured, much more expensive than she would normally have paid but she decided a hearty steak with a glass of red wine was probably just what her father needed.

As she left the butcher's shop, she thought how pretty the village looked today. Opposite her, the duck pond shimmered in the autumn sunshine, and the nearby trees looked beautiful in all their shades of gold. She crossed the road and stood watching the ducks for a while as they glided along on the surface of the pale blue water. Across the pond was a row of houses, the last of which had a traditional wooden sign hanging from a wrought iron bracket. Inscribed on it were the words, "Jonah Forman, Master Craftsman. Showroom open every day. Individual commissions welcome."

She had never noticed the sign before. Intrigued, Anna walked over and looked through the window at the furniture on display. She pushed open the door and walked in. In the centre of the showroom stood a table with six high-backed chairs. The colour of the wood was a mellow pale gold, and the wood grain was beautiful, shown to perfection in the elegant lines of the tall slim chairs. Anna put out her hand to touch their satin-smooth surface. The design was unlike any she had seen before, somehow combining traditional with contemporary style to produce a uniquely attractive effect. At that moment she realised she was being watched.

"Oh, I'm sorry!" she said to the person watching her, without thinking what she was apologizing for.

"You're welcome to touch any of the pieces," said a low quiet voice, with a warm local accent. A young man was speaking to her from further back in the showroom.

"Thank you," said Anna, looking up at him, and colouring up, "Are they your work?"

"Yes, everything here is my work," said the young man.

"They're beautiful," said Anna, stretching out her hand again to touch another smooth curved surface. "They really are works of art, not just furniture.... You're Jonah Forman then?"

"I am. Just like on the sign." His serious expression softened into a smile, "I'm glad you like them. Most people just look at the price tag and think they can get a better bargain in some cheap chain store."

"Then they don't understand what they are looking at," said Anna firmly. "If I had any money, I'd love to buy something." She looked at him apologetically, "I understand what it's like – I design and make things too. My name's Anna, I'm trying to develop my own range of designs. You put something of your own soul into each piece, don't you? Completely different from something mass-produced."

Perhaps buoyed up by her success at Moonstone Crafts, Anna put out her hand towards Jonah, who had moved forward during their brief conversation. She sensed a connection; they were both artists, or at least skilled crafts workers, sharing the common experience of devoting themselves to creating beautiful objects often unappreciated by most people.

Jonah took her hand, shaking it, and she felt the roughness of his skin, dried and hardened from his work.

"I hope your business does really well," continued Anna, "You certainly deserve it."

Then her confidence deserted her, and she dropped his hand, feeling suddenly awkward. Who did she think she was, passing judgement on this stranger's work? Had she sounded patronising?

But he smiled at her again, seemingly pleased, taking her encouraging remarks in the spirit she had made them. They talked briefly about the difficulties of getting your work noticed by people who may like it, and then she turned to leave. She had reached the door when he stopped her, calling from the back of the showroom, "Wait a moment! Take this with you!" He was holding something in his hand as he walked towards her. It was an exquisite little box, beautifully carved. It opened smoothly, the wooden surfaces gliding over one another. On the back of the box, set into the wood, was his special mark, only about a centimetre long, the tiny carving of a candle.

"I couldn't take this!" she exclaimed, almost alarmed by the gesture.

"Yes you can – you *should* – you'll enjoy it."

"But it's worth a lot of money." She hesitated. The wooden box was lovely, and Jonah had already put it in her hand. She looked down at it, and then up at him. He was looking at her earnestly, she could tell this item was something he was particularly pleased with. She decided she couldn't refuse it.

"Thank you, it's beautiful." There was an awkward pause; Anna felt the moment had become almost intimate. Perhaps she had complimented him too much. Unsure what to do next, she looked at her watch, as though suddenly aware of the pressure of an appointment elsewhere, "Is that the time!" She looked up at him again, "Sorry, I must run."

She began to move away from him, "Are you really sure about the box?"

He nodded, "Of course, yes, you take it."

"Thank you," she said again, and reached the door gratefully. She shut the door behind her, breathing a sigh of relief.

*

When Anna got back to the vicarage, her father was out visiting some of his parishioners. She went into the kitchen to make a sandwich, still feeling flustered by her encounter with Jonah Forman. He wasn't like the male students she'd studied alongside at university – he was more mature, with his own business, already highly skilled. She doubted that he had taken a degree before starting work; she imagined he had spent time learning his craft steadily, perhaps as an apprentice. The sound of the vicarage phone cut into her reverie. She left the bread on the kitchen worktop and went to answer it.

"St Gregory's Vicarage?"

A quavering voice at the other end of the line said, "Hello? I wondered if the vicar was at home?"

"Not at the moment I'm afraid. He's out visiting. I daresay he'll be in before too long. Would you like to leave a message for him?"

"Oh, I hadn't thought about that," the voice became even more unsure, "I... well... it was just to let him know, in case he didn't know already, that the old church, St Brannock's, has been cut off by the storm. I know it's not really the vicar's responsibility, but I thought he should know... such a shame. Thank you." The line went dead. The old lady, whoever she was, had not given a name, or number, but that wasn't unusual; all sorts of calls came through to the vicarage, from all sorts of people, not necessarily connected to St Gregory's, but who felt "the vicar should know" about some local event or occurrence, probably of more concern to the caller than anybody else.

Anna returned to the kitchen. Shame about the old church. The storm seemed to have caused all sorts of damage. She doubted there was anything her father could do about it, and besides, was there any point in keeping a place like that open? The church here could do with a bigger congregation; shouldn't Christians from Netherton just come over to St Gregory's to attend services instead of struggling to keep their own little parish church open part-time, as well the old pilgrims' church?

She switched the radio on, then sat down at the kitchen table to eat her late lunch. A discussion programme was being introduced; a bishop, a politician, a retired headteacher and a nurse were to discuss "Religion and Spirituality: Good, Bad or Irrelevant?" She listened to the soothing voice of the bishop, insisting that the church had a place still, giving a sense of continuity through the stages of life, "Hatching, matching and dispatching!" he quipped. The politician countered with claims of the urgent need to update our notions of the important life issues: self-awareness, mindfulness and self-empowerment were the essentials to leading a full and meaningful life, he claimed. The old intolerant, narrow way of thinking had to go, and an enlightened way be embraced.

The retired headteacher, drawing upon her long experience, said she had concluded that the acquisition of knowledge and understanding of the world made religion largely unimportant, "Knowledge is power!" she intoned, although she added that she liked to go to church at Christmas.

Only the nurse had much to say in favour of spiritual things. She said she had been with hundreds of people as they passed out of this world, and those who had the assurance of believing God loved them and would receive them tended to have much more peace.

"Self-delusion!" scoffed the politician, "Cheap comfort for desperate people."

"Doesn't that sound a bit narrow and intolerant?" asked the nurse.

Anna laughed and turned the radio off, then made some coffee to take upstairs to the room which she liked to think of as her studio.

James had visited three elderly ladies by four o'clock and was feeling tired. The effort of just making himself heard was exhausting, especially with Dorothy Clayton and Maud Clutterbuck, both being very deaf. He always prayed with each of these elderly women towards the end of his visit, but often ended up almost shouting, "Father, I ask for your PEACE and BLESSING and STRENGTH!" It detracted a little from the sense of God's peace and presence that he hoped Dorothy or Maud would feel. Once, when he had prayed about Dorothy's bad back, she interrupted, asking was he praying about haddock? Perhaps she was feeling hungry, he thought, and patted her hand, and shouted a bit louder.

His final visit of the afternoon was to the Miller family, on a farm which lay a short distance outside the village of Netherton. The grandfather had died during the night. Contrary to most people's wishes in these present days, the family did not want the body moved yet, but had laid the body out in a room downstairs in the farmhouse. James felt somewhat apprehensive about the visit. It was the daughter of the deceased who had telephoned the vicarage; she had commented that their family normally "never darkened the door of a church," but nevertheless required the services of the local church now. James only knew the family by reputation, and that was not a promising one. There were Millers in several of the villages and towns in the area. They were involved in a variety of trades and businesses, and local people knew not to cross them. There were rumours from time to time of dubious and underhand methods but nothing ever seemed to come to court.

He got out his map to look for Mill Farm. He could see his route there would involve going a considerable distance on single track roads, climbing gradually higher. He tried to memorise the turns and junctions of the lanes, and then laid the map down on the passenger seat next to him and started the engine.

He wondered if the family name Miller was derived from the farm, perhaps there had been a mill there for centuries. Ten minutes later, as he drove carefully round a bend on the potholed lane leading up to the farm, the outline of a derelict windmill came into view. The remains of the wooden sails were scattered around, apparently where they had fallen, and the mill's brickwork was beginning to crumble away. A picture of neglect, what a shame, James thought; if someone had given the windmill some care and attention it could have been transformed into a lovely home. Too late now, it was ruined.

The windmill occupied a prominent site, elevated into the wind. From the top window you would be able to see out over the landscape for miles. James parked the car, then stood for a moment looking up at the windmill before he walked over to the farmhouse, past the shabby outbuildings. He approached the door of the farmhouse feeling uneasy, wondering what the Millers would be like. He knocked tentatively then took a step backwards, waiting. The door began to open at the same moment as the sound of a large dog barking started, and a mangy-looking animal ran out of one of the outbuildings towards him. It ran unevenly, one of its legs shorter than the rest, and James glimpsed a torn ear as the animal got closer, now snarling.

"Come in, Vicar," said the person at the door, standing back to let James step in. Just in time, the dog's progress was blocked, and the inhabitant aimed a kick at the animal as it attempted to run through the door in pursuit.

James did not get a good look at his rescuer until he had stepped into the small dark entrance hall of the farmhouse. Standing on the stone floor, he looked into the face of one of the Miller family. *Was it Mr or Mrs?* he wondered. The person's voice had been rough, and fairly deep; the fleshy face had a considerable amount of long hairs growing from the chin and sprouting from the upper lip, but beneath it was a lumpy body wearing what appeared to be a woman's long green cardigan, with a kind of apron over it, slack navy blue trousers and tattered leather slippers. His or her hair was shoulder-length, grey, thin and straggly.

James held out his hand, "James Gilchrist, Vicar of St Gregory's."

"Jean Miller. John Miller's daughter. Mrs Miller to you."

A woman then, thought James, glad he hadn't addressed her as "Mr"… and she said she was Mrs…she must have kept the family name.

"I'm so sorry to hear about Mr Miller's demise."

"He's in here," said Jean Miller, opening a door to the room next to the entrance hall. She jerked her head at James, indicating that he should go in. His eyes took a moment to adjust to the gloom as he entered. In the centre of the room, he could see a long table, covered in a tablecloth. On top lay the body of John Miller, ninety-two, deceased, dressed in a black suit, arms by his sides. The curtains at the only window were half-closed, allowing only minimal light to have access. A tall unlit candlestick had been placed at either side of the corpse's head, unusual in the setting of a private home. James went over to look at the body; the skin was deathly white, as expected. There was a strange odour in the room which he could not identify.

"Mrs Miller, have you contacted an undertaker yet?"

"No, we'll keep him here tonight. We'll keep watch, that's our way."

James looked back at the brass candlesticks, thick wax candles in them, enough to last all night, he thought. He imagined the room with its dark wooden furniture, bare stone floor and thin rug as it would look that night in the darkness, lit only by the two candles. He shuddered slightly, but then wondered why, as he'd seen the bodies of many dead loved ones over the years. He reached into his pocket for the small Bible he always carried with him.

"Would you like me to pray over him?" he asked kindly.

"If you like. He won't hear you though!" Mrs Miller laughed; James was startled at the tone of it, was it awkwardness or embarrassment he detected, or derision?

He decided to pray anyway. He turned back to the body, and stood close to it, opening his Bible at Psalm 113 and read a few verses aloud: "From the rising of the sun to the place where it sets, the name of the Lord is to be praised."

Mrs Miller stood watching him, a faint smile flickering around her bristly face. A rustling by the fireplace caught his attention. He tried to pray, "Almighty God, I ask you for your peace—" His mouth became dry and he heard the rustling sound again, "and for your presence here with...."

Over in the corner a piece of paper, perhaps a letter, fell from the oak sideboard and fluttered down on to the floor, distracting him. The words James was trying to say felt stuck in his mouth, as though he could not get them out. He looked back at Jean Miller.

The smile flickered again.

"Amen," James managed to say, and closed his Bible.

"That was a short one."

"I..." James moved towards the door of the room, feeling cold, wanting to get out. "I think I'll go now." His mouth was dry, and he rubbed his forehead – he felt a sudden headache gripping him.

Back in the hallway, he put out his hand to grasp the handle of the front door, then remembered the dog.

"Would you hold on to your dog, please? I think when I arrived he wanted to take a chunk out of me."

He felt annoyed now, feeling he'd been made a fool of.

"Mick won't hurt you, Vicar, I won't let him, don't fret," she laughed her mirthless laugh again.

James opened the front door, then turned to face her, "Are you sure about wanting a funeral in church, Mrs Miller? A Christian funeral I mean?" He was aware he hadn't discussed anything to do with the funeral arrangements, but he wanted to get out of the farmhouse.

"It's our right. We've been here hundreds of years, our family, on this land. We've got people buried in the graveyards of all the villages around here. People know to respect us, and that's the way it will always be. We belong here."

"Would you come to the vicarage then, to talk about arrangements. I'm sorry, I must go now. You have my number." He began to sweat, despite feeling cold. He pulled the door wide open, and looked out anxiously, scanning the area in front of the farmhouse for any sign of Mick. There he was, about ten feet away, but James could see the dog was already fully occupied. It was crouching low on the ground, and a few inches from its mouth was a small creature squirming in the mud. It had been injured; on its side was an open wound. It made an attempt to get away, but the dog's teeth were bared and it made another swift attack, biting into its terrified prey, then dropping it and pulling back to crouch down and watch it again. The small furry animal squealed weakly and quivered. The dog snarled at it and settled down to watch its desperate struggles.

James glanced over his shoulder to see Jean Miller's reaction. Her lips were curled into an amused expression. She was enjoying this. Her eyes flicked from the dog and its prey to James, "He's entitled to his fun," she commented. "What's the point of not stringing it out a bit? Killing things is Mick's job."

James didn't reply. Careful not to go too close to the dog and its tormented prey, he made his way as quickly as he could back to his car. His fingers shook as he pulled his keys from his pocket. He fumbled as he tried to grasp his car key, and the whole bunch fell down on to the muddy ground. The sound attracted the attention of the dog. It raised its head and turned to stare at James. James grabbed his keys and pointed the car key at the door, clicking to unlock. The mechanism failed. The car remained locked. He tried again and again. He could see the car's lights flash as he clicked, but there was no corresponding clunking sound of the doors unlocking. *What was wrong with it?* James never opened his car manually with the key, he wasn't even sure it would work. He inserted the key into the door lock and turned. He heard the sound of the door unlocking. Thank God, he breathed, and pulled the door open, jumping inside quickly and slamming the door. He looked across at the dog. It was on its feet again, its head turned towards James, watching him steadily. James started the engine and began to move the car. Abruptly, the dog abandoned its quivering prey and leapt towards the car, bounding over on its uneven legs and throwing its full weight against the driver door window, crashing into the glass just inches from James' face. James flinched as the car shook with the force of the dog's attack. He accelerated hard, throwing up a spray of mud from the wheels. As he sped away, he shot a glance at the rear view mirror: the dog, left behind the car, was leaping into the air, barking angrily in the direction of the car. What if one of his wheels had run over the dog? What would the weird owner have done? At that moment he didn't care, he just needed to get away.

Chapter Three

So far it had been a very ordinary Friday morning at St Gregory's Vicarage. James had already made several phone calls about routine church matters, and had gone to the kitchen to make himself another mug of coffee. He was trying to concentrate on his Sunday sermon, but his mind kept wandering. He knew what he was trying to say, but it wouldn't take a proper shape. It felt like a muddle of separate ideas and points, with no order or connecting thread. What was wrong with him? He'd been like this since the incident at the Millers' farm; it had disturbed him in a way that he could not properly explain. He had tried to have some strong words with himself, "Come on, James, pull yourself together. You know how to do this!" But it hadn't helped; he felt muddled, confused. Anna was concerned about him. She followed him into the kitchen, and put her hand on his arm as he stood waiting for the kettle to boil, "Dad, are you OK?"

Putting his hand over hers, glad to feel the warmth of her affection, he murmured, "I'll be all right, just feeling a bit wobbly. Don't know why really."

"You'll have your fan club supporting you on Sunday – *me*, I mean! Oh, and the ladies from the Mothers' Union, who still regard you as a very nice young man!"

James couldn't help smiling; it was true, despite being fifty-three he was still "young" to this group of ladies in their seventies, eighties and even nineties!

He picked up his mug of coffee, feeling considerably better, and returned to his study. Half an hour later, James was sitting at his desk in the study, relieved that at last he was making some progress in his preparation for Sunday. From his desk he could see out over the drive and front garden, down to the double gate which was always open. Sometimes, when in meditative mood, he would gaze out of this window, watching the birds sitting on the stone birdbath in the centre of the lawn. This morning, however, his head was bent over his desk and sermon notes. What was it then, that made a feeling of unease pass over him, and cause him to look up suddenly, down the drive to the gate? Just as he did so, two people walked in through the open gate and began to walk up the drive. Before he could see the faces clearly, the shape of one of them seemed familiar – the powerfully built, almost masculine outline, and the thin straggly hair – Mrs

Miller. Next to her walked a tall thin young man, presumably her son.

As they got nearer, James could make out his thin rather mean-looking face, like a pale ferret, he thought. Although James thought he had hidden himself behind the curtain as he watched them, both of the Millers turned to look directly at him as they walked towards the front door. He jerked backwards from the window – too late to pretend he was out. Immediately he checked himself, what an inappropriate thought... these people, strange though they were, had come to see him, the vicar, God's representative. It was his duty to engage with them, not try to avoid them.

The doorbell chimed loudly. James heard Anna go to answer it, saying brightly as she opened the door, "Hello, have you come to see the vicar?"

He heard Mrs Miller's low rough voice reply, "Yes."

"Is he expecting you?"

"He should be, I said we'd come," was the rude response.

"Could you just wait here one moment; I don't remember my father mentioning he had an appointment this morning, but I'll just check to see if he's free."

Anna opened the study door and stepped in quickly, crossing over to her father and whispering, "Dad, there's an odd-looking couple wanting to see you. Should I bring them in here?" But as she spoke, the door was pushed open behind her, and Mrs Miller walked into the study, her son close behind her. Anna raised her eyebrows, "Actually, here they are already, Dad!"

Anna noticed the expression on her father's face as the Millers walked into the middle of the room. It was a mixture of distaste and fear. Who were these people? she wondered. "I'll be in the kitchen, Dad, if you need me," she said, feeling protective. Then, "In fact, shall I bring you all some tea?"

Mrs Miller gave her a withering look, as though tea at the vicarage was a ridiculous idea, "We won't be staying long."

Anna retreated from the study, leaving the Millers standing in the middle of the room despite James' invitation to sit down. Jean Miller looked around the room with something like a sneer on her face. On one wall, there hung a group of small reproductions of Greek and Russian Orthodox religious art, faces of Christ and the apostles, richly ornamented in glowing gold, and deep shades of blue and red. She curled her lip at them, then took in the framed extract from the

Lindisfarne Gospels on another wall, and finally, the cross which hung over the fireplace.

She had a shopping bag hanging on her arm. She took hold of it with both hands, moved towards James' desk and tipped the bag upside down. As James watched, several bundles of twenty pound notes fell out on to the desk. "That should cover expenses," she announced, "Whatever you want to charge for a funeral, and burial plot, and a big headstone with *this* on it." She handed him a folded scrap of paper. "We want it on Saturday, 2 o'clock. And the stone needs to be ready too, you've got one week." Her tone was rude, even aggressive. James unfolded the grubby looking piece of paper. On it was a rough sketch of an inscription for the gravestone,

John Seldon Miller
2nd January 1926 – 6th October 2018

Always remembered.

His name lives on in this county,
A prince among men.

Beneath the inscription was a sign or letter which he couldn't quite make out.Jean Miller was speaking again, "You'll see where all the Millers are. His wife is Zena Miller – put him near her, *obviously*." She spoke in a derisory way, as though James was stupid.

James opened his mouth to object to her more unreasonable demands, "Mrs Miller, firstly, stone masons normally take much longer than that, and the stone will be erected after the burial, and anyway, there's a way to do these things – I'm not sure I can just accept cash like this—"

"Why not? We like to use cash. Nobody refuses our money, you'll find, V*icar*. "She almost spat the word out.

Her son watched her and grinned, cracking his knuckles one by one, the sound making James wince. Meanwhile, Jean Miller was already moving towards the door; she clearly had no intention of talking any further.

James tried to delay her, "But what about hymns, and readings, Mrs Miller, and I need to ask for some information for the eulogy."

She turned to face him, stepping back towards him, and he caught a whiff of her foul breath as she spoke right into his face, "No hymns, no readings, and we don't want your eulogy. If we want to say something we'll say it. You've got the money – use it all – we want the biggest plot and headstone. Make sure you do it." Then she added, sarcastically, "*Please.*"

This time she was determined to leave without interruption. James was still following her, wanting some more details. She turned her head towards him once more, shouting over her shoulder at him, "And no b----- flowers!"

The son laughed at her expletive, and spoke for the first time, revealing stained brown teeth, "Bet you don't often hear that word in the vicarage!"

There was nothing James could do to stop them. They walked through the hallway, out of the front door and down the drive without speaking again. They had given their instructions.

Astounded, he sat down at his desk, heart pounding, his forehead resting on one hand. Anna found him in this position a few seconds later, "Dad! Are you all right? What an obnoxious pair – I could hear their voices from the kitchen." Then she noticed the bundles of notes on the desk, "Good grief! What's this? Are they gangsters or something?"

"God knows; I couldn't stop them giving it to me."

For the next ten minutes, James and Anna took the rubber bands off the bundles and counted each one. The total was eight thousand pounds. They looked at each other in dismay. It was like something from a film, bundles of notes being passed from one person to another in some underhand deal.

"What am I going to do with all that? They handed it over as though it was payment for some crooked transaction. It's not a donation to the church so I don't think I should include it with the normal money coming into the church; there's the burial plot to sort out, but most of it should go to the funeral director. Also, I don't like the thought of having the Millers' money on the premises."

"Ring the undertakers now," said Anna decisively. "The Millers must have spoken to them about the body. Ask them to come round as soon as possible, and see if they'll take the cash away with them."

*

As usual, George Wright carried the menu sign outside and placed it near the doorway of the Mason's Arms to attract customers. Ever since the night of the storm, business had picked up. People came to the pub to escape the effects of the storm and flooding, not just the physical mess, but the psychological distress, seeking comfort in talking it over again and again. It had generated camaraderie, even a buzz of excitement. As Wright pondered this, he smiled to himself. Long may it last, he thought, wiping the surface of the bar; he would milk the situation for everything he could get out of it.

At half past six, Mike Small and Geoff Crawshaw walked in through the door, earlier than usual. They took up their positions on the bar stools. Meg, who was cook, kitchen hand and barmaid all rolled into one low-paid, part-time job, was behind the bar, putting out some bar snacks. The landlord served the drinks and did most of the talking with the people. Meg only served behind the bar when there was a sudden rush of customers, which was not a frequent occurrence at the Mason's Arms.

"Evening Mike, evening Geoff. How are you?" Meg asked, always polite and friendly.

"We'll feel better with a pint of Bishop's inside us," said Mike. "Come on, girl, get them on the bar, fast as you like."

Meg, fifty-two and a grandmother, smiled at the term "girl." She hoped it was an indication that she still looked fairly youthful. She was by nature quiet and easy-going, so didn't find it hard to be patient with the customers, even when they were short-tempered or had drunk one pint too many. If anyone really needed to be put back in their place, she left it to George. He didn't hesitate to lay down the law, his own law, in his pub. She pulled two pints of beer, then started to turn round to unpack some small packets of peanuts. Mike Small, however, claimed her attention, "So, my love, what have you been doing lately?"

Meg hesitated. Her days were divided between working in the pub, helping with her two small grandchildren and the one or two evening groups which she attended. There was little time for anything else. Her husband had died several years ago during an evening game of football with a local team. He had always kept fit and was unaware of a congenital heart problem. At half-time he collapsed in the changing rooms, and Meg was made a widow at forty-five.

"Just the usual things," Meg answered, "My family, and the gardening club – that's about it. How about your family, Mike?"

She could guess how Mike would answer her question. It would involve indulging in a satisfying grumble.

"Fair to middling I suppose," said Mike, "You spend all your money on them and they're never grateful. My daughter's wedding cost *seven thousand pounds* last year. Daylight robbery. Now she wants a new kitchen. Just like the wife." He took a long slow drink of beer. Meg took her chance to move away further down the bar. Fortunately Geoff took over the role of listening ear.

"I know what it's like, mate. Just the same with me."

"You haven't even got a daughter," quipped Mike

"No, but my son's likely to be the same... if he ever gets married, that is, if he can get himself off his backside long enough to do anything!" Geoff laughed, "When I was his age, I'd been at work for seven years already, and was married with a kid."

"They don't know they're born these days."

They continued to enjoy a hearty session of criticizing the younger generation, only pausing when it was time to order another beer. The pub door opened, and two more people arrived, Malcolm and Barbara Morton, regulars at the Mason's Arms. Meg greeted them kindly, "Hello, Barbara. Hello Malcolm. How are you both?"

Barbara looked into Meg's face, sensing sympathy, "As well as can be expected, I suppose. I've had terrible backache since we were flooded. And the headaches... I saw the doctor, and there's nothing she can do, just increase the painkillers."

"And she told you to try to relax, love. That's the thing, try not to worry," said Malcolm gently.

"Malcolm, *don't* go on. You're making my head ache more."

"Sorry dear, just trying to help."

"Well, you're not helping. Just keep quiet Malcolm. I'm trying to talk to Meg."

Meg looked over Barbara's head at Malcolm. Their exchange of looks said everything. Meg realised what life was like for Malcolm, an endless round of trying to placate Barbara's anxious and unreasonable behaviour. Barbara always had first claim to special consideration; she believed she was easily upset, a sensitive person with health issues. Malcolm tried to help, she supposed, in his own limited way, but he just didn't understand her. She knew he wasn't a bad husband, but any romance in their relationship had died a long time ago and irritation had taken its place. They had lost sight of the young people they used to be, and set aside any hope of life ever being exciting again. Barbara had developed a habit of speaking to Malcolm with a mixture of exasperation and sharp condescension.

Meg served their drinks, a gin and tonic for Barbara and half a pint of brown ale for Malcolm. She asked Malcolm which ale he fancied, but he said just whatever she had most of, whatever was convenient. Meg smiled at his reluctance to make any demands, even when he was the customer.

Further down the bar, Geoff and Mike looked over at Malcolm, "How do Malcolm!" called Mike, "Have you got dried out yet?"

"Almost," said Malcolm, looking nervously towards Barbara, fearing correction.

"I wouldn't say that," chipped in Barbara.

"Are you covered for the damage?" pursued Mike.

"Yes, we are – well covered – thank you," replied Malcolm.

Barbara screwed up her face in annoyance, "It's not just about insurance, Mike, it's the trauma that matters."

"Well, that's your area, Barbara," retorted Mike, winking at Geoff, "You've always had a lot of trauma."

Geoff sniggered.

"Well darling," Mike continued, "if it's a new kitchen you're needing, I'm the man to come to. I'm going to set my daughter up with a top-quality designer kitchen at the best possible price. When you're got your insurance claim sorted, come to me. I can get the labour in. Nobody will beat my price, although the insurer needn't know that of course. I'll give you a nice high quote, and then we'll sort the details later, if you get my meaning."

Geoff interposed at this point, "It's true, he beats everyone's price. Nobody else round here has got Mike's connections."

Malcolm nodded his thanks, "It's very good to have neighbours at a time like this, isn't it Barb?"

Barbara gave him a sour look, and Geoff and Mike turned back to their beer.

"How's business going?" asked Geoff.

"Good, very good." He lowered his voice, "I'm bussing in thirty-odd immigrant workers every morning. They're desperate for whatever I can give them. They'll do anything, and they're grateful for what they get from me. Hard workers too."

Geoff looked suitably impressed.

Mike continued, "Got another big contract just agreed, renovating warehouses down by the river in Exton. I'll take on more workers for that, carpenters, plumbers, decorators, electricians, although a lot of them can do everything. And I'm thinking of diversifying. I can see openings in the *Catering and Hospitality* industry for some of the females."

Geoff thought for a minute, taking in the meaning behind Mike's words, "You mean—"

Mike Small lowered his voice even more, "I'm not saying anything Geoff, except, there's good business to be had, and there's some tasty-looking ones who would be willing to cater very nicely, and be *very* hospitable. Just another line of business, another niche in the marketplace. And I've got an expanding family to think of, and a wife who's got her eyes on a little place in Spain – lovely, a get-away in the sunshine, as many times a year as we want."

Ten years ago, Mike was a self-employed builder, doing private jobs and contracting himself to employers for larger jobs. He'd worked continually since leaving school at sixteen, and began to notice the toll that decades of manual labour was taking on his middle-aged body. Around that time, he started hearing about the large numbers of immigrants from Eastern Europe and beyond arriving in the nearest city. He began to think of how much easy money could be made if he could find ways of connecting this ready source of labour to all the work and businesses he had links to. He was good at networking with other businessmen and had a good grasp of the local business scene. He knew respectable companies would want to keep their hands clean of any illegal practices, but if he could be the middleman, well-known local companies would give him contracts for providing workforces for any number of projects. His small business had transformed into Heartland Development Services, the name chosen to give the impression of a friendly, dependable company.

The pub door opened again, and younger voices came in to join the hubbub of pub conversation. Rob, Tim and Jonah walked over to the bar. "Can't stay long," Jonah was saying, "Just time for a half and I'm heading back to Appleton."

"You need to slow down, Jonah. You're working all hours, overdoing it," said Rob in a mock-serious voice.

"I just want to get some more done on this new design I'm working on."

"You know what they say about all work and no play..." Rob paused meaningfully.

"Makes Jonah a dull boy," Tim finished the sentence, sniggering.

"You don't want Sandy thinking you're a dull boy, do you now?" taunted Rob, "Not when she's all hot and bothered about you," he laughed, and a lewd expression passed across his face.

"I wish you'd stop talking about her. You know I'm not interested."

"I seem to remember you weren't always like this," whispered Rob meaningfully.

Jonah looked uncomfortable and embarrassed. He took hold of the half-pint of beer which had just arrived on the bar and started to drink it immediately. He wanted to drink up and get out of the Mason's Arms as fast as possible. He wasn't sure what was happening with his old friends, but he no longer felt at ease in their company. Somehow they didn't seem to get on as well as they used to.

Rob noticed Jonah's glass was already half empty, "You're drinking fast tonight, Jonah, you'll be wanting another – I'll get it for you."

"No thanks – seriously – I need to be going soon."

Rob and Tim exchanged looks, then Tim said disparagingly, "You're getting to be a real boring old man."

Jonah got up and left without speaking.

*

Only a few hundred yards away from the sounds of the pub, in her quiet of her small cottage, Hilda was sitting in her armchair. The evening light had faded, and she had turned the lamps on. They lit the room with a warm, subtle light, adding to its comfort. The armchairs and sofa were old but still in good condition, the leather softened with age. A selection of velvet and tapestry cushions lay at the end of the sofa, together with a neatly folded woollen blanket for when the nights became colder and the old cottage let in draughts despite the warmth of the fire. Paintings in gilt frames hung on the walls, as well as two beautiful embroideries she had made. Hilda generally worked on her embroidery after her supper but this evening her hands were unoccupied, lying folded in her lap. She was deep in thought. If things had not changed, she would be looking forward to tomorrow morning when, according to her regular habit, she would walk up the High Street to the place where the old bridge crossed over the river. She would have gone over the bridge and up the track to the old church to pray for a while. At Easter or Christmas, or some other special time of celebration, she and some friends would take flowers with them to put on the altar, and take the dusters and polish out of the cupboard at the back of the church and spend two or three hours dusting the window ledges, polishing the wooden pews and arranging the flowers, preparing the church for a simple service of prayers. There was also a long tradition of remembering the feast days of certain saints and martyrs. Hilda was saddened that many Christians would frown upon honouring particular "saints" in this way, and believed it important to remember the inspiring lives of these faithful men and women who lived so long ago.

Hilda sighed. What would they do now that the bridge had gone? What would become of St Brannock's? And what would the pilgrims do when they started to arrive in spring and summer? As she sat, she began to pray, and reached for the Bible on the top of the bookcase next to her armchair. She longed for some guidance. Should she continue her commitment to the existence of St B's as a beacon of true faith in this area and a place of pilgrimage, or should she give way to what others may say was the inevitable? She opened her Bible, and her eyes fell on the verse: "I would rather be a doorkeeper in the house of my God than dwell in the tents of the wicked." Was that what her calling was? To be a doorkeeper? To keep the door of St B's open so that people seeking God's presence could still come to the ancient church where Jesus Christ had been honoured for so many centuries?

Tears welled up in her eyes. In her mind she could see the feet of hundreds of pilgrims walking up the track to the church to pray, dusty, tired feet, sore from the journey. Like the souls of people, she reflected, sore with the pains of life, coming to find rest in God. It was a precious trust she had been given. She smiled, feeling so much lighter, her mind clear.

She glanced at the grandfather clock in the corner of the room; the brass hands pointed to a quarter to ten. Time for cocoa and oat biscuits, then upstairs to bed with a favourite book, Barchester Towers. She loved the clever portrayal of characters; how fascinating people's personalities and motivations were.

*

Early the next morning, Hilda woke with the sound of birds singing outside her window. She sat up in bed, remembering her prayer the previous evening, and the call to be a doorkeeper. But how could she do it when the Ishka had destroyed the bridge? She prayed, "Lord, help me to spend this day well. Guide me and direct me. Show me your way and help me to walk in it."

As she opened her Bible, a small booklet of Bible reading notes fell out of it. She picked up the notes and looked for today's entry. It was a single verse, Exodus 23:19 "The choicest of the first-fruits of your ground you shall bring into the house of the Lord your God."

The commentary section challenged the reader, "How often do we offer second-best or even third-best to God and his kingdom, keeping the best of our time and money for our own comfort?" Hilda pondered this, and wondered how she could put this into practice on this particular day. Firstfruits of her ground? The only ground she owned was her garden. She realised that you had to look behind the literal sense of the words to get the full meaning as well as the obvious sense of it. She thought about it while she ate her breakfast, then went outside into the cottage garden. What could she offer? Was there anything here which could be her "firstfruits"? She gazed around, and her eyes were drawn to some lovely roses which had somehow survived the storm, tucked up against the garden wall. They must have been in bud that dreadful night and only now had begun to open. It was late in the season for roses to be blooming; Hilda smiled, knowing they would last for a good while yet until frosts began and shrivelled the last of the flowers. The only other flowers had been flattened by the storm – these roses were the best of what her "ground" had to offer. She went back into the cottage for her secateurs and an oval flower basket. Then she carefully snipped through the stem of each rose, and laid them in the basket, seven deep red perfect roses. I'll do it straightaway, she thought, and went out through the garden gate, basket in hand, and up the High Street. Some neighbours greeted her on the way, "Good morning!" "I see you've still got a few flowers – amazing that the storm didn't finish them off!"

She answered them politely but without stopping, and continued to head towards the pilgrims' church, to the place where the bridge had been, where she stood for a moment, watching the still swollen river Ishka. It looked cold and grey, flowing swiftly along its deep course. These flowers, she thought, should be going up to the church to be placed on the altar. But since I can't get them across, this will have to do. Taking hold of the roses she prayed, "This is the best I have to offer, Lord, these perfect roses," and, one by one, she threw them over the river, each rose cutting a high arc in the air before it landed on the other side on the muddy track which led up to the old church – bright spots of red on the dark earth. Villagers passing at the time saw her doing this and thought what a funny old thing she was, what a shame, she had always been such a dignified person. Would she be out in the street wearing only her nightdress soon, shouting at people? Hilda turned and smiled at them, saying "Good morning to you!" then returned home, satisfied for the moment.

Chapter Four

Monday morning. Martin Fielding woke at the sound of his alarm, cursing and hitting his pillow with his fist. He never got enough sleep – getting out of bed was a daily battle. He constantly went to bed very late, having eaten either too much or too little and frequently having drunk a large quantity of whisky.

He believed that the best way to make business deals was to take people out to dinner in an exclusive restaurant, with expensive wine to drink; in these relaxed circumstances his terms would seem reasonable, and the prospective client would sign the contract. Recently though, he had not had much success, certainly not any really big profitable deals. He felt thwarted. Success always energised him; he loved the feeling of walking into the Bluebird building and announcing his latest triumph. Knowing that his boss hardly ever made a positive or approving comment, he was hungry for those rare moments when Arnold Wheeler's small greedy eyes would turn towards him, glinting with satisfaction, and he would finally hear, "Well done, Martin, you cracked it – there'll be a bonus for you in this." For the briefest of moments he would feel a sweet sensation of security and acceptance; he'd soak it up like water in the desert, but a short time later Wheeler would be putting pressure on him again; a potent mixture of bullying and manipulation, always keeping him on edge.

As he made his first cup of strong coffee, to pull him out of his fuddled state, his mind ranged over the potential deals he was working on. The one that stuck out in his mind was the one near the village of Netherton. He drank the coffee while he searched on the internet for satellite maps of the Netherton area. As he drank the second cup, he decided he'd visit again today and dig for some more information. He believed it could be a very profitable venture if only he could secure this piece of prime land for residential development. Buoyed up by this thought, he showered and dressed, and, missing breakfast, he grabbed his phone and briefcase and was out of his flat by seven thirty. As he drove, he wondered about which local people of influence he could gain some leverage with. Maybe parish councillors? Or community groups? No, he thought, avoid those, they tend to object to change. What about the local vicar? If he could persuade someone who commanded some respect in the community that a carefully designed building development would be of great benefit – more children in the local school, new money to support local businesses etc., surely this would help gain planning permission. Persuading the landowner to sell was a separate issue, but even this may be easier if a respected local leader were in favour.

By eight forty-five, Fielding was sitting in his car on the High Street in Netherton. He took in the features of the old street, scanning the row of old cottages he had parked in front of. He could almost see the future sales brochure with its advertising slogans: *Desirable village setting. Steeped in history, tradition, heritage. A safe haven of peace in the English countryside.* Any of these phrases would boost potential selling prices for new houses. As he watched, he saw some children come out of a house further down the road. He left his car and followed them at a distance, expecting that they would lead him towards the local primary school. Five minutes later, he was standing outside Netherton Church of England Primary School. He ran his eye over it quickly; small, a mixture of the old building together with a more recent flat-roofed extension, standing in a tarmac yard, with a grassy area at the back. It was clearly in need of imaginative development; there was none of the attractive play equipment, wildlife garden and shaded area for the children that many primary schools enjoyed. He smiled to himself as he scanned the shabby exterior of the building, thinking that the interior probably could also do with a generous injection of cash. Bluebird Design and Construction could offer them a grant. Next to the school stood the parish church; he walked over and read the noticeboard outside. It listed the times of Sunday services, and the name, address and telephone number of the Vicar in Charge, Reverend James Gilchrist. He put the information into his phone, then walked around the village for a while before retracing his footsteps back to the High Street. As he got his keys out, he noticed an elderly lady approaching one of the cottages. She was going through the garden gate when Fielding caught up with her, "Good morning!" he tried to sound cheerful, relaxed.

"Good morning, dear," replied a pleasant Scottish voice.

"May I introduce myself, I'm Martin Fielding, visiting the area on behalf of Bluebird Design and Construction.

"I'm Morag McCulloch. Pleased to meet you." Morag smiled and continued up the garden path.

He could see the opportunity to engage her in conversation was slipping away fast, "I wonder if you could give me some directions?" he asked, a plaintive tone in his voice.

Morag couldn't resist. She stopped and turned round again, "Are you lost, dear?"

He smiled, trying to look unsure of himself, "I think I may be. I'm trying to do something for my boss, and I'll be in trouble if I go back to the office empty-handed."

"What are you trying to find?"

At that moment, the door of the cottage opened, and another old lady appeared. Morag greeted her, "Hilda – there's a young man here who's got himself lost and needs directions!"

The owner of the cottage, who he now knew was Hilda, stepped back saying, "Do bring him in, Morag, perhaps we can point him in the right direction."

How trusting they are, he remarked to himself, how easily they believed him. He followed the two ladies into the cottage, noting how clean and welcoming it was; he took in the deep armchairs with colourful cushions, and tasteful paintings on the walls. It smelt of beeswax polish. He felt himself relax as he walked into the calm atmosphere. His determination to extract as much information as possible from these vulnerable old ladies began to wane and instead he simply began to enjoy being there in the comforting ambience. Hilda was speaking, "Come through into the kitchen, and we'll sit down and have some tea."

Soon the three of them were seated around the kitchen table, a tea pot and a plate of scones set in front of them. "Help yourself to scones," said Hilda, pouring the tea, "Try the jam – Morag made it – it has a lovely flavour."

Fielding felt he had stumbled into a parallel universe, where kindly strangers accepted you without question, without any hidden agenda. So far away from his world of ruthless bargaining and dog-eat-dog mentality.

"His name is Martin," said Morag helpfully.

He had just taken a large bite of scone with butter and jam, "Sorry!" he tried to say, realising he hadn't introduced himself to the owner of the cottage whose kitchen he was now sitting in. But all that came out of his mouth was a muffled sound, and pieces of scone shot out of his mouth on to the table.

Hilda laughed, "Don't worry, just enjoy your scones!"

He felt like a small boy having tea with his aunts. It was ridiculous, but strangely pleasant. He took another bite, these scones were delicious.

Hilda and Morag exchanged looks, "You were hungry," said Hilda kindly.

"No breakfast, I bet," commented Morag.

The two ladies began to discuss gardening, so Fielding wasn't under any pressure to say anything. He watched them as they talked; clearly they were very fond of each other – how had they managed to be so old and yet so full of life and enthusiasm? He didn't expect to get beyond sixty, in fact, he often wondered if he'd make it as far as that, with his lifestyle. His plate was empty now, and as if on cue, Hilda turned back to him, "Glad you enjoyed the scones!" she said, "Now how can we help you?"

It was just the opening he had wanted and yet now he felt a peculiar sense of being unwilling to get back on his unscrupulous track and take advantage of their kindness. It wasn't like him to have any reluctance about using anybody who came his way.... He told himself to get on with the job. He began, "I work for a company that wants to do some..." he hesitated briefly, "community development work here in Netherton."

Morag cut in energetically, "I used to be in the WRVS." Then seeing his bemused look, explained, "Women's Royal Voluntary Service... happy days!"

Hilda bypassed Morag's WRVS reminiscences, "Community development," she pondered aloud. "That sounds very positive – what sort of things might that involve?"

"Better facilities for the people, bringing in more investment to the area."

"Is this a private company?" asked Morag, "What's in it for them?" she asked pointedly.

Hilda shot her a look, thinking she had sounded rather sharp.

Morag softened her tone, "I'm sorry to ask, but private companies aren't charities, so there must be away of them making a profit."

Fielding tried to sound gently reassuring, with a slightly humorous tone, "You're right of course, the company has to make something out of it, or it will go bust!" He wasn't sure what to say next, still trying to avoid saying it would involve building on a large piece of land next to the village. Just then he noticed a Bible on the worktop and spotted a likely way to lead the conversation to his advantage. "May I ask, do you go to church?"

Hilda smiled, "Yes I do, I go to the parish church here in the village, and also sometimes to the very old church just outside the village. It's rather special as well as ancient. Morag and I love it."

He hesitated, sensing a problem, "How interesting, Hilda," he said.

Hilda, warming to her theme, had an idea. Perhaps this young man could be an answer to prayer; God sometimes answers in very unexpected ways. She thought of the washed-away bridge... if someone had money to invest for a good cause.... "Would you like to see it? It's only a very short distance from here. In fact, you can't go all the way there at the moment, but we could point it out to you, if you're interestedin this locality. We think it's a very important place for the people of this area."

"I'd love to see it," said Fielding, standing up, "And thank you for the tea and scones."

The three of them left the cottage and walked up the High Street together, an unlikely group – two old ladies in raincoats and a fashionable young businessman in an expensive-looking suit.

When they got to the river Ishka, they stopped, and Hilda pointed across the water to the hill with St Brannock's standing at the top. "You can't really tell from here how beautiful it is. It has a wonderful atmosphere – it's all the hundreds of years of prayer, you see, it *changes* places, makes them special. It has stood here for all that time, a holy site for pilgrims and local people to come to. Because it's so high, it looks out over a very wide area. Actually there's a beacon tower next to it too – you can't see it until you're on the track. The beacon on the tower would have been lit to warn people of danger or maybe to celebrate a great occasion."

Fielding looked up the hill to where the church stood. He imagined it surrounded by new houses, stretching out in all directions, a smooth tarmac road replacing the track which the feet of pilgrims had worn into the earth.... More likely, though, he thought, the church would be altered beyond recognition, incorporated into part of a leisure facility, or a luxurious home, or even, if they could get away with it, bulldozed. It might be possible to have it declared unsafe, a danger to children. He'd have to look into it. Strange, when he was in Hilda's cottage, his constant habit of sly plotting, using every opportunity to his own advantage, had briefly paused; he had allowed the peace and beauty of Hilda's home somehow to invade him and influence him. Now, standing outside by the grey water of the Ishka, he had reverted to his old ways, and felt no sense of guilt as he stood next to Hilda listening to her speak about the value of the holy place across the water while surreptitiously planning its destruction. "How do people get across?" he asked, looking down at the fast-flowing water surging past.

"There was a bridge – a very simple affair of two stone pillars on opposite sides of the river gorge, and long pieces of timber, reaching across the river. Until now. The recent storm washed it away, a terrible thing, after all those centuries of carrying people across to the church."

"So actually it's unused now."

"Sadly, yes, but only temporarily," said Hilda.

Morag added with a touch of mischief in her voice, "Hilda believes we can find a way of getting there again."

Fielding looked over at Hilda, thin and frail-looking, her hair pure white and her hands knobbly with age. She didn't look like much of an opponent. He laughed inwardly. He spoke carefully, to hide his thoughts, "It's really good of you to show me a little of the area; it's helped me to *get a feel* of the place. I need to take my impressions back to my boss and see how we can help." Morag looked at him abruptly, "You still haven't told us anything about your company's plans."

He picked his words carefully, "Well, take the local primary school here – it looks like it could do with some support, maybe it needs a plan to extend and improve the buildings – we could help with that."

Morag was unimpressed, "But the school can't afford anything. They can't even stretch to an extra mobile classroom."

"We would cover the costs; we have done a large number of similar building projects."

"Ah, I see," said Morag quietly, "You would build houses here, make a big profit, and give a bit to the school."

Undeterred by her tone, he countered, "More children would come to the school, and that would help too. Also more for the local Scouts and Guides – all the community groups would benefit." Morag had been an active Guide leader for forty years, and even now was a supporter. Fielding had struck gold. "That would be wonderful – we're down to just six children in our group here. Often only five turn up on Friday nights."

Happy memories from the past flooded back into Morag's mind, of thirty-five guides pouring into the Scout and Guide Hall in the town where she used to live before she moved to Netherton, and of herself standing ready in her uniform to greet them as they arrived. She said warmly, "It could save our group here in this village."

A smile spread across his face, "All those benefits would come to the village."

Just then, rain started to fall, so they said their goodbyes, and Fielding ran back to his car and left the two ladies behind him. Neither of them had realised what his persuasive words might mean for the future.

*

As Fielding drove away from Netherton, he felt satisfied, even quite excited at the prospect of planning a huge housing development on the edge of Netherton. The potential profits would be vast, so long as they kept overheads to a minimum. He'd have to put some figures down on paper. He needed to talk to some more people about that b---- church, check it wasn't a listed building, under some sort of protection order or whatever. He must try to contact the owner; he needed to work out what kind of offer Bluebird would need to make.

He had intended to go straight back to the office, but his eye caught the sign to Appleton. Why did that ring a bell with him? Of course, that was where the vicar lived. Perhaps it would be worth calling on him for some more information.

Soon Fielding's car was turning into the vicarage drive. James, looking up from his desk in his study, saw the unfamiliar car arrive and wondered who it could be. After the Millers' unsettling visit, he did not relish the idea of strangers arriving unexpectedly. Who could it be, driving that expensive car? James watched as a young man got out of the top-of-the-range Lexus. He reminded himself that, as a vicar, he must be careful about making judgements based on people's outward appearances, but be prepared to welcome everyone equally.

Fielding walked up the steps and rang the bell. James called out to Anna, "Don't worry, I'll answer it!"

Opening the door, he greeted Fielding, taking in the slim handsome face, the well-cut suit and expensive shoes, "Do come in," he said. "How can I help you?" He didn't bother saying he was the vicar – the clerical collar said that for him.

Fielding held out his hand, "Martin Fielding."

James shook the hand, "James Gilchrist. Do come into the study." When they were sitting down in two of the well-worn armchairs, Fielding thought he would come straight to the point, "I hope it's all right to come unannounced – I saw your name on the noticeboard outside the church in Netherton."

"No problem at all, you're very welcome."

"I represent Bluebird Design and Construction, a development company. We are in the process ofdrawing up plans to provide affordable housing for the community there."

Fielding chuckled inside at his own ability to adapt his sales pitch to his audience. The word "affordable" would surely appeal to a bleeding hearts vicar-type – it brought to mind visions of helping struggling young families trying to get onto the housing ladder, moving into the first home of their own, faces lit up with gratitude. In fact, the houses he had in mind would indeed be affordable, but only to wealthy people, ambitious executives moving out from the city in search of a rural idyll befitting their upwardly mobile status, perhaps a place where their spoilt child could have a pony.

"That sounds marvellous," said James, "So many young people in areas like this have no chance of ever owning their own home. Of course people moving out of London would think they were very reasonable, but to farm workers and other—"

"Exactly," interrupted Fielding. "I felt sure that you, as a member of the clergy, would understand these things. Would we be able to count on your support?"

"Well of course, anything that's good for the local community will get my wholehearted approval and support."

"Thank you so much," said Martin, standing up as though ready to go, then added, "I noticed there is a primary school in Netherton, next to the church."

"Yes, it's a church foundation school. I often visit there, take assemblies, try to encourage the staff etc. I am also the Chair of Governors there."

"Then perhaps you could mention that if Bluebird Design and Construction could help the school in some way, perhaps with some refurbishment, or an extension to provide a better learning environment, we would be delighted to do so." He handed his business card over to James.

James felt a surge of happiness; this would be great news to share at the governors' meeting. He thought of how clever they would think he'd been to secure some extra funding for the school. It would show them he was someone who could make things happen! He had a couple of seconds enjoying the warm glow of success while they walked to the door of the study, which at that moment opened, and Anna appeared in the doorway, saying, "Sorry to disturb you." She caught sight of Fielding, and smiled at him.

"This is my daughter, Anna," James said, watching Fielding's expression as he looked at her.

"Really pleased to meet you," said Fielding quietly, admiration showing in his eyes.

Anna blushed prettily. Then turned to her father, "Dad, I just wanted to let you know I need to go out. Actually, my car's blocked in." She looked towards Fielding again.

"Very sorry! That's my fault! I'll move my car immediately."

"I don't want to hurry you."

"I'm happy to come with you now," he said, looking steadily at her, then seeing her become uncomfortable at being so obviously the focus of his attention, he added quickly, "I just wanted to ask a question about a church building."

James looked interested, "Yes, do ask and I'll try my best to answer!"

Fielding said lightly, "It's just a little old church, partly derelict I think, a few miles from here, outside Netherton."

Anna answered for her father, "You mean St Brannock's. It's a very old place, isn't it Dad, not used much, in fact not at all at the moment."

James nodded, "A small number of people, the Friends of St Brannock's, normally open it up once or twice a month, elderly people mainly. The same little group also attend the parish church in Netherton, but they have a special regard for the old church on the hill – they think of it a holy place where people can find peace with God. There is also a steady trickle of pilgrims from all over who come to visit the church, especially in the summer months. The Friends group keep it open much longer in the summer."

Anna continued, "But the recent storm has changed things; it was particularly bad in Netherton. St Brannock's has been cut off from the village – the bridge over the river has been destroyed, and there's no other access – the river almost circles it, apart from a steep drop on the far side of the church."

Fielding was listening attentively to her, as though this was all completely new to him, "Really?" he said, "Fascinating. Thank you,

I just needed to understand the background. I've just been explaining to Reverend Gilchrist that my company's hoping to address the need for affordable housing for local families. It may be that these much-needed houses end up quite near the place. So you think not many people ever really go there?"

James answered, "No, in fact, not many people go to the parish church there either. In some ways it would be better if that small congregation would be willing to join the congregation here in Appleton. Of course, I'm happy to go to Netherton to lead the services but there's a lot more to keeping churches open than that. As for the pilgrims' church, it's privately owned, not part of my responsibilities."

"I see. So it's a bit of an oddity, is it? A little isolated relic from a bygone age?"

"You could put it like that."

Fielding looked at Anna again, "I must move my car for you, Anna. So sorry to be in your way." He walked towards the door, shaking James' hand as he passed, "Thank you for all your help."

Fielding hurried through the front door after Anna. "I'm so glad we met, Anna. It would be good to talk some more about the local area."

Anna hesitated. There was no doubt about it, this young man was attractive, and seemed so polite. But something about him was almost too smooth, his manner so persuasive.

Sensing she was resisting he added quickly, "I'm determined to do my very best to get this project for local families started, so I must try to get to know the area." His tone was earnest.

"Well, I suppose I could show you one or two of the villages near here if you like – I have some time on Thursday afternoon," she offered.

"That would be lovely, Anna. May I come back here at two o'clock on Thursday?"

She looked into his eyes and felt a flutter of excitement, "Yes, that would be fine." She walked over to her car, not sure what to say next.

"See you on Thursday!" he called out to her. He watched her as she got into her car, his eyes running over every inch of her. She was lovely, he thought; young, unspoilt, perfect. He would have to be careful not to rush her. He didn't want to frighten her off. It would be worth the wait.

James watched the two cars leaving, the impressive Lexus followed by his daughter's modest blue Vauxhall. He had been impressed by the younger man, by his enthusiasm and his polite, slightly deferential manner, an unusual quality to find today. He had also seen the way he had looked at his daughter. Could he be a suitable match for her? Would he by any chance be a Christian? He certainly seemed to have respect for the church; that was a good start. There was no young man connected to Anna at present, as far as he knew. She was twenty-two; wasn't it time for her to be looking for a future husband? Then the chilling thought of losing her flitted across his mind. There's no hurry, James comforted himself, she was still very young, and seemed happy with their present arrangement; there was plenty of room at the vicarage for her to develop her fledgling design business. It was wonderful to have her here with him – how empty the vicarage would seem without her. He pushed all thoughts of losing Anna out of his mind and decided it was not too early to have lunch.

James went into the kitchen. He decided on poached eggs on toast, simple but tasty, and within his culinary skills. He turned the radio on, and listened while he poached the eggs and buttered the toast. As he sat down at the table to eat, he continued to listen to a discussion about community action. Seems to be a popular topic, he muttered to himself. A female councillor was being interviewed, "It's very important," she was insisting, "that we move away from the idea that everything will be done for us by the government, either national or local. We must all take responsibility for our own areas. If we just sit on the sidelines, grumbling that things are going downhill, then that's exactly what will happen."

"But how can ordinary people instigate change in their town, city or village? Surely they haven't got the authority or resources to do so?" queried the interviewer.

"Movement towards change for the better always starts with ordinary people, sometimes even just one person, who's willing to stand up for something they feel passionate about," the councillor replied. "It's time to get involved, enter the fray, become part of the solution."

The interview ended. Hmm, thought James, easier said than done. How could he possibly instigate change for the better around here? Sometimes, despite all his efforts, he felt he achieved very little. Perhaps partnership with other groups such as the construction company he'd heard about today was how he should be working.

Renewal, he thought, is what the Gospel should bring to people, and new hope. The restoration of what is good and life-giving... and the expulsion of harmful influences and systems. The words of Jesus in the Gospel of John came into his mind, "I came that they may have life, and have it abundantly." Beautiful words, full of promise and hope. But they followed on from the uncomfortable words, "The thief comes only to steal and kill and destroy." Who was the thief in this area? He wondered. Certainly God's church here was going through a difficult time. The doorbell sounded. Time to get back to work.

James opened the door to find a man in a dark suit standing there. "Sunnyside Funeral Services," intoned the man in that calm practised voice cultivated by those in his line of business.

"Good," said James, "Do come in."

He showed the man into the study saying, "Thank you for coming so quickly. Do sit down, I think this may take a little while to explain."

James began to tell him about John Miller's demise, but it was clear the man already knew about it. "There is a complication with this funeral," James continued, "The family want to handle things in a rather unusual way. They don't seem to want to discuss arrangements, and they have provided the money to cover all the costs in advance and... in cash."

The man didn't show any surprise.

"Is that difficult for you – a large sum of money in cash I mean?" pursued James.

"It's the Millers," said the undertaker. "They do things their way; it will be fine, we'll get it sorted out."

James handed him the grubby note with details for the headstone. "I'm afraid they want the headstone ready very quickly too – it would have to be done this week if it's to fit in with Mrs Miller's instructions. I realise this is asking for the imposs–" he stopped in the middle of the word, watching the man's face, knowing that to have individually inscribed headstones prepared normally took much longer. There was, however, no sign of surprise, just a nod of acceptance. He carried on, "The funeral is to be here on Saturday at two o'clock. Do you have a free slot at that time?"

The undertaker opened his large black and gilt diary and turned to Saturday. James could see details of services and burials written in through the day. The man looked at the crowded page, then back at James, "We'll alter some arrangements to make it possible."

"But what about the other families?" asked James.

"They'll understand, we'll say it can't be helped." He leant towards James, lowering his voice, "You haven't been here long, have you? You'll find it's better to go along with the Millers. Yes, we'll make it possible."

James was astonished. What kind of hold did the Millers have around here? He had an idea, "Are you related to the Millers?"

"Not exactly, but my grandmother and grandfather were close to them. They know all the old families round here."

James walked to the front door with the undertaker saying, "I'm not quite sure how to handle all this cash they have given me. In fact, could you wait a moment? He went back to the study, and opened the top drawer of his desk. He took out all the bundles of notes, then removed sufficient to cover the church's fee for the funeral and other costs connected to the burial plot in the graveyard. Taking hold of a carrier bag next to the desk, he emptied the contents, palm crosses left over from Palm Sunday, onto the desk and in their place tipped the bundles of notes. Then he hurried back out into hallway where the undertaker was waiting. He held out the carrier bag, "Here's the money left by Jean Miller," apart from the fees required by the church, which I've taken out, and will provide a receipt for."

The man looked into the bag, eyes widening with surprise, "That should easily cover costs. Thank you. I'll sort out the headstone."

"Glad to pass it on, to tell you the truth," said James, "Never known an arrangement like it, not happy at all about receiving this quantity of cash, I think the church treasurer will have a fit when I tell him, but they wouldn't take no for an answer."

The man nodded, tucked the bag under his arm and left. James closed the door behind him, thinking about the various forms which should have been filled in.

*

After the undertaker had left, James decided to get a breath of fresh air. It was a beautiful afternoon, the fall of leaves from the trees having dropped a golden carpet over the grass around the vicarage. He would walk over the fields to Netherton to look at the churchyard there. He had never conducted a burial there yet during his time as vicar – so many people opted for cremation now – and he wanted to feel familiar with the place before the Millers' funeral. Forty-five minutes later, he left the field footpath which ended a short distance before Netherton Parish Church. He went through the wooden gate into the churchyard and sat down for a few minutes on the bench near the church door, lifting his face for a moment to the warmth of the sun's rays, enjoying the mellow autumn sunshine. After a while, he got up and walked among the gravestones. In the warmth of the afternoon sun it was pleasant to linger, reading the names of people long gone on the lichen-covered stones. There was a sense of poignancy too, reading the record of beloved people, statements written in times of great sadness. The sharp pain of loss was diminished now by the passage of time, and the stones mainly echoed gratitude and affection.

"*To the memory of Edith Mary Shaw,*" he read, "*cherished wife of Joseph Shaw, and mother of Ann, Rachel and Esme. Always in our hearts.*" There were several graves of children lost in infancy, "*Sophie May Peasdon, aged five years. Safe in the arms of Jesus.*" How her family must have suffered at the time, thought James, but now the little one's grave is a place of peace.

Many of the modest graves near Sophie May's had small bunches of fresh flowers in a vase in front of the headstone. One area of the graveyard had larger, more elaborate graves in it. James walked over to the largest. It was in the style of a chest tomb, raised above the ground, with Grecian-style pillars at the corners and an inscription running round the edge of it. "To the memory of John Richard Miller, 1724 – 1795, Landowner of the Parish of Netherton. Remembered and honoured." The Millers again, thought James. Slightly strange wording, James mused. It didn't sound quite right; somehow it made it sound as though John Miller owned the parish, which can't possibly have been right. He remembered the Miller's farm, they were hardly landed gentry.

Nevertheless, they clearly had power of some sort. Jean Miller had been completely confident about her family's influence: "People won't refuse *our* money." She had expected that he would do whatever they instructed, that they needn't be restricted by anyone else's rules. He studied the gravestones near to John Miller's, counting fifteen separate plots, each containing a family group of Millers. Soon another John Miller would be buried here, another memorial raised to the power of the Miller dynasty.

As he turned to leave, he noticed that each of the Miller graves had a small symbol carved into the stone beneath the inscription, a circle with a dip in the centre. It could possibly be the mark of the stonemason, but it didn't seem to appear on any of the other stones.

Walking back to the church, he wondered how it had been possible for the Millers to come to this position of influence. It certainly wasn't friendship which conferred this widespread cooperation. Who would want to be friends with Jean Miller? He remembered her with a shudder.

He sat for a while on the bench again, thinking he would pray for a while. In his previous parish, he reflected, it had been so very different; there had been a sense of energy, even excitement. Various new groups had been started during his time there – a men's "Encounter" group, the women's "Destiny" group, several youth and children's groups. Even when these had only a small number of members, there was a liveliness present, the feeling of moving forward into new, positive things. Here, however, there seemed to be a drag on everything he tried to set up. Without doubt, there were some faithful Christians here, but they were very small in number. Sometimes he blamed himself – was he just too dull and boring to attract people to the church, or was it the loss of his darling Ruth? As a couple, everything had been easier. Although he had held the title of vicar, they ministered together. Ruth's prayerfulness underpinned everything. People who came to the vicarage during those years, seeking help or counsel, ended up in the kitchen with Ruth just as much as in the study with James. They would sit at the kitchen table with her, drinking coffee and opening their hearts to her. Ruth took at least half of the burden of parish work on her shoulders, and also was his own precious love. Their relationship was strong; intimacy came easily to them. Her sudden decline and death was cripplingly painful to James. It seemed to him as though they had been walking together, hand-in-hand on a long summer's day across a sunlit meadow, when suddenly a huge hole had opened up in front of them, and over the edge they had fallen, down and down.

During her brief illness, she had been at peace, accepting, in her words, that she "was going home sooner than expected." He, accompanying her during those heartbreaking few weeks, spent all his energy just trying to hold himself together in the face of gut-wrenching loss, trying to be being strong for his family.

After the funeral, the need to continue for Anna's sake kept him going from day to day, but he had questioned God ferociously from time to time about his lonely vocation as a vicar. He wasn't any good on his own, he knew. As the months passed, he immersed himself again in parish work, but privately he barely survived between

Anna's university vacations, trying not to sound too keen for each end of term to come round again, trying not to ask which day she was going to come home. Fortunately Anna had many good friends at university who seemed to enjoy coming to stay with her, so during the long holidays the vicarage would be full of activity and young voices again. Like Ruth, Anna had a quiet steady faith, without the emotion-led highs and lows which James was prone to. Nevertheless, he genuinely cared for the people in his parish, whether churchgoers or not. He wanted to see vibrant Christian faith grow, with all the accompanying new meaning in life that following Christ brings. In the parish of Appleton, reaching out to people with the hope of the Gospel seemed so difficult and problem-strewn, and in Netherton it was even harder. The greatest danger was probably that you became used to the prevailing atmosphere of disinterest in God and church and began to accept it.

Sitting alone on the bench by the church wall, he prayed for an increase of awareness of the spiritual nature of the area, and that he would be more effective as a disciple of Jesus, that he would come into direct contact with people whose hearts were in need of the power of saving grace. Then he got up and unlocked the door and went inside the church, walking towards the front, his footsteps echoing on the tiled floor in the empty building. He tried to imagine what it would be like on Saturday afternoon during John Miller's funeral. How many of the Millers' extended family would come? He would be pleased to get this funeral over with. It was so different to any other he had been involved in: no grieving family to visit and comfort, no gently exploring the life of the deceased to prepare a carefully-worded eulogy. It was peculiar, he concluded; he felt a bystander to the process, expected to stand to one side and only step forward if summoned by Jean Miller. He sensed he was getting irritated, so told himself to stop thinking about it and start walking back to the vicarage – perhaps Anna would be home.

When James arrived back, Anna had just come in. She kissed her father on the cheek, saying, "How was your afternoon, Dad?"

"Good question: it's been *interesting*," laughed James.

"Sounds intriguing – what's been happening then?" asked Anna, sensing something unusual.

"Firstly, I got rid of that pile of money, thank goodness!"

"Good, did the undertaker come and collect it?"

"Yes; it felt strange, handling all those thousands of pounds in notes, with no receipt or paperwork. But anyway, now it's up to

Sunnyside Funeral Services to deal with it. I must say the man didn't seem bothered by it at all, even accepted the funeral had to be on Saturday at two o'clock, when clearly he had other bookings in his diary. Don't know what I'll do about the forms for the church. I could try to fill them in by myself, but I should get signatures."

Anna could tell her father had something more to say.

"In fact, Anna, there's been a sort of theme running through this afternoon. Quite a disturbing one."

Anna's eyes opened wider with interest. Her father continued, "Something about the hold the Millers seem to have. Whatever they want, they seem to get, and yet... I don't see them as people with lots of friends who would want to help them out."

"Perhaps a lot of people owe them favours."

"That sounds even more like the Mafia! Bundles of banknotes, people being intimidated."

"Or maybe there are old secrets that they know about and threaten people with!" giggled Anna.

James smiled at her, "You think I'm taking this too seriously, don't you? You're probably right. Perhaps they're just a bunch of strange country folk."

"It sounds like there was something else that happened this afternoon."

"Oh, just something about the gravestones. I'll show you later – I've got a few telephone calls to make. Any thoughts about what we're going to eat later? Would you like me to cook supper this evening?" he offered, but with a thinly disguised note of resignation.

Anna laughed again, "That didn't sound like a very enthusiastic offer!"

"Sorry, but you're a much better cook than me. I always look forward to eating what you've made. But if I cook, it's always a bit of a gamble. It *may* be just about all right, or it may be a tasteless barely edible heap on the plate."

"OK, point made, I'll cook!" She went into the pantry to get some ingredients for supper while James retreated with relief, thinking of his phone calls.

By twenty minutes to six, they were eating their meal – chicken with a mushroom sauce, green beans and rice, followed by red berry fruit crumble and custard. As he collected the empty dishes together, James felt very satisfied, a delicious meal to be followed by an evening at home. Unusually, he had no meetings or visits planned for tonight.

As they began to wash the dishes, James asked, "Have you got anything on tonight, Anna? I'm happy to say I shall be watching the television – you would be welcome to join me. I may even have a glass of wine!"

"Oh what a wild life you lead, Vicar!" joked Anna, "What would your parishioners make of your dissipated lifestyle!" Then, more seriously, "It sounds great, Dad, but I've got something on; do you remember I talked with the woman who has an arts and crafts shop in Upper Exton? She's going to take me with her to an arts group tonight."

"Excellent, that sounds promising."

"Yes, I'm hoping to do a bit of networking with other designers and artists. However, I've still got time to come and see whatever it was you saw in the graveyard!"

James felt a little foolish now about his concerns about the gravestones, thinking he probably was imagining things, but thought it would be good to have Anna's opinion; if she thought he was reading too much into it, he would try to forget about it. They drove the short distance to Netherton and parked near to the parish church.

A chill wind had started to blow, and the light was fading as they walked through the gate into the graveyard. Anna wrapped her coat more tightly around her as they stepped between the headstones, some leaning at odd angles. They stopped at Sophie May's little grave, which James pointed out, "So sad, isn't it? So many children died in infancy in those days. You hope that somehow people were able to accept it better because it happened so often."

"Or did it just make it worse, losing one child after another, your heart breaking again and again," said Anna.

James led the way over to where all the large Miller graves were, indicating the one with the imposing stone memorial.

"Gosh!" commented Anna, "What a contrast to the other graves."

"Yes, that's what I thought, and look at this little symbol." He pointed to the circular mark cut into each stone.

"Oh yes, I can see it... it's on all the Miller gravestones." She walked between the graves, crouching down to examine them, "I wonder what it is?"

It was getting even darker, and they were in danger of tripping over the graves in the unlit graveyard, so they began to walk back along the path towards the car and drove back to Appleton. They turned into the vicarage drive and got out of the car, then both stopped short. In the near darkness they could see the shape of someone standing near the steps leading to the vicarage door. A shadowy figure in a long dress and cape was standing there, absolutely still. James caught his breath, and reached for Anna's arm, as though he was about to pull her away from going any nearer to this apparition. But Anna sounded relaxed when she spoke,

"Don't worry, I know exactly who that is, it's Mia. She's come to pick me up."

James breathed a sigh of relief, "Sorry, I must be feeling jumpy. She did look rather eerie standing there."

Anna called out, "Mia! I'm over here! Sorry, have you been waiting long?"

The familiar low voice reached them through the dim light, "Only a few minutes."

Anna walked towards her, saying conversationally, "We've just been to Netherton Church, well to the graveyard actually."

"How fascinating. I've always liked graveyards."

"May I introduce you to my father, James Gilchrist."

They were standing close to Mia now. Her dark hair was drawn back off her face, held in place by small silver combs. She was wearing a full-length black dress with an embroidered top and a deep red belt around her waist. A velvet cape with a metal clasp and black suede boots completed her outfit. By the light of the two lamps on either side of the steps going up to the vicarage door they could see Mia's face clearly; it was carefully made up, dark eyeliner and metallic eye shadow emphasising the shape of her eyes, and plum-coloured lipstick making her lips look full and soft. Her cape was unfastened, revealing her white neck, adorned with a gemstone hanging from an ornate silver chain. It was eye-catching, resting just above the deep neckline of her dress.

She held out her hand towards James, just as she had to Anna in the shop, but he did not respond. Anna looked at him; he was gazing at Mia. Goodness, thought Anna, he's completely taken with her. James tried to speak, "I am very... pleased to meet you," he stuttered.

Mia smiled calmly; there was something catlike about the way she was watching James. Just then James noticed Mia's hand, still held out to him. He grasped it eagerly, holding it in a very un-vicar-like way, Anna noticed. What had come over her normally shy father? She watched as Mia took a small step towards James, still holding his hand; she was standing quite close to him now, and had drawn his hand towards her so that it almost touched the front of her dress. Then she let it go, looking up into his face, her plum-coloured lips moving slightly. Did she say something? Anna wasn't sure.

Then Mia turned towards Anna, "I think we should go, we don't want to be late." Mia turned her back on James without any further conversation, leaving him standing on the drive, staring after her, his gaze fixed on her as she walked away.

"See you later, Dad," said Anna, to his apparently deaf ears.

*

The meeting of the Arts and Crafts Circle was held in the village hall. When Mia and Anna walked in, about thirty people of all ages, from about eighteen years upwards, were standing around drinking coffee. Several of them turned round and greeted Mia. She smiled, announcing confidently to the room in general, "Let me introduce Anna, our newest member! She is a designer who lives here in Netherton." It seemed that Mia was a leading light in this gathering; she had no difficulty getting everyone's attention. After a few minutes of general chat, the woman who seemed to be the organiser shouted, "Let's sit down, everyone, and we'll start." She took her place behind a small table with a notebook and pen on it. Everyone found a seat in a large circle of chairs with the little table squeezed in at the top of the circle. The organiser spoke again, waving her hand in Anna's direction, "I'd like to officially welcome Anna to the Netherton Arts and Crafts Circle. We hope you will benefit from being one of us, Anna. We may look like an odd bunch, but when you get to know us, you'll probably quite like us!" There was a titter of laughter around the room.

The first item of the evening was to look at the latest work of one of the members. This evening it was Mark Winthrop, a basket weaver who also wove ambitious objects out of natural materials. He showed some wicker animals which he hoped would sell as garden or conservatory ornaments, as well as some more abstract works, meant to evoke different aspects of the natural world. Anna could see he was very skilled at basketwork, but didn't find his work in any way attractive, especially those pieces for which he had given his imagination free rein. Some of them seemed very weird. However, they applauded him and Shelley, the organiser, thanked him for showing his work and explaining what had inspired it.

Next, they split into small groups to discuss what they were working on at present and to help one another with ideas. People in

Anna's group told her how she could set up an exhibition of her designs or perhaps even do it jointly with some of them. It was quite informative; she took notes as they talked. At half past nine, Shelley called them all back together again, and then asked if there was anything to share with the whole group. One middle-aged man with very long dreadlocks stood up and said everyone would be very welcome to come to the drumming event he was facilitating. "It's on November 4th, from about 7 o'clock, on the allotments behind my house. It's called Earth Rhythms," he said, "and it's for anyone who wants to connect with the rhythms of the earth, and indeed the universe. You don't have to know how to drum, just come along and be open."

"That sounds wonderful," commented Shelley.

A very nervous young man, perhaps even still a teenager, stood up next, "I'm having an exhibition in Exton Library from November 3rd–8th, well I've got a side-room in the library actually. It's called "Spirit, Earth and Fire." I'm showing all my pieces, some of them are very experimental, and there's an opportunity for people to write down their comments." How brave of him, thought Anna, encouraging the public to leave their comments for others to read. She hoped people would be kind to him, he looked so thin and frail.

Then Mia spoke in her low calm voice, "I want to invite all the lovely talented people here to a special evening which is all about strengthening and replenishing you. When you are a creative person, you give out *so much*," she purred. There were nods of understanding round the room. She pressed home her point, "You really need to receive something yourself, to renew your inner self so that you can continue to be creative. So, please put in your diary Thursday 25th October at 7.30pm, a "Receiving and Renewal" evening. I believe it will really help you. It's at my home, I'll give out directions, and there'll be wine and nibbles too." The teenager looked interested when she mentioned nibbles. He could do with nibbling something, thought Anna.

At the end of the evening, Mia and Anna walked back to the car. Mia said, "I hope you'll be able to come to the evening at my home. You already know where it is, it's where the shop is – the back and the upstairs are where I live. Do come, you'll find it useful."

On the journey back to Appleton, she adopted a confidential tone, telling Anna she was a single parent, "I have a beautiful daughter. She lives in an artists' community in London. Her father and I split up a long time ago – he was a musician and needed his freedom to tour the world – I just wasn't part of his destiny," she murmured sadly.

"I'm so sorry," said Anna, sensing that Mia expected sympathy.

"I've moved on," said Mia quickly, "I accept my pathway in life. If I can help other people find contentment and peace, then my life is worthwhile."

At this point they pulled up outside the vicarage. Mia turned to look at Anna, "Thank you for joining us, you've encouraged everyone by being there. Has anyone ever told you that you have a wonderful light about you?"

Anna had no idea what to say in reply so continued to get out of the car, "Thanks for taking me, Mia. I've got lots of useful notes."

"See you at my house on the 25th then!" called Mia, as she reached over and pulled the passenger door shut before Anna could answer.

Anna hadn't agreed to go, but hadn't made an excuse either; it sounded like a slightly peculiar evening – Mia hadn't made it at all clear what exactly was going to happen at her house, apart from the wine and nibbles. She unlocked the front door and went inside. It was only just after ten o'clock and yet the house seemed very quiet. She walked into the living room looking for her father. He was there, sitting in an armchair in front of the television, but the screen was blank.

"Are you OK, Dad?" she asked, going towards him.

He looked up, startled, "Anna! Sorry, I was so deep in thought, I didn't hear you come in."

She sat down next to him, "Must be very interesting thoughts Dad. Anything you want to share?" She felt concerned; it wasn't like her father to be sitting alone, apparently without anything to do, just thinking.

"I was just... well... thinking about *me*. I know that sounds peculiar. Just taking stock I suppose."

Anna touched him on the arm, "Are you sure you're all right? You seemed a bit strange earlier this evening."

"Did I? When?"

"When Mia came round. You just *stared*."

Her father looked embarrassed, "Did I really? Oh dear, I'm sorry, it's so rude to stare. Though I must say, she is a very striking woman, took me by surprise I suppose, hard *not* to stare."

Anna gave him a sideways look, smiling mischievously at him, "I think I'd better get you some nice warm *relaxing* cocoa, Dad."

Chapter Five

It was a dull grey morning; the sky was overcast with heavy dark clouds. The wind was blowing from the north, making it cold, too cold for mid-October. Hilda had planned to have coffee at Morag's house. First, however, she had to check something. She put on a warm quilted jacket, wrapped a scarf around her neck and locked the cottage door as she left.

In a few minutes, she was standing once more next to the river, studying the place where the bridge had once been. She could see there were stones from the bridge left on the steeply sloping banks, having been wrenched from their place in the supporting pillars. The river was still very full, the water flowing fast. She moved closer, looking down into its depths, watching it swirl into whirlpools near the edges, sucking downwards with irresistible force. It would be dreadful to fall into the Ishka while it was in this tumultuous mood. She stepped back from the edge, away from the pounding of the water. The need to have a bridge across the river again had never been far from her mind since the day after the storm. When the handsome young man from the development company had arrived at her cottage her hopes had risen that perhaps he would help, but she couldn't let too much time go by while she waited. The way to the pilgrims' church must be opened again quickly.

An idea had struck her during the night; if the stones could be dragged out of their places in the stone pillars, why could they not be put back in place? Now she could see them in daylight, it seemed to her that the individual stones were not so very large. Of course stones were heavy, even stones of modest proportions, but, if they could be moved one at a time, surely it would be possible to rebuild the bridge, stone by stone. Then there would be the question of how to replace the thick wooden planks to complete the bridge.

Encouraged, she looked at her watch to see if she had made herself late for Morag. No, there was still plenty of time to get there. Should she tell Morag her exciting idea? No, she decided, it was too early. She would need to have something more tangible to convince her pragmatic friend; Morag would need evidence that repairing the bridge one stone at a time was possible.

*

That same morning, Martin Fielding went into the boardroom feeling confident. He was ready to give an update on the Netherton development. Arnold Wheeler was already sitting at the large table when he arrived, even though the meeting was not due to start for another ten minutes. Once again Fielding had prepared a colourful presentation of all the information he had gathered so far, with a map of the area and how the proposed development would fit into it. He had also prepared a broad-brush financial costing: Fred and Susan Roland would work on the details of budgets. He had worked hard; he knew that the whole thing wasn't in the bag yet, but he was pleased with how it looked so far. He had contacted the Land Registry to ascertain who owned the land around Netherton, and had taken some legal advice, including a land search to learn about possible rights of way and restrictions as to land usage. The story he had uncovered went back a long way; a family called Haliwell had first owned land in the area hundreds of years ago, including the hill where St Brannock's church was, evidently a site with a long history. They also acquired a large piece of land on one side of the present village of Netherton.

"All right, Fielding, let's hear what's going on at your end of things," barked Wheeler, without bothering with any greetings or other formalities.

"No problem." He opened his laptop, which he had already connected to the projector positioned above their heads, hoping this could be the day when his preparations for the meeting would actually be viewed by the board, and he might get the recognition due to him. It was not to be so, however.

"Not that again!" sneered Wheeler," I've told you before, I don't like all that stuff." Wheeler watched Fielding's face, the colour rising in it. He decided to soften his approach for once. "Martin," he said, "You must understand I've been in this business for a very long time – since you were in nappies," he grinned, exposing his teeth, long and yellowed. His expression was half-way between a smile and an animal snarling. "I've done it all without electronic claptrap, and I'm too old and too impatient to start now." He narrowed his eyes, studying Fielding's frustration and powerlessness. He enjoyed pulling the carpet from beneath his underlings' feet, it reinforced who was boss.

Fielding spoke carefully, "Just as you like, Mr Wheeler. It was just a way of presenting the facts clearly." He hoped to indicate by this that Wheeler's method was a hindrance to clarity and efficiency. However, it wasn't so easy to wrong-foot Wheeler.

"Aren't you able to speak clearly then, Fielding? Come on, open your mouth and see how you get on!"

Fielding closed his laptop, swallowed his pride, and began, "I've done background research on the main project I'm investigating at the moment, the Netherton development. Without going into any details then," he touched his laptop as he said this, "I have found out who the land belongs to – it belongs to the Haliwell family, who arrived in the area centuries ago. It seems there aren't many direct descendants of the family left, but the land still belongs to Elise Haliwell, who lives in the United States, Colorado Springs. I'm due to visit the family's solicitor here in the UK who deals with any issues connected with their land, to inform him that we are interested in purchasing. I've got a detailed map of the area and have drawn up possible plans for our development, with broad costs."

"Good. Keep it going then. Any conflict of interests so far?"

"No, not so far. All the locals I've spoken to seem very amenable to the idea of building new houses. I've had to offer a few carrots: possible grant to the village school to help them get their building updated, or perhaps we could build an extension ourselves, and I told the vicar we were building 'affordable housing' for cash-strapped locals."

Wheeler snorted, "Fat chance of that. Still, if we stick a couple of cheap houses in at the edge to keep the country bumpkins happy it won't kill us, so long as it doesn't interfere with the high-end appeal to bring in the punters who'll deliver the profits we're after." He paused for a moment, then, "*Good*. Put it all into a report *on paper* for us, and get that solicitor to give us some definite indication from the owner that they'll sell. Then we'll need to fast-track it into a legally binding commitment, with a penalty clause built in just in case they try to back out."

Fred and Susan Roland both murmured their approval and smiled sycophantically at Wheeler. He turned back to Martin, "Good work, Martin. With Netherton and the other two current projects, we should be pulling in some really good money next year."

Fred chipped in adventurously, "Enough for Arnold to retire on very comfortably and take some well-earned rest—"

"Enough of that," interrupted Wheeler, "I've got no interest in retiring – I prefer to work – it keeps me young!" He laughed loudly, banging the table hard, making Fielding jump.

"Arnold," Fred, trying to cover his faux pas quickly, said eagerly, "Would you like Susan and me to spend some time on the Netherton development? We could start figuring out which contracts to put out to tender. We're going to need plenty of labour to complete it in the sort of timescale we prefer at Bluebird."

"Yes, get the figures done and then we'll put some feelers out to some likely providers."

Susan spoke for the first time, "You know we'll do the best job we can for you, Arnold, as always," she simpered.

There were a few minor points raised from the other projects, and then Arnold Wheeler yawned, opening his mouth wide without covering it with his hand. This signified the end of the meeting. He got up and walked to the door of the boardroom, tossing over his shoulder the remark, "Well, work to do, chop, chop!" And he was gone.

Fielding left the boardroom and went into his office to start working on the report Wheeler required, *on paper*. He would have to extract all the information he had organised in tables and charts in his colourful presentation and summarise it in plain words.

The Rolands remained for a few minutes at the table, discussing what to do next. Fred began to gather his folders together, "I think, dear, we will continue to look into the Netherton development. Let's take a trip there now – we could have lunch there while we're about it."

*

Fred and Susan Roland arrived at the Mason's Arms feeling hungry after walking around Netherton to gain an overall impression of the area. It was still quite early for lunch, and only half a dozen customers had arrived as yet for the lunchtime specials. Susan sat down at a table while Fred went to the bar to ask about ordering lunch. George Wright was behind the bar when Fred approached saying, "I see you have some tempting things on your lunchtime menu board!" Wright looked up, taking in the small man who leant over the bar; he looked fussy, thought Wright, the type who led a neat suburban life, never having got his hands dirty, but somehow raked off enough profit to live very comfortably. He curled his lip with derision, then hid his distaste and adopted his pub landlord's persona, "Yes, game pie today! I can recommend it – it's delicious. Meg will come and take your order in a moment. Anything to drink while you're waiting?" As he served their drinks, he asked if they were new to the area.

"Yes, we are new in a way; we're not actually residents, but are part of a company wanting to invest here."

Wright was immediately alert, always interested in anything which may be to his advantage. "Invest? Sounds interesting – invest in what exactly?"

"Development opportunities... luxury homes, possibly an upmarket leisure facility... it all needs to be assessed and costed," said Fred, not wanting to give too much away.

"Houses then?" pressed Wright, thinking that would bring more business for the pub.

"Yes, more customers for you!" said Fred, guessing his thoughts. "Lots of people with money to spend here in the village."

"How big a project will it be?"

Fred had started to drink his pint of beer, and it was already beginning to loosen his tongue. He was feeling at ease, a man of importance talking about big plans. "All at a very early stage, my wife and I are assessing the overall feasibility and costs: planning, materials and labour etc. – we need to be sure we can bring in the best outcome at the best price. You'll understand that as a businessman yourself," he said, with the smallest hint of condescension; obviously a pub landlord's "business" could not be compared with his own responsibilities.

"If you're needing labourers, I may be able to help you." Wright was leaning forward on the bar, his voice lowered.

"Really?" Fred leaned in closer too.

"One of my regulars brings in teams of workers, at very attractive rates. Perhaps you'd like me to have a word with him."

"Teams of workers, at a low cost?" asked Fred. "That sounds very interesting. I suppose it would have to be handled... *quietly*."

"Yes, a private arrangement, a gentleman's agreement, you could call it. And if I manage to help you get what you're wanting, I expect there would be a..."

"A 'Thank you' for yourself, of course," said Fred quickly, "for your help."

"Give me your number. I'll make some enquiries and call you when I've arranged a meeting."

Fred was excited; this was a very lucky coincidence. Arnold would be so impressed. He decided to offer their standard "sweetener" to Wright – three hundred pounds for making a vital link or key opening step for a project. He reduced his voice to little more than a whisper, "I'll wait for your call then. Our 'thank you' is three hundred, payable after a successful agreement is reached." He wrote down his mobile phone number on the back of a beer mat and slid it across the bar.

"Sounds reasonable," said Wright.

During their conversation, Meg had already gone over to the table where Fred's wife was sitting, waiting. Susan was so irritated that Fred had stayed talking at the bar without any regard for her that she ordered for him without asking him what he wanted. She was hungry and not prepared to wait any longer. She sat purse-lipped while Meg tried the usual pleasantries, "It's not a bad day for the time of year, is it? I love these autumn days."

Susan looked up at Meg standing next to the table, weighing her up, guessing she had two or three grown-up children, and maybe a few grandchildren. Probably had them all round on Sundays, squeezing them into a small house, feeding them on cheap food from the supermarket. Why did women like this choose to live such pathetic little lives, slaving away in menial jobs?

She forced a thin smile on to her lips, "Yes, beautiful time of year. My husband and I try to squeeze a little time away from our business affairs to have a run out into the country to see the autumn colours." She enjoyed the feeling of superiority; she didn't want this little woman to mistake them for retired people looking for a cheap pub lunch. She hoped they didn't look old enough to be retired. She sat up straighter in her chair and pulled her stomach in.

"Your lunch won't be long. Enjoy your break from work," Meg said kindly, thinking the woman looked strained, probably working too hard, she thought, and hurried back to the kitchen, passing George Wright and Fred Roland, still talking earnestly. Were they friends? Or was this another of the men who met in the room upstairs? The meetings of the Guild were always conducted with the door firmly closed. Despite having worked at the Mason's Arms for years, and having prepared the upper room for a great number of Guild meetings, she still had no idea what was discussed between the men who gathered there. Many of them she recognised, men from this village and beyond, linked together in some undisclosed way. Perhaps it was a bit like the Mothers' Union, she thought, for friendship and sometimes to raise money for a good cause. But why the secrecy? She thought about the secret club her son used to have in the shed in her garden; five boys from the village used to meet there and could only get into the shed if they gave a secret password. Perhaps it was an adult version of that, something men are attracted to.

*

At seven thirty, Mike Small took his usual place at the bar. "Evening, George, pint of Bishop's when you're ready."

Wright put a pint glass under the beer tap, filling it slowly, waiting for the other customers to move away from the bar, out of earshot. Then he spoke quietly, "Had a man in here today asking me if I could put him in touch with some workers for a new building project. Seems he's on a tight budget, if you know what I mean."

Mike looked around him, checking they weren't overheard. "How many is he after?"

"He's talking about a big building project, luxury homes, leisure club. He wants figures, how much a day, that sort of thing."

Mike Small thought for a minute. "Tell him I can do it, and it will show up on the books as OK. He won't get a better deal anywhere else."

"He wants to meet you."

"Fine, I'll see him. Tomorrow, seven-thirty, can we use the room upstairs?"

"No problem." Wright looked straight at Mike Small, "I'm sure you'll want to remember me with thanks, won't you Mike? You could say it was for the room hire, if you like. Write it off against tax." He laughed, but Mike Small knew he expected to be paid. It didn't bother him – they could all benefit from this – it was a goldmine, there for anyone bold enough to take from it.

Chapter Six

Anna stood in the kitchen, deep in thought. Five minutes ago, she had decided to make some toast, but here she was just standing by the toaster, thoughts racing. She was in two minds about this afternoon's arrangement with Martin Fielding. What he had said about providing houses for local families sounded so good, and she remembered his tanned skin and dark eyes, the engaging way he talked and his expensive car, suggesting a lifestyle of glamour. The other half of her whispered *calm down, what seems to be too good to be true probably is exactly that... a warm heart is worth more than wealth and good looks.* So there she was, stuck by the toaster, confused and unsure. The ringing of her mobile phone jolted her back into consciousness of her surroundings. She recognised the caller's voice immediately – Fran, a friend from university, asking her how things were going. Anna perched on the edge of the table while she told her about the promising contacts she'd made for her fledgling business. "But what about romance?" probed her friend, "Come on, spill the beans"! Anna hesitated, and Fran guessed there was something she wasn't saying. Finally, Anna weakened and told her about Martin. Her friend was suitably impressed, "Good grief! What are you hesitating for! He sounds gorgeous, obviously a successful businessman, and has a beautiful car – go for it, Anna! He sounds *heavenly!*"

So Anna did. She went upstairs immediately and washed and blow-dried her dark brown hair into long glossy curls resting on her shoulders. She put on a black tailored skirt, a beautiful white cotton blouse with tiny sprigs of embroidered flowers and then a pair of dark sheer tights, being careful not to snag them with the dry rough skin around her nails, the result of the white spirit she had used to remove paint from her fingers. She completed the look with her only pair of black high-heeled shoes. She looked at herself in the full-length mirror on her wardrobe door, aware that she looked lovely.

At ten minutes to two she put her head around the door of her father's study, calling out brightly, "Going out soon Dad, won't be long – you remember I agreed to show that property developer around the area."

"Of course," replied her father absently, "What was his name again... oh yes, *Martin.*" He got up from his desk and walked over, his hand reaching for the door handle. Anna realised she didn't want her father to open the door fully and see what she was wearing – it was so different from the usual jeans and jumper. Too late, he pulled the door open, "Goodness, Anna, you look absolutely wonderful. I can see this young man has made a deep impression!"

Anna, embarrassed, answered nonchalantly, "Just fancied smartening up for a change."

"I hope he appreciates what a privilege it is to take my beautiful daughter out."

"Dad, it's not even a date," said Anna, "I'm just being helpful, that's all."

The doorbell rang, ending their conversation.

Martin Fielding looked approvingly at her as she came out of the vicarage and walked down the steps towards his waiting car. He opened the passenger door for her, playing the part of the perfect gentleman, then got into the driver's seat and started the engine with a little more pressure on the accelerator than was necessary – the car sounded powerful. Without asking for directions, he swung it out of the drive.

*

The afternoon passed pleasantly, driving from one village to the next, Anna trying to give a running commentary on anything of interest. Around half past three they noticed a very appealing country hotel which had an "Afternoon Tea" sign outside.

"Let me treat you to a cream tea," he said, "to thank you for giving up a whole afternoon for me." Put like that, Anna could hardly refuse. They went inside together.

Sitting opposite each other at a table gave her the chance to look directly at him again. He was undeniably very good-looking, like someone in a fashion magazine. She saw his slim hands on the silver-plated knife, slicing and spreading efficiently. He noticed her watching and, without warning, reached across the table and took hold of one of her hands. She felt a kind of electric impulse as their skin touched, alarming but compelling. He spoke softly, "This afternoon has been so special." His index finger ran slowly over the back of her hand. Taken by surprise, she was glad that at that moment the waiter came across to their table, giving her the chance to move her hand quickly, embarrassed. Fielding whispered, "Sorry!" and after that kept the conversation strictly to light-hearted things, aware that he had overstepped the mark. He asked her about her university course, listening intently to her ideas on design, saying how wonderful it must be to be artistic, that his life in the business world was so harsh, it was so good to be with someone with a whole different approach to life. Then, at the end of the afternoon, about half-way home, he asked, respectfully, could he see her again? Reassured and flattered by their conversation, she smiled and said yes.

"That makes me very happy," he said, and took one hand off the steering wheel, moving it to find hers. He lifted her hand to his lips and kissed it, his eyes still on the road. It was a moment of perfect romance, the setting sun lighting the sky as they drove back through the countryside, the last of the autumn colours all around them. For the next few miles, he drove one-handed, his left hand still holding hers. She felt excited, but also nervous; without really intending to she had started a relationship with him; he had smoothly re-positioned them into being a couple. Two or three miles from Appleton, he said he could hear a vibration beneath the sound of the engine; he must stop for a moment and check it. He got out of the car, and walked round the back, stooping down to look underneath. Then he got back in, "Sorry, everything looks all right, just thought I'd better check."

Before she knew it, he had moved towards her, sliding his arms around her and drawing her towards him. His mouth found hers. She gasped, her breath taken away by the suddenness of his move, and placed a hand on his shoulder, pushing back against him, resisting him, turning her head to one side. He whispered into her ear, "I'm sorry, I couldn't resist you, you're just so lovely." She tried to reply, but he placed his finger on her lips, "Don't say anything, I don't want to make you do anything you're not happy with. Don't worry, I'll take you home."

She felt a sense of guilt, as though somehow she had let him down or behaved badly, but couldn't understand why she should feel so. She remembered what Fran had said to her when Anna had described Martin to her.

He kissed her again when he stopped the car outside the vicarage. He didn't enter the drive – perhaps he preferred to be hidden from sight of the vicarage windows. This time it was just a soft kiss on the cheek, accompanied by a half smile. "Imagine," he said mischievously, "*me*, with the vicar's daughter. Perhaps you'll make me into a better man – the love of a good woman etc.!"

Anna looked into his brown eyes. She felt all his attention focused on her... it was so flattering that she was so attractive to him, so desired. She felt beautiful, powerfully feminine, but also disturbingly like a trophy that had just been won.

*

Meg left the Mason's Arms at ten o'clock. She lived half a mile away, only about ten minutes' brisk walk. She never worried about walking home alone. She had done it for years, and the streets were generally quiet, apart from a few bored teenagers. She assumed tonight would be the same as any other night as she set off in the darkness from the pub door: all was quiet, as though the whole village had already settled down for the night. She was half-way home, walking along by the edge of the village green. At the centre was a great oak tree with heavy branches hanging down towards the grass. As she hurried along, her attention was caught by some movements near the tree. She could hear some muffled sounds. What was it? The light from the street lamps along the edge of the green did not reach very far and she could only just make out the darker outline of the huge tree. The sounds were coming from that direction. She stepped a little closer on the grass, the dew quickly soaking through her shoes, wetting her feet. Then she heard a sort of gasp, just audible. Her first thought was that she had come across a romantic liaison, a couple entwined beneath the old oak. She began to move on, but something stopped her, something about the sound that didn't seem right. What if it was a young girl caught in a situation that had got out of control? The thought flashed through her mind that, if it had been her daughter, she would want someone to intervene. She couldn't resist checking to see if the girl, if it was a girl, was all right. She could be walking into trouble of course; perhaps her good intentions would be met with aggression. As naturally as breathing, she prayed under her breath, "Jesus, be with me as I go to see if this young person is safe. Please protect me."

She began to walk towards the tree, calling out, "Excuse me! Is everything all right? I heard a sound." As she finished speaking, there was a sudden rush of movement, and she was pushed violently to one side. She fell awkwardly, sprawling on the cold wet grass. Two figures sped past her, one treading on her hand as he went. She cried out in pain then started to struggle back on to her feet. As she lifted her head, she saw something move on the trunk of the tree. She could make out a human shape there. She got up and moved closer, hearing a whimpering sound. In the dark she could only just see the pathetic outline of a boy, tied to the trunk of the tree. His head was hanging forward, his breathing laboured. She put out her hands to him, gently lifting his head up, "You poor boy. Don't worry, you're safe now. I'll get help." The boy moved his head, his mouth struggling to form words, "No, don't leave me.... *Please.*"

Meg felt along the ropes which had been tied tightly round him. In the dark she could not see how they were tied. She felt her way round to the back of the wide trunk and found they were elasticated bungee ropes, held not by knots but by hooks at their ends. Pulling hard on them, she managed to unhook them. As she did so, she heard the boy slump on to the ground on the other side of the tree. She hurried back round to the other side and sat down on the grass next to him, cradling him in her arms. "You're safe now." She fumbled in her coat pocket for her phone and dialled 999, "Ambulance, please, hurry, a boy's been beaten up on the village green, Netherton."

*

Meanwhile, in Upper Exton, Fred and Susan Roland sat together at home in their dining room, papers spread out on the table in front of them. They had put different aspects of the proposed Netherton development onto separate sheets of paper, with columns of figures on each, breakdowns of estimated costs for equipment, labourers, office personnel, sales staff, legal costs, advertising and publicity. They were excited, sensing that this could be one of their most profitable exercises so far. The main thrust of their efforts was to cut as much as possible from each of the columns representing costs, each time increasing the overall profit margin. They loved it, this intricate game of figures, with a reward at the end of it. The reward was a multiple one – firstly, a financial bonus for them, something to invest in their growing portfolio of shares, hidden away to ensure their comfort and security; secondly, the kudos gained from another personal triumph, to be bragged about in their small group of friends, and, thirdly, the achievement of pleasing Wheeler. They had been with him for decades, bending their administrative skills to his driving will and ambition. He was their leader, and he had an absolute hold over them. They never questioned his judgement, even privately. He made them feel secure, needed, occupying a reserved niche, the world made safe for them because of Wheeler's control.

They worked on into the night, their keen motivation energizing them. The hands on the gilt wall clock clicked past one o'clock, then two, but they worked on without flagging until half past two, finally stacking their sheets of paper into neat piles.

Fred Roland stretched, his back stiff from leaning over the table for so long, "The only thing that really bothers me is the labour costs. It could undermine the whole plan unless we really get on top of it. However, I have an idea about that."

She looked at him, curious, her eyes narrowing with interest.

He added a tinge of mystery, "I am making careful enquiries about a new supply of labour, but I'll be sure to keep any *complications* at a distance from ourselves. No need to mention any names at this stage. We'll keep it all on a business level, entering into a contract in good faith with the provider, according to employment law etc. We'll check the small print, make sure any liability stays away from us."

"Good," she said contentedly, "Just keep us out of any *messy bits*."

"Of course, Susan," he said, as they got up from the table and turned off the lights. They headed up the stairs to their king-size bed in the master bedroom of their comfortable suburban home. Within minutes, they would be resting their heads on their feather pillows, reaching out to turn off their bedside lamps, satisfied. Outside, the night wind blew across the closely-mown lawn and neat flower beds, picking up a few dry leaves and blowing them against the tall electric gates which locked out the rest of the world.

They slept soundly until eight o'clock when their alarm clock rang. Fred had decided to give them a little longer in bed than usual this morning on account of their late-night working the previous evening. Despite having had only a few hours' sleep, he felt refreshed, eager to get into the new day. He got up and went into the bathroom, smoothing his thinning hair over his head as he looked at himself in the mirror over the sink. He smiled at his reflection, still enjoying the feeling of pleasure at the progress they had made, looking forward to getting into the office.

"Susan!" he called from the bathroom, "Are you getting up? Lots to do!"

He needn't have bothered; she was just as eager to get to work, laying out her clothes on the bed. She called out happily, "Yes, Fred, I won't be long."

By nine o'clock, they were walking through the doors of the Bluebird building. Unusually, Wheeler was there before them, standing next to the front desk. "There you are!" he shouted to them. "Getting bad habits, are you? I didn't expect to see you two to coming in at this hour!"

Fred adjusted his glasses, pushing them further up his nose, agitated and embarrassed, "It's just nine o'clock exactly, Arnold; we allowed ourselves a slower start as we were working on the Netherton project until very late last night."

"Until half past two," added Susan quietly, irritated for a moment, then smiling weakly at Wheeler as he turned his attention towards her.

"Well! That's good to hear!" he responded. "Let's hear what you've come up with!" He started to walk in front in them towards the lift, then turned towards them again, speaking very loudly so as to get the attention of the two girls at the reception desk, "I'm *quivering* with excitement!" Exploding with laughter, he continued on his way, the Rolands scurrying to get into the lift with him.

When they were seated round the table in the boardroom, the Rolands opened their folders and took out their sheets of projections and calculations, spreading them across the table in front of Wheeler. He ran his finger down the columns, pausing every now and then to ask a pointed question, each one focused on ensuring the cheapest possible materials and methods were to be used. When his eyes fell on the costs for labour, he jerked his head up, fixing Fred with a stare. "What's going on here?" he demanded, stabbing at the columns with his finger. "There's two figures for each line."

"Yes," Fred answered quickly, "the one in black is based on the estimated cost of labour from building contractors which we have used for some of our previous projects. The red figure, which is much lower, is an alternative estimate based on the new labour market."

"What do you mean, new labour market?"

"Builders, plasterers, plumbers who have only recently become available."

Wheeler folded his arms, deep in thought, taking it in. Then said quietly, "Immigrants."

"Yes. I have a contact who could arrange it."

Wheeler looked up abruptly, "Have you talked to him already?" He spoke sharply, as though he was firing bullets at Fred, who almost winced.

"No, Arnold! I wouldn't dream of moving forward on anything without your approval."

Susan saw her opportunity to grease the wheels, and leaned toward Wheeler, speaking gently, "Fred has a friend, Arnold, a trusted friend, a very *discreet* person, who, if you would like him to, he could have a little talk with."

"That's all right then." Wheeler lowered his voice. He stood up, moving away from the table to stand by the window, looking out. Fred sensed he was meant to go and stand next to him. As he did so, Wheeler spoke again. "You understand I cannot be brought into this." He turned slightly to look into Fred's face, "I trust you to keep my name out of it, for the sake of the company, and that means all of us."

"Of course, Arnold, you can rely on me... on *us*," he said, glancing at Susan.

"Talk to your friend then and get some prices and numbers. Tell him he must handle the people, and you'll make sure he gets paid. We'll need to look at how it will appear in the books – he'll have to have a company name, bank account etc. Before you start talking to him, see our lawyer, get him to tell you how it must be done. I'll ring him now."

Wheeler pulled his mobile phone out of his pocket and pressed a speed dial number. It was answered immediately.

"Greenwood? I want you to see Fred Roland this morning- he needs some advice. I'll send him over to you now."

He finished the call without any further discussion. Whatever Greenwood had planned to do this morning would have to be put on hold. He turned back to Fred, "You go and talk with Greenwood. If you can get this sorted, we'll save on your reckoning, about two million on labour alone." He laughed,

"That will suit us very nicely."

Fred looked over at his wife, wanting her to be included in this rare moment of approval. "Susan and I have really racked our brains about how we could try to make this our best project yet."

Wheeler twisted the corners of his mouth into a forced smile, which in fact was more alarming than his usual expression, "Of course, Susan and Fred, you *two together* are the best asset this company has."

It was all that was needed. Fred shuffled his feet with pleasure, and Susan turned pink, saying, "Thank you, Arnold, you know how loyal we are to the company." Fred put his arm round his wife's shoulders while Wheeler watched them, a thin layer of disgust spreading across his face. For a ghastly moment he thought they were going to weep. He cleared his throat, wanting to move on, "Off you go then."

Their moment of glory was over. They collected their sheets of paper, stuffing them quickly into the folders and left the boardroom quietly. Wheeler was already on the phone.

*

Hilda remarked to herself how beautiful the morning was as she rolled a heavy stone a few inches at a time along the steep riverbank from where the angry Ishka had dropped it on the night of the storm. She was wearing her thickest gardening gloves. She moved it to where she had already started to lay stones tightly together, where the foundations of the stone pillars of the destroyed bridge still remained. Over the next hour, following the existing pattern of stones, she managed to push five back into position, making them interlock tightly like pieces of a jigsaw. It was quiet today; there was nobody around to see the elderly woman, her back bent as she strained to move the heavy stones. At eleven o'clock, she was exhausted, stopping to rest and catch her breath. For a moment a dizzy spell overtook her, and she reached out and grasped a branch to steady herself. The world seemed to spin around her for a while, but when it was steady again, she breathed a sigh of relief and viewed her handiwork. It wasn't much, but it was a good start. She climbed up the steep riverbank, using the branches of trees to help her. Tomorrow she would come back and continue.

She walked back to her cottage slowly, anticipating the pleasure of a pot of tea on a tray with a biscuit, to be enjoyed in the comfort of an armchair. As she went along, a familiar voice called out to her, "Good morning, Hilda!"

She looked in the direction of the voice and saw the vicar waving to her from further up the street. She waved back, another surge of tiredness washing over her at the thought of having to make conversation, even with James. She wasn't sure she had sufficient energy left. Fortunately, he didn't come any further down the street but went through one of the cottage gates further along the street. He must be visiting Mary Williams, she thought.

She had almost reached her door when James reappeared, this time on her garden path. "Hilda, just thought I'd see how you were. I knocked on Mary's door and she seems to be out – have you seen her recently? She wasn't at church on Sunday."

"She's not been well again recently, but I saw her earlier, walking in the direction of the bus stop."

"That's good, she must be feeling better at the moment."

"Come in, James, I was just about to make some tea."

Hilda unlocked the door and, hands shaking slightly, filled the kettle and put some cups on a tray. She had made a habit of being hospitable no matter what her own feelings were at the time. She found this ensured that her home was a haven for anyone who needed an escape from their troubles. Many people had left her cottage feeling so much more peaceful than when they had arrived. Perhaps James was one of them, she thought, as she poured milk into a small china jug. James sat quietly until she came to sit down next to him. "Tell me, how are you just now James?"

He looked slightly agitated at her question, not expecting that it would be his welfare that would be the focus of their conversation. He fumbled for words; he couldn't tell this dignified elderly lady the truth about his internal turmoil, so he settled for the customary "Fine, thank you."

But Hilda had spotted the hesitation. She passed him his cup, and offered him a lemon biscuit, and let a few moments of silence pass between them. Then, sensing the time was right, said quickly, "It's all right for you to be an ordinary human being, you know, even though you are the vicar. In fact, being just an ordinary human is rather exciting."

James wondered if he had heard her correctly, "Did you say *exciting*?" He wondered what could be exciting about being eighty-plus years old.

"Absolutely. There's always something to be excited about, if you can keep your eyes open."

Although James had often thought Hilda was a lively person for her age, this statement took him by surprise. What did she mean by it? What did she have to be excited about? A little bargain to be had at the local shops ... a visit by a blue tit in her garden? And what about his own life? Shouldn't they both, as long-term Christians, simply be quietly going about their normal daily round, undisturbed by excitement and surprises? Somehow this connected with the heart of his dilemma. The disturbance he was feeling, which was keeping him awake at night, was a complete surprise to him, and was very exciting in its own way, but was it something he *should* be excited about, or was the excitement forbidden? He was deep in thought, holding his teacup in front of him.

"No lemon biscuit then?" Hilda enquired, still holding the plate of slim biscuits, their golden crisp edges slightly crumbly, arranged on a flowered porcelain tea plate.

"Sorry, I was daydreaming," said James, reaching out for a biscuit hastily, and knocking two of them on to the rug. He jumped up, and spilt some of his tea in its saucer. "So sorry, Hilda, what a clumsy oaf I am."

"Just leave them on the tray, dear," said Hilda kindly when James had picked the fallen biscuits up.

"Try again, slowly this time." Her eyes almost twinkled, her tiredness ebbing away as she watched James in his comical struggle to maintain his dignity. She could see there was something troubling this poor man. Had the good Lord led him to her door at just the right moment to provide a listening ear?

"James, do you sometimes think that God has all sorts of plans and ideas?"

James was grateful, but also slightly perturbed, when a member of his congregation volunteered to talk about God. In recent times he had become more accustomed to having to somehow squeeze God into the conversation, much to most people's discomfort, even though they were regular churchgoers.

"Yes, I do think God has, as you put it, plans and ideas, Hilda." The faces of the professors of theology who had taught him during his training flitted across his mind. The terms they were familiar with in connection with God were much loftier. They were concerned with symbolism and sacramental ordinances, and hermeneutics. Would they have been happy about God having all sorts of plans and ideas? It certainly sounded much more interesting than hermeneutics, he thought, then realised his thoughts had been straying again, while Hilda sat quietly watching him. "Sorry, Hilda, did you have anything in particular in mind? Or was it just generally?"

"I think there's a great danger in considering everything just as 'generally'," she answered mischievously. "You see, 'generally' reduces things to a kind of uninteresting sludge – a little bit boring and tame."

James didn't know how to reply. Was the dear old thing going round the bend a bit? He settled for saying, "Oh, I see," while thinking he hadn't a clue what she was talking about.

Hilda chuckled, "In the spring and summer, my garden is full of flowers. But if someone a long way from here telephoned me and said, 'Tell me what a flower generally looks like,' I would have to reply that I couldn't possibly give a general description, they're all so completely different, different colours, red and blue and yellow. If you tried to lump them all together, you'd end up with a muddy colour, do you see? You'd lose the wonder of them, the differentness."

"I *think* I see what you mean," said James.

"Poor you, I've thrown you in the deep end," said Hilda.

James fidgeted in his chair, completely confused as to where the conversation was going.

Hilda was unperturbed, "I mean, although I think God does 'generally' have some things in mind for us... but don't you think God had some special individual plans and ideas in mind *just for you* and *just for me*?"

"I'm sure you're right," James replied quickly. "You're quite a theologian."

"Not really, but I do think God is very close to us, and cares about every little thing in our lives, and has some very good ideas for us."

James blushed; could Mia, the woman who was disturbing his sleep, be one of God's very good ideas? He felt his safe predictable world was rocking on its foundations. Could this be part of God's plan for him? Or was it a terrible temptation? He looked at Hilda's bright eyes behind her gold-rimmed spectacles. Could he confide in her? He opened his mouth and began, "Sometimes, however, it's difficult to tell the good ideas from the pitfalls, isn't it?"

"It is, especially when the pitfalls sometimes look so tempting," she said gently.

James wondered if somebody had been whispering to Hilda. It was as though someone had been spying on him, it was so peculiar that she seemed to have guessed his inner thoughts.

Hilda put out her hand and patted James' arm, "We just need to ask the Good Shepherd, don't we? Ask him to guide us away from the pitfalls."

"Yes of course." James stood up, feeling he needed to go. "Thank you for the tea, Hilda, and sorry about the biscuits."

"Not at all... you know my door is always open, James."

"Yes." This time he spoke from the heart, "I appreciate it, Hilda." He left the cottage feeling a little lighter, a little less alone.

Chapter Seven

Anna saw the text pop up on her phone. Martin was asking her to go to see a play with him in Exton that evening. It was an Agatha Christie, he said, nothing too demanding, just right for a relaxing Friday evening. She guessed he must be trying to put her at ease about the pace of their developing relationship – what could be more reassuring than a good old-fashioned Agatha Christie mystery? She put any feelings of unease about his previous behaviour aside and texted back, *OK, that sounds like fun.* He picked her up at six thirty, so that they would have plenty of time to park. In fact, he drove so fast they had more than enough time, so he suggested going to a cocktail bar. Anna was not at all sure what this would be like, but imagined it would be simply a smaller, perhaps smarter setting than a traditional pub. As they went through the door of the Jazz Nights bar, she realised it was much more sophisticated than she had anticipated. The decor was black and gold, very tasteful art deco. The barman greeted Martin as though he remembered him from many other nights. Anna looked around; on the walls were groups of large black and white photographs of musicians from the 1930s, all very stylish. The lighting was subdued, a mellow glow provided by gold-shaded wall lights and slim lamps on the tables and at the ends of the long bar. A few people were already there, chatting in low voices, drinking cocktails of different colours. In the corner of the bar a pianist was playing songs from the 1930s, sweet jazz melodies drifting over the sound of the customers' chatter, subtly changing the mood of the people, drawing them away from the stresses of the week into the relaxed, romantic ambience.

"I feel a little under-dressed," she said, looking at the attractive women there wearing close-fitting dresses and sparkling earrings.

"Don't worry, you look lovely." He placed his hand gently on her back, steering her towards the bar, "What would you like?" he asked.

"I've no idea – I've never had a cocktail before."

He smiled at her, leaning down quickly to plant the tiniest of kisses on the tip of her nose, "You are such an innocent," he said, "Let me be your guide to the wonders of cocktails."

He showed her the long list of cocktails, pointing out those which were particularly popular with young women.

"I'd better have whatever you think I'd like," she said simply, "since I'm so totally ignorant."

He moved down the long bar for a moment to where the barman was serving another customer and gave their order. Anna didn't know what he had chosen for her. He was back at her side in a moment, suggesting they go over to a table in the window. It gave them a view out on to the street and the bustle of people going out for the evening. Rain started to fall, soaking the pavement outside. The lights of the restaurants and bars were reflected on it in long bright streaks, adding another dimension to the bright nightlife scene.

"Are you warm enough?" he asked her, putting his hand on her arm gently, feeling its temperature, looking concerned.

In fact, the bar was very warm. How kind of him to be wondering if I'm feeling chilly, she thought, it must be because we're sitting by the window. The cocktails arrived; hers was a delicate pink, in an elegant slim-stemmed glass, with tiny pieces of fruit impaled on a cocktail stick. She sipped it tentatively, it was delicious. "Which one is this?" she asked.

"It's a house special," he said. "An original, unique, just like you!"

She laughed, and took another sip.

The cocktail soon had the intended effect; as the music played on Anna became totally relaxed. He reached across the table and took her hand, and when a waiter came across to ask them if they would like more drinks, Martin nodded and murmured, "Same again."

She didn't object, despite the fuzziness in her head; she was enjoying the romantic atmosphere.

She was half-way through the second cocktail when she remembered the play, "Goodness! We should go! We'll miss the start." She started to get up.

He reached across to catch hold of her hand again, "We don't have to go, we can just stay here."

Without thinking, she brushed the suggestion aside, "No, not at all, it's such a nice idea of yours to go to a play." She turned away from him to retrieve her jacket and handbag, so missed the look of disappointment, even annoyance, that flitted across his face.

"Finish your cocktail first." He pushed the glass towards her.

"I don't think I'd better. I feel a bit light-headed already – I won't be able to follow the plot!"

He didn't answer. He was irritated, partly because the cocktail had just cost him nine pounds, but more so that he was enjoying the mellowing effect it was having on Anna.

They walked to the theatre from the cocktail bar as the rain had eased up, and Anna was pleased to have some fresh air to clear her head. The theatre was small and tired looking, which surprised Anna, seeming so out of character for someone with Martin's tastes. He must have chosen it as a venue that she would be likely to agree to when he invited her, a local theatre company which needed support. Or had he ever intended to come at all? Was he really hoping to spend the evening in the Jazz Nights bar, drinking cocktails? He certainly didn't seem very keen to see the play. During the performance he sat very passively, glancing at his phone every now and then. He didn't turn it off, despite the plea from the director of the theatre company before the performance. He merely put it on silent, but continued to send texts. Each time the phone's screen lit up, a woman sitting next to him tutted. Anna thought he would probably take the hint and turn it off, but he was not so easily swayed. In the interval they went to the theatre bar and Martin ordered drinks for them while Anna was in the Ladies' room. It was too late for her to say she didn't want another drink; he had bought her a large glass of chilled white wine. Anna thought she had better drink it, it was so kind of him, he was obviously trying to please her. They only had a few minutes so she emptied her glass quickly, and they returned to their seats for the second half.

Anna felt considerably tipsy now, and was grateful to have a shoulder to lean against. She felt his arm slip around her, and his hand stroking her hair. The woman sitting on the other side of Martin got up and moved seats. On the stage, the actors continued, and Anna drifted into a doze, vaguely aware of the soothing effect of his hand on her hair, and neck... The sound of a gunshot on stage jolted her upright. She sat up straight, apologising to Martin, "Sorry, that made me jump! I must have been asleep."

He looked back at her, a dull, bored look coming into his eyes.

She searched in her handbag for the chocolates she had brought with her. They watched the last twenty minutes of the play with the box in between them. He didn't eat many. Soon the actors gathered on stage to take their final bow, and Anna picked up her handbag, ready to leave.

As they retraced their footsteps back to the car he said, looking towards the cocktail bar, that they just had time for a quick drink before the drive home. She was surprised, "But you're driving – it will put you over the limit."

He smiled and drew her towards him, "Don't worry, my cocktails were alcohol-free. They're not as good, but I wanted to be careful about consumption, and for you to enjoy the real thing. But now, I probably can risk a small one, just to round off this evening. Mustn't let you catch cold though," he said, taking off his jacket and putting it round her, then drawing her towards him and kissing her. She thought, how unselfish of him to want her to have the fun of trying cocktails whilst he did without – she hadn't thought there was such a thing as alcohol-free cocktails... her father would approve of Martin's restraint.

The lights seemed lower now in the bar. The barman began to prepare their cocktails, and they settled on a leather sofa in a corner of the room. Nobody seemed to mind that, as they drank their drinks, he kissed her; they were after all, tucked into a private corner. Her cocktail added its effect to the previous drinks, and Anna, lulled and disinhibited, began to kiss him back. He wanted to order some more drinks, but she roused herself sufficiently from her sleepy state to say drowsily that this time they *must* go home; her father would wonder where she was. He seemed to accept this, albeit reluctantly. Another time, he said.

*

Earlier that evening, Fred Roland had arrived at the Mason's Arms. As he and Susan tended to do most things together, he felt strangely alone as he walked in. He had made the arrangement to meet with this stranger without consulting Susan, which did not fit with their usual pattern of discussing things together in advance. He had been feeling excited by the idea of doing this on his own, relying on his own wits, but now that the time for the meeting had arrived, he felt exposed without her; she always was so sure about making the right decisions. He felt nervous, sweat breaking out on his forehead as he stood by the bar waiting to catch George Wright's attention.

After Wright had finished serving some customers, he nodded towards Fred, and came out from behind the bar. "You can wait upstairs," he said, "It's the room on the left."

Fred walked up the stairs and turned left at the top. There was a heavy wooden door at the end of a corridor. He opened it and walked into the room. It was furnished formally as a meeting room, a large polished wooden table occupying the centre of the room with an ornately carved chair at one end of it and fifteen carved wooden dining chairs around the rest of the table. On the walls hung paintings, portraits of local dignitaries apparently. The most impressive hung over the fireplace. Fred walked over to read the inscription beneath it. "John Richard Miller, Master of the Guild. 1770-1795." The face which looked out from the painting was a fearsome one, thick eyebrows low over hooded eyes, deep lines etched into the skin, set into an intimidating expression. The man was wearing a dark gown with wide sleeves. One sleeve had a band of purple fabric on it, with a symbol of some sort embroidered onto it. The meeting room itself was also a surprise; he had expected just an extra room for accommodating larger parties of people, or at most a room adapted to be hired out for meetings of local community groups, perhaps stretching to provide a flipchart and pens. But this room was something completely different to anything Fred would have imagined – Fred felt very small as he stood under the portrait, daunted by the atmosphere of the place, as though he had stumbled into somewhere he had no right to be, where influence or power of some sort resided.

He turned away from the painting as he heard the sound of someone approaching the room. He moved back towards the table, his hand resting for a moment on the high back of the chair at the head of the table. As he did his fingers felt the intricate carving, including the small centrepiece, a simple circular shape with a dip in the middle. At that moment, the door of the room opened and Mike Small walked in. He walked down the room to Fred and held out his hand to him, "Pleased to meet you, let's sit down and see how I can help you." He pointed to two winged chairs on either side of the fireplace. Mike Small sat down and lounged back in his, confident, affable. Fred sat on the edge of his, unsure how to start.

Mike Small was watching him steadily, weighing him up, enjoying Fred's discomfort, "I hear you need some workers for a building project."

"Yes, that's right. My company is hoping to start a large development on the edge of Netherton. We are in the process of drawing up plans but need to know we can find a workforce at short notice at an affordable price."

"No problem, that's my line of business, providing workers." Mike Small reached into the inside pocket of his jacket and took out a handwritten sheet of paper with figures on it. He held it out to Fred

"Here's an outline of what we could provide, numbers of workers, skilled and unskilled, cost per day. No overheads. We would provide transport to get them on site for the beginning of the day, and remove them at the end of the day." Fred quickly perused the figures, pleased with what he saw. "This looks promising. I spoke with our legal advisor, and there are certain reassurances we would need. He called it a 'firewall' between my company and your services. We would need to be able to pay into the bank account of a legally registered company which undertook to comply with employment regulations, and we'd need evidence of insurance against liabilities."

"I can do that for you; we've worked with several big companies, providing workers. We've had no complaints about our services," he said confidently.

Fred rubbed the palms of his hands, damp with sweat, on the sides of his trouser legs, saying, "Obviously I would have to take all this to our board, but in the meantime, would you be able to provide samples of the necessary documents, and details of your company?"

Mike Small talked for a few more minutes, reiterating his experience and success in this business, and then they shook hands again. Small gave Fred a contact number, and his name as simply 'Mike.' Fred decided to take a similar approach, and gave his own name just as 'Fred.' By now Fred was feeling confident again, a frisson of excitement energising him at being involved in cutting such a profitable deal, right on the edge of what would be accepted as legal. He felt clever and sophisticated. Arnold would be pleased.

*

James was unable to sleep much that Friday night. He fidgeted, turning over in his bed, unable to keep still and relax; his thoughts kept drifting back to the funeral of John Miller the next day. When he finally dropped into a fitful sleep he dreamt he was standing next to the open coffin during the funeral service, trying to pray, much as he had done at the Millers' farmhouse, and was struggling to get his words out, unable to form them, his tongue stuck. All the eyes of the people in the congregation were on him, and suddenly raucous laughter broke out all around him in the church, reverberating around the building, everyone mocking him and enjoying his acute embarrassment, culminating in the corpse in the coffin sitting up, and the dead face of John Seldon Miller breaking into a grin. James woke up in a cold sweat, glad to discover it was a dream, but still shaken by it. Surely the actual funeral couldn't be quite so horrific.

The following day, when the time of the funeral approached, James stood by the lych-gate of Netherton Church, waiting for the funeral cars to arrive, just as he had done on many other occasions. At last, he saw the black limousines coming. The undertaker's men stepped out of their cars and opened the back doors for the passengers to get out. James stood waiting quietly, hands folded in front of him. Normally he would have a few quiet words with the grieving family, but none of the Millers so much as glanced at him. They lined up behind the coffin, then stood waiting while other mourners continued to arrive, all dressed in black. A group of men in dark suits assembled around the coffin. With a ceremonial flourish, they unrolled a piece of black cloth with a now-familiar circular emblem on it. Feeling a little foolish, James realised what the symbol was – a millstone. The small, weathered versions of it on the gravestones it had not been so obvious, but the large gold embroidered one was without doubt perhaps the most likely symbol for a family of millers – the millstone which signified their power. In the past, the local miller would have wielded considerable influence over his neighbourhood. Without the good favour of the miller, a local farmer would not be able to have his grain milled. The miller could set his own price for his services. People would be unwise to make an enemy of him. This may have been the beginning of the weird hold which the Miller clan still enjoyed.

The men spread the cloth over the coffin so that the Millers' emblem was clearly displayed but then James noticed there was a second symbol which lay over the centre of the coffin, an ornate triangle with a gothic G. James studied it, G for what? he wondered. One of the men in dark suits stepped towards James. James turned towards him, glad that someone seemed to have noticed he was there. The man's face was solemn; he leant towards James, saying quietly, "The grandson of the deceased will say a few words at the end of the service."

"Of course," said James, gratified that a little input from the family was to happen after all. He moved towards the church door, to take up his position, ready to precede the coffin into the church. What actually happened next was that, instead of the undertakers taking their lead from James, they looked towards the group of men in dark suits who now hoisted it on to their shoulders. They waited for the man who had spoken to James, and, in front of him, a thin young man, to take their position in front of the coffin. James hesitated, feeling like a bystander. Should he stop and wait? No, he decided, he would precede the coffin as usual. He went in through the open doors and walked at a steady respectful pace down to the altar. He arrived there alone and stood by the bier which had been placed in front of the altar, ready to receive the coffin. He turned and waited for the coffin procession to come. After a minute or so, six of the men in dark suits, acting as pallbearers, entered with the coffin, the thin young man walking a few paces ahead of it. People already seated in the church stood without any prompting. Since Jean Miller had ordered that no hymns should be sung, and no flowers either, the church seemed very dark and sombre, with everyone dressed in black around the black-draped coffin.

James began the familiar opening words of the funeral service. Within minutes the service was drawing to a close as there was no sermon, hymns or readings. James glanced towards the young man now sitting on the front row. He was wearing a neat black suit and a black hat, which partly obscured his face. At that moment he got up from his seat, walked to the front of the church and took off his hat. James realised he had seen him before – it was the unpleasant, sneering son of Jean Miller who had come to the vicarage to see him about the funeral. Today, however, his manner was very different; he walked with a new confidence, almost a slight swagger, as though, like an actor, he had adopted a different role. He took up his place at the head of the coffin, stood still, then nodded to the man who had spoken to James outside the church. The man stepped forward with a wicker basket full of green branches. One by one, twelve men got up from their seats and came forward to take an evergreen branch from the basket and lay it on the coffin, bowing before they retreated to their seat. James felt completely excluded from this, and very uneasy that a ceremony was being enacted of which he had no understanding.

At that point an open book was handed ceremoniously to John Miller, who began to read aloud from it. The words seemed to be from some kind of religious ritual. He talked about the thread of this life being broken, the body returning to dust but the spirit of John Seldon Miller going on forever. What was the book he was reading from? James leaned towards him, to try to see it. Abruptly, John Miller finished reading, closing the book. James caught a glimpse of the front cover as it was passed back respectfully to the first man. There was a golden shape embossed on the front cover. The men in dark suits moved forward again to lift the coffin onto their shoulders and begin the short journey into the graveyard where the grave had been prepared.

James turned to pick up his Bible but before he had turned back to face the coffin, the bearers had already started to move away down the aisle, and the mourners had begun to cluster behind the coffin to follow it. James was left at the back, trying gently to squeeze through the people to get to where he normally would have been positioned. It took him the whole of the short walk to the graveyard before he had managed this, only catching up with the coffin as the straps were being put in place to lower it into the waiting grave. In accordance with the family's instructions, the impressive headstone was already in place with the bold inscription announcing the name of the deceased, the dates of his birth and death, and the phrases Jean Miller had specified. In addition was the sign of the Millers and also the triangular sign with a capital G. The branches of evergreen were left on the coffin as it was lowered. No tears were shed, there were just a few moments of silence. James stood a few feet away from the grave; he had intended to say the comforting words he was accustomed to recite at the graveside, but he sensed they would not be welcomed by the people who stood around John Miller's grave. Unnoticed, and unsure what to do, he slipped away.

He walked back along the graveyard path, trying not to look as if he were in a hurry to get away. He found himself walking faster and faster until by the time he reached the inside of the church he was almost running. He went immediately to the small room set aside for the clergy to robe and disrobe. James closed the door behind him, heaving a sigh of relief, then sat down in the sanctuary of the little room to wait until the mourners had left. He longed to go home, but had to wait until everyone had gone so that he could lock the church. Fortunately this did not take long – the black funeral cars and the other cars in attendance glided slowly away and there was complete silence. James poked his head out through the door to check the church was empty, then hurried down the aisle towards the door. Within minutes he was back at the vicarage.

Anna heard him come in and called down to him, "Dad! Are you OK? You're back sooner than I expected."

She started to come downstairs while he was still in the hallway, panting a little. He called back, "I'm all right ... I think. Just another weird experience with the Millers."

Anna was next to him now, looking at him with concern, "What was the funeral like, then?"

"Just weird, there seemed to be a lot of men in black suits. I know that doesn't sound unusual, people wearing black at a funeral, but it was different; they were a distinct group, behaving in an organised way. And the revolting young John Miller (I know, I shouldn't say that) read out something from a book – I can't quite describe it – it was just *odd*."

What did he say?"

"Hard to remember really, about the body returning to dust etc."

"Isn't it your job to say things like that?"

"I hardly had any part in it, especially with no hymns, no eulogy, no sermon. And then up jumps John Miller with his black book, as though he had every right to take over. And they did this strange thing with a basket of evergreens."

"That does sound very weird, like some sort of ancient folklore. Perhaps it's something they do around here, their equivalent to Morris dancing!" She laughed, and suddenly James saw a funny side to it.

"Morris dancing, for the first time in my life, would seem relatively very attractive! At least I would feel I knew what was going on. At this moment, Anna, if I could exchange these villages for the roughest part of Manchester or London, I'd do it like a shot."

"Poor you, Dad. And I bet they didn't even offer you a cup of tea and a slice of cake afterwards."

"Absolutely nothing so normal as an after-funeral tea. And if there had been some refreshments, I expect it would have been bat wings and nettle tea."

"Oh dear, the strain's really getting to you!"

Anna persuaded him to come and sit down in the kitchen while she made him tea and a toasted teacake to cheer him up.

"You're a treasure, Anna. Thank goodness I have you here keeping a level head."

Anna felt a twinge of guilt – if she was as level-headed as her father believed, how she could be enticed so quickly into a relationship with Martin Fielding?

After twenty minutes, James went to change into his off-duty clothes of jeans and jumper. He would try to relax for the rest of the day, he decided. He just had a few things to finish off in his study first. He had only been back at his desk for ten minutes when the telephone rang in the hallway. Anna heard it ring from upstairs and considered running down to answer it but heard her father's voice saying the usual, "St Gregory's Vicarage; how may I help you?" There was a pause, and she heard the tone of her father's voice lower slightly, and then the sound of the study door closing as he took the phone into the study. It must be a private call, she thought, or maybe he needed to look in his diary. Inside the study, out of Anna's earshot, James was saying, "That would be very welcome, thank you, an evening of music sounds wonderful. I'll see you on Monday evening, yes, I am definitely free. Thank you for inviting me, Mia." He put the phone down, his heart beating fast. Mia, he thought, lovely, dark-eyed Mia, asking *him* to go to an evening of folk music. He hadn't hesitated for a moment before agreeing to go. His hand was on his diary next to the phone, open to show Monday 22nd October. Clearly written on the page was "Mothers' Union 7.30pm Special meeting – must attend." A moment ago it had seemed so obvious, just go with Mia. Now a guilty conscience assailed him. He had agreed to be at the Mothers' Union ages ago. He tried to brush off the thought. He would just have to make an excuse. After all, it was ages since he had been out for a – what was it exactly? A mixture of embarrassment and excitement swept over him as he realised he had just agreed to go out for a *date*. How strange that such an event would seem ordinary for a younger single man, but to James, bereaved and in his fifties, it seemed almost shameless.

He sat at his desk for a while, unable to concentrate. Before long he gave up and went back to the kitchen where he found Anna beginning to prepare supper.

"Dad, I've been thinking, why don't you and I have a treat on Monday evening – it would do you good. Let's go to the Italian restaurant in Exton. The food is delicious."

James experienced a jolt of panic. What should he say? He played for time, getting some plates out of the cupboard. Then he sighed, "Anna, that sounds really wonderful." *But not as wonderful as spending the evening with Mia*, whispered another thought. "Unfortunately, I did promise to be at this month's meeting of the Mother's Union." *Ouch!* That was a lie, said James to himself, or at least a deliberate deceit, which is surely the same thing.

Adding to his guilty feelings, Anna kissed him fondly on the cheek, "Dad, you must have some time off soon. You really are a hero, always putting other people first." She turned back to the cooker without seeing the look on his face.

Chapter Eight

Meg had been thinking about the boy ever since she had found him on the green on Thursday night. While she was working, serving meals, pouring drinks, or making light conversation with customers, his battered face would come back into her mind. She decided she would find out how he was. It shouldn't be too hard to do – surely he must still be in the local hospital. If she got there and found he'd been sent home, then at least she would know he was recovering well from his injuries.

She caught the bus to Exton from the bus stop near the Mason's Arms. The bus took almost an hour, stopping at various villages on the way. After getting off the bus, she stopped to buy a box of chocolates, just as rain was starting to fall. She ran through the steadily increasing rain towards the hospital, wishing she had an umbrella with her.

The hospital receptionist asked Meg if she was a family member. Meg feared at first that she would not be allowed to visit him; so she told the story of her involvement with Steven and the woman said she would give directions to the ward, but that the staff may not let her in. Meg walked down the long hospital corridors, her feet squelching in her wet shoes. When she reached the security door, she pressed the button and waited, leaning forward to hear the reply over the intercom. At first the nurse who answered said, sorry, only family members, the patient is too poorly to see other visitors. Meg told her story again, and the nurse said, wait a minute, and came to the ward door. It was probably only Meg's pleasant face and manner that persuaded the nurse to allow her to come in for "just a minute or two."

Meg walked down the hospital ward, looking to the right and left of her, her eyes scanning the patients in the beds. The nurse she had spoken to had said the boy was about five beds down, you can't miss him. But she couldn't see the boy she had held in her arms on the village green. She knew his name was Steven, he had told her so through trembling lips, covered with blood. She had better look for his name at the end of each bed. Just then the fair hair of a boy with a massively swollen bruised face caught her eye. Steven had fair hair, she remembered; she had noticed its fine texture as the paramedics strapped him onto a stretcher and lifted him into the ambulance. She moved closer. Despite the purple bruises and swollen, almost closed eyes she could imagine Steven's face. Not quite sure, however, she said quietly to the boy, who was lying down, absolutely still, "Steven?"

He murmured something, and turned his head towards her slowly.

"Hello, Steven. I've come to see how you are. It's Meg – do you remember me from the other night?"

There was no answer, but a tear squeezed through one of his swollen eye slits.

Meg pulled up a chair to sit down next to the bed. "It's all right. Don't try to talk." She put out her hand and held his slim pale hand in hers. To her surprise he responded to her, holding on to her fingers. "I brought you some chocolates. You probably don't feel like them now, but you will soon, I'm sure. My son always liked chocolates, still does actually."

Still holding his hand, she reached into her bag for the chocolates, and put them on the bedside cabinet. He was trying to say something. It looked as though he couldn't get his jaw to do what he wanted. After a couple of attempts, he managed to say something which sounded like "Shankoo," the nearest he could get to thanking her.

Meg spoke to him gently, "I'm just so pleased that I was there at the right moment. Thank God I heard something and stopped."

Another tear rolled down the boy's face. Perhaps she should try to change the subject. She was saved from trying to make more conversation by the arrival of a woman by the bed. A small neatly-dressed woman quietly leaned over Steven and kissed his forehead tenderly, "Hello, darling, were you wondering when I'd be back?" She looked over at Meg, who was still holding Steven's hand.

Meg quickly took her hand away, not wishing to offend – this must be Steven's mother. She stood up and went round the bed to stand next to her. "I'm Meg Somers. I don't know whether the police mentioned my name to you, but I found Steven on the green."

The woman's eyes filled with tears and she touched Meg's arm, "I'm so grateful that you were there.... I can't imagine what might have happened if you didn't see what was going on." She started to cry. "Netherton has got worse recently. Steven and I have lived there for five years. We thought it would be a peaceful place for Steven to grow up in, but it's not. Steven's the third boy to be beaten up this year. They'll pick on someone for any reason, or no reason at all." She reached out to stroke Steven's hair. "He's not tough, not like some of them. He's done no harm to anyone. He's quiet, likes to play the piano. Why did they do it? They broke his ribs, and his cheekbone." Her sobs burst out from her, shaking her, leaving her gasping. She struggled to control herself, to stop the sobbing which shook her body as she stood by her battered son, lying quietly in the hospital bed.

Meg instinctively put her arms round this heartbroken stranger, holding her until she was calmer. Then she spoke gently, "I'm so sorry. If there's anything I can do.... I work at the Mason's Arms most evenings – you could find me there. Or, would you like my number?"

Steven's mother put Meg's number in her phone, her fingers trembling, thanking her again. She said her name was Cheryl. She would let Meg know how Steven was.

Meg left the hospital with a heavy heart. She felt very emotional about the injured, even disfigured, state she had found Steven in, and also felt something like shame for the village she lived in. She walked back to the bus stop in the gloomy half-light as the day faded away, deep in thought. What kind of a place was Netherton? Evidently a place where an inoffensive teenager was tied up and savagely beaten right in the middle of the village. Were things really getting worse, just as Steven's mother thought? Feeling disturbed, she decided on the spot to go to the parish church the following evening. It had been a while since she had gone to the service; somehow with all her work and responsibilities with her family, she had drifted away from church in recent times but just now she felt she needed to be there. Unless it had changed, the service would be at six o'clock, she remembered, just enough time for her to catch most of it before she hurried to the Mason's Arms for her evening shift.

*

Anna read his message again. He wanted her to have dinner with him at The Rose Hotel. It was at least twenty miles away and had been given wonderful reviews in the Sunday newspapers. Anna knew this because she immediately searched on the internet for the Rose Hotel; she guessed he was trying to impress her, or was it just that Martin Fielding wouldn't ever consider going to eat in the kind of restaurants she would go to with her father or friends? She felt trapped in a state of confusion about Martin Fielding. Last night, in the dimly-lit romantic setting of the cocktail bar, listening to the music, the touch of his hand upon hers, she had experienced a dreamlike pleasure. It was exciting, almost overwhelming – was this what falling in love felt like? But the familiar pattern of her life had been interrupted, and it disturbed her. She found her behaviour was changing; by nature, she liked to think things through carefully, she preferred not to make quick decisions and she normally drank very little. With Martin, however, she seemed to behave almost like a different personality, or was it her true personality that she had somehow repressed? Before last night, she had never even tasted cocktails before, but with him she'd drunk whatever he had suggested. The headache she woke with this morning indicated that perhaps the drinks were even stronger than she had realised.

She sat in her room, trying to think calmly about him. He was so confident, at times showing such ease socially, but at other times withdrawing. She remembered how bored he had been during the play and his insistence on keeping his phone on, despite the annoyance it had caused to the woman next to him. She recalled the way he had persuaded her to drink in the interval, and to go back to the bar again. Was he really just "spoiling" her, or was he just good at getting his own way? Despite her mixed feelings, she knew she would go. He was drawing her towards him, she could feel it, a strong silken thread which he had attached to her, and he was slowly winding it in. She was lost, there was no point in resisting.

At seven o'clock, she began to get ready; a shower in some expensive shower gel and then a careful choice of dress. She wore a hair band of alternating blue stones and pearls. It made her look younger than her years – was it too unsophisticated? She hesitated, looking at her reflection in the long mirror in her room. She noticed her face was very pale, her eyes like deep pools, distant, the usual warmth gone out of them. *Am I happy?* She asked herself. She no longer knew. She picked up her coat and went downstairs to wait for him.

His car pulled into the drive at exactly five minutes to eight. He jumped out and came round the car to open the passenger door for her, then waited to close it after she had got in, quickly enveloping her in the heated interior of his luxurious car. He paused at the end of the drive, leaning across to give her a long kiss. Then the car glided onto the road and on into the dark countryside.

After ten miles, the car's engine stuttered. Fielding's face tightened with tension as the car lost power and slowed down. He thrust his foot down on the accelerator, but to no avail. Then suddenly he hit the dashboard with his fist, shouting "No!"

Anna watched him, shocked by his reaction. The car slowed even more, then the engine cut out completely leaving the car coasting downhill fifty yards or so into a secluded lay-by bordered by hedges. He got out of the car, slamming the door and walking round it, as though he would be able to see the cause of the sudden failure. She saw him pull out his phone and then his wallet, searching through it. She pressed her window button to lower her window a couple of inches to find out who he was calling. He found a card and then dialled the number on it. What she saw next alarmed her – looking at the display on the phone screen, he became even more angry. Watching, Anna realised the phone must not be working. His face distorted with rage, and he launched the phone high into the air. He threw it with such force it made an audible sound as it cut through the air, and then fell, disappearing into the bushes at the side.

Sitting in the car, Anna didn't know what to do – watching his rage, she realised how vulnerable she was. She shrank further back into the comparative safety of the car; she didn't want him anywhere near her. For a moment she considered locking herself in the car. Then she thought maybe she should do the opposite – get out and stand with him, try to be supportive, perhaps that would calm him. She got out her own phone but could not get a signal. The lay-by was a long one with trees and hedges, completely screened from the road. Because the car had come to rest there, they should not be in danger of being hit by other traffic, but they were also hidden from sight – nobody would know they were there. She opened the car door and got out, just as he landed a hefty kick on the other side of the car, swearing at it. She made a quick decision, "I'm going to walk back along the road."

"No, you're not. Get back in the car," he shouted at her. His voice was harsh, ugly. Nothing of his velvet charm remained.

At that moment the power he seemed to have over her started to crumble. He was no longer the smooth confident male who had so easily gained such influence over her but an undignified, peevish man who could not control his temper, standing by the car shouting. Even in the dark she could see his face was twisted with rage.

From deep within, she mustered enough calm to repeat, "I'm walking back."

She began to walk, leaving him behind her still shouting. She increased her pace, trying to put some distance between them as she heard him getting closer, walking fast, his footsteps loud in the dark. She increased her pace again, desperate now to get away from him; she heard him break into a run. Then he was grabbing hold of her, pulling her into his arms, "Sorry, *sorry*, I shouldn't get so mad." He kissed her face, "Please, Anna, you know I didn't mean to get mad." He looked at her, the whites of his eyes showing up starkly in the dark, the white of his shirt almost luminous. Then he grinned, and whispered, "I'm scared of the dark, please stay with me." The change in him was sudden, and absolute, the rage was gone, the charm was back. He reached for her hand, "Let's walk together," he said. Frightened that his violent mood might return, she allowed him to keep hold of her hand, her mind racing, trying to work out her next move. She would have done anything to have been back home with her father. What on earth had possessed her to come out with him? Inside, she began to pray desperately, "Help me God, please get me out of this. I don't know why I'm with this man, please help me get away from him."

She still had her phone in her right hand. She held it up as she walked – still no signal. But soon it will be back, she thought, I just need to hold on. Her heart was pounding; he appeared to have calmed down, but she was not convinced that this wasn't just an act, that maybe the anger was still just beneath the surface and would break out again. They continued walking, the dark country road completely empty, its black surface stretching out before them, dark bushes and trees at either side. Her high-heeled shoes were already hurting her feet. Would she be able to run in them, or would she be better kicking them off if she needed to try to escape?

After another few minutes, a weak signal showed on her phone screen. He noticed her glancing at it and said eagerly, "Have you got a signal? Let me have it so I can phone for help." He reached out for the phone, but at the same moment she moved it out of his reach. If he took her phone, she reasoned, her one link with other people would be gone – she would be entirely at his mercy. He spoke in a wheedling tone, "Just one call, it won't cost much, honestly." Seeing her still holding on to her phone tightly, he grabbed for it, wrenching it away from her. She felt a stinging pain as he tore it from her grasp, but at the same second, headlights shone over the next rise in the road. She broke into a sprint, running towards the headlights, waving her arms and shouting. The car braked hard, its tyres screeching on the road. She saw the shape of a man get out. Fielding was already alongside her.

Before she knew it, he had put his arm round her, calling out to the driver of the car, "Thank heavens you stopped, my girlfriend and I were just getting a bit desperate – we've broken down – I don't suppose you could give us a lift?" He sounded so pleasant, who would know how frightened she was? The man's face was impossible to see behind the glare of the headlights, but then he stepped forward, and she recognised him, the young man from the furniture shop. He looked from Fielding back to her, she could see him weighing up the situation.

"Sure, I can give you a lift," he said, walking back towards the passenger door and opening it, "You can come in the front seat," he said to Anna. Fielding reacted quickly, squeezing Anna closer to him, "No, she's had a bit of a shock, I'll keep her with me." He was speaking gently, protectively, "We'll sit in the back."

"Like I said," Jonah replied, "Anna can come in the front with me." His voice was serious. How did he know something was wrong? She got into the seat quickly, and Jonah closed the door after her. Fielding moved towards the rear passenger door.

"Wait!" said Jonah, "I think you'd better stay with your car."

"Oh *come on*! Surely you could stretch to giving me a lift too!"

But Jonah was already back in the driver's seat and had started the engine, shaking his head and pressing the button which locked the car doors. He drove off as Fielding smacked his hand down on the rear wing of the car.

"Are you all right?" he asked her.

"Yes, thanks to you. How did you know? I mean what made you think..." she ran out of words.

"The look on your face. Whatever he said, it was clear something was wrong, that you needed to get away."

"Thank you, Jonah," she said again, and put her head back against the headrest. "I feel so exhausted." She felt she owed him an explanation, but she didn't know where to start.

He saved her the trouble by asking, "Is it serious then, between you and him?"

"No... I hardly know him really.... I thought he was interesting, and I thought...." She was running out of words, "I didn't realise what he could be like."

"Best rid of him, by what I could see," he said abruptly.

"Perhaps it was my fault, I don't know, perhaps I gave him the wrong impression. Really, I'm happy to be in my studio, well, my bedroom really, working on a design project, or cooking supper for my father, but he – Martin – likes other things, expensive restaurants, cars—"

Jonah cut off her chatter by taking her hand and lifting it up gently as he drove, "Was this your fault too then?"

She looked down at her hand. Unnoticed in the stress of the last few minutes, her hand had a nasty cut on it. It had bled on to her dress and swollen up. It must have happened when Martin had torn her phone out of her grasp.

He put her hand back down gently, "I think we'd better call in at the hospital."

Anna groaned, "Oh what a mess."

*

They waited for an hour and a half at the hospital before Anna's hand was cleaned and the cut pulled together with adhesive strips and covered with a dressing. Afterwards, Jonah drove her back to the vicarage. He didn't come in with her; she felt it would be better not to make too much of what had happened. She thanked him again and then went quickly inside, closing the front door firmly behind her, then leaned back on it, her eyes closed, breathing a sigh of relief and a prayer of thanks for her narrow escape.

It was late but she knew her father would be waiting for her to come home before he went to bed. She called out softly to him, "I'm home, Dad, safe and sound."

She heard his voice coming from the living room, sounding sleepy; he must have fallen asleep in his chair while waiting for her, "Good night, Anna, glad you're home. Sleep tight."

Anna went upstairs quickly, not wanting her father to see her in case he noticed her hand or asked awkward questions about the evening. She would have had to give an explanation for her bloodstained dress and injured hand. She heard her father on the stairs as she reached her room, closing the door behind her.

Chapter Nine

Hilda was tired but happy as she prepared her meal. It was only five o'clock, but she was hungry; her appetite had grown since she had begun working on the bridge. She worked only for a short time each morning and would have liked to have worked for longer but this seemed to be the limit of her endurance. At the end of each session her old hands were sore and her back very stiff. Despite this, she thought her arms and back were getting stronger. Even at her age, she concluded, muscles were designed for work. Because the site of the bridge was right at the end of the village, there were few passers-by and anyway, she was hidden from view working below the level of the riverbank. Morag still didn't know what she was doing; Hilda was reluctant to tell her until she had made some more progress. Then Morag would have to admit that rebuilding the bridge looked possible and perhaps other people would catch her enthusiasm and begin to help.

By quarter to six, Hilda had washed and dried the few pieces of crockery from her meal and was getting ready to leave her cottage. She aimed to be at the parish church for five minutes to six. As she got to the end of the High Street, and turned into Church Lane, she saw a few other people walking towards the church. Good, perhaps there would be one or two extra people this Sunday evening. Often there were just five or six of them, including the vicar.

Hilda opened the church door and walked down the aisle. She could see there were indeed two or three more people than usual. Morag was there, and two other ladies who often attended. She smiled when she saw that the vicar's daughter had come with him this evening, and there was a pretty woman with a friendly face she recognised but who she hadn't seen for a while. *What was her name?* She was sure she had known it at some point in the past. Hilda smiled at her as she sat down. They were seated in a semi-circle of chairs arranged on the carpeted area in front of the altar. This gave an informal, more intimate feeling for this evening service. As they were sitting so closely together, Hilda overheard the woman say to James, "Please don't think there's anything wrong if I have to leave just before the end of the service – I need to be at the Mason's Arms at quarter to seven to prepare the bar meals."

"Thank you for warning me," replied James. "I might have thought I'd said something to offend you!"

He sounds happy, thought Hilda. He's probably delighted to see a new face.

"I'm James, by the way," continued James.

"I'm Meg Somers."

She has a kind face, and a kind voice too, mused Hilda.

James welcomed them and began the opening prayers. The service finished in just over thirty-five minutes. Meg left the moment after James had spoken the words of the blessing. The service had been very quiet but there seemed to James to be a new warmth in the responses made by the congregation, as though the people were more engaged than usual. James said this to Anna as he drove them back to the vicarage in Appleton.

"I think I know what you mean," Anna responded. "I wonder if a few of us really *needed* to be there, so... it meant more to us."

James glanced across at her, surprised, not sure what she meant.

*

Meg hurried in through the door of the Mason's Arms; she didn't want to be late. Somehow, she knew that the excuse of having been to church would not have gone down well with George Wright. They had never discussed anything spiritual, but Meg sensed that Wright would not have any time or respect for the church.

She went straight to the kitchen to turn on the two ovens. Having finished her routine preparations, she went back out to the bar in case Wright needed her help. He called her over to him at the other end of the bar counter. "A word, Meg." Then, quietly, "We've got a meeting of the Guild tonight at nine o'clock. Finish serving meals a bit earlier than usual; I'll need you to take over the bar – I'll be upstairs at the meeting. Bring up a couple of bottles of decent red wine, and beer for those who want it."

Meg had taken drinks up to the Guild meeting before. Wright liked her to knock on the door and wait for someone to answer it as they had confidential business to discuss. She was surprised that the group never advertised any of their activities in the pub. One day she ought to find the courage to ask George Wright about it, but so far she had always felt reluctant to enquire about it, probably because of the unusual, even secretive nature of the meetings. She noticed they were never put on the noticeboard; the men must come by private invitation only.

There were always about a dozen or so men at each meeting. They would all sit around the large table, with the leader in the large carved chair at the head of the table. Meg always found the meeting and the meeting room strange and unsettling. On the occasions when she had taken drinks up to the meeting and had been able to get a glimpse of the gathering, she had seen that the person in charge of the meeting always wore a dark gown. He sat at the head of the table in the largest, most ornate carved chair, as though he was a judge in court. There were objects lying on the table in front of the leader, for which she couldn't imagine a purpose. Although she knew many of the faces round the table, at Guild meetings they treated her as a stranger. There was no chatter as she went into room. Everyone stopped talking as she tapped on the door and then carried the tray of drinks in. There was a serious edge to the atmosphere, quite intimidating. It certainly wasn't welcoming to a woman or, Meg surmised, to anyone who wasn't a member of the Guild.

The next couple of hours passed quickly. At a quarter to nine she collected the last plates up and loaded the dishwasher. At ten minutes to nine, men who were to attend the meeting upstairs began to arrive. Some of them stopped to buy a drink at the bar, and then went straight to the meeting, drink in hand. They didn't stop to speak to anyone in the pub lounge, and nobody commented on them passing through. At the same time, George Wright left the bar and went upstairs to his own accommodation to change his clothes, ready for the meeting. All the members came dressed smartly in dark jackets and ties. Wright returned to the bar to say abruptly, "Bring the drinks up as soon as you can."

Meg had a few more customers to serve before she was able to pull out a tray from under the bar counter and put on it two good bottles of wine, glasses and some bottles of beer. She glanced around at the people who were sitting at the tables or on the bar stools, talking, laughing, eating and drinking; everything looked settled, a good time to leave things unattended for a few moments.

She carried the heavy tray upstairs carefully and turned left down the corridor to the Guild meeting room. As she approached, she could hear raised voices. Unusual, she thought, the meetings were generally very quiet, consistent with their covert nature. Trying to balance her tray, she managed to stretch one hand forward towards the door sufficiently to tap on the door. Because of the weight and awkwardness of the laden tray, she couldn't knock very hard. Nobody came to answer the door. Using her elbow, she pushed down on the door handle, and leant against the heavy door. As it opened, the voices in the room got even louder. No one noticed her standing in the doorway. The scene that greeted her was astonishing; two men were standing at the head of the long table shouting. One of the men was wearing the black gown that featured in the portrait above the fireplace. His face was red with anger, contrasting with his white hair. As Meg watched, he took hold of the arm of the great carved chair, clearly trying to sit down in it. The younger man moved forward, blocking his way, a sneering expression on his face. The other men in the room were all talking or shouting at the same time, the anger and alarm palpable.

"I am the elected Master of the Guild!" exclaimed the red-faced man, "I have been a full member for decades! You weren't even at the last meeting. The whole Guild voted, and I was chosen!"

"Whose name is *that* then?" snarled the thin-faced young man, pointing to the painting above the fireplace. "Is it Piper or Cullingworth or Melbury?" The room had fallen quiet. "No!" he continued, "It's John Miller, Master of the Guild – *I* am John Miller, and now my grandfather's dead, I am the Master." He grinned, showing brown teeth, shocking at his young age. The men were stunned by the breach in protocol. The previous Master was indeed John Miller, recently deceased, but nobody expected his grandson, who because of his young age had attended only a small number of meetings and been inducted as a member just two months ago, to seek to be the next Master. No one could deny that over the last three hundred years, there had hardly ever been a Master who was not from the Miller family, but all had been elected by the assembled members of the Guild. This youngest John Miller was assuming it was his right to preside over them. All the eyes in the room were on the two men standing by the Master's chair. John Miller was taller than the older man. He leaned towards him, smiling eerily, and put his hand out towards him. There was a gasp in the room, *was he about to strike the old man in the dark robe?* The tension in the room was almost unbearable. George Wright broke it, stepping forward quickly, putting an affable tone into his voice, the tone of the friendly landlord, "Now, now! Gentleman of the Guild! Let's not have any discord. We must stand *together!* There's business to be done. Prosperity and mutual benefits are ours to be had, but our strength is that we are one! We are a brotherhood."

John Miller lowered his hand, but at that moment the other man put his own hand on his chest, grimacing.

Wright was quickly at his side, "Are you all right? Here, sit down a moment, catch your breath."

Wright pulled out one of the chairs from the side of the table towards Harold Williams and helped him to it.

"Just the old angina," said Harold, "Shouldn't get so excited."

While the old man settled himself on the chair, Wright, seeing Meg in the doorway, motioned her to come into the room. He took hold of one of the bottles of wine and opened it, pouring some into a glass. "Have a spot of this. They say red wine is good for the heart, don't they?"

While several of the men fussed over the old man, John Miller slid into the Master's chair, resting one hand on each of the carved arms, a satisfied expression on his face, as though he belonged there.

Wright indicated that Meg should offer everyone a drink. He was eager to restore a sense of order and calm. Then he hurried her out of the room, saying, "Bring another couple of bottles up, but leave them outside the door."

When he had shut the door firmly behind her, he addressed the room, "Gentlemen, it is not really my place to speak, but if you would allow me a few words – first, may I ask if Mr Williams is feeling better?" He turned to Harold, who looked older and more frail than when he had arrived a short time ago.

"I am recovering nicely, thank you." He looked across at John Miller, still sitting in the Master's chair. "But I must say I am shocked." He waved a bony hand in the direction of the usurper. "Never in all these years have we had anything like this."

George Wright was quick to take back the initiative and change the tone of the meeting, "We have all been more than a little shocked. Although Mr John Miller Senior was a great age, we were not ready for him to be taken from us. I would like to propose a toast to his memory. Gentlemen, let us stand and honour Mr John Seldon Miller."

Everyone stood to their feet as one. This removed John Miller from the Master's chair. They raised their glasses. Sensing he was leading the room, Wright pressed on, "Now may we toast our revered elder, Mr Harold Williams, who has been a guiding light among us." They all raised their glasses again. "Mr Williams," he continued in a steady formal tone, "may I ask you to say a few words?" Wright was taking a calculated risk. He wanted to catch a moment when Harold felt old and weak but was enjoying the respect of the other men. Wouldn't this be just the moment for him to step aside with dignity rather than the indignity of fighting for the position of Master. By asking Harold to speak, Wright hoped the other men would understand he was indicating he was the senior person there.

Harold cleared his throat and started to speak, his voice surprisingly strong after his attack of angina. "Gentlemen, let us remember with the deepest respect the Master of this Guild, Mr John Seldon Miller, who led us for forty years. He kept order and under his leadership many generous benefits came to us as members sworn together by blood oath. Forgetting that they had already toasted him, Harold declared, "To John Seldon Miller!" He raised his glass and the others followed suit, drinking solemnly. He paused, and then continued in a statesmanlike tone, "Remembering the strong leadership we have had for so long, I must ask you gentlemen to reconsider. I thank you all for casting your votes for me as Master at the last meeting, but perhaps after all I am not the person to lead us into the future." He glanced at the young John Miller, whose ferret-like eyes were watching him greedily. "You need someone who can bring not only experience but also strength."

Wright smiled inwardly. Clever, he thought, mentioning experience. He's trying to cast doubt on the young upstart.

Harold was commanding everyone's attention, "I suggest the Guild has a few moments to consider the way forward. Then let us recite the Guild's oath and vote again."

There were murmurs of assent around the room. Wright, not wanting another unpleasant scene around the Master's chair, moved his solid frame towards the head of the table and raised his voice again, "Members of the Guild, may we ask our present elected Master to sit in the Master's chair for these moments of deliberation leading to the vote." He watched John Miller's eyes flick round the room, hesitating for a moment, calculating whether it was in his interests to refuse. Everyone was already nodding agreement with the suggestion and Wright was already standing back respectfully, ushering Harold back towards the Master's chair. Miller moved away scowling while the old man sat down, a satisfied expression on his face.

For a few minutes the whole assembly of men kept still and silent. Silence was a key characteristic of the Guild. Their motto was emblazoned on the long wall of their meeting room: *Loyalty, Obedience, Silence*. The ability to keep silent was essential in order to protect the interests of the members. It fitted exactly with the other two values; firstly, absolute loyalty to one another and above all the Master, taking priority over loyalty to family and friends, and secondly, obedience to the commands of the Master and the decisions of the Guild. A cloak of silence covered all their activities, and protected members from threats of any kind from those outside the Guild. Promotions were gained, deals were agreed, and legal actions turned aside because of the sworn allegiance to one another.

Young John Miller's action in opposing the Master was contrary to the oath and could have had severe repercussions. As secretary, George Wright should have put this on record, and disciplinary action would have followed. Tonight however, Wright had not followed their rules; had the person involved been any other but a member of the Miller family, he would have done so, but the Millers had such a long history of being Masters of the Guild that Wright had known instinctively he should try to resolve the breach in procedure in a different way.

The Master, his black gown wrapped around him, took hold of the rod which lay on a pad of black velvet on the table in front of him. Alongside it lay a gavel like that of a judge. Although made of dark wood, the rod was shaped and carved like a sceptre, and symbolised the power of the Master. The gavel represented his authority to make judgements, which would be acted on without question. He held up the rod in his right hand, drawing all the eyes in the room to it. "Brothers in blood, let us stand and speak again the oath which binds us together, in the presence and hearing of the great Power which directs us."

The men stood up in one movement and each pulled back the sleeve of his right arm, exposing his wrist, where the veins of the wrist were close to the surface of the skin. The wrist of each man bore a small livid scar. They began to intone the oath of the Guild. They spoke in absolute unison, "We bind ourselves by solemn oath to obey the Master, who represents the great Power which directs us, and to honour each other above all other ties, in loyalty, obedience and silence. May death overcome us if we break the oath."

It was a solemn and chilling moment, as the group of men all pledged their first allegiance and obedience to an unnamed power and to each other, even above their love for their wives and children. Most did not consider what this truly meant, but enjoyed the intense feeling of fellowship, of brotherhood.

"Now, gentlemen, please be seated. I ask our secretary, George Wright, to call us to vote."

Wright was sitting to the right of the Master, a leather-bound ledger open in front of him. This was the only record of Guild meetings. He opened it at the entry of the last meeting. Only one person, Harold Williams, had stood for election, and the vote for him as the new Master had been unanimous. Wright spoke clearly and seriously, "I call upon you to consider this decision very carefully. All those who wish to offer themselves for election as Master, please stand. This is not about power for yourself as an individual person, but about representing the Power over us all, and to uphold this body of men bound together by an eternal oath."

John Miller and Mike Small stood to their feet.

George Wright noted their names in the ledger, then said formally, "Every man here will have one vote to cast. Those who are standing may not vote for themselves."

"Votes for Mike Small."

Hands were raised.

"Votes for John Miller."

More men indicated their preference, looking towards John Miller as they did so, hoping he would remember their loyalty. Wright recorded the votes for each man, then raised his head, looking round the room, "I declare that John Miller has been elected as Master of this Guild." Miller's supporters began to applaud, but Wright raised a hand to stop them. "Would all members of the Guild show their appreciation to Harold for holding the position of Master following the demise of our previous Master." There was applause. Now we welcome John Miller to step up to the Master's chair and receive the robe of office." Harold began to disrobe, assisted by Wright. John Miller held his hand out for the robe, but Wright held on to it, indicating that he would put it on to John Miller, with due ceremony. Harold stepped away from the Master's chair and John Miller moved to stand in front of it. With everyone else in the room still standing, George Wright said solemnly, "We, the members of the Guild, bound together by blood oath, invest you, John Miller, with the robe of office of Master." He placed the robe around Miller, then walked over to a cupboard on the wall, opened it, and took out a silver box and brought it across to the table. He bowed his head towards the box, then lifted its lid and took out a roll of parchment, handing it to Miller, and bowed again.

John Miller held the roll between his fingers, the smallest of grins appearing at one side of his mouth. He had never seen anyone be inducted as Master. What was he expected to do now? All the eyes in the room were on him.

Wright said quietly, "The sacred scroll contains the words of the Master's oath. You must bind yourself to it for all the years you are Master. The penalty for breaking it is death." The silence in the room thickened with expectation. The word death cut through the atmosphere, inducing a chilling excitement in the men. All of them sensed how powerful this moment was.

John Miller unrolled the parchment and read aloud what was written on it in black, quilled script, inserting his own name, "I, John Miller, pledge myself to be Master of the Guild of Netherton, to be lord over the men of the Guild, to command their loyalty, obedience and silence, so as a single body we will rule this village and land, and will dispense all power at our command to overcome any that oppose us. I give allegiance to the Grand Master of England, and to the Power that directs us. This vow will bind me for life unless for the strengthening of the Guild I should step down. The Guild is my blood family more than those of my flesh. Let death overcome me if I break this oath."

The men nodded their approval. Wright bowed again towards Miller, and held out his hands to receive the scroll, which he placed ceremoniously back in the silver box, and closed the lid. Then he picked up the rod from where it lay on the black velvet and gave it to Miller, who gripped it tightly, raising it up.

Wright watched him. It was strange to be going through this ceremony again so soon, but Harold looked content despite the struggle earlier in the meeting, now seeming to view his brief time as Master was as a caretaker until a younger, stronger man stepped up. Wright saw the grin still lingering on Miller's face as he gripped the sceptre-like rod denoting his position. Would he be able to lead them? Clearly some men thought that the Millers had the right to lead, and there was no doubt that many of the older families in the area still feared the Millers, despite their diminishing number. Young John Miller had so little experience – Wright couldn't recall him ever saying even a word at the Guild meetings before now, he had just watched his grandfather presiding. It seemed that suddenly he had begun to see himself in a new light, as a figure of importance with the right to be heard and respected, although he didn't yet have the presence of his grandfather, who had made people nervous just by standing near them. Wright wondered what had triggered the change in Miller.

A subdued ripple of applause began, and Miller sat down in the Master's chair, this time with the right to do so. All round the room, those present settled down again on their high-backed chairs around the long table. Now they would get to the business of the evening.

Wright quickly wrote a summary of what had just happened in the minutes of the meeting in his ledger and recorded that John Miller of Mill Farm was the new Master, and underneath the names of all present.

Just then Miller grabbed the gavel and banged it on the table, even though there was no need to do so. "Now for business!" he said in a loud voice, "What business have we got this evening?" He sounded lacking in gravitas, like an ignorant youngster playing at being an adult.

Wright decided to rescue him, saying quickly, "We could start with the first item on the agenda, which is, any issues to do with membership – any prospective members and so on." He spoke calmly, covering up the complete lack of appropriate behaviour displayed by John Miller. Wright opened a slim red book on the table and pointed to a sheet of paper which had been inserted into it before the start of the meeting; it was the agenda. Miller grabbed hold of it, wanting to assert his control, "Anyone got any new members to propose?"

Mike Small spoke up, "I would like to permission to introduce someone new to the Guild. He is going to be working, although probably not living, in this area. It's unusual I know for someone new to the area to be brought to the meeting, but a connection like this may be of benefit to many of the members."

"What kind of work is he in?" demanded Miller.

"Building development – a very large development on the edge of Netherton."

"What, on the Haliwell land?"

"Yes, his company are buying it."

"That's right next to our land," said Miller, "Nobody's talked to us about it." He sounded affronted.

Small continued, smoothly, "I'm sure they will, and you may prefer it, *Master,* if one of their key people belongs to us, if the brotherhood approves his membership."

Miller smiled an unpleasant smile," Of course, that would be very *useful,*" he said, laughing. Round the room, men fidgeted in their seats; Miller was being too obvious, their desire to have influence was never usually spoken about so clumsily. It was better to make oblique references to things, to imply meanings rather than to state them openly.

One of the other men spoke, "Would we just have him to the first part of the meeting, as we have done with other men being introduced, so we could meet him without letting him hear more confidential items?"

Wright started to answer, "Yes, that—" but stopped, realising John Miller should be doing so.

Miller stepped in, "Nobody must hear what we don't want them to hear. Not when they haven't taken the oath." Again, he spoke without subtlety; faces round the table looked away, embarrassed.

This time Harold Williams stepped in to cover up Miller's clumsiness, "Quite right, Master, we must be sure we can count on everyone's loyalty. We would expect that perhaps our brother Mr Small will develop his knowledge of this man before the next meeting, and sound him out on various things, to see how likely it is that we could welcome him among us."

Harold sounded so calm and dignified after John Miller's comments.

"I'll do that," said Small, "I'll get to know him better and even if he comes to the first part of the meeting, we still needn't include him at all if anyone has objections."

Wright was speaking to John Miller again in a low voice. The other men waited, still uneasy at what had transpired at the meeting. It had lacked the solemnity which accompanied the formal part of all their meetings. The atmosphere had been disturbed.

George Wright finished speaking and John Miller spoke to their meeting in a loud voice, "Having spoken with the secretary, I have decided, in view of the recent death of my grandfather, Master John Seldon Miller, we cut this meeting short as a sign of respect and meet again in a week's time."

There was an air of relief in the room, and murmurs of approval. Wright leant over and turned to a fresh page in the red book, pointing to the words which with the Master should close the meeting. With a little more dignity this time, Miller read out the final exhortation to the men of the Guild, reminding them of their binding oaths. Soon afterwards, they dispersed silently from the room.

Chapter Ten

It was a clear sunny morning. Jonah had been working since eight o'clock sanding the surface of a desk. About eleven o'clock he decided to take a break from the workshop. He'd recently had an idea that he could make some original items using wood still in a very natural state, using the unique shape of branches and trunks to make some unusual but functional pieces of furniture. Since the storm he had noticed there were several fallen trees still lying on the ground in various places, particularly around Netherton. If these trees had obstructed a road or path, they had already been cleared away by the local council. But in other places they had been left where they fell. He hoped that he may be able to use some wood from these. Perhaps he could form a small exhibition of the finished work, *Survivors of the storm.* He turned the *Open* sign on the door to *Closed* then climbed into his van and drove the short distance to Netherton.

Having parked the van at the far end of the High Street he stood for a moment looking up towards the old church standing high up on the hill beyond the river gorge. The morning sunshine was lighting up the old stonework with a warm glow, the tower of the church reaching up towards the clear blue autumn sky. He walked to where the River Ishka ran across at the bottom of the track leading up to the church and looked down into the water running several feet below. Something down below and to the left caught his eye... there was an old woman down the side of the steep bank. Had she slipped and fallen? He stepped on to the edge of the bank and called down to her, "Are you all right? Do you need some help?"

The elderly face looked up at him. "Since you so kindly offer, thank you. I would appreciate some help."

He climbed down to her, expecting her to need help clambering back up the steep bank. Instead she pointed to some large stones strewn along the edge of the water. "If you could just help me move one or two of these, that would be wonderful."

Nonplussed, he picked up a large stone, "Where would you like me to put it?"

"Just over there. As you can see, I'm rebuilding the bridge."

Jonah, convinced that the poor old bird must have senile dementia, carried the stone to where she directed. No harm in humouring her for a few minutes, he thought. As he got to where she was pointing, he could see she was not imagining things. It was obvious that she had been trying to reconstruct a stone pillar which had been demolished by the storm-surge of the river. She'd been working on the second layer of stones, fitting them together tightly, like pieces of a jigsaw. The foundations of the stone pillars were still intact, embedded in the banks of the narrow river gorge.

Jonah moved a few more stones and then said tentatively, "This seems like a very big job to take on."

"Yes, indeed," said Hilda, "And, in fact, nobody apart from yourself knows I'm doing it. I don't think anyone, at this stage, would agree it was a good idea. But as things progress, I'm sure they will. A bit like Noah building the ark!" She laughed breezily.

"Yes, I can see that," said Jonah, thinking that at least Noah probably had some help, and did eventually finish the job. There was no chance of this old lady getting very far with this. He jumped on top of the layer of stones, shifting his weight between his feet to see how much movement there was between the stones. He was surprised at how steady it was.

"It's really all a matter of doing what you believe is the right thing," the old lady was saying. "I am convinced that this is what I must do, as a Christian."

He looked at her smiling face, thinking that the lines around her eyes were arranged in a very pleasant way. Maybe if you smiled and laughed enough, it made your wrinkles turn out better than if you were miserable. He looked back at the stones, pondering, "Have you thought about using cement between the stones?"

She looked at him, surprised. "The original stonework had no cement. The stones just fitted together very tightly, like the stones in a dry-stone wall."

"Dry stone walls don't bear the weight of a bridge," mused Jonah.

"But surely, if we can replace the stones exactly as they were, they will do the same job as they have done for centuries."

"But nobody thought about public liability in those days." Jonah straightened up from working on the stones, thinking as he did so, *What was he doing, talking to her as though this bridge building thing was even a possibility?* He also noticed she had just used the word 'we'.

Hilda was watching him thoughtfully. She had prayed all week, asking God to send someone to help her, someone who would

116

understand why she was trying to do this. If this young man was the answer to her prayer, she didn't want to offend him.

"I think you have a very good point. I wonder, would you be able to tell me more about adding cement to the pillars? By the way, my name is Hilda." She took off her glove and held out her hand to him. It was in the next moment that something happened that changed Jonah's attitude. Not liking to be rude, he took her right hand in his to shake it and as he did so held the frail knobbly fingers in his. He felt the dry swollen knuckles, fragile in his strong grip, vulnerable as a bird with broken wings, lying helpless in the palm of his hand. How could he not help her? And yet, this whole thing was ridiculous.

Hilda looked up at the sky, which was clouding over, "Aha! Here's the rain coming! At just the right time, thank the Lord, for a coffee break. Do come and have a cup of coffee with me. It's the least I can do after your help."

Jonah started to make an excuse, but she didn't seem to take any notice.

"My cottage is only along the High Street there. And it's raining now, you need to get out of the rain for a few minutes."

They climbed back up the riverbank, Jonah giving Hilda his arm for support. He could feel the effort she was making, gaining footholds in the wet grass. He sighed; he hadn't even begun looking for fallen trees. The rain fell harder on his head and started to trickle down the back of his neck. Coffee in a cosy cottage suddenly sounded attractive, even with this strange old lady.

They hurried back along the High Street together, heads bent against the driving rain.

"Here we are, Honeysuckle Cottage, said Hilda, pushing open the garden gate. A moment later they were inside, and she was urging Jonah to take off his jacket, "Hang it over a fireside chair." There was a fire in the grate and the room was warm. As Jonah took his shoes off and hung his jacket over a chair where it could begin to dry, Hilda was already busy making coffee in the kitchen. "Do sit down and make yourself at home!" she called out.

He sat down in one of the armchairs, looking round at the paintings and furnishings. His eye, accustomed to studying style and design, was taken by the tasteful bringing together of colours and fabric. What an interesting person she must be, he thought.

She came back in with coffee and cake for each of them, saying, "I'm so sorry, I don't think I remember your name."

Jonah knew he hadn't told her his name. "It's Jonah Forman. I'm from Appleton."

"You are the master craftsman, with the lovely furniture shop," she said. "How perfect. How good God is," she added, mysteriously.

Seeing him look confused by this comment, she said, "You have a very special calling in life, Jonah; to create beautiful things from pieces of wood which other people would not have even noticed. In your lifetime, you will add so much beauty to this world."

*

The same morning, Anna was sitting at her desk working on a set of drawings for a range of bags of different sizes. They were to be an autumn range, made out of felted wool in rich browns, reds and gold. By the time she had these ready for sale it would be too late for this autumn. She realised this, and that maybe she should be working on a range for the next season instead, but while the leaves were falling outside she felt attuned to this season and inspired to use its colours.

She left her desk for a moment and walked over to the window to look down on to the drive and front garden. She remembered the feeling of excitement and anticipation of just a few days ago when she'd left the house and got into Martin Fielding's car, the sensation of being swept into a world of luxury beyond the familiarity of the vicarage. She remembered, and shuddered to think, of how easily she had been seduced into being led wherever he wanted to take her, like a foolish lamb being led away from the flock. She felt tainted by him.

She moved away from the window and sat down again at her desk. The little carved box which Jonah had given her lay there next to her pencils. She ran her finger over its delicately worked surface, and looked again at the tiny candle carved there, thinking, candles are a symbol of hope... and light in the darkness. She sighed. She felt that the darkness around her was gradually snuffing out the light and hope in her life. Since Jonah had brought her home that dreadful night, she had hidden herself away in her room much of the time, pretending she was working, while the truth was that she didn't want to risk bumping into Jonah and feeling acutely embarrassed. She supposed she ought to thank him, but preferred to avoid him rather than talk about that horrible evening. It was not until the following day that she'd realised Fielding still had her mobile phone. Rather than try to contact him to ask him for her phone she'd cancelled her phone contract and ordered a new phone.

One of the few times she had ventured outside was to go to the Netherton evening service with her father. She had gone along to keep him company, knowing that the number of people attending was always very small, but also because she needed the comfort of being in the company of good people. She wanted to feel safe, surrounded by prayer and the warmth of kind steady hearts, drawing her away from the dark influence she felt Martin had spread over her. She recognised now how easy it was to be attracted away from what is reliable and true into what appears fascinating but beneath the surface is bitter and harmful. She wanted to feel clean and innocent again. She felt she had only narrowly escaped, but was still concerned that she had given him a foothold in her life. Sitting at her desk, she recalled what she had experienced when she was sitting in the church in Netherton on Sunday evening – quite suddenly she had a picture in her mind, the strong sensation that the small congregation were in a ship on a dark sea. Inside the cabin, they were warm and dry, lit by the light of the ship, but outside was darkness, with deep black waters underneath.

Her thoughts were interrupted by the doorbell downstairs. She heard her father's voice welcoming someone in. She was straining her ears to hear who it might be when her father called upstairs to her, "Anna! Have you got a moment? There's someone down here hoping to see you!"

Instantly, her heart started to pound – who was it? Could it be Fran, arriving unannounced on a surprise visit, or maybe another friend? Might it be Jonah? She left her room reluctantly, holding tightly on to the banister, walking down the stairs with the sound of her heartbeat loud in her ears. As she neared the bottom, she could see her father's back as he stood in the hallway talking with the visitor. Another two steps down, and she could see who it was – a man with a large bouquet of flowers in his hand – Martin Fielding. She felt tension rising in the back of her head and neck. The conversation between him and James was animated; her father was clearly enjoying it. As Fielding caught sight of Anna, he stopped talking and smiled at her, the same admiration in his eyes as when he had first seen her in her father's study.

"Anna," he said, his voice tinged with emotion, "I'm so glad you're here. I've come to plead for forgiveness. I've just been explaining to your father how incompetent and inconsiderate I was the other night. My car was due for a service, but I was so preoccupied with work I failed to get it organised. The result was that it broke down. I was so angry with myself, with my stupidity. I behaved like an idiot."

Anna could see her father smiling sympathetically as he listened. Fielding's words reflected his own situation, being so busy with so many pressures; James understood exactly how that felt, that it meant you missed important things, things that should be done. He also knew how it left you feeling incompetent, stupid, not fit to do your job or look after people properly. Poor young chap, thought James, he's embarrassed himself and is trying to make amends. He watched Fielding move towards Anna with the beautiful bouquet, holding it out to her. Anna remained where she was on the bottom stair, not smiling.

James looked at his daughter; there was something about her manner which he couldn't quite make out. Why did she look so unhappy? He looked at the young businessman again, with his winning smile, then back to his daughter. He had noticed that she had been quiet lately, but assumed she was concentrating on her work. Surely it would be good for her to take a break from being alone in her room and enjoy the attention of this young man. He saw Fielding reach out to take her hand as he tried to pass the flowers to her, then, just for a second, he saw a strange look on her face, something between fear and distaste. Something was wrong. James had the strong impression that he should intervene.

"Anna has a lot of work to do at the moment," he said, moving past Fielding to stand next to Anna, putting his arm round her shoulders protectively. "Another time, perhaps, I would agree that going out would give her a welcome break, but I feel I should insist that she stays at home resting with her ancient parent." He felt the tension in Anna's shoulders relax as he said this, but saw the smile disappear from Fielding's face. In its place appeared an appealing expression, a mixture of embarrassment and disappointment; his body language was apologetic as he leant forward to lay the lovely flowers at the bottom of the stairs.

"Please let me leave the flowers with you, Anna. I chose the colours specially for you." Then, to James, "So sorry to disturb you, Reverend Gilchrist. May I call again at a better time?"

His request was so polite, it was difficult not to agree instantly. But James felt a small sense of foreboding, an internal check on his usual affability. "Ring me, would you, Martin, and I'll let you know how things are."

Fielding was livid as he drove away from St Gregory's vicarage, accelerating hard. A string of expletives burst from his lips, all focused on the vicar and his daughter. His phone rang but he was in no mood to talk to anybody; he ignored it. He heard the sound of a voicemail, and guessed it was Wheeler. He knew he'd better listen to it quickly – nobody ignored Wheeler. He looked down at his phone and selected the voicemail icon. The familiar loud voice came through, "Fielding? Answer your phone next time! What do I pay you for! I want to see you within the hour – we've got word that we can get that land. I'm on my way to the office and I expect you to be there."

This could be the key moment for the Netherton project. If they really had got a green light for the purchase of the land, Wheeler would want all the plans for the site to be finished within a matter of days. His impatience for quick profits would overrule any other considerations. Anyone who tried to stand in the way would be frightened off or paid off, whichever was easiest.

Soon Fielding was turning into the car park at the Bluebird building. Wheeler's car had already arrived, occupying the reserved place nearest to the double entrance doors. Fielding got out quickly, feeling the same sense of anxiety he always felt when about to meet Wheeler. He hurried past the reception desk, ignoring the cheerful greeting from the receptionist, and took the stairs two at a time up to the first floor. He arrived feeling flustered, going through the door still a little breathless, and saw Arnold Wheeler, Fred and Susan Roland and the company lawyer already sitting round the table. It was unusual for Philip Greenwood to join them for a meeting; Wheeler must want some legal details to be given directly to them.

"Fielding! Kind of you to join us!" called out Wheeler sarcastically as Fielding entered, then looked around at the others expecting them to appreciate his wit. They all laughed dutifully, taking in Fielding's discomfort and feeling relieved that he was on the receiving end of Wheeler's jibe and not themselves.

"Right, now we'll hear what Greenwood has to say."

The lawyer shuffled his papers importantly and began, "I am very pleased that negotiations regarding the purchase of the Haliwell estate next to the village of Netherton have been successful so far. Acting on your instructions, I have drawn up a contract for all partners to sign. He passed copies of the contract to each of the people around the table. I have also been in communication with the planning department of the district and have received, unofficially, a favourable reaction to the notion of Bluebird Design and Construction submitting a planning application for a major development on the site, provided certain elements are included.

"Elements?" interrupted Wheeler, "Plain English, Greenwood, if you don't mind too much! Elements means metals, something from a school chemistry lesson."

"I beg your pardon, Mr Wheeler. I mean certain things included in the proposal."

"Such as?" snapped Wheeler.

"Socially responsible housing."

"Ha!" shouted Wheeler derisively, "Rubbish! What's that about? Houses for spongers?"

"Houses for local people on a lower income."

Wheeler continued to make disparaging noises, "The planning department must be mad – where's the profit in building little boxes for no-hopers!"

"This would represent only a small percentage of the total – the rest of the houses could be aimed at high-income buyers from outside the area."

"So we have to blight the luxury homes by sticking some cheap ones right next to them? We'd have to put a whacking great wall round them to keep the low-lifes and losers away from the folks with decent cars!" Wheeler was in his element now, sneering and insulting.

Philip Greenwood tried to mollify him, "The plan for the site could indeed be designed in such a way as to take account of the different types of housing, in a sensitive way, allowing privacy and space for the different housing needs."

"Absolute bilge!" exploded Wheeler, "Get me the name of the head of planning! I'll have a word in his ear. He'll soon see sense. Any more 'elements'?"

"The house designs should reflect the traditional character of the village. Also, the old pilgrims' church and ground around it are subject to restrictions with regards to purchase – building plans must stop short of interfering with the church being used as a place of worship and pilgrimage."

Fielding spoke up, "According to my informal investigations, there are very few people still using it."

"How many?" barked Wheeler.

"Couldn't give the exact number, but maybe ten or even less."

"What about 'pilgrims'?"

"That's mainly a seasonal thing – mostly during the warmer months."

Wheeler started to grin slyly, "But we're approaching winter, aren't we? If someone did a count of pilgrims for the next couple of months, there might not be any to count!" he announced triumphantly.

"There'd still be the locals – a small number of them seem to be very attached to the place."

"Find out some more about them, see if you can persuade them to see things our way – we don't want any protesters chaining themselves to the diggers, or any rubbish like that. Remember how much this means to each of us in this room." He looked round the table as he spoke, making eye-contact with each of them, expecting them to catch his full meaning, that they were bound to benefit a great deal personally if they succeeded, or, if they failed, to lose the position they enjoyed at present.

Fielding nodded, "I'll get on to it."

There was a knock on the door.

"Enter!" shouted Wheeler. A girl from one of the offices came in carrying some large sheets of paper.

"Bring them over here to the table," ordered Wheeler.

The girl hurried forward, saying nervously, "Mr Patterson asked if you wanted him to come up." She worked in the architectural design and planning section; Ed Patterson was the lead architect.

"Yes, get him up here, we'll need to get some answers from him."

Wheeler never thanked anyone; the girl was no exception. She hesitated for a moment then hurried away again, overawed by being in the boardroom, and especially having the onerous task of speaking to Arnold Wheeler. Fielding watched her go, *like a mouse scurrying away*, he thought.

Ed Patterson arrived a minute later. The plans his department had worked overtime to prepare were spread across the table.

"Tell us what we're looking at," said Wheeler, tapping a large plan with his index finger, displaying a heavy gold signet ring on his right hand, AW engraved boldly on it.

"Certainly. Hello, everyone," said Ed Patterson pleasantly, "You can see the outline plan for the site, drawn up as accurately as we could manage with the information we have at present. Many of the houses, all with five, six or seven bedrooms with ensuite bathrooms, will have spectacular views over the county; I have placed the houses on the plan in such a way as to get maximum advantage from this, in effect making two crescents at the most elevated end of the site, near the old church, assuming it is no longer in use. I've allowed for a wall to be put around it, thinking of any health and safety concerns. Otherwise, we're looking at demolition, in which case...." He placed a smaller sheet of paper on top of the plan. "The space could be utilised like this." The new sheet covered the church and the area round it, overlaying it with a further group of luxury homes occupying the highest part of the land. "Or even...," he produced another sheet to overlay the first one, this time showing an artist's impression of the church radically altered to form part of the front elevation of a large stone building. The original stonework of the church, incorporated into the whole, gave character and a sense of tradition to it. "This building could include a restaurant, bar and fitness/spa resort. All very high-class, attracting the same income bracket as the housing."

Wheeler leaned forward, spreading his short wide fingers over the page, the gold signet ring gleaming. He was excited; a slow smile spread across his face and a sheen of perspiration appeared on his forehead. "This is very good, Patterson. I can tell that you and Martin have taken seriously my idea of hitting the high end of the market, and maximising profit margins."

Martin noted Wheeler's use of his first name; this denoted a change in Wheeler's mood. Better enjoy it as long as it lasts, which probably won't be very long, he thought to himself.

"Yes indeed," replied Patterson, in his usual affable way, "Always good to work as a team."

Wheeler flashed him a patronising look. "Anyway, it's good, I like it. It makes financial sense, especially that notion of giving views right over the countryside – that translates into a lot of extra money. And I like this section here—," stabbing a fleshy finger at the additional sheets overlaying the site of the church. "I need to see detailed estimates of the costs of each of these two options – one for demolition and building twelve additional houses, and one for incorporating the old building into a fancy leisure club, restaurant etc." That'll be *your* job," he nodded towards Fred and Susan Roland, who smiled back eagerly. "And to finish off securing the use of the church – that's one for you, Martin." He grinned at Fielding.

Ed Patterson looked up questioningly, "Oh, I'm sorry, I thought we already had a free hand with the church site as an abandoned building."

"Almost, don't worry about it. Martin's on to it." Wheeler slapped Fielding on the back in an apparently friendly gesture, but much too hard for comfort. "Now I'll let you get back to work, Patterson. Keep your office working on all the individual house designs. I want it ready to be rolled out as soon as I give the word."

Ed Patterson took the hint immediately – he was being dismissed. Quickly, he started to gather up the plans.

Wheeler interrupted him, "Just leave them there – you've got copies, haven't you?" There was something in the tone of voice which was saying, you're surely not such an *idiot* as to have only one copy, are you?

"Absolutely," answered Patterson, never ruffled by Wheeler's rudeness.

Wheeler then ignored the architect, turning his attention to the Rolands, "Now tell me about labour costs."

Fred coughed, drawing attention to himself, enjoying being in the spotlight, "I have had some very useful conversations and have secured the offer of the full range of labourers for the project at very attractive rates. I've explained the need for the supply company to provide all the legal safeguards we need. If I have your approval, Arnold, I would like to pass the details of the company over to Philip to prepare a legally binding contract between us."

"What kind of supply company is it?"

"It specialises in the provision of workers, skilled and unskilled, for a range of projects. I am getting to know the managing director socially and feel he will be a good reliable source, understanding that our company's reputation is paramount."

"The buck stops with him, then," summarised Wheeler. "We don't want any mess reaching us."

"Just what I commented," murmured Susan, "My very words."

"Very *wise*, Susan," said Wheeler, with a note of sarcasm, which she missed and took it as a compliment.

Fred added, "I absolutely agree, Arnold. This man arranges work opportunities for people who find it hard to get into the labour market but are ready to work hard for... perhaps less than others would expect."

Wheeler laughed, "You've got a nice way of putting it, Fred! You make it sound like Social Services!"

Susan said primly, "They should be grateful – any job's better than no job. Nobody should expect to get anything for nothing. Why should decent people like us put up with half the population being scroungers?"

"You're all heart, Susan," Wheeler laughed his mirthless laugh again, then turned to look at the company lawyer. "So, Greenwood, start on that contract – as far as we're concerned these are workers approved to work here, provided by a registered company, and we will have the paperwork to prove it. Check out that they're registered, and put in the contract that the liability, insurance, training, health and safety, all that kind of thing, rests with the provider. Get it in the small print.

"Fred, get some rates of pay down on paper and pass them to Greenwood for inclusion. And one more thing, let your contact know that we won't be messed about with. Penalties will apply if necessary. Greenwood, make sure you get penalty clauses put in the contract. Glad you're socialising with your contact, Fred. Find out where he lives."

Their discussion moved on to other projects, but it was the Netherton project which had gripped Wheeler's imagination. He sensed a battle, and he intended to win.

*

Jonah heard the telephone ringing. He put down the cloth he was using to oil the surface of a small table and walked through the connecting doorway from his workshop into the showroom to answer the call. It was another enquiry about a possible commission. Business was picking up. Soon he would be able to afford a mortgage on a small house as well as the rent for his business premises. It was time to move out of his parents' house – perhaps he should start searching for a property on the internet, he mused. He glanced at his watch. It was already ten forty-five. Time for a coffee break.

As he switched on the electric kettle, he remembered the coffee he'd drunk with the old lady, Hilda, a couple of days ago. Would she be back down by the river, struggling with those stones? He shook his head, trying to dismiss the thought, but in vain. As he carried his mug over to his desk, about to browse for houses on the internet, the idea of Hilda working all on her own by the river kept popping up in his head. He could see her in her raincoat and gloves, tugging against the weight of a stone, trying to lift one. He felt again the frailty of

126

her hand when he had taken it in his. It was no good, he would have to go and see if she had gone back down to the river. Perhaps he could persuade her to stop. He left his coffee untouched and took his keys from the desk. He would have to work a bit later tonight.

When he reached the riverbank in Netherton he found Hilda at work again, just as he had suspected. He went down to join her. When she heard him coming, she looked up eagerly, "I hoped you would come! In fact, for the last half-hour, I've been praying you would!"

Jonah smiled with amused resignation, "No wonder I couldn't concentrate, with your prayers interfering."

He worked alongside her again, following her directions, for almost an hour. They talked as they laboured, and only stopped when once again rain intervened. He helped Hilda climb back up the bank and was about to leave when, to his own amazement, he heard himself offer to come and help again. What was happening to him? He wondered if he was going soft, spending time with this old lady when he should be building up his business. But the fact was Jonah had found himself enjoying their conversations; Hilda had a particular way of seeing things which was different to anyone else he knew. She often seemed to see *behind* what was obvious and superficial to another level of perception. What other people would miss, or dismiss, she spotted and saw the significance of. Sometimes she said things which mystified him, and sounded odd, or slightly crazy, but the more he listened to her, the more he came to understand how she perceived things, what she believed in, and what fascinated her. Most of it seemed to hinge on her absolute faith in Jesus Christ; he was a real person to her, not a shadowy historical figure. She was, she said, in a sort of ongoing conversation with him. Jonah found this peculiar, but every objection he raised to her beliefs she gently brushed aside with a penetrating reply. He began to hear his own comments as sounding immature and ignorant compared with hers. She had an advantage over him, a particular source of time-honoured wisdom – she often slipped into their conversation a quotation from the Bible. Formerly, he would have regarded the Bible as a quaint remnant from a bygone age, irrelevant to life today. When Hilda repeated excerpts from it, however, it seemed to make thought-provoking comments on a wide range of things. This happened most pointedly when she quoted things Jesus said; his words seemed to have a different quality to anyone else's.

Jonah, without ever intending to do so, fell into a pattern of coming down to the river to find Hilda, to check whether she was all right, and to help her for a while. He still thought it was a hopeless cause but couldn't find it in his heart to abandon her to her lone task. After three more sessions of helping Hilda with her endless struggle to rebuild the bridge, Jonah quipped, about some minor point of discussion, "Go on then, tell me what Jesus would say about it!"

Hilda replied, "Why don't you come and find out? You'd find a lot more answers if you came along to the church sometimes."

Jonah laughed, "Hilda, I probably will – I seem to end up going along with any crackpot idea you come up with! If I told my mum, she'd think you must be twenty-one and have long blonde hair."

Hilda chuckled, "Come with me, just try it once, six o'clock on Sunday evening."

"This will probably ruin my reputation with the lads in the Mason's Arms."

She waved goodbye, saying, "Ten to six, then, see you at my cottage!"

Chapter Eleven

Monday afternoon. The natural light was fading fast in Anna's room. Although she would continue working by electric light, she always felt frustrated by the shortness of the autumn and winter days, when the sharp white daylight abruptly retreated from the room, leaving dim grey light which was so difficult to work in, straining her eyes until at last she had to give in and turn on the harsh electric light which overlaid the natural lines and colours with its own spectrum and shades. She sighed, deciding to take a break.

As her attention moved from the design in front of her, she thought again about her thwarted plan to remove her father from his duties for an evening. She shouldn't have given up so easily. What a shame he had committed himself to going to the Mothers' Union meeting this evening. He had seemed so disappointed when she had asked him about it. Although the older ladies who attended would undoubtedly be very pleased to have the vicar with them, surely they didn't really need him, Anna pondered. If they knew how much an evening at an Italian restaurant would benefit him, they would be very likely to tell him to take up Anna's offer. Thinking this, she decided to act straightaway.

She slipped downstairs quietly to find the copy of the parish magazine which always lay on the little hall table and brought it back up to the privacy of her room. Then she closed the door and flicked through the pages, looking for the monthly article by the president of the Mothers' Union. She picked up her mobile phone and moved away from the door, just in case her father was passing. Betty Lawson answered on the third ring. Anna explained that she wanted to give her father a surprise treat by booking a table for a meal out together, and then had realised that her father was due to come to their meeting. Would Betty be willing to accept her father's apologies on this occasion? She hinted that her father was working a little too hard. Betty immediately sympathised, "Of course, dear, we'll give him the evening off – we don't want any breakdowns, do we? I have heard it happens to some vicars – they are working hard as usual, and suddenly, while nobody is taking any notice – bang! Down they go, like a popped balloon! And then there's no vicar for *years* while the bishop tries to find one somewhere."

Anna almost laughed aloud at this description. She managed to keep serious, however, replying, "I knew you'd understand, Betty." She decided she would keep the arrangement a surprise until the last minute so that her father couldn't succumb to a fit of guilt and try to ring Betty again to say he would go after all.

At five past seven, Anna heard the doorbell ring and hurried into the hallway at exactly the same time as her father, almost colliding with him. "I can go and see who it is if you like," she said, then, "You look really smart, Dad, a bit over the top for the Mothers' Union – the ladies will be swooning!"

James seemed not to hear and was already almost at the door, "Sorry, Anna, I really must be off."

"Hold on, Dad!" called Anna, "I need to tell you something!"

Her father seemed to be deaf to her protest; he shouted, "Goodbye, see you later!"

She dashed after him, catching him up as he pulled open the front door, revealing who was standing outside on the doorstep. It was Jonah Forman. James looked momentarily shocked, then, recovering himself quickly, held out his hand and said, "Good evening, I'm the vicar, can I help you?"

Jonah looked past him towards Anna, saying, "I'm Jonah – I was just passing and thought I'd knock and see how Anna is."

James looked confused, "I think Anna's fine. Ah – here she is." He realised Anna was at his elbow, "Someone for you, dear."

He was looking beyond Jonah, down the drive.

Anna asked Jonah to come in while watching her father, who seemed to be acting very strangely. "Dad, I really do need to speak to you before you go."

James checked the drive one more time, then closed the front door again and turned back to Jonah. "Do come into the living room. I'm afraid I'm just about to leave – I must go, or I'll be late."

"No, Dad, you've no need to go. It was meant to be a surprise. I spoke to the president of the Mother's Union and gave your apologies – hope you don't mind – I just felt you needed a break. I explained I was taking you out for an Italian meal."

James' face fell. Anna began to think she had made a mistake when the doorbell rang again.

"Ah!" said James, and without another word exited through the door before his daughter could stop him again.

She sighed, "I'm sorry, Jonah, this is turning into a farce."

At that point, James suddenly reappeared, saying abruptly. "Sorry – another call – must go!"

"Who is it?" asked Anna, but he had already gone.

Jonah had been watching the confusion with amusement, "Your dad seems to have a busy evening planned."

"Yes, that was a bit peculiar. I don't understand what just happened... and I've booked a table."

"At an Italian restaurant? Sounds good." There was a pause during which both of them stood thinking for a few moments. Then Jonah said, "By pure coincidence, I'd been hoping to get the chance to go for an Italian meal soon." He smiled. "If you'd still like to go, I'd be happy to stand in for your dad."

"Let me get my coat," she said, laughing.

By the time Anna had fetched her coat and gone outside with Jonah, James had got into Mia's car and was half a mile away. He had felt a potent mixture of excitement and panic when he had opened the front door and seen her standing on the steps. He had taken in her attractive form, wearing a similar outfit to when he had first seen her, a long tightly-fitting dress, clinging to her ample contours. Her eyes were heavily made-up, as before, the black kohl eyeliner making them dark and mysterious, and, he thought, his heart beginning to thump, sensuous. He had tried to get away from the house as quickly as possible so that Anna would not see who he was with. He had hoped she would assume a parishioner had turned up requiring his immediate help. He had turned to pull the front door closed behind him, but on turning back found that Mia had decided to do what so many people did nowadays, even with relative strangers, that is, to greet them with a kiss. Before he could do anything about it, she had raised her arms to embrace him, pressing her full lips against his cheek, perilously close to his mouth. "Hello James," she breathed.

He almost gasped, trying to breathe normally and also attempting to look back at the door behind him, while still encircled by her arms. He turned back to her, and said unsteadily, still feeling her breath against her face, "Good evening, Mia." Then panic got the better of him and he grabbed her arm and started to propel her down the steps, saying, "I suppose we'd better get going."

Her full mouth curved into an amused smile. "You're right, let's get started, no time to lose."

She drove quite slowly, asking him if he would mind if she put some music on while they drove – it would relax him, it was a special recording, compiled by a friend. It didn't sound anything like music, James thought, just a never-ending series of sounds. He couldn't decide what it was, but then he remembered how fond some people were of whale music and similar things, so decided it must be that. For a while, he thought he had better not speak, since the music must be a favourite of Mia's, but after about ten minutes of trying to enjoy it, he was beginning to get irritated by it. "Very interesting," he said, in a fairly decisive way, hoping she would get the hint that he had listened to enough of it to form an opinion, and maybe it was time to turn it off.

She turned sideways to look at him, and smiled as she turned back towards the road. "I think you find it very hard to relax, James. I'll have to see if I can help you with that. It's something I'm very fascinated by – relaxation techniques."

"Really? I suppose you're right, I do tend to always be thinking my work, the next person to visit, or funeral to arrange, or baby to christen, although I must admit there haven't been many babies for a long time."

"Ah, babies, I love baby-naming ceremonies. I took part in one only recently."

James nodded, "Yes, I enjoy them myself, a time to celebrate new life. You're a godmother then?"

"Not exactly, but a bit like that."

James frowned, wondering how you could be a bit like a godmother, but not exactly. It must be a modern re-wording of the liturgy, he concluded, one that the bishop had neglected to notify him of. No matter, what does a difference of a few words make?

Mia turned the whale music down, much to James' relief, but then he was concerned that maybe he had offended her. He thought he had better indicate that he didn't strongly dislike it. "I am actually quite interested in whales, and in marine life in general," he said amicably.

Mia started to laugh, a low quiet chuckle. She reached out her hand and let it rest for a second on James' knee, saying, "You are so funny, James. Marine life, is that what you thought it was?"

James looked down at her hand, with its unusual rings, the gemstones reflecting flashes of light in the dark car. How long would she keep it there? What should he do? He thought of moving his leg so that her hand slipped off, but it would seem so rude. His main concern was about what anyone would think about a vicar being alone in a car in the dark with an attractive and unusual woman whose hand was touching his leg. After a few moments of frozen indecision, he decided that nobody could see them, even if the car had stopped, so no one could be offended or confused by it. He looked across at Mia, her strong features, the shape of her lips in profile and her dark hair. He breathed in her perfume, a mixture of flowers and incense, slightly intoxicating. At that moment, she removed her hand. He felt a small sigh of disappointment escape his lips. She was speaking again, "Tell me, James, what else are you interested in, apart from marine life?" She chuckled again.

He tried to think of engaging things to say, to present himself as an even mildly interesting person, but their conversation in her car only served to convince him that he was actually very boring, with hardly any interests outside his work for the church. He felt deflated, a dull middle-aged man with his best years behind him. He considered this as they continued to travel through the dark evening; how could he change, he wondered, and make the most of his life while it lasted?

*

Anna got into Jonah's car, and they headed towards Exton. Being in his car again had felt strange at first, bringing back the unwelcome memory of the night he had rescued her from Martin Fielding. It filled her with embarrassment that she had put herself in that position in the first place, but it also reminded her how grateful she was that Jonah had arrived at just the right moment. Nevertheless, she didn't want it to dominate her thoughts; she didn't want to think about it at all but wanted to relax and enjoy this fresh new friendship, so different from the dark place she had been experiencing in her mind and emotions.

The Italian restaurant was small with a welcoming atmosphere, light opera music playing in the background and genial waiters who talked to the customers almost as though they were friends. From the moment they stepped into the place, Anna and Jonah felt relaxed, ready to enjoy themselves. It seemed as if they spent most of the time laughing as they ate a three-course meal. She described to him some of the things that had happened at the vicarage recently, from the quavery old ladies who rang up with funny muddled messages for the vicar, to the weird Miller family, as well as other peculiar things that had happened over the years her father had worked full-time for the church, including pets' funeral services, a bishop who roller-

133

skated in the cathedral and the church where they had so many bats, which they were not allowed to get rid of, living in the roof space, that members of the congregation had to be given waterproof capes and hats as they came in, to wear during the service to protect them from the bat droppings falling on their heads. With hindsight, this and all the other things seemed side-achingly funny, especially when Anna told him about the churchwarden of the bat-ridden church finally cracking and bringing his shotgun to church one night, along with some night-sight goggles, to try to shoot all the bats, resulting in two medieval stained-glass windows needing ten thousand pounds worth of repair and an armed police unit bursting into the church. While two armed policemen were sitting on top of him to restrain him, the churchwarden said, wide-eyed, "I am trying to do my job, and I will be happy to shoot anything else that is misbehaving in church."

At the end of the meal, they split the cost – Anna insisted she wouldn't let Jonah pay, and then they drove back to Appleton, still full of lively conversation. When he stopped the car in the drive and got out to walk to the steps with her, she wondered if he would expect a kiss, but he just paused for a moment and said, "That was a really good evening. Hope your dad turns up sometime!"

Anna remembered the odd way her father had been behaving earlier that evening before he left. "Yes, I wonder if he's back yet. Do you want to come in and say hello to him?"

Jonah declined, saying it was quite late already, and he had an early start the next day. He had hesitated for a moment, then he raised his hand in a brief wave and went to his car.

Just then something had happened to Anna that made no sense to her. As she watched him turn and walk away from her, she experienced a profound sinking of heart, a physical ache. A feeling of sadness and loneliness swept over her, as she saw him going back down the drive, getting smaller as the distance between them grew. How silly of me, she thought, I hardly know him.

When she unlocked the front door and pushed it open, the interior of the vicarage was in darkness. She wished she had thought to leave a lamp on. Her father must still be out. She felt for the light switch, then looked at her watch. It was half past eleven! Her father never stayed out late. Where could he be? Immediately she felt a stab of anxiety and wondered what on earth she should do. As he had not gone in his own car, perhaps whoever was driving him was a careless driver. Her thoughts began to race – they could have had an accident, and be stuck on some country road unconscious, or maybe he was injured and unable to call for help because the mobile phone coverage was so bad around here. Calling one of her father's parishioners to ask for help and advice about the vicar would be unacceptable to her father, and all her friends lived far away from here. She decided she must calm down and simply wait. If it got to one o'clock, and he still had not returned, perhaps she should call the police. She tried to occupy her time by wiping all the kitchen surfaces and cupboard fronts, then doing all the ironing that had been sitting in the ironing basket for weeks.

*

Mia's car reached the edge of Exton, then through the streets towards the centre. She parked in a car park opposite the Victoria Theatre, an old, slightly dilapidated building, down a side street from where the main theatre and other arts venues were. There was a board outside advertising current and future performances there. "For one night only," it announced, "Soul Music from the East."

"Excellent," commented James, "A secret favourite of mine."

Mia looked at him, raising her eyebrows enquiringly, "I must admit I'm surprised, *pleasantly* surprised."

"Yes, it's true," said James, pleased that he had finally struck a chord with her, "I've always loved Al Green, Marvin Gaye, Aretha Franklin."

Mia started to laugh at him again, coming towards him to whisper, "But *they're* not from the East, my poor innocent. What you'll hear tonight will be another kind of soul." She came closer to him, slipping her arm through his and guiding him through the doors.

The auditorium was hung with long gossamer-thin lengths of fabrics, waving gently in currents of warm air. A similar kind of scent to Mia's filled the air, and, very subtly, the low sounds of a stringed instrument could be heard playing softly and unseen. James had expected that they would go and sit in one of the rows of seats, but Mia led him towards the front, where the open space in front of the stage had been covered with various oriental rugs and carpets. Several people were already seated on these rugs.

"We'll sit here," said Mia confidently, indicating a spot towards the back of this area. She took James by the hand and walked towards a brightly-coloured rug where she sat down cross-legged.

"Come on, join in, you're not too old for this, you soul-music lover."
She gave him a mischievous look. He sat down next to her, trying to
fold his long legs into position, crossing them at the ankles like she
had, but found the unaccustomed arrangement very awkward. He
would have much preferred to move to one of the comfortable
cinema-style seats further back but knew this would make him seem
very boring indeed, so decided he would have to stick it out.

After five minutes or so, some musicians began to arrive on the
stage, carrying various drums, sitars and other instruments James
couldn't have put a name to. A row of small clay oil lamps were
carried to the front of the stage and were lit by a man with a long
beard and a lit taper. He chanted as he went from lamp to lamp. As
each lamp was lit, and the small flame flickered into life, a new scent
joined the smell of incense. Then the man blew out the taper and
turned to face the audience, joining his hands together, palm to palm.
He bowed to the people, then began to dance slowly and
rhythmically as the musicians began to play. At first, James had to
stifle his amusement, seeing this bearded man begin to twist and turn
on the stage, lifting his feet off the ground in turn and bending first
backwards then forward, raising his arms and moving his head from
side to side. It was peculiar, but after a while James found himself
lulled into a relaxed state.

Gradually, people stood up and began to join in, moving in time
with the music. No words were spoken at any point, nor were any
introductions or directions given. The curtain at the back of the stage
was suddenly lit up with lights behind it, illuminating the silhouette
of a large statue. About half an hour into the performance, the curtain
was pulled back and the statue revealed. It was a pale stone statue
with a long face. Lamps were burning in front of it, and bowls of
flowers and fruit were arranged in a semicircle around it.

As the evening went on, the tempo of the music increased,
changing into a pounding rhythm, leading the dancers into a more
energetic dance. Many of them were old, James noticed, but they did
not seem to get tired. Mia had tried to get him to join in, holding out
her hands to him as she stood up and started to move. He shook his
head apologetically, and tried to speak to her, but she turned away
from him. He watched her as she seemed to become part of the
music, moving her hips sinuously. He saw that she had taken off her
shoes; as she danced, he noticed she was wearing metal anklets. It
reminded him of the girl Salome in the Bible, who danced before
King Herod and had pleased him so much that he had promised her

anything she asked for, and she had asked for the head of John the Baptist on a plate. James imagined the scene as he watched the whirling dancers in front of him. Could dance lead people to do strange, even terrible things? he pondered. He looked at Mia's face as she moved past him, her eyes closed as though she was in a trance. At that moment, she turned back towards him, and her eyes opened again, and fixed on him, those deep dark eyes which had fascinated him when he had first seen her. His own eyes met hers, taking in the paleness of her skin, and her full red lips. She was so beautiful, he told himself, more beautiful in that moment than anything else. When James had first arrived at this unusual musical event, he had resigned himself to enduring it as politely and patiently as possible, not wanting to appear to be narrow-minded, but as the evening advanced, he found himself quite mesmerised by it.

At eleven o'clock, the curtain slowly closed, and the bearded man blew out the lamps on the stage and put his hands together, bowing to the audience. The musicians began to leave the stage quietly, one by one, while the dancers from the audience sank down on to the rugs, still at last. Mia came back towards James, and to his surprise, wrapped her arms around him, glowing with heat from her exertions. James closed his eyes for a few seconds, basking in the thrill of the moment. He could smell her hair, brushing against his face. She lifted her head, bringing her mouth close to his, "Hasn't it been wonderful?" she breathed. "I want you to share it with me, James, the wonder of it, the *worship*." Her voice had a different sound to her usual voice, as though she had somehow changed. James looked down into her eyes, disconcerted. He needed to clear his head, needed to think; he couldn't get his thoughts straight in here. He wanted to get away from Mia.

"I need some air, Mia, I'll just go outside."

He started to walk, almost drunkenly, towards the back of the auditorium, passing bleary-eyed people on the way. It was as though they had been drugged, he thought. When he emerged into the darkness outside, he leant back against the stone wall of the building, inhaling the cold night air, drawing it deep inside him. After that strange moment a few minutes ago, he wanted to flush out the heavy incense-filled air of the interior of the theatre and fill his lungs with clean sharp air. He rubbed his eyes vigorously, trying to force himself into a fully awake state.

He began to walk a few steps along the pavement, thinking it would help him to feel better. He got to the corner and hesitated. He wanted to walk further, to put some distance between himself and the event at the theatre and the confused state it had induced. He crossed the road and then paused again, looking to his right and left. In the cold late October evening air, mist had begun to form, hanging over the dark street. He walked on a little further, feeling disorientated.

Several minutes later he stopped again, feeling chilled and confused, a ridiculous figure in his smart evening clothes, without even an outdoor coat. Where was he? Where had they parked the car? He didn't recognise this part of Exton. The lights in some of the houses on the street were already turned off. Another light went out as he watched. He realised he was lost, and it was far too late to knock on someone's door to ask for directions. He looked around him. The street was empty and silent. Which way should he go, up or down the street? He wasn't even sure which way he had just come. At that moment he felt a hand on his arm, and a voice spoke close to his ear, "James, are you all right? I've been looking for you – I've been searching all over." Mia's low voice seemed just as it had when he first met her. He turned round to look at her. Her features were indistinct in the dim light, but he could see her eyes and the curve of her mouth. Her other hand reached up towards his shoulder, and then to his face, "You're cold, James, you've walked a long way, further than you think, and the mist is getting thicker. Let's go inside for a few minutes, to warm up. He nodded, realising he was beginning to shiver. He didn't question what "inside" meant. At that moment, he was grateful to see anyone, and the offer of getting out of the cold and creeping mist was very tempting. She put her arm through his before he could reply, and began to steer him along the street, saying, "It's just around the corner."

He did not know where she was leading him but thought vaguely perhaps it was to a pub that was still open, or even back into the foyer of the theatre; perhaps he had wandered in a circle and was back where he started. However, after a few more minutes' walking, Mia stopped outside a shop which had a narrow passage next to it. She tugged at his arm, "Don't worry, just come in for a minute for a hot drink."

He still expected to see the entrance to a small bar tucked away down this passage, but he found they were standing outside the back door of the same property as the shop, and Mia had put a key in the lock. He was reluctant to go in, but what was the alternative? A freezing wind began to blow along the passage, whipping round his legs, chilling him even further, making his teeth chatter. Mia had the door open, and gently pulled him inside, closing it quietly behind him. "Welcome to my little home," she said.

James looked around him. They were in the kitchen of the house. It was clean and welcoming, lamps already lit. Bunches of dried flowers and herbs were hanging from the ceiling and a large dome-shaped cage hung on a stand in the corner. Inside a bird sat on a perch, its head turned towards them watchfully. Mia had followed his eyes, "That's Igor," she said, "He's my guard dog. He must like you. He hasn't called out to me." She picked up the kettle and filled it with water. "Sit by the fire while I make you a drink." There was a small sofa, covered with throws and with large cushions, in front of a wood-burning stove with a neat stack of logs next to it. While the kettle boiled, Mia opened the doors of the stove and added more logs to it, then left the doors open so that they could see the flames leaping up from the dry wood. James sat down on the sofa and held his hands out towards the fire, enjoying the warmth. After a couple of minutes, feeling his body warming pleasantly, he leant back against the cushions, closing his eyes for a moment in relief. He sat up again sharply when he felt Mia sit down next to him. She had a mug in each hand for them.

"Try this. Warming herbal tea, just what you need."

He had expected ordinary tea, the sort they always had in the vicarage kitchen and made hundreds of cups of throughout the year for anyone who came to see him. This was very different. It had a warm gingery flavour which was quite pleasant, and a bitter tang to it as well as a hint of sweetness, probably honey, he thought. He sipped it and watched the fire. Drowsiness began to creep over him. He sat up straighter, "I can't stay long, Mia. I must go home – Anna will wonder where I am."

Mia smiled, "You're not a teenager, James, you are allowed to go out without getting permission." Her tone was humorous, careful not to make him defensive. She watched him thinking, weighing her words. She waited for his reply.

He looked at her, considering the whole notion of *going out*, and felt his emotions rising, making his voice unsteady, "I know, you're right, but I haven't made a habit of going out...." He ran out of words, not wanting to mention the loss of his wife, that they used to go out together, long ago. How things had changed since he had become a widower. What a sad word, *widower*.

Mia touched his hand, comfortingly, just as he might to a bereaved member of his church. "I know how lonely it can be, when you have been loved... when you still *need* love." Then she leaned forward and gently, slowly, kissed his cheek.

He could smell her perfume again, that heady mixture of spicy fragrances. She stroked his cheek, her fingers moving to his neck. The soporific effect of the warmth of the fire and the herbal tea seemed to swirl around him, drawing him in closer to her. Inside his head, he could hear music and see the movement of the dancers at the theatre, Mia moving rhythmically among them. Then suddenly he saw the face of Jean Miller, grinning at him, and snapped back into full consciousness. Mia's fingers were still touching his face. He stood up, a wave of heat passing through him, "I must go."

She stood up and said kindly, disarmingly, "I'll get my keys and drive you home."

"No," he said abruptly, not wanting to be next to her again, in the close confines of a car, not trusting himself. "It's far too late for you to walk back to the car and drive all the way to Appleton. I'll get a taxi."

"It will cost a fortune."

"Never mind. It's my fault for letting you do all the driving."

"At least let me ring for a taxi then." She reached for her handbag and pulled out her phone, speed-dialling the number for a taxi. She spoke briefly to the person who answered, then said to James, "He'll be here in two minutes."

"Goodness, that's very quick."

"Yes, a local cab. Do you want to sit down again for a minute while you wait?"

James declined, preferring to stand. He made a few remarks about her kitchen, asked her about the herbs hanging from the ceiling and to his relief was interrupted mid-sentence by the sound of a car outside.

"Here he is," said Mia. "I hope you enjoyed the evening. I know it was not something you'd experienced before, but it will grow on you. I promise."

Then, before he could move, she had slipped her arms around him, and kissed him on the lips, lingering for a few seconds before moving away again. In those seconds the room began to spin around James, and he was intensely aware of the softness of her full lips. Then she moved back from him, crossing the room to open the door to the cold night and the taxi driver standing outside.

The taxi ride seemed very long, and James dreaded what the cost would be. He didn't give his precise address to the driver, feeling awkward about the idea of being driven so late at night directly from Mia's house to the vicarage. He merely asked for Church Road in Appleton.

For most of the ride, they kept silent, not going through the motions of the usual taxi conversation between driver and passenger. As they neared Appleton, the driver surprised James by asking, "Are you sure you don't want me to take you all the way?"

"No, just drop me off on Church Road," replied James.

"I just thought you may want to go right to the vicarage."

"What made you think I wanted the vicarage? I didn't say the vicarage," said James, panicking slightly.

"It's entirely up to you, Vicar, you do what you like, it's none of my business."

James felt deeply embarrassed as well as caught out. He fumbled for something to say, to explain his behaviour, which clearly wasn't what was expected of a man of the cloth. He decided he had better sound dignified, as though he was merely trying to not cause any bother to anyone.

"Certainly, that may be best after all, it just seems rather late, and I don't want to disturb anyone. I don't usually have to be out until this hour," he said, purposefully giving the impression that he may have been out on church business, then immediately felt even more guilty for being deceitful.

The man was not so easily put off the scent, "A late night out in the line of duty then was it, Vicar?"

James thought he detected a note of glee in the taxi driver's voice. Things in his life seemed to be sliding rapidly out of control. He decided to avoid any further conversation, and so simply kept quiet, wondering what connection the driver, clearly from Exton, had with the church in Appleton. He was a youngish man, perhaps it was a wedding or christening he had attended.

It was only when the taxi stopped outside the vicarage, and James had given the driver every last pound he had on him to cover the cost of the trip that he had another look at his face and recognised him as the man from Sunnyside Funeral Services. This must be a job he did on the side to get some extra money. Both his jobs would give him ample opportunity to tell his story of how he had picked up the vicar of Appleton and Netherton from the house of an attractive woman in Upper Exton, at around midnight.

*

It was after half past twelve when James approached the front door and tried to open it without making a sound. Nevertheless, Anna heard him coming in, breathed a sigh of relief and hurried into the hallway. The questions that were on her lips to ask her father were, what had happened, was he all right? But she checked herself – what right had she to ask him where he had been and why was he so late? She settled for merely giving him a hug.

"Anna – I thought you'd be fast asleep in bed," he said.

"Not yet, just getting a few jobs done. Did your evening out go well?" She looked at his pale face, "You look wiped out."

"Yes, not used to staying out late." He smiled faintly, "A home-bird, that's what I am, not cut out for all this adventure."

Adventure, thought Anna, whatever has Dad been up to? "Let me get you some tea, Dad. Would you like some toast?"

His face lightened a little, "That sounds really good, Anna, will you have some with me?"

"Of course."

James locked the front door, grateful to shut out the outside world and retreat into the security of home. They went into the kitchen where the warmth from the Aga range made it the cosiest room in the house. The central heating had turned off hours ago, and the old vicarage with its solid walls was poorly insulated and never heated up properly, even during the day in the few hours that James could afford to keep the central heating running.

They sat together companionably at the kitchen table, hardly speaking at first, just enjoying the homeliness of the kitchen, and the taste of the hot buttered toast. Anna was still being careful not to ask him about his evening, which clearly had not been a happy one. Instead, she started to tell him about her evening at Italian restaurant. He looked guilty at first, saying "I'm so sorry, I had no idea you were planning to take your poor old dad out."

"Don't worry, it all worked out in the end."

"Who is that young man?"

"It's Jonah. He makes beautiful furniture. He has a showroom here in the village."

"You are getting very popular, Anna. Being hotly pursued, it seems, by a succession of suitors."

"Bit of an exaggeration, Dad, don't you think? Anyway, time for bed for me at least." She grinned at him, "It might still be a bit early for some people."

He shook his head, smiling at the irony. The hands on the kitchen clock on the wall clicked on to one o'clock as they got up from the table, hugged one another goodnight, and each went upstairs to bed, full of their own thoughts.

Chapter Twelve

The days following James' evening out in Exton with Mia were packed with church business. He made sure this was the case. He made appointments with people he had been meaning to see for a long time and did more visits than usual, so that he spent very little time in the vicarage study. This meant that he was not there to answer calls, but he advised Anna not to keep running down to answer the phone, but leave the answer machine to pick up any messages from unanswered calls. All of this was with the purpose of avoiding Mia. He was in turmoil about the events of the evening and couldn't even think about it without panic sweeping over him. He wasn't even sure he knew confidently what had happened, so he tried to block it out of his mind. As long as he could avoid Mia, he didn't have to face it, or make a decision about it.

Meanwhile Jonah called to see Anna again. He was passing, he said, and wondered if she'd like to come out for coffee. She left what she was doing, and they went to the cafe near the duck pond in Appleton.

It was a fine bright day, and they sat at a table near the window, talking and looking out at the ducks.

"Any more amusing or weird things happening at the vicarage?" he joked.

"Not today," she replied, "Not yet anyway. How about you?"

"Lots of work, the business is building up nicely, it seems like I hardly ever stop." As he said this, he remembered the haranguing he had got from Rob and Tim, about him becoming dull. He said defensively, "It's what I want though, and what I love doing."

"Of course," she said, wondering at his change in tone, "Did I just hit a sore spot?"

"No, sorry, it's just some old mates of mine – I've known them since primary school. They think I've become boring because I don't want to hang around with them. To me, they seem to be aimless, stuck in the same old pattern of work, which they aren't interested in – they don't seem to want anything beyond that. I do, I want more in my life, and that seems to be annoying them. They apparently dislike everything about me these days."

"They don't sound like very good friends to me."

"The friendship seemed fine in the past, but it seems to have soured, or maybe I've changed."

"Is there any point in spending time with them if it's become so negative?"

He looked at her thoughtfully, "I'll tell you something peculiar – this will make you laugh – I've got to know an old lady, I've been helping her with something, and I enjoy spending time with her more than with my old friends." He laughed, "Isn't that something? She's got to be in her eighties, like a little old bird, but she's really interesting. She always gets me thinking about things, things beyond the everyday stuff. If the lads ever found out, they'd really give me a hard time."

"Well, I think I'd prefer your old lady too." But as she spoke, she thought of Martin Fielding, who she had allowed into her life and even now hadn't found the strength to tell directly never to contact her again. Why did people like her and Jonah let themselves get tangled up with people who much of the time made them feel miserable?

The fact that Jonah was kind to an older person would have impressed her father no end, Anna reflected, and asked, "So what do you help this lady with?" She expected him to say gardening or odd jobs in the house which she couldn't manage and was surprised at the answer.

"It sounds strange but, I'm helping her to build something."

"*Build* something, and she's in her eighties?"

"Yes, I know it sounds crazy... it actually *is* crazy, and it won't work, but I just can't leave her on her own."

"Well, that's really nice, I hope I have someone like you looking after me when I'm old." Then she realised what she'd said and felt herself blush. For a moment she looked directly at him, and then away, embarrassed.

"At the risk of sounding boring, I'll have to get on, I've got a sixty-mile journey to deliver a table."

"Of course. Me too, well not a table, but a small evening bag I've got to sort out." She giggled, pleased to recover from her previous remark.

They paid and left then stood for a moment outside the cafe. He caught hold of her hand, "Anna, do you want to see me again? Or are you still seeing that – I was going to say idiot – but I suppose you must have seen something in him."

Anna hesitated; he was waiting for her reply, watching her face. She opened her mouth, trying to find the right words, but, sensing her reluctance, he had let go of her hand and begun to look away, already guessing her answer.

"I'm not still seeing him," she mumbled, "But I haven't told him."

He looked at her, studying her face. "When you're sure, you know where to find me. Take care of yourself." He turned and began to walk away, and she felt the same wrench inside as she had felt before. She watched him cross the road and walk toward the showroom just beyond the village pond.

She walked back to the vicarage slowly, deep in thought and regret that, even now, her brief relationship with Martin Fielding still had a hold on her. She had hoped that the Martin situation would just fade away, and she wouldn't have to do anything about it, but now she wondered whether this approach would suffice, or whether she would have to make some definite gesture which made it clear to everyone that she did not want to see him again.

She arrived back just as the phone was ringing. Her father was out and, because she was so preoccupied thinking of other things, she forgot about what her father had said about leaving the phone unanswered, and that serious callers would leave a message for him, and went to answer it. She answered with the usual, "St Gregory's Vicarage," and waited for the caller to speak. There was a slight hesitation at the other end, and then a familiar low, almost purring voice said, "Hello, Anna." It was Mia.

"Hello, Mia, how kind of you to phone. Is it about the evening at your house?"

Again, there was a slight hesitation, and then Mia replied, "Of course, I just wanted to remind you of the time. You are still going to come, aren't you? – I'd be so disappointed if you couldn't."

Anna wasn't quick enough to think of a good excuse, and she was grateful to Mia for including her with the other people in the Arts and Crafts Circle, so she reassured Mia that, yes, she had remembered the time and she would be there.

"Lovely," said Mia, "Give my very best wishes to your father."

Anna smiled, remembering James' reaction when he first saw Mia, "I'll do that," she said.

*

147

The evening of "Receiving and Renewal" was to start at 7.30pm. Anna would have much preferred to stay at home with her father, who she was still concerned about. Recently he had taken to sitting staring into mid-air, apparently thinking deeply about something, and didn't notice her until she touched him, which would startle him back into the present moment. She had no idea what was on his mind, but whatever it was seemed to have a very tight grip on his attention. Anna thought if she didn't turn up it may offend not only Mia herself but also the other people who had welcomed her among them as a fellow artist.

She arrived a few minutes late on purpose, hoping that most other people would already be there and she could slip in quietly among them. However, when she parked outside Moonstone Crafts, she could only see two cars parked anywhere nearby and wondered if she had got the time wrong after all. As she got out of her car, she heard a squeaking sound from further up the street. As it got nearer, she could see by the light of the streetlamps that the squeak was coming from a rickety bicycle which was coming unsteadily down the street towards her. As it juddered to a halt by the shop, she saw it was ridden by the nervous young man with holes in his jumper that she had seen at the Crafts Circle meeting. She called out hello to him, but then immediately regretted it as he was so alarmed, he almost fell off his bike.

"Sorry," said Anna, "I didn't mean to scare you. Do you remember me? I was at the Arts and Crafts Circle meeting."

He looked at her quizzically, then, "Oh yes, I do now – you're Angela, aren't you? I didn't see you standing there."

"It's Anna, actually."

She followed him down the narrow passage next to the shop then waited while he tried to secure his old bicycle to a drainpipe with a heavy chain and padlock. Anna doubted whether anyone would bother stealing such a wreck. He dropped the padlock twice as he struggled to attach it to the slightly too short chain.

"Can I help?" enquired Anna, "Let me holds the ends of the chain while you pick up the padlock."

Between them, they managed to lock the bicycle up, but then realised the back of the bicycle was partly blocking the passage.

"Oh dear, I'll have to move it," he said, sounding flustered.

At that moment the back door opened, and Mia stepped out into the backyard, saying, "I thought I heard some more people arriving. Come upstairs – there are other folks here already."

She took Anna by the hand, "Anna, I'm so glad you could come, let me show you the way. Matthew, you come up when you're happy with where you've put your bike."

Matthew, far from taking offence at being left, just nodded and started to try and unlock his big padlock again.

As they went inside, Anna asked, "Will he be all right? He does seem to be struggling."

"Oh, don't worry, Matthew's always like that. No one would want his bike anyway. He has a problem relaxing and letting things go. I've tried to help him with it, I'm sure it's all connected to things that happened to him in the past, but he has to be willing to accept that."

"Oh poor Matthew, has he had a tough start in life?"

Mia murmured, half to herself, "Well maybe not *this* life," and hurried Anna towards the stairs which led to the upstairs room where a group of ten people were sitting, talking and drinking glasses of wine.

"Come and join us," said Mia, "At the moment just enjoy the snacks and some wine, and then we'll start." Anna looked at the snacks; there was a bowlful of grey shrivelled-looking morsels which she couldn't identify, and next to it a bowl of brown wrinkly strips. She peered at them.

"Parsnip Slivers," a man standing near her announced, "the earth's holistic alternative to crisps." He took one and bit into it, "Delicious. You can tell they're grown organically, no chemicals, just good honest dung on those parsnips – you can taste it."

Anna moved the dry corrugated treat round her mouth, trying not to think about dung. Then she surreptitiously took it back out of her mouth and threw it under the table when she thought no one was looking. Scanning the room, she recognised Mark Winthrop, the man who created wicker sculptures, and also the drumming enthusiast with dreadlocks who had organised his *Earth Rhythms* event, open to all comers to participate. Anna wondered if anyone had come and taken part, or whether he'd been left alone in the field behind the allotments, drumming. He caught her looking at him, and came across to her, holding out his hand. She shook it politely, trying not to notice how grubby it looked, and felt. The rims of his nails were black with dirt, and as he leant forward to speak to her, she glanced at his dreadlocks, wondering if he ever combed them out and washed them, or if they just stayed as they were indefinitely, growing bigger and crustier. He seemed to guess her line of thought, and stroked his

149

hair fondly, saying, "I bet I know what you're thinking – how has he managed to grow these, and does he use special shampoo, or something like that." He spoke patiently, as though explaining a difficult concept to a struggling learner. "The thing is, dreadlocks like these *don't need* to be washed. They have achieved a state of *equilibrium*. Hair actually doesn't need to be washed anyway. Washing hair is a recent idea – nobody used to do it. It actually damages your hair, removes all sorts of things from it."

Anna gazed at the matted brownish lumps – were there things in there which needed to be removed? Were they crawling about right now, inches away from her? At this point, his shook his hair, which was greying in parts, as though shaking it would demonstrate what good condition it was in. "See?" he said, "It's absolutely fine."

Anna wasn't sure what to say in reply, so tried to change the subject, "How did the drumming go?"

"Very well. The connection was there, which was what it was all about."

"Oh. Good. And people came to join in? I remember you said it wasn't necessary to have any previous drumming experience."

"Absolutely. You just open up and connect with yourself and the earth. Both of us said it was moving."

"Both of you?"

"It's not about numbers."

"No, of course."

Anna noted, with gratitude, that someone else was heading in her direction; she didn't think there was anything else she could think of to ask about this man's hairstyle or drumming habits.

It was Shelley, the meeting organiser, who squeezed in between her and the drummer, saying, merrily, "Anna, how nice to see you again. How is your design work going?"

Anna, relieved to return to a subject that made more sense said, "Fine, thank you. I'm trying to get a wide enough range ready for sale."

"Have you got plenty of shops wanting to offer them for sale, or do you concentrate on craft markets?"

"It's early days yet. Mia is going to take some, which is wonderful, and I'm making a list of craft markets. I still need to build up more stock, and it all takes so much time. I love it though. It feels like the right thing for me to be doing, making things." She spoke truthfully; she did love it, but it disturbed her that there were others here in this strange assortment of people who also loved arts and crafts and did not seem to be very grounded in reality. She didn't want to become another slightly weird person creating things nobody wanted. Shelley, however, was not in that camp. She seemed to be a very ordinary happy individual who simply wanted to encourage people to enjoy the creative arts. Mia was more unusual but clearly also wanted to help young designers like Anna. Without people like Mia, Anna reflected, how would new designers ever get their work seen at all, apart from on the internet, which was not the same as seeing textures, form and colours in reality.

After a while Matthew joined the group; he must have had a terrible struggle with his padlock and the positioning of his bicycle, or was the struggle mainly inside his head, some sort of desperate anxiety, Anna wondered as she watched him come nervously into the room. She crossed over to him and enquired, "Matthew, are you all right? Did you manage to get your bike and the padlock sorted out?"

"Yes, thank you," he said, "I just like to know that it's in a safe place."

"I'm sure it will be fine, tucked away behind the shop here. By the way, how is your exhibition at the library going?"

A look of sadness and disappointment clouded his face, "It didn't actually go ahead in the end. I was supposed to get all my exhibits there by nine o'clock on that first morning, and my friend was going to come round in his van, but he wasn't well, and so I didn't know what to do, and I just panicked really. I couldn't work out how I could get things there, so I phoned them and said I couldn't do it."

"I'm sorry, Matthew. What a shame – it was such a good opportunity."

Matthew lowered his head like a child in trouble.

Anna said, "I'm sure another chance will come your way. If it happens again, and you're stuck, ring me and I'll try to help."

He looked up at her, brightening, "Thank you, that's really good of you."

Across the room, Mia was getting to her feet, and everyone's eyes gradually turned towards her. She looked round the room, making eye contact with each person as her gaze swept round the room. The chatter quietened and everyone listened as she spoke quietly in her purring voice, "I'd like to thank you all for coming to my home this evening. It is so precious to be among friends who appreciate the same things... who love creativity and honour other creative spirits." She paused and smiled around her, almost glowing with warmth towards everyone present. "It's lovely to talk together, to share some food and wine, but there's something more here this evening. We come together, a gathering, a *union* of souls and spirits. Let's have a time of quiet, joining together, open to receive strength and inspiration."

She swept her arm around in a circle towards the chairs which were round the edges of the room, and everyone sat down together as though she was conducting an orchestra. Anna followed suit, sitting down in a small chair in the corner of the room. She noticed Mia had started to pull a low table into the centre of the room, forming a centrepiece. On it was a round beaded mat, with a bowl of water standing on it. Floating on the water were several round candles. With a ceremonial air, Mia walked towards the doorway, disappeared through it momentarily, then returned holding a tall lit candle in a black wrought iron candlestick in one hand and a long wax taper in the other. As she walked back slowly into the room she nodded towards Matthew, standing near the door, who caught her meaning and switched off the lights. Mia came into the centre of the room and put the candlestick on the table. Everyone watched with rapt attention as she used her wax taper to transfer a light from her candle to each of the floating candles in the bowl, murmuring as she did so.

Anna could not catch what Mia was saying but, gradually, all around the room, other voices were joining Mia's, whispering the same low chanting of words in a kind of repeated chorus. This continued for several long minutes. Anna listened hard, trying to make out individual words, but failed to do so. Was it another language? Or was it more like a poem, or folk song? She looked round the room at the other people there. All of them seemed to know the words, and were moving their lips in unison, completely transported by this odd activity. She felt a mixture of curiosity and a growing disquiet as the atmosphere seemed to change. She became aware of some sort of mist in the room, and to her amazement the candles seemed to begin to move, as the water in the bowl began to stir and ripple. *What was this? What was happening?* Anna looked again at the faces around her. Most of them had closed their eyes, and were sitting absolutely still, completely focused on whatever it was they were experiencing.

Mia had stopped chanting and now had a serene expression on her face as she watched the candles moving. Then she said, "Yes. Yes, we want to hear."

At that moment, from the pocket of Anna's jeans, the jangling of her mobile phone ringtone broke into the proceedings. Anna jumped up, relieved to have a reason to escape from this odd gathering. She exited from the room as quickly as she could, treading on Matthew's foot as she left, which seemed to startle him out of the semi-trance he was sinking into. She raced downstairs, her phone still ringing in her back pocket, grabbed her jacket from a row of hooks in the kitchen, and shot out through the back door. Once outside, she grabbed her phone to answer the call. There was no one on the other end of the line. She looked at the call list and saw there was a missed call from her father. Never mind, she'd be home soon and would talk to him then. Anna hurried to her car and got inside, grateful to be back in a familiar place. She started the engine and turned the heater up to the highest setting. She felt chilled and strange. Thank goodness her phone had given her a reason to escape. The more she got to know Mia, the more weird she seemed. Anna accepted that artistic people often were slightly, or even very, unusual in some way, but the gathering at Mia's place was surely beyond the sort of bohemian lifestyle she could feel at ease with. It had left her feeling disturbed; she didn't even want to think about it – she just wanted to get back home and lock the door.

When Anna arrived back, she found her father sitting at his desk in the vicarage study, looking thoughtful.

"Still working, Dad? It's getting late. You should have stopped by now."

He noticed the clock on the wall behind her, "Goodness, I had no idea it was that time already. Did you have a good evening? I'm sorry, I shouldn't have tried to ring you, I hope I didn't disturb your evening, but I could hardly stop myself. I had an awful feeling you were in some sort of difficulty. I think I must have had an attack of the disease of over-protective father." He looked at her sheepishly.

She walked over to him and kissed him fondly on the top of his forehead, "Thanks, Dad. It just happens that I am very grateful for your call – it got me out of an awkward moment."

"Really? I'm glad to hear it. I've had enough 'awkward moments' recently to last me for a very long time. I'm feeling in urgent need of some moments of home comfort, preferably involving something from the fridge and the company of my daughter."

Anna laughed, "Would a cheese and pickle sandwich be comforting enough? Or do you need a chocolate éclair as well?"

"Both, definitely both. This is a comfort emergency."

They went into the kitchen, still enjoying the joke, and made hot drinks and sandwiches, to be followed by fresh cream chocolate éclairs. They had settled down at the table to enjoy their impromptu supper when James asked lightly, "So what was your 'awkward moment', or is that an awkward question?"

"It was more a bit weird really," replied Anna, then hesitated. "I'm not sure what to make of it. Some kind of peculiar new age spirituality I think – the Arts and Crafts Circle people. Anyway, I left before it went any further."

"What was going on then? Describe it," said her father, intrigued.

"I think they were singing together, or rather *droning* – a song, or chant, I don't know which – I couldn't catch the words. And lots of candles, and everyone closing their eyes."

"So, group singing by candlelight, and a bit of meditation?" quipped James, "Sounds like the daily routine of a monastery or convent – plainchant and some contemplation."

"No, not like that at all. Monastic singing sounds lovely. This was not peaceful and holy. It was... I don't know, I didn't like it."

"Perhaps you should just stick to the practical side of art and design, and steer clear of the weird fringe in future."

"I will. I don't want to offend Mia but—"

"Did you say Mia?"

"Yes, it was at Mia's house. She seems to be into this alternative spirituality, or whatever."

"I see." Her father sounded serious. He stopped eating and put a half-eaten sandwich back on his plate. The dreadful evening with Mia was flooding back into his mind.

Anna could see he was looking disturbed. "What is it, Dad?"

"Oh, nothing really."

"You really liked her, didn't you? I could see you did. I'm sorry, I don't want to spoil your image of her."

"No, no, not at all. My image of Mia has changed anyway."

Anna was confused, wondering what could have caused this. Surely her father had only had the briefest encounter with Mia when she had come to pick Anna up for the meeting last month.

James continued decisively, "Nothing for you to worry about Anna." He looked down at his abandoned sandwich, "I think I've eaten enough – don't want to eat too much cheese before bedtime, bad dreams and all that."

"Isn't that just an old wives' tale?"

"Perhaps we're just about to find out."

A couple of minutes later, they had left their plates and mugs in the sink and gone to bed.

*

Whether it was the cheese for supper or not, Anna found herself dreaming vividly that night. She dreamed that she was back at Mia's house at exactly the point when her phone had rung, but this time there was no welcome interruption. Instead, Mia continued speaking to whoever or whatever it was, repeating, "We're listening." As the dream continued, the water in the bowl swirled more and more until it began to boil, and mist rose out of it, and hung over it. As it coiled about in the air, a face appeared in it and began to speak. Anna woke up abruptly, sweating. She sat up in bed, glad to be awake. Is that what would have happened next? She was shivering. She pulled her duvet around her. What had really happened earlier that evening? Was it some kind of elaborate hoax, or something much more strange? She lay down again, trying to dismiss the fear which had gripped her, but found she couldn't. Sitting up again, she reached out for her bedside lamp and turned it on. Beside it was a book of Psalms which used to belong to her mother. She opened it at Psalm 124, and began to read it aloud:

"If it had not been the Lord who was on our side
  when our enemies attacked us,
then they would have swallowed us up alive,
when their anger was kindled against us
then the flood would have swept us away
the torrent would have gone over us
then over us would have gone the raging waters."
She thought of the swirling water in the bowl on the table at Mia's house, and read on...

"Blessed be the Lord.
We have escaped like a bird
from the snare of the fowlers;
the snare is broken,
and we have escaped.
Our help is in the name of the Lord...."

She started to pray, thanking God for her escape, feeling just like the bird in the psalm, trapped in a snare, but who by God's grace had been rescued. *Again*, she thought, once from Martin Fielding, and now from the strange event at Mia's.

After a while, still holding the book, she fell asleep.

Chapter Thirteen

Fred Roland had a call on his mobile phone. Mike Small was asking if he would be able to come to a meeting of local men – businesspeople and others – in Netherton. It may be a very useful source of contacts for him. Fred was flattered – clearly he was being viewed as a person of significance in the Netherton area. "I would be delighted to come, thank you," he said happily. *Men only*, he thought. Well, Susan would have to accept that sometimes men needed some time on their own to do business, to make connections. She couldn't always be involved in everything. He felt confident, superior; he didn't need Susan for this anyway.

The meeting was to be that Sunday evening in a meeting room at the Mason's Arms. It was a well-established men's association, Fred understood. It sounded very much like the sort of group he had always wanted to be part of. It would be ideal, a good environment for networking, and probably enjoyable too, he thought. He imagined a gentlemen's club, winged leather armchairs, men of substance standing around wearing tweed jackets, discussing the grouse season, or the government's unreasonable regulations about their employees.

He explained to Susan that this could be an important link for Bluebird Design and Construction, and that, as it was men only, she couldn't come with him; it was merely a tradition – she wouldn't want him to go with her to the Women's Institute, would she?"

"*I* wouldn't want to go to the WI, Fred," replied Susan in a withering tone.

"No, quite," said Fred, "I would never suggest that, Susan."

Fred arrived a few minutes early for the meeting, but not too early, he thought as he walked towards the Mason's Arms. He didn't want to put himself in the potentially embarrassing position of arriving first and not being sure what to do. As it turned out, his timing was perfect. Just as he arrived at the door, he looked up the street and could see Mike Small coming towards him from the opposite direction. He risked giving him a friendly wave, but then immediately regretted it. After all, this was strictly a business meeting, wasn't it? On the other hand, he seemed to be about to be welcomed into a social group. Tricky, he thought, but also surely a personal compliment; he must have made a very favourable impression on Mike to be accepted not only as an influential man of business, but also as a friend. Thinking this served to increase Fred's self-confidence as he paused for a moment by the door, straightening his tie. He delayed just long enough so that he and Mike Small went through the double doors together. Mike Small patted him on the shoulder companionably as they walked into the bar, saying warmly, "Good to see you, Fred. Glad you could come tonight – I think you'll enjoy meeting the other men."

"I'm so glad you invited me, Mike"

"Let me get you something to drink; we can take it up to the meeting with us."

Fred looked at the names of ales displayed on the beer pumps. He didn't drink much beer, didn't really like it very much, apart from a cold lager and lime when he was on holiday with Susan. Tonight, however, he wanted to be one of the men, and, he supposed, real men drink ale, not gin and tonic, which was what he drank with Susan at the end of the day's work. He studied the names on the pumps: *Ishka Special Ale,* he read, "That's an unusual name – is it a locally-brewed ale?" he asked.

"It is, it's brewed just a couple of miles from here at a very old brewery. Every pint is said to have a little of the water from the Ishka in it, that's our river which runs round the edge of the village, and then right underneath it. The water from the river is said to have special power," laughed Small, not expecting to be taken seriously.

Fred, however, was intrigued, "What an interesting history – I must try some of that. I've never heard the word Ishka before."

"People say it's an old word for water, Celtic or something like that. The old people round here say the river is supposed to have water spirits in it. I don't take much notice of that sort of superstitious stuff."

Fred was nodding enthusiastically, "I'm sure it's a very nice river. Let's see what it tastes like!" He reached for the pint glass of ale which had just been put on the bar and lifted it to his lips. It had a strong bitter taste. "Goodness!" commented Fred, "The Ishka spirit must be a tough old thing."

George Wright, standing behind the bar, was listening to their conversation and added, "It was certainly tough a while ago – it flooded part of the village."

"Better kept inside a beer glass then," quipped Fred, "like a genie in a bottle – once you let it out, it runs wild, and goes around destroying things." He already felt a little tipsy, the strong ale going straight to his head, making him talk too much.

Small smiled genially at him. "Fred, when we go up to the meeting, I'll need to introduce you to the other members, and there's a sort of formal shape to the meeting. You'll be asked to say something about yourself."

Feeling pleasantly relaxed, Fred replied happily, "Of course, Mike, I could say, 'I'm Fred Roland, married to Susan, I live at Magnolia House, The Crescent, Upper Exton, and I work for Bluebird Design and Construction, North Park Avenue, Exton." Fred had completely forgotten Arnold's strict instruction about keeping a firewall between the company and the local source of labour. While Fred drank some more beer and took some peanuts from a bowl on the bar counter, Mike Small took a notepad from his pocket and noted down Fred's details.

At that moment, Wright, from his position behind the bar, nodded at Small, who took the hint that it was time to go upstairs to the meeting. Other men had already begun to slip quietly through the bar to the stairs which led up to the meeting room.

The room was lit by candles in brass candle holders at regular intervals along the walls of the room. The subdued, flickering light lent a clandestine ambience to the room, quite different to when Fred had been in it before. All the men were talking together in groups standing around the room when Fred walked in with Mike Small, so he did not realise at first that the meeting was going to be according to a rigid protocol. Feeling very jovial as he stood drinking his ale, he started to tell Small that he had just booked a holiday for himself and Susan in the Canary Islands, the same hotel as last year, when he saw out of the corner of his eye a very thin young man dressed in a black gown move down the length of the room to the head of the large table which occupied the centre of the room. Fred watched in amazement as this odd-looking person stood in front of a large carved chair, took something like a small hammer from the table, and banged it hard on a wooden block which stood on the shiny dark surface of the table. Everyone looked up, stopping their conversation mid-sentence.

The young man grinned, exposing his badly stained teeth, and all the men moved as one towards the table and sat down. Small indicated a chair at the very bottom of the table, tapping the back of it so that Fred would know his place. He stood behind the adjacent chair, clearly expecting Fred to follow suit. Fred noticed the landlord of the pub, now in a smart jacket, had taken the chair to the right of the strange young man, and had opened a leather-bound ledger on the table in front of him. Still nobody spoke, apparently waiting for something to happen. Glasses had been put down on the table when the gavel had called them to order. Suddenly the thin young man spoke in an unnecessarily loud voice, "Welcome, brothers, to the meeting of the Guild." After saying this, he did not seem to know what to do next. Fred watched as the landlord, who seemed to have adopted a different persona now from the man serving behind the bar only minutes ago, slid a thin red book in front of his young leader, and opened it, pointing to a particular place in it. The younger man looked down at it, and began to read from it:

"All who are not brothers, step back."

Small took Fred by the arm, and gently but firmly pulled him back three steps from the table. He nodded to him, indicating that he must remain there, and returned to stand behind his own chair.

The leader was reading aloud again, "Brothers of the Guild, and of blood, let us re-take our oath."

All the men began to recite in a low tone, perfectly together, "We swear by all our power, to uphold above all other loyalties, one another and the Great Power. We will strive, by thought and purpose, by our work and everything we own, to protect one another and preserve the bond between us."

A thrill ran through Fred as he listened. He had never heard anything like this before.

"Let us announce our values."

All the men spoke again, their voices seeming to rise, "We will be true at all times to our values of Loyalty, Obedience and Silence."

"Brothers, as Master I demand your loyalty, not for my own pleasure, but for the protection of all, under the direction and guidance of the Power above us."

Fred shuddered as he took in the sound of deep male voices rising again, filling the room. The tremor seemed to resonate inside him, chilling and exciting him at the same time.

"We pledge ourselves to you, Master, and to the Power above us, above all other loyalties and ties, above family and friends, as long as life endures, and may death pursue any brother who turns his back on the brotherhood."

Fred shivered again as the last vibration of sound died away in the long room. The Master, which Fred now knew him to be, sat down in his ornate carved high-backed chair. Around the table, the men began to take their seats. Mike Small turned and beckoned Fred forward, pointing to the chair at the bottom of the table. Fred tiptoed the three paces back towards his chair and slipped respectfully into it, mesmerised by the proceedings. The Master spoke again, reading from the red book, "Are there strangers at the meeting tonight?"

Mike Small spoke up, confidently, "Yes, Master, I have brought a friend to make him known to the brothers."

"Let the stranger stand and make himself known to us."

Mike Small nudged Fred and whispered, "Introduce yourself to the Master and the brotherhood."

Fred stood up, his knees trembling. He swallowed, his mouth suddenly dry. He opened his mouth to speak, but only a squeaky voice came out. He coughed and started again, "My name is Fred Roland." He tried to remember what else he should say, but couldn't recall anything.

The Master watched him. Fred saw his expression change and thought for a moment he was going to laugh at him, but then the Master's face returned to seriousness. Around Fred, everyone waited. George Wright came to his rescue, "Perhaps we could hear a little more about you," he suggested.

"Oh yes, certainly," said Fred, suddenly remembering what he might say. "I am married to Susan, my wife of course," he giggled nervously, "And I live in Upper Exton, and I am proud to work for a very active company in this area called Bluebird Design and Construction, alongside the company director." He heard a murmur of approval in the room at this description.

Fred looked at Mike Small, sitting next to him, hoping for an indication as to whether he had said enough. At that moment George Wright spoke again. Fred deduced that he held the role of secretary of the meeting.

"Thank you. You are welcome to stay for the first part of this Guild Meeting." Wright bowed his head slightly towards Fred and began to clap his hands appreciatively; everyone joined in, smiling at Fred encouragingly. Fred looked round the room at the faces of all the men turned towards him and felt a glow of well-being. They liked him, he thought, they wanted him with them, part of the group. To his surprise, he felt tears begin to well up in his eyes. Mike Small rose to his feet next to him, and gave him a manly hug, as the Master spoke above the sound of applause, reading again from the red book, "Thank you, you can sit down now. You are not permitted to speak during the meeting but can listen to the members of the Guild until we enter the closed part of the meeting."

Fred said squeakily, not quite in control of his emotions, "Thank you very much... Master."

Wright, in his role as secretary of the Guild, read some brief minutes of the previous meeting. There wasn't much to read out; it sounded as though the meeting had been devoted to discussion about the election of the new Master following the death of the old Master, and that other items had been deferred to tonight's meeting.

The first item on the agenda was the village Winter Gala. They discussed how much money the Guild would give for the event. Some members wanted the Guild to be thanked in public by the leader of the Parish Council as well as have the name of the Guild on the programme. Others preferred to maintain their usual low profile.

"Remember one of our values is Silence," advised an elderly member. "All our activities are cloaked with silence. We don't want to trumpet our presence."

How refreshing, thought Fred, wanting to do things without being seen to do them. These men are quiet heroes.

After another agenda item, George Wright leant towards the Master and whispered something to him, pointing to something in the red book that still lay on the table in front of him. The Master looked towards Fred and then said firmly, "This concludes the first part of the meeting to which we may give access to those who are not yet brothers. Such people must leave at this point."

Fred experienced a horrible sinking of heart. He suddenly felt small and lonely. He longed to stay, to be included in this brotherhood. How soon could he be part of them, he wondered? Mike Small had already stood up, ready to escort Fred from the room. He held out his hand, pointing away from the table indicating they should go towards the door. Fred opened his mouth, thinking he would say something, perhaps thank the meeting, but Small gave the slightest shake of his head, as if reading Fred's thought. Quietly, they slipped out through the door and down the stairs. In seconds, Fred found himself guided out through the pub door on to the street outside where it was cold and dark. Small didn't say anything other than, "Good night, Fred. I'll be in touch," and disappeared back inside the warmth of the Mason's Arms.

Fred stood looking after him, at the closed door, the light shining through the glass panes and the muffled sounds of voices and laughter within. He felt lonelier than he had ever felt since he was a little boy, wanting to be included with the popular confident boys, who always seemed to be bigger than him and able to make other children do what they wanted. He turned away and started to walk towards his car. When he had got in and closed the door, he spoke aloud to himself, "Never mind Fred, soon you'll be able to join them, you'll be one of the brothers." He smiled, he liked that idea, he had never had a brother.

*

Jonah wondered if he had left it too late as he arrived at Honeysuckle Cottage at five minutes to six. He generally was on time and knew it was no accident that he was late. Although he had agreed to go to an evening service with Hilda, he had had second thoughts since then, and, consciously or subconsciously, had delayed leaving home. He knocked at the door softly – another attempt at avoidance. However, his efforts to evade her were useless; she answered the door immediately.

"Jonah, how lovely to see you."

"Sorry I'm late. I thought I might have missed you."

"Not at all. I didn't mind waiting – I was sure you'd come." She smiled in her bright pleasant way, "We can still just about get there on time!"

They set off together, walking to the church, Hilda setting a cracking pace for someone her age.

A small number of people had gathered for the service, occupying a semi-circle of chairs at the front of the church. The vicar was already about to begin but looked up as Hilda and Jonah entered. He called out to them in a friendly way, "Good evening! Don't worry, we haven't started yet."

They made their way to the front and sat down on the remaining two empty chairs. It was only then that Jonah realised why the vicar seemed familiar, *of course*, it was Anna's father. Jonah looked round the group of people, whose faces were all visible as they sat in the curve of chairs. He noticed Anna, sitting next to her father. Her eyes were closed for a moment, only opening when her father spoke.

"Welcome, everyone, in the name of Jesus Christ."

Jonah looked down at the booklet Hilda had placed in his hands.

"All the words are in there," she whispered to him, "Well maybe not all, but a good number of them, enough to start with."

The church was not very warm, but fortunately everyone was dressed for the low temperature outside, wearing thick coats and scarves, which nobody removed. The atmosphere inside the church was warm, however, in a different way – Jonah felt a sense of belonging, even homecoming, which was strange since it was years since he'd been inside a church.

James led them through the service, following what was written in the booklet, until the time came for communion. Jonah watched as the bread was held up for them to see as it was broken, and James repeated the words of Jesus, "This is my body, broken for the forgiveness of sins." Then he lifted up the cup of wine, a simple piece of glazed pottery, saying, "This is the cup of my blood, poured out for you."

The words seemed to echo inside Jonah... what did they mean? How could the blood of Jesus Christ be poured out for him?" He watched as the vicar stopped, and saw the other people look surprised, as though he shouldn't have stopped at this point.

James put the communion cup back down on the table slowly, then looked up at his small congregation. He clearly was doing something unusual – Jonah could tell by the way others were watching him.

"Brothers and sisters, I wouldn't normally say anything of a personal nature at this point, but I feel compelled to do so this evening." His voice was shaking a little as he continued, "The point of the communion service... in a nutshell... is this, that Jesus poured out his blood, his life-blood, so that our sins, your sins, *my* sins could be forgiven, washed away, and we could come home to God. We can't understand it, but it's very real. And tonight, as your vicar, I want to say I am so glad that my sins can be got rid of, and I can be given a new start. I am a sinful man." He paused, searching for words, "I'm sorry, I don't want to shock you, but of course I am, and recently it's become even more obvious to me. I'm the vicar, but I'm nothing special, it's Jesus Christ who is special. But if we can just hang on to him, he will take us with him, away from the old habits, the things that mess us up, and he can make us free and clean." His hands as well as his voice were shaking now. He carried on, the people listening, fascinated by this unexpected outpouring, hanging on to every word. "We're all in the same boat, every one of us, whatever our lives have been like. We need Jesus, I need Jesus. We need him to forgive us, and free us from our sins. That's why he poured out his blood, for you and for me."

He halted, as though he had run out of strength. Jonah was riveted. This was unlike anything he may have expected – the rawness, the passion, the words of a man who was almost breaking, but was not blaming anyone else, rather was saying it was himself who was at fault, his own sin that was messing him up, and that mysteriously, Jesus Christ could put things right. Jonah's head was almost reeling, he had never heard this before.

There was a minute or two of silence while the vicar stood with his head bowed. Jonah knew that soon the regular churchgoers would go forward and take communion, he had read it in the booklet he held in his hands. But he wouldn't go; he was an outsider. The vicar's words were still rolling around in his head, bouncing backwards and forwards, "The blood of Jesus, poured out for you", "I am a sinful man"... he'd never thought of that before – images flashed into his mind, scenes from his life, late nights out with Tim and Rob, the mornings after, Sandy, and others too. *I am a sinful man*. Deep inside him, he was moved, and something like a sob almost rose to his lips. He wanted what James had been talking about. He wanted to be made clean, and free. He felt tears welling up, even though he hadn't cried since he was a child.

James was speaking again, "Draw near with faith," he was saying. "You are welcome to come to the Lord's table."

Jonah felt Hilda's eyes on him. He looked up at her, "I can't come," he said, "Not me, I'm not a Christian."

Hilda whispered, "Remember what our dear vicar said, '*We're all in the same boat, we need Jesus, none of us is special, only Jesus is special.*' All we need to do is trust him, Jesus I mean."

Jonah felt another impulse to weep. He closed his eyes, and deep inside himself, prayed, "I don't understand this, but if you're real, Jesus, please help me, forgive me, I need this."

A sense of peace passed over him, and when Hilda stood up and turned round to him, a question in her eyes, he got to his feet and went with her to receive the bread and wine. He forgot everyone else in the room, and when the vicar held out the piece of bread to him, saying, "The body of Christ, broken for love of you," he whispered in reply *Thank you.*

The service finished a few minutes later, James going to stand by the door to have a few words with each person as they left. Anna stayed at the front of the church with the church warden to help clear away. Hilda and Jonah were the last in the short line of people leaving. As they drew level, James held out his hand to shake

Jonah's, about to say the usual "I'm so glad you could join us this evening," but was arrested in this by Jonah holding on and shaking his hand vigorously, saying, "That was... incredible. I didn't realise church was like this, well this church anyway. I've never heard anything like that before. And the communion... about Jesus' blood, and what it does to you." He paused, suddenly feeling embarrassed, "Sorry, I'm not normally like this, I just can't really put it into words."

James stood looking at the young man in front of him. It was obvious that he had just had a very significant spiritual experience – in this church! In Netherton! James could almost have jumped up and down and shouted. As it was, he couldn't think of anything to say, apart from, "Perhaps you would like to come again?"

"Of course, when's the next one?" asked Jonah eagerly.

James immediately worried that Jonah's intense spiritual experience may not be repeated, and this may result in disappointment. Then it struck him that tonight's service had not exactly gone smoothly – he had almost broken down in tears and had been very close to making a public confession of lust and perhaps other things during the communion. Still God had used it all somehow, and this young man's heart had been touched.

Hilda fetched a list of the times of services at Netherton and Appleton and handed them to Jonah before they left the church. She offered him tea and cake with her before he went home, which he accepted happily, wanting more time to discuss what had happened to him that evening. They talked for two hours, Hilda showing him some Bible passages and Jonah asking her if she thought he could get a Bible anywhere that evening.

On the way back to the vicarage Anna asked her father what Jonah had been talking about at the back of the church.

"In a nutshell—" James began.

"That's two nutshells you've had tonight, Dad," she said, laughing.

"Yes, in a nutshell," he continued, unperturbed, "Jonah met with God tonight."

"Are you serious? That's amazing! He's the only gorgeous male I've met who is also a Christian! Present company excluded of course, Dad!"

"Gorgeous, is he Anna? Well, well, I had no idea."

He began to sing loudly and happily, a thing he never did, so Anna gave up trying to question him further, and sang along with him.

Chapter Fourteen

All week, Fred looked forward to Sunday evening. He had met with Mike Small during the week before, to be briefed about what he must do to become a member of the Guild. Everything had been explained to him, the objects he would be presented with, the cut that would be made and the binding nature of the ceremony. There was plenty of time for him to change his mind, Mike Small said, only join us if it's what you really want. He added, however, that he had never regretted becoming one of the brotherhood – it gave him strength and new meaning in his life, not to mention the business advantages. The phrase which warmed Fred's heart the most was, "You'll never be alone again, Fred. You'll always be connected to us, and the Power which links us all together as brothers." Fred didn't understand, or care to know more about the origins of the Guild, but he did know there was a powerful atmosphere at the meetings, and felt a deep respect, even awe, with regards to this. He wanted it, he wanted to join it and know he belonged. He didn't mind about being cut as part of the joining ceremony – it would probably only be a small cut, he told himself, no more than he might get when shaving clumsily.

He hadn't explained all the details to Susan but had given her the general outline of him joining a local businessman's club, and that it would be good for their social standing in the area. The Guild connected with a large number of similar groups, spread through the county and beyond, and they all gathered together for conferences periodically, at large country estates, so Mike told him. Incongruously, the strange young man who had recently taken over as Master seemed to have little "social standing." He supposed that the Miller family connection made up for John Miller Junior's lack of social skills, and that over time he would show more of the lofty status and gravitas that he understood the Master of the Guild was expected to present to the brothers. In the meantime, the office he held would confer upon him all the power he needed to hold the respect of the men.

On Friday morning, at half past ten, two days before the meeting, he was in high spirits as he left the Bluebird building to drive to Netherton to visit the building site. Despite there being difficulties which still needed to be sorted out with the owners of the land with regards to the old church which stood on it, Mike Small had two vans bringing workers to start work on the site that day. Bluebird's contract with Mike Small's company had been carefully constructed by Bluebird's lawyer and approved by Arnold Wheeler. It was, on the surface, a model of respectability and good business practice. Philip Greenwood had spent days composing the details of the contract, its clauses running to many pages of precise wording. Its purpose was to protect Bluebird from any possible responsibility and liability for working conditions. Bluebird's arrangements included having "daughter" companies which in fact were still Bluebird, but which entered into the contracts to keep the mother company free from taint in the event of difficulty.

It was entirely consistent with Wheeler's style that work was to start on the land before the contract of sale between the landowner and Bluebird was complete and signed. So long as there was no risk to the company, getting some labourers started on digging out foundations presented only a small risk of wasting a little money if the Haliwells refused to sign at the last moment. At the rates Wheeler had agreed to pay Small's company, there wouldn't be much of a loss, and Bluebird would gain a substantial advantage by getting the project started without delay. Winter weather tended to delay any building work, but Wheeler was determined the labourers would be on site working every day regardless.

Fred knew all this as he stepped on what was still Haliwell land, crossing over on to it by means of a temporary arrangement of steel girders lowered into position across the River Ishka, just stable enough to allow labourers to cross with spades and pickaxes, but not giving vehicle access. It was raining hard when Fred arrived. He was wearing wellington boots and a waxed jacket to keep out the heavy rain as he walked gingerly across the wet girders. It felt dangerous to be balanced above the fast-flowing river. Fred reflected that this particular risk had been covered by making all health and safety measures the responsibility of the company supplying the workers, Mike's company in fact. Fred hoped that his new friend would take care no accidents occurred – he would hate him to be blamed for any unforeseen incident.

Formerly, any breaches in health and safety arrangements might have bothered him, especially one so blatant as this precarious makeshift bridge of girders. Of course Arnold always had his contacts in the local council departments who would make sure that the right inspection forms were filled in, the necessary boxes having been ticked, and afterwards the person would receive an envelope which only ever was referred to as a "thank you" from Wheeler, passed across quietly to the appropriate council officer.

Fred generally felt secure that Wheeler would protect him because he was important to the company. Now, however, he felt a new and even better source of security; if anything threatened him, or Mike, or any of the brothers, there would be a large body of men who would come alongside and use their combined influence to protect him.

Fred reached the end of the wobbly girders and began to squelch through the mud on the other side of the river, going to the right of the track which led up the steep hill, and walking instead to where the first houses would be built, with other rows planned to be in progressively higher crescents behind them. The workers, fourteen in total, were already measuring and putting in marker posts under the direction of a foreman, a rough-looking man with a loud coarse voice. Fred's boots were getting stuck in the deep mud, making walking difficult. The foreman had just instructed the workers to start digging trenches along the line of the markers. They began as directed, forcing their spades into the heavy mud and then throwing the mud on to piles as directed. Every time their spades went in, the hole filled with muddy water. Fred watched them as they laboured. How were they managing to dig in these appalling conditions? He was glad his wellingtons were of the longer variety that reached all the way to his knees. He approached three of the men as they were digging. They glanced up at him as he came near them. He noticed all three had two things in common – one was that all of them looked pale and exhausted; the other was that they were not wearing boots, just shoes in varying degrees of dilapidation, caked with dark sticky mud. They slid about as they tried to plant their feet firmly in order to dig. It looked more like a scene from First World War trenches than a modern building site.

Fred was quite shocked – something must have gone wrong – their equipment must have been delayed. He was sure that Mike Small would get this sorted out, maybe he would mention it to him on Sunday evening. Thinking about the Guild meeting distracted him from the men in front of him, and he retraced his footsteps back across the river. As he did so he tried not to look at the deep grey water beneath him but keep his eyes straight ahead, so he missed entirely the layers of neat stonework low down on the banks of the river.

*

The Guild meeting began as usual at 9pm on Sunday evening. There was a particular air of excitement as the men gathered; there always was when a new person was to be inducted as a member. At one end of the room a kind of high table, almost an altar, had been prepared. It was covered with a black and gold cloth. In the centre of it lay a black marble slab with gold symbols engraved on it. To the left of it was a metal bowl and to the right a sharp knife with an ornate ivory handle. Fred looked towards this display eagerly, almost hungrily, as he entered the room and went to stand with the others. He felt his attention constantly being drawn back towards it as he tried to make light conversation during the minutes before the meeting started.

Soon the time to start arrived, they assembled around the large table and the meeting began. Fred noticed that John Miller was much less excitable than he had been the first time he had seen him. He seemed to be growing into his role, changing into a more dignified and authoritative figure.

After several minutes of regular items on the agenda for discussion the Master drew that part of the evening to a close and nodded to George Wright who rose to his feet, all the men following suit with that peculiar ability they all seemed to have to act at times as one person. Fred rose to his feet with them. Only the Master remained seated. All of the men apart from Fred moved from the table to stand near the high table at the end of the room. John Miller then got to his feet, picking up the rod of his office, and walked towards the high table, his black robe flaring out around him as he moved. The room was silent, waiting. The men had formed a semi-circle behind the table, apart from Fred, who was standing on his own as instructed, waiting. The Master approached the altar-like table and bowed down low towards it, touching his forehead onto the black marble slab. Then he stepped back again, and turned round so that he was facing down the room towards Fred, his rod raised up in his hand. George Wright, looking impressive in his dark suit, stepped forward to stand on the right of the Master and, raising his voice to an imperious level, called out, "Who is the man who wishes to join the brotherhood of this Guild?"

Fred knew what he must do next; he walked respectfully to the Master and stood in front of him.

"Say your name," ordered George Wright.

"Frederick Mervyn Roland," said Fred nervously.

The Master looked at him, a half-grin flickering over his face, and said, with a hint of anticipated enjoyment, "Bare your right arm, and put it on the altar."

Fred took off his jacket. He had been prepared for this by Mike Small and knew what would happen next. He rolled up his shirt sleeve, exposing his pale forearm which he laid on the marble, wrist upwards. Fred's arm was trembling as the Master picked up the knife while Wright took hold of the bowl. Seeing the Master raise the knife caused Fred to make a little gasping sound. Momentarily, he doubted. Was he sure this was all right? Suddenly his sureness about the warm fellowship which this group of men seemed to offer started to evaporate. It was his last chance – he could still pull his arm back. At that same second there was a movement at his side. Mike Small had moved next to him, putting his hand on Fred's shoulder, whispering, don't worry, this is a *good* thing – the sign of brotherhood." Fred felt the pressure of Small's hand, strong and firm on his shoulder. The idea of brotherhood, the sureness of belonging to something bigger than himself, which would stand by him and protect him, drew him on.

The Master was speaking again, "Let us all repeat our oath."

The men's voices rose in unison, repeating the oath of eternal loyalty to the Power above them and to one other, binding themselves to accept discipline and punishment if they broke their oath.

Then it was Fred's turn to recite the oath in front of the others. He had practised it all week and was word-perfect. His normally weak voice seemed to gather strength and his trembling almost stopped. As he pronounced the last words, he felt the blade of the Master's knife. The atmosphere in the room seemed to change, the empty space in it now appeared to be filled, as though more than just the men of the Guild had gathered into it, an unseen audience to witness the initiation. Blood began to ooze from Fred's arm. The Master told hold of it and held it over the metal bowl so that blood dripped into it. Then another member of the Guild came forward, baring his arm. The knife's blade advanced again, this time cutting the other man's arm and those present looked on while blood from both men dripped, thick and red, into the bowl. The Master dipped his forefinger into it, mixing the blood together. Then he used the bloody finger to smear it on to Fred's forehead, saying,

"Marked with the blood, to serve the eternal Power and the Brotherhood."

Fred felt a deep sense of fear and awe. He knew he had entered into something powerful, something he had never experienced before. Some antiseptic was dabbed onto his arm, and a strip of cloth was tied deftly over Fred's cut to staunch the blood. The men were applauding, and George Wright was the first to offer him the "right hand of fellowship." The other men gathered round him, shaking his hand. Then two trays of glasses of red wine were produced and placed on the large table; all the men took one and a toast was proposed. There was a sense of relief and bonhomie. A cloth was placed over the ceremonial table, covering up the knife and marble slab and bloody bowl. It was as though the grim ceremony was swept away, and the heavy brooding atmosphere gave way to chatter, much like any other gathering.

*

John Miller returned from the Guild meeting that night in high spirits. Mick started barking, announcing his arrival while he was still several hundred yards away from the farmhouse. To reward the dog's enthusiasm, Miller aimed a half-hearted kick in Mick's direction as he went into the house. Mick wagged his tail – he had learned to interpret this behaviour as encouraging and would have been disturbed by soft words.

"That you, John?" his mother's gruff voice called out.

"Who else would it be?" he responded, "Unless you were thinking of some late-night entertaining," he mocked. "No chance of that I think, Mother." He walked into the large kitchen at the back of the farmhouse. His mother was still up, despite the lateness of the hour, stirring something in a pot on the stove. She turned towards him, "Hold your tongue, John. Treat your mother with some respect."

"You need to treat *me* with respect now I'm Master of the Guild."

Jean Miller looked at him with a mixture of pride and incomprehension.

"Don't look like that – it's what Grandad wanted, isn't it?"

"You're not like your Grandad. He was a born leader. Nobody crossed him, ever. You're twenty years old John, a puppy. How are you going to get them to do what you say?"

"You don't know, Mother, you're not a man. Women don't understand these things – the weaker sex, that's what you are."

His mother took the wooden spoon out of the cooking pot and came towards him with it, brandishing it in the air, "Weak, am I?" she said, aiming to hit him on the side of the head, laughing roughly.

He put up his hand to fend it off, "Watch you don't get that filthy brew on my suit. What are you doing anyway, up at this time?"

I can't sleep properly since your grandfather passed. L keep thinking he's downstairs. He always said he'd never leave this place, sometimes I think he hasn't."

"He should be feeling happy, shouldn't he? He said to me to step into his shoes – I'm doing what he wanted. And – before you say anything – I *am* old enough, whatever you say. The Guild's accepted me. And our workers will too."

"You'd better sort them out then John. Show all of them who's boss. Go and visit the clubs... take a couple of the men with you."

She looked at him, studying his face as though she would be able to tell whether any of his grandfather's ability to dominate people, even when in his nineties, was showing signs of being present in John Miller Junior. She had noticed some changes in her son recently. He had surprised her in his determination to carry out her father's wishes to keep the family's tradition of being Master of the Guild. He also seemed to be spending less time in his room on his computer and more time on the farm. He was more focused. The farm was not what it used to be; they only had a few people working on it now, enough to keep the pig farm going, in addition to running the clubs in Exton. She didn't know much about that side of the family business; in recent years she had managed the pigs while her father saw to the clubs. Between them, they'd kept their little empire running, but now there had to be changes. The important thing was to continue their family's traditions. John was young, he could father a new generation of Millers who could extend their influence further than it had ever been.

She took the pot off the stove and carried it into the pantry to cool overnight. Then she came back and put the kettle on to boil,

"Want some tea, John?"

"No, Mother, whisky for this time of night."

"Since when have you started drinking whisky?"

"Since tonight, where is it?"

She got his grandfather's bottle of single malt out of the cupboard and poured some into the same glass as her father had drunk out of every night. John had already sat down in the rocking chair by the kitchen range. She stood still and watched him for a moment as he leaned back comfortably, setting the chair into a slow steady motion. It was happening, she thought, there was a John Miller back in charge. She carried the glass to him, grinning.

Chapter Fifteen

The Guild was controlled by an inner circle. There was no election involved in the formation of this. Men were included in it by the decision of those already in it. The lesser members of the brotherhood were not sure who exactly was in this inner circle but sensed that some brothers were accorded more respect than others. Only if a brother was called for disciplinary action did he discover more about the inner circle of authority. The Master was always at the centre of it, with longstanding members of the Guild joining him to form a small ruling council. Although every member of the Guild was bound to keep silence about the affairs and concerns of the brotherhood, the inner circle alone handled the most sensitive and important issues which were considered too onerous for younger or less experienced members.

On Tuesday evening, the inner circle gathered round the fireplace in the upper room. There were five of them – John Miller, George Wright, Mike Small, Harold Williams and Peter Melbury. Two others were absent, so they numbered less than their usual seven. The Guild placed considerable importance on numbers: seven for the inner circle, twelve senior members of the Guild and forty was the maximum number for the whole Guild, beyond which prospective members had to join a neighbouring Guild which they linked with for regional gatherings. Keeping to the required numbers ensured that relationships and accountability were kept strong; it also reflected the mystical nature of the brotherhood.

The scene was one of comfort, the large fireplace having been carefully tended earlier in the evening, the brassware polished and the grate swept clean before a fire of dry logs had been lit, ready for the men coming. This was one of Meg's tasks. George Wright never told her who exactly was coming or what the function of the inner circle was, but she understood what he wanted when he said she should prepare the upper room for a "small meeting." It meant that in the autumn and winter months she must prepare the fire and armchairs and put out drinks and small bowls of snacks, all arranged cosily around the fireplace end of the room. The attendees would arrive in a similar way to the men arriving for the meeting of the full Guild, coming quietly through the bar and slipping up the stairs. Her only use was to serve them and to keep quiet. On other nights, the same men might be in the pub and talk to her in quite a friendly way but not on Guild nights.

The inner circle never kept a record of what they discussed. This evening they had two things which engaged their attention. The first was the development of the land next to Netherton. John Miller wanted to know the details of what was happening. Mike Small was happy to give an update.

"I hope it will generate some good business opportunities for us. I've already got workers on the site. I'm offering a good deal to the construction company, which as you know Fred Roland is high up in. Later, there should be other contracts up for grabs. And when the new residents move in, they will be the right sort of people to keep house prices going up, good for all of us."

Melbury commented, "We don't want too much building going on in our area. That would have the opposite effect - a glut of houses on the market, too much availability, prices going down."

John Miller scratched his neck thoughtfully, "I could tell you a story about that land."

The eyes of the other men turned towards him.

"Ages ago the Millers owned that land, as well as the farm. Didn't my grandfather tell you?"

The others looked at him, only half believing it. But he was the Master now, he must be respected.

Mike Small said quietly, "How did that happen then?"

"My ancestor, whoever that was, probably John Miller..." he laughed, amused by his own joke, "had the farm *and* the mill of course, and people had to get their grain milled, so I guess they all owed him. And if you owe someone, you need to pay them with something. Maybe if their crops failed, and they got poor, they paid him with something else." He grinned at them. "So, John Miller got more and more land... and had them all in the palm of his hand." He was repeating what he had heard his grandfather say many times.

The others listened, in silence, thinking how in the present-day John Miller, so young, had also gained power over them.

Then Harold Williams spoke up, his voice a little shaky, "But then you lost some of the land to the Haliwells."

John Miller reacted with disdain, "Religious maniacs. Troublemakers."

"Troublemakers?"

"My grandfather said they got their lawyers onto my family. They claimed that we'd cheated people, that us Millers had used light weights for the mill. So my ancestor was fined and had to sell land to pay off the fine. Guess who bought the land? The stinking God-bothering Haliwells. The land they got off us was the big piece with that church on it. That land was ours. They wanted to keep that cross on it, and let the pilgrims get up the hill. We should have knocked that cross down, got rid of it all while we had the chance. Serves them right that they're losing it now. About time. My mother says they never could profit from it, not after we'd had it." He gave a kind of derisory snort.

The others said nothing.... They had no regard for the pilgrims' church but once again felt uncomfortable with the lack of subtlety of their new Master.

John Miller was warming to his theme, however. He leaned forward in his chair towards Mike Small, lowering his voice as though they were in a private conversation, "In fact, if your business contact is looking for any partners or shareholders, the Miller family would be interested in getting a stake in that land again. A bit of revenge for what was done to us all that time ago."

Mike Small shook his head, "I don't have that kind of relationship with them. I don't know much about them. I deal with them through our newest member, Fred Roland. He arranged all the paperwork, and I just provide the workforce, no more contact between the two companies needed, just a regular cheque in the bank from them to me, job done."

He hoped that this would finish the conversation, but Miller was in pursuit: "Fred Roland – let's get more information from him."

Small looked doubtful – he didn't want any unnecessary complications in his deal with Bluebird. He was keeping Fred close to him, tied into the brotherhood, and that was enough.

Harold Williams spoke up again however, "Fred is one of us now, and will no doubt be happy to give us more information about the company. Since they are active in our area, and changing the landscape here, we need to know more. For instance, do they have any other plans for around Netherton that we don't know about – we don't want a takeover here, do we?"

There was a pause. One of the men refilled the glasses, then Harold spoke again. "There's another thing we need to discuss – the incidents of violence in Netherton?"

John Miller looked interested, "What incidents?"

"Among the youth of the village – beatings. We're not against some high spirits, horseplay, after all we were all at that stage once.

Even I, at my great age, can still remember going out at night to enjoy myself and having a bit of rough and tumble—"

"Rough and tumble eh Harold!" Miller guffawed.

Harold risked ignoring him, "But I've been told of some serious attacks on young people. This could mean gangs, and we don't want gangs getting a hold here. This is *our* village; we don't want outsiders gaining a foothold here."

John Miller thought Harold had talked for long enough and decided to assert his authority again. "If it's young lads causing it, I think I'm more likely to find out what's going on than you, wouldn't you say?" There was a tinge of sarcasm in his voice, not enough to provoke a disagreement, but enough to undermine Harold's confidence. It worked. Harold mumbled something and lapsed into silence.

John Miller, eager to show himself a man of action, said, "I'll have a word with some people, and we'll settle things."

"Don't you need names?"

John Miller decided to be magnanimous, "If anyone knows the name of someone involved, that would be helpful to me."

George Wright, unusually silent tonight, said quietly, "I bet I know who can tell us. Hold on a minute."

He left the room, the others looking after him, surprised. A minute later he returned, leaving the door half open behind him. He said to the other men in a low voice, "Do you mind if I bring someone in?"

The others shook their heads, wondering who it was. Wright went back to the door and beckoned. "Come in. This will only take a minute."

Meg came into the room, looking apprehensive, "Did you need me for something?"

"Just a couple of questions. Do you know about any young people in the village getting set upon, beaten up, anything like that?"

Meg looked surprised. She had always felt intimidated by these secretive, all male meetings, but, if they were concerned about young people's safety then that could only be a good thing. She nodded, "Yes, there was a really sad situation just recently, a young lad, beaten up badly, for no reason at all."

The men around the fireplace were all sitting back comfortably in their armchairs in the warmth of the open fire, while she stood in front of the half open door, a cold draught coming up the stairs, blowing against the black skirt she wore when on duty in the pub. She reached down and pulled the fabric back over her knees.

They took their time before asking another question. Wright had returned to his place by the fire, leaving Meg standing alone. She felt embarrassed, scrutinised by five seated men while she stood awkwardly in front of them. John Miller and the others seemed to be enjoying their moment of superiority. He addressed her, almost like a judge, taking no account that she was old enough to be his mother, "His name?"

She hesitated, thinking, why did they want to know? After the trauma they had been through, Steven and his mother just wanted to be left alone. Should she tell them his name?"

From down below them in the bar there was a sound of breaking glass.

Meg jumped, startled, "I'd better see what's going on."

"You stay here. I'll see to it." Wright got up and left the room. She suddenly felt very vulnerable. She recognised every face in the room but they all were acting like complete strangers, and, worse than that, like some sort of ruling council which had authority to make her answer their questions. She decided on the spot that she wouldn't cooperate. She told herself George Wright was her employer, a publican, nothing else. She would not be coerced into giving them Steven's name or anything else.

John Miller said seriously, "Still waiting for a name."

"Sorry, I can't help you."

"Can't or won't?"

"Both," she replied quietly, and followed Wright downstairs.

Chapter Sixteen

Fielding saw the message from Arnold Wheeler pop up on his phone while he was driving at eighty miles an hour on the motorway. It said he must come to an emergency meeting at the Bluebird building, due to start fifty minutes from now. He was sixty miles away when the message arrived on his phone, on his way to another of their building projects. He cursed loudly. He took the next exit off the motorway to head back towards Exton, anger and anxiety making him break out in a sweat. He accelerated to ninety, then ninety-five. Wheeler would not forgive him for arriving late.

When he arrived at the building, he ran up the stairs to the boardroom. Wheeler, the Rolands and Philip Greenwood were already sitting at the conference table. There was an angry mood in the room. Fielding could almost taste the atmosphere as he walked in. He would have to be careful not to irritate Wheeler in any way – any provocation would be dangerous.

"Fielding!" barked Wheeler. "Sit down! I don't know how much time you think I've got to waste!"

Fielding opened his mouth to protest that he had driven over the speed limit all the way ever since he'd got Wheeler's message, but closed it again, resigned to taking the brunt of the present outburst rather than provoke an even worse one.

"*Finally,*" continued Wheeler sarcastically, "We can get on with discussing this serious development, this attempted *blockage* of our plans." He sounded affronted, as though on the receiving end of some unwarranted personal attack.

Fred and Susan Roland dutifully shook their heads, as though sad that their boss should be the victim of this offence. How could anyone be so crass, their attitude suggested, as to interfere with his plans.

Wheeler banged on the table with his fist, words exploding from his mouth, "That stupid American 'lawyer' has sent us a 'letter'!" The heavily sarcastic way he emphasised the words seemed to indicate that he doubted the validity of both the man's legal qualification and his ability to write a letter. This was despite the fact that the missive in front of him on the table contained details of extensive legal qualifications that the American lawyer had, and the style of written communication was undoubtedly an elegant and precise letter.

Wheeler hit the letter with the flat of his hand, then picked it up and began to read it aloud angrily, "With regards to the proposed sale of a large piece of land adjacent to the village of Netherton, this land being the property of Mrs Elise Haliwell, we have instructions from our client that while she is willing in principle to sell this land, there are certain binding restrictions which must be agreed to in the contract of sale, the main components of these restrictions being: firstly, that the church, St Brannock's, must be protected in such a manner as to ensure continual free access to worshippers from the area of Netherton and to pilgrims who walk the pilgrims' way to the church; secondly, that any proposed development on land in the vicinity of St Brannock's must be approved as to its observance of these restrictions by the Friends of St Brannock's Church; thirdly, no construction on the land on which the ancient church of St Brannock stands, whether temporary or permanent, may obstruct the view of the church, the cross or watchtower from the surrounding areas."

Wheeler stopped, waving the letter about angrily, "Preposterous!" he shouted, "Idiots! Do they think they can stand in the way of progress with their pathetic restrictions? Are they seriously suggesting the proposals of a well-respected British company, providing work for a very large number of workers, should be tossed aside because of their precious decaying old church that nobody wants to go to anyway? They want our money but they're saying we can't do anything without the permission of a bunch of pensioners who creep up the hill once in a blue moon!"

He turned to Greenwood, "Greenwood, offer them some more money – everyone's got their price."

Philip Greenwood shook his head, "With respect, Mr Wheeler, I anticipated you may need a response to a proposal of that sort, so I "tested the waters" with regards to an increase in the offer from Bluebird in return for a relaxation in the restrictive clauses. The answer was absolutely not, the protection of the role of the church and free access to it, are, Mrs Haliwell insists, non-negotiable."

Arnold Wheeler's face darkened with rage. "I won't be beaten by one old woman in America." There was a pause, the tension in the room making them hold their breath.

"Fielding – I expect you to come up with a solution." He grinned at Fielding, which did nothing to make his face appear softer or more friendly. "Come on, you're on the team as our bright boy, our fixer. I expect you to have something for us by tomorrow morning."

Fielding swallowed hard – how on earth could he "fix" this? Especially by tomorrow morning – it was a ridiculous expectation.

Wheeler was watching him, his sharp beady eyes fixed on Fielding's face, which was downcast. He spoke again, "You've just reminded me, I've decided to introduce a special Christmas bonus for my most loyal senior employee, enough for a substantial treat, new car, a boat to sail in, whatever a top executive fancies.... I'm thinking forty thousand, to be awarded on Christmas Eve." He was still looking at Fielding.

Fielding nodded, "I'll get on to it, I just need a few hours, one or two people to talk to."

Wheeler howled with laughter, "There you are!" he said triumphantly. "I don't make mistakes when I hire people. Eight o'clock tomorrow morning... *Martin*," emphasising his use of Fielding's first name. He knew the combination of primal fear of Wheeler's displeasure and the prospect of a fat cheque had secured Fielding's absolute obedience. Fielding got up and left, aware that after his desperate high speed sixty-mile dash back he had only been in the meeting room for a few minutes at most. He comforted himself with the thought that the most important thing was that Wheeler had expressed his confidence in him, that he could fix the problem, and in front of the others. He had the longed-for sense of well-being that went with one of Wheeler's rare expressions of praise. His boss would give him a handsome bonus if he could give him what he wanted. He went back to his car in the car park to drive to Netherton.

*

Fielding walked up the path leading to the door of Honeysuckle Cottage, hoping that the old lady – he wished he could remember her name – would be at home. He would have to turn the charm on, persuade her that he really did only have the best of intentions. He hoped the other old woman wouldn't be with her, the Scottish one; she seemed to be quite sharp, although she'd soon succumbed when he implied Bluebird's involvement would benefit the local Scouts – amazing how little some people needed to make them change their minds.

The door opened in response to his knock, and there stood Hilda, a smile on her face, "How lovely to see you again, Martin," she said, stepping back to make room for him to come into the cottage. "Do come in, dear."

Fielding went inside, noticing again the pleasant interior but this time, he reminded himself, he mustn't get too comfortable here. There was something about this place that calmed him down and took away his fighting instinct, his aggressive edge that gave him the inner compulsion to succeed.

Hilda invited him to sit down, "Would you like some tea?"

He hesitated, remembering his decision not to let his guard down too much. *I must stay focused on what I've come for, not get distracted.* However, he thought, drinking tea together would help to develop some sort of rapport with this old bird, so he replied, "Thank you – just what I need – it's been a really busy day so far."

"Sit by the fire then; I won't be a moment."

Just like before, she gave him tea and home baking. He wondered whether she always baked cakes and scones just in case she had visitors. Again, he was in danger of forgetting why he had come as he enjoyed this cosy interlude in his frenetic, self-absorbed working day.

Hilda took a sip of tea, then put her cup down and looked at him enquiringly, "How can I help you today?"

He wondered if it should be so obvious to her that he had come to get something from her. He stalled for a moment.

She was still looking at him directly, her clear blue eyes studying him, "I expect you've got something to ask me. Is that right?"

Fielding smiled at her, with what he hoped was a disarming expression, "You're absolutely right. I would love to find out a little more about the area, especially about the little old church near here. I know you're very fond of it, so I knew you were the right person to ask."

Hilda nodded. To Fielding's eyes, she looked like a helpless old person, easily hoodwinked. He expected that she would never doubt his intentions. Hilda was indeed by nature someone who thought the best of people, giving them the benefit of any doubt about their motivations. She was pleased to welcome this young businessman into her home and give him every encouragement and assistance, but something about him did not ring true with her. She decided, however, that there were few better topics of conversation to engage in with him than the lovely pilgrims' church.

"St Brannock's, of course. A holy and precious place. What would you like to know about it?"

"For a start, how on earth is it looked after? It's in quite an awkward spot, isn't it?"

"Some people may think that, people who don't really – forgive me for saying so – understand what its purpose is. It has to be where it is to do its job, you see."

"Oh, I see," said Fielding, not seeing at all.

"The church was built hundreds of years ago, right up on a hill, to be a sign of faith in Jesus Christ. People would be able to see it from miles around, and be reminded of the Christian faith, of God's love and help. The watchtower standing next to it would be lit at special times, or to warn people of danger. For centuries, people have walked across neighbouring counties, stopping at various abbeys along the way, and ended up at the village of Netherton. They would walk over the bridge, across the River Ishka, and up the hill to the church. Many took their shoes off and walked the final stretch barefoot on the stony track. The track would have been spotted with the blood of many pilgrims' feet over the years. In fact, some pilgrims still walk barefoot up the hill even now, as a sign of faith and willingness to sacrifice for the love of God."

Fielding was stuck for words for a few moments. What a quaint old practice. Were these people mad? He thought that sort of thing had gone out with medieval times. While he tried to work out what to say next, Hilda continued, "I know it's hard to understand, Martin..."

He was amazed that she remembered his name.

"...but keeping this precious place of worship and pilgrimage open is not *awkward*; it's a privilege, a calling from God."

Fielding's mind started to race – how could he turn this round? How could he make a connection between the restrictions on the land imposed by Mrs Elise Haliwell, far away in America, and this old woman's convictions about the importance of the church, some way of getting both of them to play into his hands. His mind wasn't working as fast and aggressively as usual. Something about being here in this cottage was taking the edge of his usual ruthless capacity to re-package things to his advantage. He decided to put out another feeler, "So you and your friends, I suppose, are determined to keep it running?"

"Yes, absolutely. The Friends of St Brannock's will faithfully take care of the place, keeping it open for Christians to come to, and as a sign pointing towards Jesus for the whole area. It's a lifelong commitment for us."

He felt stumped. He couldn't see a way through. He got up to go. "Well, thank you for your advice. I had thought that perhaps we could help you in some way."

Hilda thought for a moment, "Actually, you could."

He was alert suddenly, was this a way forward?

Hilda continued, "As you know, the only way to the church is across the river. The River Ishka is not wide, but it's deep and fast-flowing. At the moment the way to the church is impassable because the bridge is lost, although that is beginning to be remedied, I believe."

"How do you mean?"

"I've started to re-build the bridge," said Hilda calmly. "At first, I was entirely on my own, but recently someone has begun to help me. Perhaps you could help too." She watched him for his reaction.

He had been about to leave, but he sat down again, saying earnestly, "Let me see what I can arrange." He stayed another minute or two, trying to impress her with his good intentions, but then took his leave, thoughts racing through his mind. Before going back to his car, he walked along the street towards the river. He wanted to look at it again. The water looked calmer today, flowing low down beneath the level of the road. He looked down the steep banks of the river, not really expecting there to be evidence of what the old woman had been talking about. He didn't think it was credible that she was in fact trying to rebuild anything; he inwardly mocked the idea – it was more likely she was just going senile. What he saw convinced him otherwise; at the lowest part of the steep riverbank, he could see that the decimated stone pillars of the old bridge were being reconstructed. The work was at an early stage, but he could see that the stones were being fitted together again methodically. He could also see that further along there were some girders straddling the river, a temporary arrangement for the labourers to cross over onto the site. He raised his head and looked up the hill on the other side of the river to where the old church stood. It was obvious that at present no one could reach it as this was the only access point, an access point which was about to be restored, he thought grimly, and was protected by the ancient covenant put in place by the Haliwell family. They must have been fanatics, he thought.

A plan was forming in his head: clearly the attempts of the old woman and whoever was helping her would not get much further, but, if Bluebird were to rebuild the bridge, they could build it to a standard ready to take the heavy construction vehicles. Offering to rebuild the bridge would gain the support of the old woman who seemed to be the leading light of the "Friends of St Brannock's," the group that had the trust of Mrs Haliwell. This would give Bluebird suitable and convenient access to the site, which was needed anyway. Having gained proper access and started building the houses, they could deal with the other restrictions in the contract. Mrs Haliwell was a long way from here and would apparently trust her contacts here to represent her. If her contacts could be persuaded....

He smiled inwardly. This would form the basis of his "solution" to present to Wheeler. He took a photograph of the river and track, and headed back to his car, energised by his own cleverness.

*

Fielding was back at the Bluebird building. It was eight thirty in the morning and time to report back to the meeting with his "solution," as directed by Wheeler at the previous meeting.

"After more investigations," Fielding began, "this is what I propose."

"I don't want to marry you," quipped Wheeler. "Handsome young devil though you are."

Fielding smiled and tried to laugh at Wheeler's little joke. "Not a proposal then, just a solution to our problem."

"Now you're talking my language!" exclaimed Wheeler.

"An access road to the land next to the village of Netherton should be started immediately, and Mrs Elise Haliwell notified as follows: "In line with the clauses attached to the deeds of the land on which the ancient church of St Brannock's stands, Bluebird Construction and Development, the proposed purchaser of this land, is responding to the immediate crisis caused by a severe storm. The effect of this storm surge was to completely destroy the bridge which provides the only access to the church. Since this time not a single Christian, whether pilgrim from afar or from the local community, has been able to get to the church. Bluebird Construction and Design, in accordance with its commitment to the protection of the church, seeks to restore access by means of a new road and bridge of the best quality construction, built at our own expense as a gift, no matter the outcome of our ongoing negotiations."

"Clever. Very clever. I see where you're going with this," interpolated Wheeler.

"Furthermore, it is our hope that this goodwill gesture will demonstrate sufficiently our great concern for the continued purpose of the church and will reassure the Haliwell family as to our trustworthy intentions as we enter into the final stage of our contract together for the purchase of the land."

"Excellent. Knew you could do it. You've got a way with words – you should write books, Martin, you nearly brought a tear to my eye." Wheeler was delighted, and Fielding could bask in the sunshine of his approval for however many minutes it lasted.

"Tell me Martin, how did you think of this angle? It's brilliant. Don't start getting big-headed, mind."

"I've been talking with an old lady, an influential member of the 'Friends of St Brannock's.' We drank some tea together and she told me all her worries about the church needing to be kept open and the bridge being demolished in the storm.... It occurred to me that instead of thinking her group were in our way, we could offer them help."

"Offer to help them?" Wheeler sounded disdainful.

Fielding was undeterred, "By building a new bridge and a proper access road leading to the building site. The old lady in question is delighted. We can expect all the 'Friends of St Brannock's will be similarly pleased with us and will communicate this to the Haliwells over in America."

"Very good work – I can see that bonus is half-way into your pocket already." Wheeler was exuding satisfaction. Everyone was falling in with his wishes, this was how he liked his business to run, without anyone resisting him. "While we wait for the contract to be signed at the Haliwell end, we'll press on with getting the groundwork done, and get our architect onto planning a new bridge and access road."

"Just a point of information, there is still an old track leading all the way up from the river crossing to the church – just wondered what you wanted to do about that?"

Wheeler sounded irritated, "That will just be buried under the new road – can't have a muddy track messing up the look of the place."

"And the church?"

"Continue with plan A – stick a big wall around it. We don't want health and safety jobs-worths creeping about bleating about the dangers of having a crumbling old building on the site. As far as the local kids go, there is no way in. As far as the Haliwells are concerned, we've given it a brand-new access road and bridge."

Wheeler grinned, "Right, full steam ahead. Greenwood, get everything that Martin said into a letter to the Haliwells, reminding them that the old bridge has been swept away and nobody apart from Bluebird is willing to replace it. It doesn't sound like the few old biddies who are supposed to be so keen on the old wreck are capable of doing anything about it."

Fielding thought of Hilda and her bridge building efforts. Should he mention it at this point? Wheeler hated anything being kept from him. He decided he had better say something.

"The old biddies, that is, the Friends of St Brannock's—"

"Yes, yes, what's your point?" interrupted Wheeler crossly.

"They, well one of them, has been trying to rebuild the bridge. It's pathetic of course, doesn't stand a snowball's chance in hell."

"Tell me about it."

"It's just one old woman trying to get the stones back together again."

"One old woman," repeated Wheeler, "Is she senile or something?"

"Seems to be just a harmless old bird, believes she is on some kind of holy mission."

Wheeler burst out laughing, "So she's the local village idiot!"

A ripple of sycophantic laughter went around the table. Wheeler warmed to his theme, "I don't think we'll waste any time talking about her – we can always send for the men in white coats to take the old bat away and lock her up somewhere."

Everyone laughed again. Fielding said quietly, "Absolutely, Mr Wheeler, just thought you would want to know."

Wheeler decided the meeting had gone on long enough and dismissed Greenwood to write a letter to Mrs Haliwell. He wanted it done before the end of the afternoon, so he could sign it and have it sent electronically. He wanted this whole thing moved on quickly.

"Fred – make sure the work continues and get the architect up there – we need to get a road bridge and wide access road added into the plans."

He pressed a button on his phone to speak to his secretary, "Put a call through to my friend in the County Planning Department. I need to have another little word with him."

Chapter Seventeen

Anna wanted to start her Christmas shopping early. This year, because she was on such a limited budget, based on the few sales she had made at the small number of crafts markets and a few items sold at Moonstone Crafts, she was under pressure to find gifts at bargain prices. As much as she could, she would give her own crafts as gifts, but these would not cover everyone. She decided to spend a whole day in Exton entirely devoted to Christmas shopping.

She had arrived early and by half past twelve had already spent more than three hours searching for gifts. Hungry and in need of a break, she dropped into a small café. There were only five small tables, all visible from the street. Anna spotted a space at a table, paid for her soup and bread roll at the counter and made her way to her seat. There were already two people sitting at the table, but they were happy for Anna to share with them. She had only just begun her soup when someone came and stood near her, asking the couple if they would mind if he occupied the one remaining chair at the table. Anna heard the polite attractive voice and looked up nervously. Martin Fielding slid into the empty seat next to her, smiling. "Hello Anna. I saw you sitting here as I was passing. I'm so glad to have the chance to talk with you again." He slipped his hand over hers, glancing over at the couple as he did so. They exchanged a knowing look with each other as they saw how this handsome young man looked at the pretty girl sitting at their table. With Christmas music playing in the background and the twinkling festive lights around them, they looked at the young people and remembered when they first met, many years ago.

Anna was trapped. She tried to extricate her hand from his, but he held on to it.

"I think I should go," she said, putting down her soup spoon and attempting to stand up.

He responded touchingly, "Please don't leave. Finish your soup. I'll just sit with you while you have it."

The middle-aged couple, sensing a possible lovers' tiff, were listening intently; had there been a disagreement? Would she forgive him? He seemed such a lovely young man.

Fielding looked across the table at them briefly, trying to show them by the expression on his face that he needed their support. The response was immediate; the woman leant forward and gently pushed the salt and pepper towards Anna, saying, "Don't hurry, dear, we'll soon be going and you two can have a bit of privacy to talk. We remember how it was. Christmas is such a lovely time to be young, isn't it?" She only just managed to restrain herself from adding "and in love."

Anna blushed – how was it that he had so easily got these strangers to believe his little charade? Embarrassed and irritated, she took a few spoonfuls of soup hurriedly. He had to let go of her hand to let her take hold of her bread roll. No matter what these people thought, she was determined not to be drawn into conversation with Martin Fielding. However, he had a captive audience.

"Anna," he whispered, just loud enough for the couple to overhear, "I haven't been in touch because your father made it clear he doesn't approve of our being together."

The tiniest of sighs escaped the older woman as she heard this account of thwarted romance.

"But nothing has changed. I still need you... so much." He spoke with muted passion, his tone urgent.

Anna was half-way through her soup but was finding it harder to swallow. "Martin, please don't."

She stood up, reaching for her shopping bags. He was quickly on his feet, "At least let me help you to your car with all this shopping." Then, plaintively, "But if you want me to go away..."

The couple were hanging onto every word, willing Anna to relent, to let this poor man have a second chance, not to snatch away his chance of happiness. The sound of a Christmas song surged a little, *"It'll be a cold and lonely Christmas without you..."*

Anna was already trying to extricate herself, laden with bags, from the table which was hemmed in tightly by chairs. As she struggled, she accidentally knocked her chair over. "Sorry," she mumbled to the couple.

"Don't worry, dear – have a happy Christmas," the woman said, and to Anna's dismay the woman's eyes filled with sympathetic tears.

Anna didn't stop to try to retrieve the chair, which had fallen against the café's window bringing a waitress hurrying over in alarm. She moved towards the café door, dragging her shopping bags clumsily past the seated people. Having got outside onto the street she began to walk quickly in the direction of the car park, Fielding in pursuit. She rounded the corner, aware that he was only two or three paces behind her. They must have made an odd spectacle, she thought, almost comical except for the feeling of panic intensifying inside her as they left the main shopping area. She dodged quickly across the road causing a motorist to hoot at her. The car park was in sight. Fielding drew level with her. "Anna, stop a moment – just give me one moment of your time. Don't you owe me that?" The question triggered something in Anna. She stopped and spun round. "Owe you! Why *owe you*? I don't owe you anything Martin!"

"I think you do. You led me on with the way you behaved, tantalising me."

"I don't know what you mean."

"But you do. You know what you did to me, making me believe you wanted – *love* – that you wanted me to love you." His tone hovered on a thin line between passion and threat. She felt the confusion he had induced before in her closing around her again. Had she led him on? Had her behaviour signalled her hidden desires? Was it her fault after all?

He put his hands up to her face, touching it, coming close to her. The sense of being enclosed grew, as though she was being enveloped again, separated from the ordinary world around her. Deep inside her she felt the impulse to escape – now, before it was too late. She ducked out of his embrace, "No. I want you to leave me alone!"

"I can't do that Anna."

She was running now towards her car in the car park. She heard him calling out after her, his voice suddenly aggressive, "You can't get rid of me like that you little -------!" The last word was lost as she reached the safe haven of her car. She started the engine immediately and accelerated towards the exit, leaving Fielding standing in the car park on his own.

*

James woke up suddenly, hearing a noise – was it downstairs? He threw his bedcovers off and got up, standing perfectly still on the cold bedroom floor to listen. Everything was silent – had he imagined it? He reached over to his bedside lamp and turned it on. The hands on his alarm clock showed it was half past one. He was so wide awake now he doubted that he would be able to get back to sleep. Besides, if there really had been a noise downstairs he should go and investigate. However the idea of searching the cold dark vicarage for a possible intruder was not an attractive one, and the weaker side of James longed to get back into his warm bed. Should he take some sort of weapon with him? He looked around his bedroom for anything suitable to tackle a burglar and spotted his school cricket bat in its usual place on top of the wardrobe. He tiptoed across the floorboards, trying to avoid those which he remembered creaked loudly. He reached the wardrobe and stretched up to get the cricket bat, but it was just out of his reach. He lunged at it a bit too wildly and it clattered to the floor. Immediately Anna called out from the bedroom on the other side of the landing, "Dad! Are you all right?"

A couple of seconds later, she came rushing into the bedroom, looking shocked.

"Sorry!" whispered James, "I was trying to be quiet."

"Dad, whatever are you doing? And why are you whispering?"

"I heard a noise – at least I think I did – downstairs. I was trying to get my cricket bat down to arm myself against any intruders."

Anna looked at her father in his crumpled striped pyjamas, his hair standing up on end from being in bed. "I don't think you'd scare anyone, even with a cricket bat. Are you sure you heard something?"

"Not absolutely sure, but I did wake up suddenly, thinking I heard a noise."

"Ring the police then. They'll come and check."

"But what if I'm wrong? I'll be wasting their time."

"Isn't it part of their job, to come out and check suspected burglaries?"

"I'd feel very stupid if there was nothing at all. I think I'll just check round myself." He got his dressing-gown down from where it always hung on the back of his bedroom door and put it on.

She said, "I'm coming with you."

"No, you stay here. I'll call out to give you the *all clear* when I've looked round." He put on his black leather shoes without stopping to look for socks and picked up his old cricket bat.

Anna knew there was no point in arguing so waited for him to creep out of his bedroom, then hurried across to her room to grab her coat and stuff her feet into trainers before going downstairs behind him. They reached the hall and stood still to listen for any sounds. Everything seemed quiet. They checked the study, the dining room and living room, then went into the kitchen and unlocked the back door to look outside. There was no sign of anything suspicious, not even a cat prowling. They came back into the hall, about to give up when James noticed there was an envelope on the doormat. He was sure he would have noticed it if it had been there when he went upstairs to bed.

He went to pick it up, "Perhaps this was it – the noise of the letter box. Things always sound louder at night. Who would be delivering a letter at this time?"

He carried the letter into the kitchen, turning the light back on. Anna followed him. It was addressed to 'Reverend James Gilchrist', in attractive handwriting, probably a woman, he thought – it must be some troubled person needing help. He sat down at the kitchen table and tore the envelope open. There was a thick cream-coloured sheet of writing paper inside. "Expensive stationery," commented James. Anna stood next to him, looking over his shoulder as he unfolded the sheet. They read silently,

My dear James,

I felt I had to try to write down what I feel for you. When we are together it is so hard to express properly what is in my heart.

I have treasured the brief times we have shared together, whether going out together or in tender moments in the privacy of my home.

I know it is hard for you to love again when your heart has been broken by the loss of your first love, but you are safe in my arms, and together we can find healing.

Please trust me, my heart is in your hands,
Mia.

James looked up at Anna when he had finished reading. There was silence between them for a moment, then she said, "Dad, is there something we should talk about?"

"I don't know what to say."

"I knew you liked Mia, but I didn't realise it had gone this far."

"It hasn't. It's not like this."

"But you must have been seeing her. She hasn't made it all up."

"Yes, I suppose I have."

"Has it been going on for long?"

"No, of course not."

"But you have been going out together, and... going back home with her, she says."

James was about to deny it, because he knew it sounded as though it was a very deep relationship, but he stopped himself. The truth was, he had gone to her house alone with her, at night.

"Yes, it's true, I have been to her house."

Anna asked in a small voice, "Often?"

"No! Just once."

"She makes it sounds more than that... but then, once is enough." Anna sounded sad, disappointed.

"I'm so sorry, Anna. I can't deny it. I went there, but – I can't really expect you to believe this – it wasn't like what you're thinking."

Anna sat down, rubbing her forehead as though she had a headache. "I don't know what's happening to us Dad. We seem to be caught up in some kind of ... weird trap we can't escape from. When we least expect it, something sneaks up and grabs us. I'm not saying it's not our fault too, but it feels like, behind the scenes, there's a plot to drag us into... dark places that we never intended to get into."

She started to cry.

Her father, alarmed, reached over to put his arm around her shoulders. "I'm so sorry," he said again, "This is all my fault."

"No, it's not. Some of it's our fault, but not all of it. It's as though traps keep being laid for us, and we keep stumbling into them. I'm just as much to blame as you, Dad, I've been stupid too." She got up and started pacing to and fro, wiping her eyes with her hand. "But there's something about this area, it's full of – strange things, people, pressure. You think something's going to be all right, and then – it turns nasty."

She sat down again at the table, heaving a sigh as though she had suddenly become exhausted. Her father took her hand in his, "Let's pray, Anna, it's all we can do at this point I think."

They continued to sit at the kitchen table while they poured out their concerns to the God who, at that moment, felt far away. Their prayers were heartfelt and disjointed, a cry for help from a pit of mess and confusion. Anna hadn't even begun to tell her father about the tangled painful snare she had fallen into with Martin Fielding. It made her feel ill to think about it, especially his parting remarks to her.

After a while they felt calmer, and Anna made them a hot drink; the cold of the vicarage had chilled them almost to the point of shivering. Looking at Mia's letter lying on the table, Anna asked, "What will you do about the letter? She clearly feels very strongly about you, coming here at half past one in the morning to deliver it."

"I don't know. I don't really want to have any contact with her. When I met Mia, I thought she was fascinating. I was spell-bound, you could say – I don't mean that literally of course. She is unusual, I could see that, but I even hoped at one point that maybe God had sent her into my life. Nobody could ever replace your mother of course," he said with emphasis, "but I thought, perhaps someone to be with. I know you won't stay at home for ever, Anna."

Thoughts of the weird evening at Mia's house whirled around in Anna's mind and made her father's remarks seem comical. "Somehow I don't think Mia would make a very good wife for a vicar," she said wryly.

James tried to sound resolute, "Since I have allowed myself to get into an embarrassing situation I must find a way, with God's help, to extricate myself from it. And not to fall into any more traps." He folded the letter up and put it in his pocket.

Still feeling very cold, they decided they would take their cocoa upstairs and drink it while tucked up in the warmth of their beds.

James found it hard to sleep at all for the rest of the night, his mind racing, full of uncomfortable recollections about the last few weeks. Was it true that there was something odd about this whole area that made living the Christian way difficult and strewn with problems? But surely this was only what Jesus had warned his followers about? *In this world you will have troubles, but do not be afraid, little flock, for I have overcome the world.*

So, wherever you were, there would be troubles he reflected. But were some places more troubled than others? James tossed and turned in his bed, thinking how Jesus warned us to be on our guard, that the enemy was like a lion prowling about looking for people to devour. A chilling thought, and what form might the enemy take? The Bible referred to the devil masquerading as an 'angel of light'. This must mean someone good, helpful, attractive.... Did some places attract more 'angels of light' than others? Safe in the comfort of his bed, a Bible next to him and still benefitting from the time of prayer he had shared with Anna in the kitchen, he could bear this thought with fortitude, but tomorrow would arrive soon, and bring new challenges.

*

James looked at his alarm clock – seven o'clock. Despite the very disturbed night, he decided to give up any idea of more sleep and got out of bed into the cold of the dark December morning. He made the quick decision to keep prayer at the top of the day's agenda. If he and Anna were to come through this difficult time, and the church was to grow in faith, they must all spend more time in prayer. He put on his thick dressing gown and knelt down by his bed to commit the day to God.

Later, he met Anna in the kitchen. Had she also had a bad night's sleep? He enquired.

She answered, trying to sound upbeat, "Pretty bad, yes, but I've used the time I've lain awake to think and pray, so it hasn't been wasted. What have you got on today, Dad?"

"Seeing Mary Williams. She's been ill for some time; I think it's time to go and pray for her."

"Don't you go regularly to do that anyway?"

"Yes and no. I do go to see her, and I do generally say a prayer, but I mean a bit more than that today."

"It sounds fascinating. Would you like me to come too?"

"Have you time? It would be wonderful if you could – I was wondering about asking Hilda to accompany me, but if you're able to come, I'll ask Hilda another time. We'll need to pray before we go."

After breakfast, James suggested they went into the study to pray. He said he wanted to use some prayers of preparation, including prayers of confession. "I hope you don't think this is a bit too pointed, Anna, but we've both been caught up in 'messy' situations, and if we're going to help Mary Williams, we need to 'clear the decks'."

"I know what you're saying, Dad, and you're right."

For the next hour they prayed – prayers from books of prayer on the shelves in the study, and prayers for the Christians in Netherton and Appleton, that they would grow in faith and strength and would reflect the light of Christ in the area. They prayed for the Holy Spirit to flow freely in them as they got ready to go to see Mary Williams in Netherton.

When they arrived at Mary's cottage, they found her lying on the sofa in the living room. She had been ill for weeks and seldom left the house. A while ago she had seemed to recover a little but had soon relapsed again into weakness and constant fatigue. Medical tests had revealed no cause for her sickness and she and her husband had been left to cope by themselves.

She was always pleased to have a visit from the vicar and today even more so when she saw that the vicar's daughter had come too. She looked up at them from the sofa, smiling weakly, "It's lovely to see you, especially you, Anna – not that I'm not pleased to see you, James – I always love you to come – oh dear, what am I saying!" She stopped, fearing she'd given offence.

James took her hand reassuringly, "I know what you mean, Mary, and it's always lovely to see you too."

Mary's husband Sam brought in a tray of tea and biscuits for them all and they sat talking for a while. He asked if they had heard about the events of the previous evening.

"Which events do you mean?" asked James.

"The fight," he answered. Then, seeing James' blank look, said, "The two gangs of locals, really nasty stuff. Someone we know who works in the Accident and Emergency department of the hospital said the injuries were horrible – knife wounds. And it was only a few hundred yards from this cottage. Unbelievable. There's something gone wrong with this place – it's a village for heaven's sake, not an inner-city estate. I don't know where it's coming from, this outbreak of violence. And as you know, it's not the only thing that's happened."

Wanting to leave behind this depressing subject and move things on to a more positive note, James asked if Mary was any better.

"I'm afraid I'm not, James. My doctor has been very good and sent me for lots of tests, but everything has come back negative and most days I can hardly walk."

"Would you like us to pray for you?"

"Yes, I always like it when you pray when you come to see me."

"I mean, pray for healing."

"Yes, I would love to be well again; Sam wouldn't have to do everything for me, which he must find very irritating." She smiled again, the same weak smile.

"Good, that's what we'll do then. I'd like Sam to be involved too, if you're both all right about that."

James pulled a small glass bottle out of his pocket.

"In a few minutes I'll anoint you with oil, Mary. Nothing odd or magic about it, but it's mentioned in the Bible as part of the normal ministry of the church, to pray for the sick and anoint them with oil, and that praying in faith in this way will restore the person to health."

Sam took a step forward, frowning, "I've not come across this before."

"Well, that could partly be my fault – I have been too worried about offending people, making them think I'm too extreme, and by behaving like that, I've not explained to the church that Jesus Christ still has power to heal today."

Mary and Sam Williams looked surprised but agreed that it would be a good thing for James to try, and watched with interest as he took Mary's hand in his, and Anna took her other hand. James began to pray, thanking God for the life he had given to Mary and Sam and for the love they shared together. Then he asked Mary if she believed in Jesus, and then, did she believe he loved her? She answered yes to both these questions. Then James said Jesus healed everyone who came to him for healing, and Jesus is with us today by his Spirit. James asked the Holy Spirit to come with healing power to Mary and encouraged Mary to receive God's healing. As he prayed, Anna prayed silently. Sam stood watching as his wife closed her eyes, an expression of peace on her face as she was anointed with oil in the name of the Father, the Son and the Holy Spirit.

They left soon afterwards, the small bottle of oil back inside James' pocket.

Driving back, they both had a sense that they had been present at a powerful moment.

Anna said contentedly, "That was wonderful, Dad. Thank you so much for taking me with you. It felt like stepping back in time to when Christians had much more faith in God's power."

"I know what you mean Anna, and I'm more and more convinced that's the kind of faith we need to have here and now."

Within minutes they were back in Appleton, ready for an early lunch.

During the afternoon both James and Anna had been busy with their work, him in his study and her in her studio/bedroom. At four o'clock both arrived in the kitchen for a tea break and stood waiting for the kettle to boil. "Have you managed to get much done?" asked James.

Anna answered in a disappointed voice, "Yes, although it doesn't matter so much now anyway – I won't need to supply any more things to sell at Moonstone Crafts over the Christmas period, in fact

I'm going to collect what I've left there. It's a shame, as Christmas is the best time for sales."

"Oh, I hadn't realised you were going to do that."

"Of course, Dad – it's time to make a clean break from Mia, for *both* of us."

"You're right. I'd better do it straightaway."

James returned to his study, sat down at his desk and got out a sheet of paper and pen, ready to compose a letter. He wrote the address of the vicarage at the top, then—

Dear Mia,

I am afraid I have allowed a misunderstanding to develop with regards to accepting your invitation to a musical evening, and afterwards a hot drink at your house. I did not intend to give the impression that I was in a position to develop a personal relationship with yourself or anyone else. I am a widower, still recovering from the loss of my wife.

Please accept my apologies for failing to make this clear.

James Gilchrist (Revd)

He looked at what he had just written, then tore it up, *No, this is dishonest! I must admit my part in this, I went along with it, it was my fault.* He started again,

Dear Mia,

You deserve my sincere apologies. I realise now that, by accepting your invitation to an evening with you, and indeed enjoying your interest and attention, I must have given you the impression that an ongoing attachment between us was possible.

He stopped, imagining for a moment the consequences if Mia presented his letter to the Bishop, as evidence of a supposed fully-fledged affair, or at least a one-night fling. Wouldn't he have been wiser to have kept to the cooler language of the first letter which did not admit to any blame on his part? He shook his head, as though trying to shake out of it the temptation to deny the truth. The truth was that he had been very attracted to Mia, flattered, excited. Part of him wanted to state this plainly, but he thought such details would only increase Mia's fixation on him. He was embarrassed now to think of how easily he had been enticed by Mia's looks, and something else about her.... But no matter what she was like, whatever kind of influence was at work in her, he must treat her with respect. He continued,

Thank you for considering me. I hope you can accept that I must avoid any further contact with you.

If you would like to attend church, or need pastoral care, may I suggest the neighbouring parish of All Saints.

James Gilchrist

He sealed the letter in an envelope, praying that this would me the last he would ever hear of Mia; from now on, he would be wiser, and more aware. He would post the letter immediately.

Chapter Eighteen

Another Guild meeting night: Meg did the usual preparations with a pronounced sense of unease. Ever since the meeting of the inner circle of the Guild she had been disturbed by the whole idea of the Guild. Previously she had thought them little more than a rather quaint old-fashioned but harmless group which gained a sense of significance from being secretive – a grown-up version of a boys' secret club held in a shed at the bottom of someone's garden. After experiencing at first hand their controlling, even intimidating, behaviour, she now held a different opinion of them. She was concerned that there may be some consequence from her refusal to cooperate with them.

The members arrived as usual. Meg could not help paying more attention to them than normal, especially the unpleasant young man who was now their leader. He pushed past her rudely as she was carrying a box of crisps into the bar, jamming her hand against its wooden edge. She was sure he must have known what he had done, but he didn't apologise, just stared at her coldly for a moment then continued walking towards the stairs.

The upper room filled up quickly; almost every member had come. The places around the long table were soon occupied and the rest of the men remained standing. George Wright was seated towards the head of the table, in his usual place next to John Miller, who was wearing the Master's black gown and had the rod and gavel laid on the table in front of him. He seemed to be increasingly confident and assertive in his position as Master of the Guild. He led them through the agenda which had been prepared by George Wright in his role of secretary. When they got to the item on the incidents of violence in the village he leaned forward, as though about to share some confidential information.

"I have had some of my people – people who work for me – make some enquiries," he started with an air of self-importance, "about the increase of violence in Netherton. They have found some useful information about the people involved." He paused for effect, then added, "And I must, as the Master here, point out that people who work for us, even though not members of the Guild, should reflect some of our values, as they serve us." He looked at George Wright, "That's right, isn't it, Mr Secretary?"

George Wright looked surprised, wondering where this was leading, but mumbled something in agreement and busied himself with the minutes in his ledger.

Miller was enjoying himself, "Which value do I mean, you are wondering." He asked, looking round the room, then back to Wright, "I mean obedience. People who work for us must *obey* us. Or it brings disgrace on the Guild. For example, when I tell people who work for me to do something, they do it."

There were murmurs of agreement all round the large table and looks of approval. Many of them were warming to the leadership of John Miller – he was young and inexperienced it was true, they were thinking, but he understood that members of the Guild should always be respected. He seemed to be focusing on George Wright – had George Wright been doing something to let the Guild down?

John Miller lapsed pointedly into silence, staring at Wright, who was utterly taken by surprise at this change in treatment. Only a short time ago he had been acting quietly as a mentor for this much younger man. But already Miller had turned on him. Despite this, Wright was bound by the oath of loyalty. He stood to his feet, as was required when a member was accused of misconduct. A ripple of excitement passed through the room; discipline and punishment always served to stimulate new interest and intensity.

John Miller's face was stern. He picked up the rod which signified his position of authority. Wright stood with his head lowered. Miller held the rod up, looking directly in front of him and said coldly, "George Wright I accuse you of bringing disgrace on this brotherhood by allowing your servant to refuse to obey your authority, even while the Master of the Guild was present."

George Wright was a self-confident and determined man, but he knew he was caught in a trap with this and would have to bear the consequences. He understood now what the nature of his misdemeanour was. He had been so sure that Meg, his "servant," as John Miller phrased it, would have cooperated with them. He'd left her in the room alone with the inner circle... she must have refused. Very unlike Meg, he pondered, she was normally so docile, did whatever he wanted.

Abruptly, John Miller's attitude changed. He stood up next to Wright and put his hand on his shoulder, like a father speaking to a wayward son. "George, we are brothers here, and we know you are loyal to the Guild. But for the sake of the brotherhood, it is our duty to punish you." Around the room there was a release of tension, and a warm feeling suffused the men, righteous anger coloured with patriarchal authority. John Miller was totally at ease in his role, as though the spirit of his grandfather was back with them again.

"As your Master and guide, I must give you this punishment." His tone became more serious as he pronounced judgement, "Dismiss your disobedient servant."

George nodded without raising his head, "Yes, Master."

"Today."

"Yes, Master." George Wright waited until John Miller sat down again, then shrunk down into his own seat, feeling small and humiliated, trying not to think of the immediate consequences – who would prepare and serve the bar meals, who would clean the kitchen and tidy up generally?

The atmosphere in the room was tense, a mixture of shock and excitement at the drama of seeing George Wright being disciplined. John Miller looked calmly around the table, satisfaction brightening his unattractive face. "Let's move on to the next item, something which is much more... pleasant." He was choosing his words carefully, cleverly using each for maximum effect, controlling the room, all the men listening to every word. "Let us return to the important issue of people being victims of violent attacks. It is our business to have oversight of our area, and we don't want anything disturbing that. It seems to me that it would be a good thing if we took positive action."

There was a stirring of interest about this news.

"A recent victim was a young lad called Steven. He lives alone with his mother here in Netherton, and was beaten up by a gang, needing a stay in hospital to recover." His tone had changed to concerned. It was reflected by tutting and shaking of heads in response. "I suggest we make a gift from the Guild to the boy's mother. I've been told he is musical – we could give a gift towards music tuition, showing support from the Netherton Guild to law-abiding people. Also, there was an incident at the late-night store on Water Lane, with the owners being terrorised by three burglars. They hit Maurice Smith over the head with a hammer. We should give the Smiths a gift too, to help with repairing the mess, giving the shop a facelift. Who is in favour?" Hands shot up, eager to be seen as supporters.

"Who would like to deliver the gift?" Two of the men put their hands up showing their willingness to be seen giving this generous gift from the Guild.

"Thank you, our treasurer will provide you with the money. The village needs to be aware the Guild will protect the interests of our own people."

One of the men asked, "The people responsible – these 'rogue elements' – will we be taking positive action about them too?"

John Miller looked around at the members and said, with studied concern, "Do you think we should?"

The answer was immediate. The single word 'yes' resounded around the room. They considered it their business to dispense justice as they saw it, to keep control.

"Good. We will return to that at the next meeting when we have all the information."

Towards the bottom of the table, Fred was sitting enthralled with the events of tonight's meeting. Fred still found it all a little strange, but also mesmerising, the unquestioning acquiescence of these men with such an uncompromising authority; Fred found it made him feel secure – someone else, a greater authority, was making the decisions according to an agreed set of rules. So long as you kept the rules, you were safe. It was even better than being under Arnold's authority. Arnold was his boss, no question about it, but sometimes Arnold's moods were hard to read, and there was no rule book. Here everyone knew the rules; Fred believed all he had to do was to keep to them, and he would be a protected member of this closely bonded group.

*

It was not long until the Guild was assembled again. Since John Miller had become Master, the meetings had been far more frequent – he wanted to consolidate his influence as leader. There was a buzz of anticipation as the men sat down around the long table. According to their rules, any matters of discipline had to be reported to the whole meeting, so George Wright had the humiliating experience of recording in the minutes the recent disciplinary action involving himself. When it came up on tonight's agenda, he told the meeting that he had carried out what the Master had told him to do and dismissed Meg Somers from his employment. John Miller's thin lips curved into a smile, revealing his stained teeth. Whatever his appearance, he had gained the respect of the men. He had, just as he claimed was his grandfather's wish, stepped into his dead grandfather's shoes.

The next item for discussion was the issue of the perpetrators of the violent attacks in the village. John Miller asked everyone present to reveal everything they knew about the possible identity of the culprits. "You don't have to worry about naming names – everything said here is only between us. It is your duty to reveal what you know, even if those involved are in your family.

Nobody spoke for a few moments, then one after another, several of the men started to say the names of local young men, followed by where they lived.

"Write it all down," Miller instructed Wright. "Any more names?"

There was a pause, then Geoff Crawshaw spoke up, resignation in his voice,

"Mark Crawshaw."

There were expressions of shock around the table by those who recognised the name of Crawshaw's son. John Miller was unmoved by this, saying calmly, "We'll need his address."

Crawshaw gave his son's address, which was with Crawshaw's ex-wife. They had split up years ago.

Harold Williams commented in a reassuring tone, "This is difficult but if we handle it in the right way, Geoff, it could be a turning point for young Mark."

Miller spoke again, "We'll pay a visit to all of these, and explain the seriousness of the situation, that we know who they are, and that this behaviour has got to stop."

Fred Roland asked shyly, "Shouldn't the police be involved?"

Miller gave him a pitying look, which made Fred look towards Mike Small for reassurance. Small said briefly, "No, we'll handle this ourselves."

Fred nodded. Of course, the Guild would be able to do more with this local situation than the police, who probably would have to come all the way from Exton and also might not know any of the local families.

Miller was already moving on. "Next item, the gifts to the families of victims."

The two men who had been given the task of delivering the gifts to the families looked pleased with themselves. They reported how grateful Steven and his mother had been when they heard that his music tuition would be paid for. The family who owned the shop which had been burgled had also expressed their gratitude. The father of the family said he would not forget what the Guild had done to help them.

John Miller said, sounding pleased, "Put that in the minutes."

Chapter Nineteen

Over the last few weeks Hilda had been watching the progress of the work on the building site. Initially she had seen the labourers only in the distance on the other side of the makeshift bridge of steel girders. Now she could see that work had started on a new bridge. When she realised that her efforts were no longer required, she felt a huge sense of relief but tinged with sadness. Her attempt to rebuild the bridge, had been a test of her faith in the power of God to use a weak vessel such as herself. It was an intense experience which she had immersed herself in wholeheartedly, believing that the Lord would bless the work and bring it to completion. She had imagined what the rebuilt bridge would look like, made from the old stones but renewed, even stronger than before. Part of her was disappointed that the bridge which Bluebird Construction and Design were building was a modern design, totally different from the old bridge of stones and timber. Neither did it bear any resemblance to the old church it was to give access to. But then, she thought, the important thing was that access was restored and people could go to the church again.

In a surprisingly short time, the bridge was completed, and the following day Hilda noticed that work had started on a road on the other side of the bridge. Hilda decided she would like to talk to the workers as something about the position of some marker posts for the road was bothering her. The surface layer of the bridge was not yet finished so Hilda picked her way carefully over it to the land on the other side. She saw a group of workers at some distance away and headed towards them across the mud. Fortunately she was wearing her wellingtons but the going was still hard. As she got near to the labourers, she opened her mouth to speak to them but then stopped abruptly. She looked at the poor state they were in, their thin soiled clothes – quite unsuitable for the winter and for tough manual work, and the worn shoes which they had on their feet. Admittedly all of them wore yellow plastic safety helmets, and from a distance this is what anyone would notice, but on getting closer to them it was obvious that they weren't dressed properly for their work.

"Goodness, haven't you got proper jackets and boots?" asked Hilda. The two men closest to her didn't seem to understand what she had said but another man called over and said in broken English, "Safety wear coming soon. On order."

From across the site there was the sound of an engine starting. Hilda turned round towards the noise and saw a digger approaching. It passed where Hilda was standing and headed towards the track that led up to the church. Hilda watched as the man who was driving the machine manoeuvred it into position next to the track and started digging.

"Wait!" Hilda called out and began to make her way over as quickly as the mud would allow her. She arrived next to the vehicle and shouted up to the driver, "What are you doing?"

He looked down at her, surprised to see the elderly woman standing there in the mud.

"Digging new road," he shouted down to her in broken English. "New road for houses. This one no good."

"No, no!" she shouted back, then pointed at the rough track, "This old road must stay. It is hundreds of years old and is the way to the church." She pointed up the hill to show him.

He shook his head, "Boss says we make a new big road here to houses."

At that moment Hilda knew she had been tricked. The driver moved the digger round sending a thick spray of mud up into the air and over Hilda. She gasped – some of it had even hit her face. She tasted the gritty dirt on her lips. She fumbled in her pocket for a handkerchief to wipe her face and started to walk back towards the new bridge. She felt a mixture of shock, hurt and anger. She had been manipulated into supporting what she was committed to opposing, into destroying what she was trying to protect. No doubt Martin Fielding had told a very convincing version of events to the Haliwell family lawyer, that the bridge had been destroyed and that the construction company wanted to come to the aid of the Friends of St Brannock's Church and build a new bridge so that access could be restored. In fact, they were only seeking to get the landowner to sign a contract of sale and intended to destroy the old pilgrims' way in the process. And what about the church itself? Hilda wondered. Would that be next on their list to get rid of?

By now she had crossed the bridge and was walking towards her cottage, hot with anger and indignation. It seemed there was a web of conspiracy closing around them. At first it had seemed to be only the storm surge from the River Ishka which was against them, but now she believed there were people involved too.

She thought of the vicar, no wonder he was troubled, surrounded by such forces. But there were points of light in all this darkness; she smiled as she remembered Jonah's experience during the evening communion service – what a remarkable thing, and she had been given the privilege of being involved in this young man's journey into faith in Jesus. There was a battle on for the control of this village, but the dear Lord would lead them through, she announced to herself as she pushed open the garden gate. The words of the Letter to the Ephesians came to her mind, "For our struggle is not against flesh and blood, but against rulers, against the authorities, against the powers of this dark world and against the spiritual forces of evil in the heavenly realms." (Ephesians 6:12 NIV)

This battle may prove to be harder and more complicated than she could have anticipated, and it would need a great deal of discernment and wisdom, or she and the other Christian people here would be tricked again. We must be more persistent in prayer, she decided. The moment she got inside the cottage, she went to the phone and dialled the number of the vicarage.

"St Gregory's Vicarage. How can I help you?" It was James' voice.

"Hello, James. I hope I haven't caught you at a busy moment."

"It's Hilda, isn't it? Not at all, lovely to hear from you. Is everything all right?"

"Well, I'm not sure I can give a short answer to that question. In fact, that is exactly why I have rung."

James thought, *oh dear, another mysterious conversation with Hilda, I wonder what she means.*

"Do you need me to come round to see you, Hilda? Would you like to talk about something?"

"That would be wonderful. We need to talk seriously about this, James, and devise a plan."

"Right.... Do we need to do this straightaway, or is it a longer-term thing?" asked James, completely confused.

"Both, dear," replied Hilda, "We would be wise to start immediately, and also to keep going for as long as it takes."

James scratched his head, unsure how to respond.

Hilda continued undaunted, "I don't suppose you have some free time this afternoon?"

James agreed to go round to see her at half past two.

*

James arrived promptly at Honeysuckle Cottage, hoping that whatever was on Hilda's mind wouldn't take long to discuss and he would be heading home by three o'clock. He couldn't have been more wrong. First, as was her habit, Hilda insisted they have tea and home-made scones and jam. Although it wasn't long since he had eaten lunch, and despite his initial protest, he ate the scones with relish and felt himself unwinding, ready to listen to Hilda. What she told him was nothing like the usual conversation between vicars and elderly members of their congregation.

"I'd like to start at the beginning," said Hilda, putting her teacup back down on its saucer.

"Sounds very sensible," said James pleasantly.

"I don't know how much you know about the Christian heritage of this area."

"Not very much I much admit – I haven't lived here for long – I'm always meaning to find out about the history of the region, but never seem to have the time."

"I know a little about it. For instance, the Church has been here since around the sixth century."

"Goodness me, that's astonishing. Are you sure?"

James immediately thought of how hard it seemed to encourage people to come to church at all in Netherton; if the place had such a long Christian history, anyone might have expected a larger presence.

"Yes, I am absolutely sure. In fact, I can show you. Do you have time to come up to the old church on the other side of the river?"

James was intrigued – if there was evidence of Christians having been in Netherton so many hundreds of years ago, he would like to know about it.

They left the cottage together and walked to the bridge, talking as they went.

"Hilda, was this what you wanted to talk to me about – the Christian heritage of the area?"

"It's part of what we need to talk about, certainly."

"You said something about us needing a plan."

"We need a plan because in this area some bad things have been happening. That's what you notice on the surface, but I believe there's more to it than that, that there's a kind of battle on for the heart and soul of this place, but let's start nearer to the beginning, which is related to what I want to show you."

They were walking over the new bridge as they said this, and Hilda paused for a moment to look over the side at the river. "The Ishka looks calm and harmless at the moment," she observed.

"Are you comparing it to the night of the storm?"

"Yes, it became an instrument of destruction, didn't it?"

"You're not trying to suggest that the river is somehow evil, are you?" asked James, concerned now at where the conversation was leading.

"No, not at all."

He breathed out, relieved. "What does the name mean, anyway, *Ishka*, it sounds very unusual."

"It's a Celtic word for water."

"So, whoever originally named the river spoke the Celtic tongue then."

They left the bridge and walked towards the church.

"You see the track we are walking on, James – imagine this for a moment – for much longer than a thousand years pilgrims have been walking here, just like us, and then have climbed up the hill to pray."

"What a wonderful thought."

"The same stones, the same mud, were trodden by faithful Christians who were living surrounded by the pagan people who used to live here, people long before the Vikings or Normans arrived."

James looked at the marker posts which were driven into the track at various points and formed a continuous line leading to where digging had already started, and stacks of building materials lay. "The building work has already started," he said.

They were climbing up the hill, and Hilda was breathing heavily as she continued, "I believe the Gospel first reached this area years before Augustine landed on English shores. There were some wonderful missionary saints here in this part of the country. They would have come up against deeply-rooted pagan beliefs and rituals and would have needed to have been people of great faith and prayer to win through against all that spiritual resistance."

They walked around the outside of the church to the east-facing end, Hilda going first until she stopped next to a Celtic stone cross. It was about eight feet high, standing on a square stone base. Despite the effects of wind and weather in that exposed position, its intricate engraving in Celtic knot-work was still clear. It was angled so that it faced outwards over the landscape. James went closer to it, "It's beautiful, Hilda. I haven't been to this side of the old church before; I've never seen this cross before."

213

"A Celtic high cross. In the cupboard at the back of the church there's a history of St Brannock's church. It says the cross is sixth century, dating back to a monk who came to this area from Wales. It seems he erected stone crosses at various points in this part of the country and built a small chapel here on top of this hill. Of course, the chapel would have been wooden, so has disappeared a long time ago, but the cross remains. The present stone church, although very old, is in fact only the most recent building on this holy site. All through the centuries there has been a continuous stream of faithful believers wanting to preserve the Christian identity of this area, which at times has been under threat from aggressive unbelievers. The Haliwells are the latest protectors of this place, and the Friends of St Brannock's of course! What I wanted to show you James, is that for an extremely long period of time in this spot, faithful Christians have been shining the light of Christ out over this area. And it probably has always been a struggle."

"I can identify with that certainly," said James, "I have had a struggle here ever since I arrived."

"That's the next part of the conversation I need to have with you," said Hilda.

As they walked back down the hill, Hilda talked to James about Jonah. "I think it's the first sign of a breakthrough – first, he turns up at the precise moment I was praying for help in my efforts to re-build the bridge here after the storm destroyed it –"

At this point James gave her a startled look, not quite believing what she had just said. She dismissed his reaction with a wave of her hand, wanting to continue, "It must have been God leading Jonah to exactly the right place at the right time. Then he has a wonderful conversion experience, right in the middle of the communion service—"

"Yes, I've never seen anything as dramatic as that in a service."

"Although I must say you yourself were swept up into something pretty dramatic that evening, weren't you?"

James immediately felt embarrassed, "I'm sorry if I behaved inappropriately – I don't know what came over me."

"Don't apologise, James. What came over you was the Holy Spirit. It's wonderful, nothing to be embarrassed about."

"How is Jonah getting on with studying the Bible with you, Hilda? – it's good of you to take this on – I suppose Jonah should be coming to me really."

"He is hungry for the Word, just as I was when I committed my life to Jesus Christ. I know it's a bit unusual, a young man like Jonah getting together around the Word of God with a woman of my age, but it's something the good Lord has arranged, and I have learnt not to question God's will, but to go along with it, just the same as re-building the bridge together."

"I still can't believe you even attempted it, Hilda."

"It was very hard, but I knew it was the right thing, and look what happened – Jonah came along."

They reached the cottage again and James held open the gate for Hilda, thinking he would leave at this point. However, she caught hold of his arm, "Do come in again for a few minutes James. There are some other things I need to tell you about."

They went in and she urged him to make himself comfortable. While she was in the kitchen making tea there was a knock at the front door.

Shall I answer the door, Hilda?" called James.

"Thank you, I'll be there in a moment."

When James opened the door he found a familiar face there – Sam Williams.

"Hello, James – I saw you come in a moment ago and wanted to catch you with some news."

"Sam, good to see you, I'm sure Hilda will be pleased to see you too."

James stepped back to let Sam come in, saying, "How is Mary?"

"That's what I wanted to tell you – she is so much better. From the afternoon you and Anna came to pray for her she has picked up strength and, well, what can I say, she's doing absolutely everything – cooking, shopping, even some gardening. It's absolutely wonderful."

Hilda had come back into the room and heard the news, "Thank God, she's well again, she's free of that awful sickness. Have a cup of tea to celebrate!"

Sam laughed and sat down next to James while Hilda went back to the kitchen. "I can't get over it, I've got my wife back, the woman I married. Please don't think I resented looking after Mary, it's not that – but it was difficult at times. We'd have the occasional good day when she would even feel well enough to catch the bus and go shopping for a short time, and I would be really pleased, and then she would come back totally exhausted and spend the next two days in bed. And there were days she had never even got out of bed at all

215

and would be in pain and feverish again. None of the doctors she saw ever got to the bottom of it. But now every day is a good day, since you prayed for her. Have you prayed for a lot of people? I suppose you must have, being a vicar. Although I must say, even though I've been to church every now and then over the years I've never come across this before."

James hesitated, then said resolutely, "To be perfectly honest, Sam, I have never prayed for anyone to be healed in this way before. I mean, I've prayed at a distance, but this biblical way of laying hands on people and praying for them to be healed – I've read about it, but I just ignored it, or perhaps avoided it."

"So, you're saying you've never done it before – so how did you know it would work?"

"I had faith that something good would happen. I suppose my faith in God's power has gone up a level recently. I had faith that if I did what it says in the letter of James chapter 5 – that if someone is sick and we pray the prayer of faith over them – that there would be healing of some kind."

Hilda carried the tea in saying, "Isn't it lovely, two wonderful things in a short time."

James explained that he and Hilda had been talking about various things before Sam arrived. "We've just walked up to the pilgrims' church to see the ancient stone Celtic cross – I didn't even know it was there – Hilda has been telling me a little of the local history."

Sam took a sip of tea, "I didn't know about the cross, in fact I must admit I have never even walked up to the old church. I am very pleased that old bridge which was destroyed in the storm has been replaced so that anyone who wants to walk up there can do so.... The builders have built the bridge, haven't they – the people who are going to build the new houses."

Hilda asked them both, "How much do you know about the building company Bluebird Design and Construction?"

James looked surprised, "Not much really. In many ways they seem to be very helpful," he said. "You must be delighted about the new bridge. And they've offered to help build an extension for the school. They do seem to want to play their part in helping this community as well as building their houses."

"That's what I thought too James. In fact, that's what the young man from Bluebird Design and Construction persuaded me to believe. I told him about how the pilgrims have come to the church for many hundreds of years and how precious it was. Morag and I explained that we are both Friends of St Brannock's and our task is to make sure the church continues to be a beacon of faith in this area and a place for pilgrims to come and pray. He seemed to be sympathetic and when he saw the access to Saint Brannock's was destroyed by the river he offered on behalf of his company to restore it. But, James, you saw what they are about to do to the ancient track to the church."

"The young man – is this the same person who came to see me? His name is Martin."

"That's right. Martin Fielding."

"Do we know anything else about the company? Perhaps we can contact them and explain they must not destroy the track up to the church."

Hilda shook her head, "I'm afraid they are not what they seemed to be. We have been duped – they never intended to help the village, or to preserve the old church. They have been quite treacherous."

Sam looked thoughtful for a moment, then said, "I could ask my father if he knows anything about them – he knows quite a lot of businesspeople through the Guild."

"The Guild?" asked James.

"It's a local group of men who meet in the Mason's Arms."

James looked a little concerned, "The *Guild* – you are not a member yourself?"

"No, not into the funny handshakes and all that sort of thing, if you know what I mean. But my father has been a member as long as I can remember."

Hilda caught James' eye and said lightly, "We certainly do need to find a way of stopping Bluebird Construction from destroying the pilgrims' way and, I fear, from perhaps even being a threat to the church itself. And there's something else too – I'm concerned about the workers on the site – they don't have proper boots or clothing. I spoke to them, and they made some excuse, poor souls. It sounded like something they had been told to say if anyone asked, but, put all our concerns together and it all points in the same direction – the company we thought was absolutely fine is turning out to be anything but."

They fell into silence for a few moments, each of them deep in thought.

Then Sam stood up, ready to leave.

Hilda walked with him to the door, "Give my love to Mary," she said brightly, "Tell her I'm so pleased and I will call round to see her soon - and I'll see her at church and perhaps I'll see you there too," she added, smiling.

"Yes, you will; after what's happened to Mary, I don't think I could stay away."

Hilda closed the door and returned to her armchair.

James was looking serious, "Martin Fielding came to the vicarage more than once, Hilda. He came the first time to talk to me about his company's plans; he told me they wanted to build affordable housing for local young people."

"That sounds very laudable, if it were true," she chuckled, "I wonder what their plans actually look like."

"While he was in my study my daughter came in and he...," James hesitated, trying to find the right words, "took rather a shine to her. He asked her if she would show him a little of the locality as it would be very helpful. At the time, you understand, I thought his company was genuinely going to work very positively with the community. Now of course I realise I was very gullible."

"What impression did Anna have of him?"

"At first, she seemed to like him very much, and I even hoped that he may be a possible good match for her – he was so respectful towards me as the vicar. I hoped he may be kindly disposed towards the Church – quite a rarity among young men nowadays. But then, something seemed to change, and I sensed I should, at least temporarily, stand in the way of him contacting Anna. It was quite odd, nothing Anna said at the time, but since then she has indicated she made a mistake."

"Hmm," said Hilda, "How interesting. Do you see, James – that there is a sort of web of unpleasantness and trickery that this company seem to have brought with it? And add to that the attacks that have happened recently in this village, especially that very nasty one on the village green, and even the river smashing the bridge and cutting off the way to St B's. I have a growing sense that it is all connected to the spiritual battle over this place."

She paused, looking at him to check that he was following her meaning, then continued, "The old church may not look significant to many people, but it is a very obvious sign of faith in Jesus Christ. It strikes me that the forces of darkness are gathering to try and get rid of it and to cause mischief and harm to the people here. We are seeing symptoms of this around us, probably a lot more than you or I know about – trouble of different sorts cropping up."

"This is what you wanted to talk about, wasn't it?"

"Yes, and I have a proposal." She leaned forward a little, an earnest look on her face, "We must rise up against this by increasing our prayer. You've already seen the powerful effects of prayer when you and Anna prayed for Mary. Imagine what God might do if we have an extended period of prayer."

James nodded, "You're right, there have been a lot of very strange things happening. But I have to admit we haven't got a great many people to call upon to engage in extended prayer."

"But remember '*If two or three are gathered together in My name...*'"

"*I am there in the midst of them.*" (Matthew 18:20 NKJV) James finished the verse for her. He tried to imagine what was in his diary, then decided this was more important than most of what he did anyway. "We could start on Friday evening, let's say seven o'clock in the parish church."

*

When Sam arrived home in his own cottage, he told Mary about the conversation with Hilda.

"She's very unusual," he said. "Normally, I would say she was just a slightly strange old lady..."

"But a very kind one" added Mary, "I can't tell you how many times she has offered to get some shopping for me, or even do some housework – imagine – a lady of her age! And when I felt low, she would knock on the door and leave a little plant on the doorstep with a note from her saying she was thinking about me and would remember me in her prayers."

"Yes, a kind person. But what she was saying was a bit fanciful. She is *very* suspicious of the people behind the building development up near that little old church up the hill. She's convinced they have an evil plan to get rid of the place!" he laughed. "And that the construction workers have no boots!"

"Maybe she's right."

"I doubt it. It's much more likely that she's imagining things. Anyway," he added, seeing that Mary looked unhappy about his lack of respect for Hilda, "I've agreed to see if my dad has heard anything at the Guild meetings about the construction company."

"I thought they were secret meetings."

"Yes, but he's my dad, I think he could tell *me*, surely!" He laughed again, thinking his wife was taking everything too seriously.

He sat down next to her and took her hand, "Sorry to laugh at everybody – I just feel so happy that you're well again."

She smiled back at him, "It's wonderful, isn't it? In fact, while you're still feeling so happy, I have something to ask you. You know it's mostly just me who goes to church? In future, out of thankfulness, I'd like us to go together each Sunday."

He kissed her on the forehead, "Funny, that's the second person who's said that inside ten minutes. Of course, in future it will be both of us."

*

Sam Williams decided to call round to see his father. Since retiring from the police force, he found he had more time to spend with his dad. Sam knocked on his door – his father always kept it locked for security even though Netherton had always been a safe place to live – but maybe not in recent times, he reflected, as he stood outside the door.

After a minute or so Harold came to the door, "Sam! Come in – good to see you."

They went into the kitchen together and Harold made coffee for them both.

"How are you keeping Dad?"

"Not bad at all," said Harold. "For a man of my great age."

"I hope I'll be doing as well as you when I'm your age."

"Talking about age, I meant to tell you son, I decided to step aside from being Master of the Guild and let a younger man in."

"But you had only just become Master, hadn't you Dad?"

"True, but there was someone else more able to lead. It's what's best for the Guild that matters. I can't really tell you any more about it."

"Yes – the bond of secrecy and all that," said Sam, trying not to smile.

His father looked at him sadly, "I've always been a little disappointed, son, that you never wanted to join the Guild. Can't understand it. There are a lot of policemen in the different branches. Both retired and still in service."

"Secret societies just don't appeal to me. But I did want to ask you something about the Guild."

His father looked at him, "What do you want to know?"

"Sorry, it's not about joining. Just wondered if through your Guild friends you knew anything about the construction company that's started to build houses in the area."

"Of course, I can't divulge any confidential information, you understand that, other than to say there are members of the Guild in many local companies, and recently we have made contact with the company you're interested in."

"And do you think the company is legit?"

"You mean is it legal?"

"I mean a bit more than that, not just obeying enough of the law to be left alone. I mean is it straight in its dealings?"

"There's a difference?"

"Yes, huge difference, like the difference between an unkind parent who makes a child's life a misery, and the rotten parent who actually is taken to court for neglect and even abuse. In fact, both are them are rotten, but only one has been taken to court for it, with evidence to prove they're guilty."

"I see. All I can tell you is that as far as I know they are keeping within the law. It would be inappropriate for me to say any more."

"Dad, if you knew something dodgy was going on, would you tell me?"

Harold hesitated – in all his years of belonging to the Guild, his son had never asked him this question.

Sam pressed his point, "You know it's against the law to withhold information about a crime."

"As I said," said Harold, sounding tetchy, "I believe they are obeying the law."

Sam was uneasy – his father's attitude confirmed his opinion of organisations like the Guild. The fact that Harold had always emphasised that many police officers belonged to either the Guild or a similar group did nothing to convince him this was a good thing to be part of.

They lapsed into an awkward silence. Sam decided to change the subject. "I've got some good news – Mary's loads better."

"Really? Have the doctors given her some new tablets?"

"No, the doctors had more or less given up. You may know more about this than me, Dad, you've been an Anglican all your life, but she had people from the church pray for her – prayer for healing – and she instantly started to get better."

"Goodness me, were they from the church here in Netherton?" He sounded incredulous.

"Yes, the vicar and his daughter."

"It sounds more like what people from a strange religious cult might do."

"Evidently it's in the Bible for the church to do it, but mostly it's forgotten about. All I know is it's worked for Mary – she's absolutely fine now."

"After all these years – that's very odd. You know what some people would say – that it must have all been in her mind and when she got a bit of attention through somebody praying for her it did something psychosomatic or psychological."

"It's still healing, though, isn't it? To be honest, I don't care what kind of healing it is, I am just delighted that she is well again."

"So am I, so am I, said Harold quickly, "It's very good news – glad to hear it."

"Well, must be going, Mary wants me to take her with me to the golf course today – she fancies a crack at golf! Imagine that – two golf players in the family."

"Tell her I'm pleased for her, not about golf, about her health I mean."

Sam returned home, somewhat disquieted by part of their conversation.

Harold stood on the doorstep watching his son walk away, saddened that they did not have more in common. Why was his son so suspicious of the Guild? He couldn't understand it.

Chapter Twenty

Hilda spent the evening designing a poster to publicise the Friday evening prayer. She had asked James if he minded if she did this, and he said it would be a good thing for as many people as possible to know that there was prayer for the village. Hilda thought about it as she prepared the poster, which would be displayed to the general public rather than just the "insiders" of the church. Some may have worried that it may attract the wrong sort of person, but then what is the wrong sort of person, she pondered – confused people, difficult people, people who had lost their faith in God or never found it? All of these sorts would be exactly the right ones to come – Jesus would certainly want them to. The church shouldn't be like the Guild, a secret closed group. No, let everyone come into the presence of Jesus.

Hilda was artistic; she worked carefully and skilfully until satisfied with the finished product. The posters were attractive, advertising in eye-catching but tasteful lettering 'Prayer for the Village' on Friday nights at 7 o'clock in Netherton Parish Church. Everyone welcome. Tomorrow she would persuade the lady in the post office to display one in the window and she would also put one in the glass-fronted noticeboard outside the church. It would be good to have something in it besides the advance notice of the parish church council meeting and times of services. It didn't give much time for people to see the posters before this Friday's meeting but there would be other Fridays too.

After she had put the posters to one side ready for the following day, Hilda sat down by the fire to think for a while. She recalled the events and conversations of the day, from when she had gone over the bridge to the point she had reached now, not long before bedtime.

She was convinced now that Martin Fielding and his construction company had tricked her and Morag, but had they tricked other people too? What about the people who owned the land that the pilgrims' church stood on? Perhaps they had been tricked too. There must be a solicitor involved – someone must have drawn up a contract. Thinking this, Hilda knew what her next step must be – she must find out the name of law firm and also contact the landowners. But how would she achieve this?

She got up and went to the cupboard in the corner of the room which held her important documents in a metal filing box. She lifted out the box and opened it, looking for the hanging file which was labelled 'Friends of St Brannock's Church'. There were copies of some old documents relating to the church as well as notes from the quarterly meetings of the Friends. Among these she found what she was looking for – she hadn't seen it for many years as the times had been uneventful and the Friends had been happy to carry on their duties of caring for the church in the same way each year, funding minor expenses between themselves without recourse to the owners of the land the church stood on. Now she remembered it – a letter from a firm of solicitors in Exton affirming the right of the Friends to make minor maintenance decisions concerning the upkeep of the old church, and with the name and contact details of the owner, Mrs Elise Haliwell, of Colorado Springs, U.S.A.

She was excited. The moment she had dealt with the posters about prayer tomorrow morning she would go and tell Morag they must call an urgent meeting of the Friends.

*

The following morning was the coldest they had had so far that year; ice had formed on the road and pavements outside the cottage. On any other day she would have waited for the morning sun to thaw the ice, but not today, she thought – it would take too long, and what if it remained frozen all day? There was too much to do for her to have the privilege of putting things off until a more convenient time. She ate her breakfast quickly and began to put on layers of outdoor clothing against the December cold.

As she stepped outside into the freezing temperature, she thought of the workers on the building site. Would they already be there, trying to work in this biting cold?

She started to walk along her garden path, slowly, tentatively, the posters in a large envelope tucked under her arm. She reached the gate safely, then began to walk along the pavement towards the centre of the village. After a few hundred yards, she had to cross the road. The surface had the greasy sheen of black ice. With nothing to hold on to, she started out across the road. Half-way across her foot slipped. She reached out into thin air as though to grab something to hold on to, but in vain. She twisted, stumbled and fell on to the rock-hard surface of the road, striking her face against it. She felt the sharp stinging of the skin of her cheek scraped by the hard road. Shocked, she stayed there sprawled on the road for a few moments, then realised she was in further danger from any vehicles who came that way and could not stop on the icy surface. "Oh Lord, please send some help." She looked around her but couldn't see much from her position flat out on the road. She was sure God would help her if she could just hang on for a few minutes. Had she broken anything? She could not tell, the shock had made her feel numb, apart from her skinned cheek. The road was remarkably quiet – normally there would be some passing traffic or pedestrians at this time in the morning, but the severe weather had kept most people indoors unless they couldn't avoid going out. It seemed that only Hilda had braved the winter freeze. Another few minutes passed, then there was the sound of a car engine – was it coming this way?

She heard a car stopping suddenly and someone opening a car door, then a familiar Scottish voice coming towards her exclaiming, "I knew it! Only you Hilda! *Only you* would be daft enough to come out on day like today."

"Morag." Hilda's eyes filled with tears as she continued to lie on the road. She had never been so glad to see her friend. "I don't seem to be able to get up."

"You silly old thing, I've a good mind to leave you there to teach you a bit of common sense," said Morag as she got down beside Hilda and put her arm around her protectively.

"You can't lift me, dear, I'm too heavy for you."

"I can't leave you with your face on the road. Here–". She took off her silk scarf and slid it between Hilda's face and the road. "Now, can you feel your fingers and toes? Can you wriggle them?" Hilda tried and thought she could.

"Good, now to get help to get you off this road, don't worry, I've got a first-aid certificate."

Hilda was not filled with confidence by this reassurance but knew Morag would do her best. "I've just spotted someone–hoi! Over here! Yes you! Come and lend a hand!" A man had just come out of a nearby house. Hearing Morag's imperious voice, he came straight over and looked at Hilda. "You need an ambulance," he said, "have you called one?"

Morag gave him a slightly withering look, "No mobile phone; wrong generation I'm afraid. Do you have one yourself?"

The man pulled a phone out of his pocket.

"Wait!" said Hilda, trying to look up at him from her position lying face down on the road and thinking a trip to the hospital may take all day and she had more important things to do. "Do you think you could try to prise me up from here?"

The man looked down at her, a worried look on his face.

She persisted, "I really don't want to go to hospital."

"So stubborn." commented Morag. "Let's try to roll her, and see what happens."

They crouched down next to Hilda, Morag's knees clicking alarmingly as they did so, then they took hold of Hilda's coat and rolled her on to her back. To their relief Hilda did not yelp with pain.

"So far so good," remarked Morag, "now, one on each side, under the armpits and let's get her sitting up."

With a lot of panting on Morag's part, they got Hilda into a sitting position.

"How do you feel?" asked Morag.

"A bit dizzy" said Hilda, "But it's good to sit up."

By now three other people had gathered to watch.

"Let's have some more hands!" called Morag, getting into her role as leader of the rescue.

The people gathered round, each getting a grip on a different bit of Hilda's anatomy.

"Don't drop her!" ordered Morag. "You might break something."

"Thanks very much," said Hilda, steeling herself for whatever might happen next.

"Heave!" shouted Morag, and the group of people hoisted Hilda off the road and planted her back on her feet. They let go immediately and Hilda felt herself stagger, feeling dizzy after her ordeal.

"Don't worry, hold on to my arm, and we'll get you into my car." The crowd around Hilda had grown some more – she was proving to be quite an attraction. People from houses nearby had flung their coats on and come to see what was going on in the middle of the road. Eager hands opened the car door and helped Hilda in, closing the door after her. There was a hubbub of excited conversation, "Poor old dear, did you see her? Flat out on the road, had she been run over?"

Morag reversed her car away from the people and turned in the direction of her house.

"Are you sure you don't need to go to the hospital? Can you move everything? Do you feel dopey?"

"No more than usual, thank you, Morag," said Hilda.

"Oh, I see you've got your sense of humour back," said Morag. "Let's get you a drink of sweet tea."

Sitting in Morag's comfortable living room, drinking the sweet tea she had made, Hilda began to feel much better. Despite her fall she was determined to carry on with everything she had planned to do that day.

Morag had other ideas, however. First she insisted on bathing Hilda's face and applying some antiseptic, then she made her friend sit down by the fire again to rest.

"Tell me, Hilda, just what were you hurrying along to this morning? What was it that just couldn't wait until better weather?"

"Two very important things, well three actually."

"*Three* vitally important things. Hmmm...." Morag sounded unconvinced.

"Firstly, to display two special posters, one at the church and one in the post office window."

"What are the posters for?"

"For a series of prayer meetings – it's a very important call to pray for this village."

"Any particular reason?"

"Lots of good reasons." She explained her concerns.

Morag listened carefully, weighing it up. Then she said thoughtfully, "Do you remember when we first met Martin Fielding, when he asked for our help. At first I thought – *this doesn't ring true* – he's talking about his firm as though they are a charitable foundation, not a business. But then he mentioned the Scouts and Guides and I wanted to believe what he said. Now I realise I was too ready to accept whatever he said."

"We both were taken for a ride, Morag. I am now convinced that he is a very skilled confidence trickster, the front man for a business which is probably very ruthless indeed."

"So how does this relate to these prayer meetings?"

"When you think about the threat to St B's and the outbreaks of violence in the village, and some other things too, we really must start praying urgently to turn back this upsurge of evil in this village."

"That sounds very dramatic, Hilda."

"You see, that's the problem with spiritual things – once you start to acknowledge that there's more to life than what is immediately obvious, and some things can only be responded to on a spiritual level, even your best friend thinks you're being dramatic."

"Ouch, Hilda, you're not talking about me, by any chance?"

"I don't want to offend you, but would you think Jesus was a bit dramatic, going around healing people, challenging injustice, casting out demons...."

"I suppose I probably would."

"But we are followers of Jesus, and he wants us to do what he did. He said so."

"Hmm. All right, you've convinced me. I must start thinking more spiritually."

"Good. And we know prayer changes things, including changing the spiritual atmosphere. So, let's start with calling Christians to pray for this village. Will you help me put the posters up? I would appreciate some company, especially now I look like I've been beaten up. And we need to contact all the Friends of St B's and get them to start praying about the situation with the church. Some of them are hundreds of miles away, aren't they, but prayer travels well!"

"No problem at all."

"I had planned to go and see the lawyer in Exton that deals with the Haliwell land here to find out about what the contract is for the sale of the land where the church is, but I don't think we'll manage that as well today now. We also must contact Mrs Elise Haliwell to tell her what is really happening on her land."

"Let's start with the posters. Are you sure you've recovered sufficiently from your fall?"

Hilda got up from her chair, trying not to wince as she did so. "Don't worry about me, Morag – I'll be fine."

Putting up the posters did not take long, especially as the ice had melted as the temperature rose a few degrees. Afterwards they returned to Morag's house to begin telephoning all the Friends to urge them to pray for the continued existence of the church and the ancient pilgrims' way which led up to it. They had a sandwich lunch while they worked their way through the list of names. Some of the people lived far away, even in other countries, but retained their support for the pilgrims' church. By half past three they had completed the list and the light outside was fading fast.

"Let me take you home, Hilda. I know it's not far and you like to walk, but you've had an awful shock today and you look tired."

Unusually, Hilda accepted without any resistance. Morag drove her to the garden gate of Honeysuckle Cottage.

"Thank you, Morag, you're such a good friend. I don't know what I would have done without you today. God has put us together, hasn't he?"

"He has indeed. Sleep well, Hilda."

*

Hilda slept solidly until 8 o'clock the next morning and woke refreshed, remembering immediately what her first task of the day must be. By half past eight she had already dressed and eaten breakfast and was sitting at her little writing desk in the living room. Her fountain pen, which she had used since school days, was ready in her hand and a sheet of ivory-coloured writing paper in front of her. She began to write:

Honeysuckle Cottage
The High Street
Netherton

Dear Mrs Haliwell,

I apologise for the recent lack of contact from the Friends of St Brannock's Church. In the light of recent developments, I realise that this has been unwise. We have recently discovered that the company "Bluebird Design and Construction" have applied to you to purchase the land on which St Brannock's stands. I am sure they have persuaded you that they will respect the church in line with the restrictions which your legal representative has stipulated, including access to the church. In fact, they have already broken their promises by beginning to destroy the ancient track used by pilgrims to reach the church.

It is true that the company has built a new bridge over the River Ishka, but this was not inspired by the need to provide a way to the church following the destruction of the old bridge by a storm surge of the river, but rather to give access to construction vehicles for their building site.

A further concern is the treatment of the labourers - the poor workers look exhausted and are without proper work clothes or safety boots.

I implore you to reconsider and withdraw your agreement to sell the land as these unscrupulous people certainly intend to destroy this ancient place dedicated to Our Lord.

With sincere regards,

Hilda Marshall (On behalf of the Friends of St Brannock's Church)

Hilda placed the letter in an envelope and sealed it, praying as she did so, "Lord, please may this letter reach Mrs Haliwell quickly. Please use it to save St B's, and to protect those poor workers." She would ask at the post office for the fastest post to America.

The next job on Hilda's list was to contact the firm of solicitors in Exton who dealt with the Haliwells' interests in England. She had written down the telephone number from the details she had found two days ago. She picked up her phone and dialled the number.

The person who was dealing with the sale of the Haliwells' land was happy to speak to her. She quickly told him about her visit to the building site and what she had seen there. He listened without comment, then said smoothly, "Let me take your name and some contact details. Clearly there must have been a mistake of some kind."

"No mistake, Mr Kirton. These people are tricksters. They have tricked you, and everybody else too."

She expected some surprise to be expressed by the lawyer, but he merely thanked her again and reassured her that they would be in touch with her, no need for her to take any further action, just leave it with them to sort out. She thanked him and had hung up before she realised she had forgotten to tell him that she had written to Elise Haliwell.

Chapter Twenty-One

On Friday evening James left the vicarage at six fifteen. He wanted to arrive early at Netherton church, at least half an hour before the start of the prayer meeting, to make sure everything was ready. He was feeling a mixture of excitement and nervousness. As he walked down the steps from the front door of the vicarage, he pulled his scarf more closely around his neck. It was bitterly cold again. The dark evening had the sharp clearness that only freezing temperatures bring. He hurried towards his car, chiding himself for forgetting that his windscreen would probably have frozen by now. He unlocked the car and felt for the can of de-icer which had rolled under the seat. He found it and walked around the car with it spraying the windows. Fortunately the layer of ice was thin and melted immediately. He got into his car and started the engine. It spluttered reluctantly into life. He turned the heater on full and drove slowly out of the drive as mist had formed immediately on the inside of the windows. Perhaps that was why he failed to recognise the car which was parked opposite the vicarage drive, or the person who was sitting in it.

Anna's car was still in the drive. She had said she would come a little later to the prayer meeting. Like James, she forgot about her car being iced over and when she went outside gave an exasperated sigh when she realised she must de-ice it. Unknown to her, the sigh was heard by someone standing nearby. The car across the road was empty.

A few minutes later than she had hoped, Anna set off, driving slowly out of the drive onto the road. At that speed, her face was clearly visible to Martin Fielding as he stood watching, hidden behind the bushes which clustered around the end of the drive.

James unlocked the church, wondering what this first prayer meeting would be like. He was used to having a set liturgy to follow all the way from the beginning to the end of a service. Only very rarely in the past had he tried to have times of open prayer. Would people join in? Or just sit in silence while he was left to do all the praying? He thought Hilda would join in – so that would be two of them at least, he estimated.

"Lord," he prayed, as he put the chairs out in the same arrangement as for the Sunday evening communion service, "please help us all to pray."

At ten minutes to seven people started to arrive. First to arrive was Anna, who walked in chatting quietly with Morag and Hilda, then three more of the Sunday evening service regulars. Sam and Mary Williams were next, followed by Meg, then Stephen's mother, Cheryl. Just before seven Jonah hurried in, almost closing the door on the last person, coming a few steps behind him. Harold Williams had decided after a very long period of non-attendance, that it was time to put in an appearance again at the local church, especially after his conversation with his son. He had seen the prayer meeting advertised in the post office. It was wise for senior members of the Guild to stay abreast of what was going on locally.

When they were all sitting on the chairs near the front of the church, James welcomed them and said a few words about the importance of prayer, adding, "It's especially important for the village at this particular time. There are changes happening here and also there have been some events which have not been good. We must, as the Bible says, bring our requests, our concerns before God, who will hear our prayer and help us. As this is the first Friday night meeting some of us are feeling a bit nervous, maybe it's not the sort of thing we're used to, but I'm sure the Lord will guide us as to what to pray."

He sat down and was quiet for a few moments, praying silently for inspiration, then heard Mary's voice, "I want to say thank you to Jesus for making me well again. I don't know how it happened, but I am so grateful, and I want other people to know that even when you have given up yourself, Our Lord hasn't given up." Her voice broke with emotion, but she was smiling at the same time.

Hilda followed on, "Thank you Lord that when I fell down this week none of my bones were broken. Thank you for sending help and getting me back on my feet. Thank you that nothing will stop your work, your mission in this world."

Listening to the prayers, James was amazed. He had half-expected that there would merely be a long 'shopping list' of petitions, but instead the first prayers were packed with heartfelt thanks.

Anna prayed next with emotion in her voice, "Thank you Jesus," she prayed, "for saving me when I couldn't help myself."

Then Jonah prayed, "Thank you for dying for me, for opening up my eyes."

James was moved by the raw nature of the prayers. Each person, one by one, was being completely open and unguarded as they prayed. Even the woman who he had never seen in the church before prayed a simple prayer of thanks. The atmosphere in the church was worshipful, intense, powerful as they poured out to God their thanks and longings for the presence of God to drive out anything unwholesome from the area. They prayed for the people, for the church, and for what was happening to the land where the old pilgrims' church stood.

The only person who was silent throughout the proceedings was Harold Williams. He sat slightly behind the semicircle of chairs where the rest of the people were. He listened astonished at the fervour and outpouring of faith from the others. He had never witnessed anything like this before. He had always considered it a good thing to be in the Church of England but thought of it as a kind of allegiance to English heritage and history, not to a way of living, and certainly not to this kind of faith. He did not understand it and felt a complete outsider.

Some time later James glanced at his watch and was amazed to see it was already eight o'clock. He waited for a pause in the prayers and then suggested they said the Lord's Prayer together to end the prayer meeting. James led them as they prayed. Those who were not familiar with the words listened. Then they got up from their seats, not in a hurry to leave despite knowing that the freezing wintry weather was waiting for them outside, meaning their journey home was getting worse by the minute. There was still a buzz of something like excitement in the air. James watched as various individuals introduced themselves to others they did not know. He caught Meg's eye, "Meg – good to see you – you must have the evening off from your duties at the Mason's Arms." She looked uncomfortable, "I don't work there any more," she said.

"I see. Sorry, have I hit a raw nerve?"

"In a way – yes. It's complicated. I can't really explain it in a few words." She looked at him with concern and confusion in her eyes. "It's something to do with the Guild. I don't know whether you've heard of it. Perhaps I should talk to you about it one day."

"Do. Pop round to the vicarage and have some coffee. I'm at home tomorrow morning – could you come?"

"Yes, I'd like to, thank you."

Then Meg went over to Steven's mother, who Hilda was talking with. "I mustn't interrupt, just wanted to say it's good to see you." On an impulse, she hugged her warmly. Hilda watched approvingly, "You two obviously have met before."

"Yes, not in quite such a comfortable situation. It was in the hospital."

At that moment James raised his voice over the sound of conversation, saying, "If anyone needs a lift home, bearing in mind this awful weather, please tell me, it's no trouble."

The older ladies present made a beeline for James, Hilda was about to say she would walk but was pre-empted by Morag, who said decisively that she would not hear of it.

James saw Sam and Mary Williams were talking with the older gentleman who he thought was vaguely familiar but couldn't remember who he was. He went towards them to introduce himself, but Harold Williams was already leaving and had gone out of the door before James could catch him. "Did you get his name?" he asked them.

"Yes, I did," said Sam lightly, "Harold Williams, my father."

"Wonderful, I thought I recognised him – your whole family is gravitating towards the church!"

"I think my father might take a bit longer to become a regular," laughed Sam, "But it's amazing that he came tonight. Normally it's just Christmas and maybe Easter. Not that I've been any better, I must admit. I've left all the church stuff to Mary and thought that would do for both of us."

"But you're here tonight, and your father was here too – goodness, God is really on the move in the Williams family."

Jonah waited at the back of the church hoping to catch Anna. She was talking to two of the older members of the congregation. After a couple of minutes they began to walk towards the door and Anna saw him waiting. She smiled at him, "Hello, Jonah."

He decided not to ask her anything related to their last conversation, but to keep to less sensitive subjects. "It was good this evening, wasn't it? I've never been to anything like this before, well obviously I haven't. Anyway, I'm going to keep coming to these Friday nights."

"So am I, and I think we'll see all sorts of things happening because of the prayer."

They walked out through the church door together and were hit immediately by a blast of bitterly cold wind. Jonah turned the collar of his jacket up and Anna felt in her pockets for her gloves. "It's absolutely freezing!" exclaimed Anna. Jonah walked with Anna to her car and risked saying, "Have you thought any more about what I asked you?"

"I have, Jonah, and I'd like to talk to you properly about it."

"That's good – we could talk now if it wasn't so cold – we'd probably die from hypothermia." He grinned at her. She was starting to shiver. "You'd better get in your car." He took her gloved hand in his for a second, "Let's talk soon."

He watched as she drove away, unaware that they in turn had been watched. A sleek black car had been parked a short distance from the church, positioned so that the occupant could see the people as they left. When Anna's car drove off, the black car followed it, leaving a cloud of exhaust behind it in the frozen air.

James got back later than Anna, having delivered two elderly people safely home after locking up the church in Netherton. As he came into the vicarage he commented to Anna, "Did you see a black car just now? I thought it might have been a late caller at the vicarage – it seemed to be waiting just outside on the road."

"No, I didn't see a car – it must have been for one of the other houses nearby."

"Hmm, funny, I thought it was familiar somehow, but yes, you must be right."

They began to talk about the evening – they were excited about it. It felt as though things were finally beginning to move forward for the church. James went to bed that evening with a light heart, while Anna thought of Jonah's hand holding hers.

Chapter Twenty-Two

At eleven o'clock Meg rang the vicarage doorbell. James went to answer it, "Come in, Meg, good to see you. Would you prefer to be in the study or the kitchen? I ought to warn you, the kitchen is much warmer!"

"The kitchen then, easy decision," said Meg, laughing.

"I was hoping you would say that," said James, smiling. He looked relaxed in a warm woollen jumper and jeans. This look suits him, thought Meg – it must be a relief to not be wearing a clerical collar for a while.

James called out to Anna; did she want some coffee?

"Yes please!" came the reply from upstairs. "I'll be down in a minute."

He had put three cups of coffee on the table by the time Anna arrived in the kitchen.

"Meg! Nice to see you – I didn't know you were here. Should I leave you in peace to talk, Dad?"

"Meg does need to talk to me about something."

Meg looked at Anna, "Actually it would be nice if Anna stayed."

Anna sat down with them, and Meg started to talk.

"You asked me last night about whether I had an evening off from working at the Mason's Arms. I couldn't explain with other people overhearing. I don't work there any more – I've been sacked."

"*Sacked*? Why?" James sounded incredulous.

"I was sacked for not doing what I was told."

"As in, not carrying out your duties?"

"My duties are serving meals, helping out behind the bar when needed, keeping the place neat and tidy, being welcoming to customers. I was still doing all those things."

"So was it something else that you were told to do?"

"It was on a Guild night – did you know the Guild meets at the Mason's Arms?"

"The Guild... that's the second time it's been mentioned to me this week, but no, I had no idea where it meets."

"There's a large room upstairs where they all gather, whether it's the full meeting or the inner circle."

"The *inner circle* – that sounds quite sinister."

"I've always accepted the Guild as a bit peculiar but basically harmless, but recently I've changed my mind. It's strictly men-only so I never hear anything about what goes on at the meetings, and even if I was a man, I still wouldn't know – it's very secretive. What led to George Wright sacking me happened on an evening when the inner circle was meeting in the upper room."

James and Anna listened, fascinated.

Meg continued, "I'd prepared the room as usual; six members were upstairs that night and the door to the room was closed. The men never let me see what's going on, so I was surprised when they called me upstairs."

Their conversation was interrupted by the front doorbell. James got up from the table, "Sorry, I'll just go and see who that is."

He hurried to open the door but when he did so, found there was nobody there, just a bouquet of flowers with an envelope attached. He picked it up and went back inside, calling out to Anna, "It's for you Anna!"

Anna came from the kitchen but stopped when she saw her father holding the flowers. "Who are they from," she asked.

"I don't know," said James, "you'd better have a look."

He held out the bouquet, expecting her to take it.

"Can you look to see who sent them?" said Anna, not sounding at all pleased.

"Are you sure? I'm sure it's meant for your eyes only."

"Please Dad."

"All right." He detached the dainty envelope from the cellophane wrapping and opened it, removing the small card from inside. He unfolded it. On it was written two words, *Remember me.*

"It doesn't give a name." He handed it to Anna. She looked at it despondently, then gave it back to her father, "Can you get rid of them please? I don't want them."

She turned and moved in the direction of the staircase as though she was going to go up to her room, but her father stopped her, "Anna, why is this upsetting? Please tell me."

She turned round and looked at him, a dull defeated look on her face, "It's him, Dad – Martin. I told him I wanted him to leave me alone, but he won't."

"Then I shall have to speak to him."

"No, don't."

"Why not? I'm your father – if someone is bothering you I can tell them to stop."

"Just leave it, Dad. He'll give up in the end. I hope." She sounded unconvinced by her own words. She continued going up the stairs leaving her father standing at the bottom .

He called after her, "Come back to the kitchen with Meg and me, Anna, and finish your coffee. Don't go to your room on your own."

She spoke to him down the stairs, her voice sounding agitated, "I'm not a child, Dad. There are some things I have to sort out on my own."

He persisted, calling after her, "Perhaps that's part of our difficulty, Anna, trying to sort things out on our own instead of sharing them, tackling them together."

He heard her pause, and then begin coming back down slowly. She still looked sad and burdened but put her arms round her father.

He patted her on the back gently, "Come on, let's go and hear the rest of what Meg needs to tell us."

They went back to the kitchen together. James put the flowers in the bin by the back door, watched by Meg, who looked bemused by this odd action. She looked from one to the other and asked, "Have I chosen a bad time to come?"

"Nothing to worry about just now," said James. "Sorry, we interrupted you."

Meg hesitated, feeling less confident now about what she was about to say.

"You were telling us about the 'inner circle'. You can't stop now Meg," he encouraged.

She started again, "It was quiet in the pub, and nobody wanted any drinks at that moment when George Wright came back downstairs and said, 'Can you just come upstairs for a few moments?' I'd no idea what they wanted, but it was very unusual. I assumed they must want something more to eat or drink, but when I went into the room, they wanted to ask me questions."

"What did they ask?" James was frowning, suspecting he was about to hear something shocking, or at least inappropriate.

"About the attacks that have happened recently in the village. They wanted me to give them information about the people involved, especially the boy who was beaten up on the village green."

"What did they want to know?"

"His name and address."

"Do you know why?"

"I don't know. It could have been to offer help of some sort I suppose but the way they spoke to me was intimidating. They

239

behaved as though they had the right to make me answer their questions, and their leader acted like a judge. They sat around in their comfortable chairs while I stood in front of them and was questioned, as though I was in court. It felt horrible. When they wanted Steven's details, I felt I shouldn't reveal them. I wanted to protect him from these men."

"You're not saying you think they had anything to do with him being beaten up?"

"I don't think so. But I felt it would be wrong to just give Steven's name and address to them. The way they expected me to obey them was *weird*. So I refused. Fortunately at that moment there was a sound of breaking glass in the bar, so I had an excuse to come back downstairs. Then, a few days later, I was given the sack."

"Without giving a reason?"

"He said he would have to let me go, nothing he could do about it, he'd give me a month's pay but wanted me to leave immediately. When I tried to get him to tell me why, he said part of my job was to do whatever was required, and that I hadn't done that."

"And you're sure it was connected to the Guild's inner circle?"

"Yes I am. When John Miller – he seems to be their leader – passed me in the bar the other day, he barged into me, quite aggressively. I'm sure he did it on purpose. I know it sounds fanciful, but I think the whole thing's to do with wanting to control people."

"I see. Another weird aspect of this place."

"You don't think I'm crazy then?"

"No, not at all. I'm sorry you've lost your job, Meg, but from what you've told us you may be better off without it. It seems the Mason's Arms is not a very pleasant place to be."

"I wanted you to know about it because I thought it somehow is—" she paused, trying to think of the correct word, "*connected* to the other things some of us are concerned about. Do you think it could be?"

"I'm not sure. I don't want to start being someone who sees a demon popping up behind everything that goes wrong, but I fear there is something about this area, something menacing, something spoiling things."

Meg looked disturbed, "Most people would laugh at what we're thinking, wouldn't they?"

James put his arm around Meg's shoulders reassuringly. "Perhaps they wouldn't laugh if they lived in Netherton. Don't worry, you're not going crazy, or anything like that. I'm really glad you came to the vicarage."

She looked happier, but then frowned as she said, "Did you know a member of the Guild comes to church?"

It was James' turn to look disturbed. He thought for a moment, then remembered what Sam Williams had said about his father Harold.

Meg continued, "I noticed him at the evening of prayer on Friday – Harold Williams. He's one of the inner circle."

"Goodness me. The Guild has tentacles that reach everywhere, it seems."

Anna had been listening without comment all the time. Now she suggested quietly, "Can we pray about all this? It feels distinctly creepy."

They sat down again, each closing their eyes, about to pray. Then Anna opened her eyes again, saying, "Do you mind if we join hands while we're praying – it would to be good to show we're together in this."

They joined hands across the kitchen table and bowed their heads in prayer. They prayed urgently, just like on the previous Friday, asking for protection and strength. James prayed that God would give them insight and wisdom as to what to do next.

After ten minutes or so they got up from the table, Anna wiping a tear away, hoping it would go unnoticed.

"I must go," said Meg, "I've taken up enough of your time."

"It's been very good," reassured James. Anna hugged Meg, "I'm sorry about the job, although I agree with Dad – I'm sure God has a better job for you."

*

It was another Guild meeting night. Now that he was working on his own at the pub, George Wright had no choice but to do the preparations for the meeting hours in advance before the pub opened. He was annoyed – he shouldn't have to do this kind of work – he was the pub *landlord*. He was above kneeling down on the floor sweeping the hearth. Over the years he had become oblivious to the extent of menial tasks Meg covered. Now she was gone he was exhausted trying to do all the endless cleaning and tidying she had done. He knew his efforts did not come near to matching her standards, and he had given up offering bar meals. Some of the customers had remarked on the difference since Meg had left.

"You lost a hard worker there, George, you should have given her a pay rise. I bet she got a better offer somewhere else," one commented.

"All right, all right, people make their own choices, don't they?" he replied testily, implying that Meg had left of her own accord.

"The place is different without her, somehow more... *miserable,*" continued the customer, undeterred by Wright's ill temper.

Now, struggling to get the upper room ready, he was wondering what he was going to do when the Guild members arrived and he had to singlehandedly look after the pub and act as secretary. He had tried to find a replacement for Meg, but without success. He knew that the customers were right – Meg had been an extremely capable and cheerful worker – but instead of feeling a sense of fondness or gratitude, he merely felt irritated that he could not use her services any more. There must have been a lot more to her than he had realised. Somehow she had defied the Master, and it was this that had led to him kneeling on the floor now, sweeping the large hearthstone in front of the fire. When he attempted to light it, having stacked plenty of dry wood in the grate, it refused to catch. He bent down to blow on it and only succeeded in making a blast of smoke and ash come out of the fire all over him. He coughed, cursing Meg for being the cause of so much trouble.

Later, when all the men had assembled upstairs and were drinking their customary glass of wine or beer before the meeting, George Wright excused himself for a moment and hurried back down to the bar. He looked around at the small number of people sitting in the pub. Was there a regular customer who he could ask to cover for him? It was a desperate measure, but it was the best he could think of. Rob Beccles and Tim Hallthorpe were sitting in the corner, laughing coarsely at some joke. Could he trust them to be honest? He wasn't sure. Malcolm and Barbara Morton sat at the opposite end, away from the young men. Perhaps Malcolm would help out – he certainly wouldn't pocket any cash. He walked over to them.

"Evening, Malcolm, Barbara," he said pleasantly, "I find myself in a very embarrassing situation this evening. I'm on my own here, and I must attend to a special meeting upstairs. I don't suppose, Malcolm, you could keep an eye on the bar for a short time? We're very quiet here this evening, but if there was any emergency, I would come straight down again."

Malcolm looked quite shocked. "I'm not sure I would know what to do, George. I've never stepped behind a bar before. Is Meg unwell?"

Wright didn't hesitate to lie, "Left me in the lurch, Malcolm."

"Really?" He sounded concerned, "There must be a good reason, I'm sure. Have you tried ringing her? Meg has always struck me as a reliable person. She could have been taken ill." There was genuine concern in Malcolm's voice. Wright tried to keep the irritation out of his.

"No, Malcolm, she's not ill. If you would just help me out this once."

Malcolm got up, looking at Barbara to see her reaction. She didn't raise any immediate objection, so he walked gingerly over to the bar and passed through the lifted section which gave access to where the beer taps were, their brasswork still polished from when Meg had worked there.

"Just stand here Malcolm for a while. Perhaps nobody will want anything at all. I'll be back down as soon as I can." Wright abruptly left the bar.

To Malcolm's surprise Barbara had not uttered a word. He stood behind the bar, straightening his shoulders and adopting a proprietorial air. He ran his fingers over the shining beer taps and then over the keys of the till next to him. Now she came over to the counter and stood opposite her husband.

"I'd never thought I'd see you being a barman, Malcolm. How are you going to deal with awkward customers?" Her tone was for once not barbed with criticism. She looked quite amused by this unexpected turn of events and was enjoying seeing Malcolm in a new light.

He caught this note and said lightly, "Don't worry, Barbara, I'll handle it."

His wife gave him a studied look, "Try getting me a bitter lemon then, with ice,"

Malcolm looked behind him at the glass-fronted fridge containing small bottles of juices. He opened it and took out a slim bottle of bitter lemon, spotting at the same time a long-stemmed glass on a rack above. He held the glass under the ice dispenser next to the fridge, letting a generous amount of ice gush into the glass, then placed it on the counter while he swiftly removed the top from the bitter lemon using the mounted bottle opener under the bar. With a flourish he poured the bitter lemon over the ice so that it reached nearly to the top, but not too full so that he could add, using some metal tongs, the final touch – a fresh slice of lemon. Barbara watched in amazement.

He put it on the bar, "There you are, my dear, that will be one pound and fifty pence."

"How do you know?" asked Barbra.

"I guessed," said Malcolm triumphantly.

Barbara was impressed at her husband's total confidence in a situation he had never been in before, and by his cheek. She rather liked this version of Malcolm.

Malcolm was enjoying being approved of, a rare experience in his marriage in recent years. Buoyed up by his success, he tackled the till next, putting Barbara's money in it and closing it with a satisfying ting!

In truth, there weren't many drinks ordered during the next hour, but the few which were required Malcolm served without hesitation; his usual nervous deference to Barbara had disappeared. Meanwhile she sat on a bar stool watching him.

Upstairs in the upper room the meeting was in progress, George Wright taking notes. There was a separate item for an update on the Bluebird building project – this was of key interest to many of the members who saw it as potentially profitable for them. Fred Roland proudly reported that progress had already been made; the legal side was, he believed, all in order and access to the site had been completed.

One of the men commented, "We could have done the legal side for you, Fred. Who did you use?"

This was the general way business contracts were passed around between the members of the Guild. Discussions at the meetings led directly to deals being done.

"That's good of you," said Fred politely, "another time I may certainly be interested but this time we already had someone working on it."

Some other members had already approached Fred Roland to offer equipment at special prices to be arranged privately among members of the Guild.

Downstairs, all was going smoothly as Malcolm looked after the bar until a customer gave him a twenty-pound note to pay for a bag of crisps. He looked in the till – there wasn't sufficient change left to give to the customer. He would have to ask George for some more.

"Barbara, I must get more change for the till. I won't be a second." Malcolm started up the stairs confidently. As he reached the top and started to walk along the corridor, he noticed dark wooden panelling which lined the walls and the heavy velvet curtains over the windows, the whole ambience being so different to the bar below. There was a hushed reverential quality to the upstairs of the Mason's Arms, as though he had entered a different building altogether. He had a feeling of apprehension and found himself walking on tiptoe towards the heavy wooden door at the end of the corridor. When he reached it he stopped and listened for voices. He moved closer and pressed his ear against the door, finding he could hear the conversation inside. He listened, fascinated.

Towards the end of the meeting the members had the chance to raise any other issues. A point was made about the near demise of the uniformed youth groups. The Guild made an award to the best Scout in the village each year. Many Guild members had once been Scouts themselves and had initially viewed the Guild as a kind of progression from their early years and expected the Guild oath to be not dissimilar to the Scout promise. The discussion became anecdotal, members reminiscing about days gone by when more people were willing to give their allegiance to a cause. Almost unintentionally, Harold Williams, perhaps because he was tired, mentioned that the church in the village was another example, with a congregation almost slipping into nothingness.

At this, John Miller, sitting enrobed in the Master's chair, sneered, "No tears shed for that. Religious foolery. Old biddies mumbling prayers in a boring 'service' nobody wants anyway. We don't want fancy Church of England with its prayer books. We have older ways of respecting and worshipping."

Outside the door, Malcolm raised an eyebrow – what kind of a meeting was this? *Older ways of worshipping*? What did that mean? Was it something to do with the little old church that stood on the hill next to the village?

Harold Williams was surprised by the ferocity of the Master's comment and said with hesitation, "I was only going to add, 'until recently'."

John Miller shot him a look, "What about 'recently'?"

"There's been a surge of interest in the church."

Miller sneered again, "Like what – a flower-arranging festival, or is it baking cakes?"

Harold Williams hesitated again, feeling embarrassed, but not sure why he should be so, "Prayer meetings."

Miller burst out laughing, "That's *really* going to rock the village, isn't it, Harold?"

His tone was mocking, intended to pour scorn on both Harold and the small local church.

Harold gathered up what remained of his dignity, "I have always believed it was quite possible to be a dedicated brother in the Guild and an Anglican. In fact, I don't generally attend the church, but I feel I have a place there."

"That's the point, brother," Miller was speaking in a patronising tone. "We do have a place there, a *right* there, like all over this village."

Harold thought hard, trying to unpick what lay beneath their young Master's comment – was he saying he thought it was absolutely acceptable to belong both to the Guild and the church? or was he saying something very different, that the Guild had rights and influence over the church? Over all the years he had come to Guild meetings, Harold had never considered this, but now it seemed important, something that needed to be sorted out.

He looked down the table at the Master, sitting in the great carved chair, and noticed how unpleasant the sight was – there was a dark and brooding quality he'd not been aware of before. What had always seemed redolent with time-honoured tradition and order now looked different. What had changed? Was it the arrival of this new younger Master, or had he, Harold, changed?

John Miller was watching him, "Harold."

Harold jumped at the sound of his name.

"You've reminded me of something we should have had on the agenda." He turned his head to look pointedly at George Wright. "Put this on for every meeting, Secretary – new members of the Guild. It's time to expand, gather more strength. Can't have the church mice outnumbering us, can we?" He laughed again, derisively.

Why does the church bother him so much? wondered Harold. He thought back to the conversation within the inner circle and Miller's account of his family's hatred of the Haliwells.

"Harold!" Miller's voice broke through the haze of Harold's private thoughts. "Are you still with us?"

Harold sat up straighter in his chair, embarrassed. "I'm sorry, Master, my thoughts were wandering – it must be my age."

Miller grinned, "Just what I was thinking. Before you nod off–" he chuckled, taking the edge off his cutting remark, "I was thinking

246

that it's time to invite your son, Sam. Surely you want to share the benefits of the brotherhood with future generations of your own family."

"Thank you, Master, I have spoken to him before about it, and I will talk to him again."

"Good. And the rest of us – look out for any likely men who we could include in the Guild. The village is growing, and we must grow too."

Malcolm was developing a stiff neck from keeping his ear pressed against the door. He had given up the idea of disturbing George Wright at this meeting – he couldn't understand what kind of organisation it was that had gathered there but felt uncomfortable at the tone of the conversation. There was a mocking, bullying quality to one of the voices and some of the comments about the local church and the Guild seemed very strange. He moved backwards silently from the door – he sensed that if anyone came out of the room and found him there, they might be very angry. He retreated downstairs.

Back in the bar the customer with the twenty-pound note had looked through his pockets again and found sufficient change to pay for his crisps and left the money on the bar counter.

"You took a long time," said Barbara, but not unkindly. "Don't worry, I watched things for you."

She looked at her husband, this new, impressively capable version, and noticed he was thinking hard about something. "What is it? Has something happened?"

"Yes. Something about George's meeting. Something... not right about it."

"What kind of meeting was it?" She asked, all attention.

"I'm not sure. I heard them mention something called *The Guild*. I can't describe it, but it sounded like a secret society of some sort, and it seemed... a bit nasty somehow."

"Really? Did you go into the meeting?"

"No," he dropped his voice, "I listened at the door."

Barbara giggled. Malcolm smiled at her conspiratorially. He hadn't heard her giggle like that for years. Something about the events of this evening had revived Barbara, brought back aspects of her that he hadn't seen for a very long time. The middle-aged, neurotic Barbara had been rolled back, and a younger light-hearted Barbara been revealed.

247

"Malcolm, I can't believe it, first you've suddenly become a barman, now you're eavesdropping at people's doors, listening in on private meetings! All in one evening – you wild thing!"

Both of them started to laugh, which is how George Wright found them when he re-entered the bar. He looked at them suspiciously, "What's going on here? Have you been helping yourself to a few drinks?"

This remark caused them both to laugh harder, Malcolm just managing to say, "No George, haven't touched a drop. How was your meeting?"

This caused a fresh gale of laughter to burst out of the normally miserable and critical Barbara. Wright watched her, "There's something going on around here that I don't get. I think you two ought to go home. Thanks for stepping in. I'll get a new barmaid soon."

Malcolm and Barbara collected their coats, still smiling. Wright was convinced they must be drunk, whatever they said – he had never seen them so united and happy. Another unexpected change, he thought resentfully, things getting out of control. What was happening? The settled order was changing.

They hurried home through the frozen streets, the frosty air sparkling around them. They too sensed that things were changing and were excited – they had been pulled out of the rut they had lived in for so long. But would they be able to sustain it in the familiarity of their home?

Twenty minutes later they were standing in their kitchen together, waiting for their bedtime milk drinks to heat up in the microwave oven. Normally Malcolm would have done this on his own, and carried their drinks through to the living room where Barbara would be watching the television. Tonight, however, was different. They didn't want to sink back into their routine – it was as though they had been woken up and didn't want to go back to sleep again.

"So, Malcolm, tell me more about what happened – what did you hear when you went upstairs?"

The microwave's *ping* signalled that their drinks were ready. "Shall we have our drinks here, and I'll tell you all about it?"

Barbara sat down eagerly, taking her mug between her hands and looking at him brightly. She looks so much younger tonight, thought Malcolm, my Barbara.

He sat down opposite her and began, "You remember I said they referred to *the Guild*? I think that must be the name of the meeting, or group. You know we have seen men slipping up the stairs next to the bar on other evenings? I've never really thought much about it, just assumed it was a committee of a local group needing somewhere to meet. But I think it's more than that, a secret organisation."

Barbara's eyes widened with increased interest, "Good heavens, what have you stumbled on, Malcolm?"

"They were holding a formal meeting, with an agenda, and talking about things going on in the village, and about having influence over things."

"What sort of things?"

"For example, the building development next to the village. They're involved in it."

"So it's not just an outside company which happens to be building some houses here – they've actually got dealings with it?"

"Yes, it sounded like it. There's *behind the scenes* deals going on."

"What else were they talking about?"

"The church."

"The church here in Netherton?"

"Yes, they seemed to hate it, well some of them. There was one who sounded like their leader who talked about it really bitterly, as though he wanted to get rid of it."

"How awful. Do you think they know it's mainly a group of old ladies?"

"Actually, that's one of the things that seems to be getting them angry. Recently the church has started growing, one of them said so."

"Malcolm, you don't think they'll do something to the church, they're not terrorists, are they?"

"No, I don't think so, I think they're people from the village, or at least from nearby. They sounded like local people."

"What are we going to do?"

"I hadn't thought about doing anything."

"Malcolm, after what you've been up to this evening, I would have thought you'd want to spring into action."

"Would you Barbara?" he sounded pleased. "Well then, what I suggest is...." He paused, having no idea what to say but wanted to sound decisive. In the nick of time, an idea occurred to him. "We will start attending the church. We will join the congregation to take a stand against this vindictive secret society."

Barbara agreed. "Let's find out when the next church service is. Do you think it's too late to go and look at the notice board outside the church?"

They both laughed at their new carefree attitude – where would this change in direction lead them?

*

Harold walked through the dark village streets back to his house, trying to make sense of what had troubled him about tonight's meeting. His head ached with the strain of attempting to step back from all the assumptions he had held on to for so many years. He was struggling to take an objective view. The night was very cold, and he felt more alone than usual. His route took him past the parish church, and he paused for a minute, looking at the building, remembering the prayer meeting a few days ago. He had felt alone that night too, as though he didn't belong. Tonight at the Guild meeting he had experienced the same feeling, but why? He had been a member of the Guild for sixty years, almost a lifetime. At twenty-one he had been so proud to be included as a member. The ritual of joining had been an exciting event, calling to mind the Knights of the Round Table, belonging to an elite group with their own way of life, sworn to stand together against all odds. It appealed to his youthful sense of romance and passion. The letting of blood, mixing it with that of his brothers, seemed a noble thing for men to do. Over the years he had enjoyed a level of friendship with the other brothers. Nothing too close, but enough to enjoy meeting together and bringing their wives to social events, especially the grand annual ball which the women particularly appreciated. He had never thought deeply about the words of the oath or the allegiance he had bound himself into, until death and even beyond.

Harold had been christened in the parish church here at a time when this was the normal thing for every baby born in the area. His attendance had been sparse, but he had counted his appearance at Christmas and the Harvest Festival as sufficient for the average Anglican. His attendance at the prayer meeting was without doubt a new experience. He felt some of the most enduring habits of his life were being disturbed; he had the sensation that he was rocking on his foundations. Was this how you were bound to feel as you moved through old age – helpless, disturbed, rootless? His feet were getting stiff with cold as he stood on his own in the dark.

"Come on, old man," he said to himself, "Time to go home."

As he approached his house, he could see someone walking towards him. His eyes were not as good as they used to be, and he strained to see whether it was anyone he knew. Then the person called out to him, "Dad! Are you OK?"

He had never felt so pleased to hear his son's voice. "Samuel!" He held out his hand towards him, and his son hurried forward and told hold of his arm.

"It's late for you to be out on a night like this, Dad. I thought it might be a Guild night and I had a feeling you were still out, so I thought I'd walk round and check. When I found you weren't home, I started searching the streets looking for you."

Normally Harold would have chided him for fussing, but tonight he held on to Sam's arm, grateful for his concern. Sam insisted on coming inside Harold's house and making him a hot drink. He sat down opposite his father, "Is everything all right, Dad? Are you feeling well?"

"Just age I suppose. A feeling that things are crumbling."

"Crumbling?"

"Yes – things I thought were solid crumbling around me, things I thought were all right." Harold looked at his son with a deeply tired look. Then he tried to rouse himself, not wanting to be feeble, "How is Mary?"

"She's fine, thanks."

"It hasn't... *worn off* then?"

"The prayer for healing you mean? No." Sam laughed. "It worked, Dad, I don't know how exactly, but it did, and I've got a healthy wife again."

Harold shook his head, thinking, another sure thing crumbling around him. He had got used to Mary's ill health. There were rare times of slight improvement when their hopes were raised, only to be dashed again when Mary returned to her sick bed. This time however, she had apparently become strong again and showed no sign of weakening. Her attitude had changed too, but how? It was beyond him and made his head start aching again.

Sam was talking again, "Dad, I can see you're feeling rotten at the moment, but I have an idea about something which I think will help."

His father looked up at him, his white hair, normally neatly combed, looking unkempt where he had been running his fingers through it.

251

"I think you should come to the evening communion service this next Sunday. Shall I come and walk there with you?"

"Let me think about it."

"OK." Sam knew never to try to push his father. He had said as much as he dared. Harold was a very determined man; he must make up his own mind.

Chapter Twenty-Three

Monday afternoon. Anna arrived home just as it was getting dark. It was bitterly cold, and she didn't have her coat on. She ran up the steps to the front door of the vicarage carrying a bag of arts and crafts materials, shivering as she tried to find the right key for the front door among the keys on her key ring. She was just about to put it in the lock when someone ran up the steps behind her and snatched the keys out of her hand. She gasped and turned her head to look straight into the face of Martin Fielding.

"Give them back to me!"

"Steady," he said smoothly, "I'm just trying to help. Let me unlock the door for you."

"No. Give them back to me."

He ignored her and put the key in the lock, then opened the door for her. She didn't think quickly enough to realise what he was doing; as she went inside, he stepped in behind her, pulling the door shut after him, and re-locking it from the inside. Panic gripped her as she realised she was locked inside the house with him. She dropped her bags on to the floor, the contents spilling out around her feet, and lunged towards him, trying to grab her keys from him. He held them above his head out of her reach.

"Wouldn't you like to make me some coffee, Anna. Come on, isn't hospitality a Christian virtue?"

He whisked the keys down from over his head and put them in his trouser pocket. He folded his arms and stood in front of the locked door, a half-smile still on his face.

Anna stood still, determined not to do what he wanted, then realised if they went through to the kitchen perhaps she could try to make her escape through the kitchen door. "All right, I'll make you coffee."

She went ahead of him towards the kitchen. Once there she picked up the kettle to take it to the sink to fill it. He followed her and stood behind her as she held the kettle under the tap, moving closer to her until she could feel his breath on the back of her neck. "I still think you're beautiful," he said in a low voice.

Hurry up, hurry up, she thought as she watched the water filling the kettle. It seemed to slow down as she watched it. He reached around her to the tap and turned it off.

"I don't need coffee... you know what I need – what we both need." His tone was threatening. He moved closer, blocking her against the sink, hands reaching over her, touching her, pressing against her. Inside she was screaming. She knew she must act quickly. She tightened her grip on the kettle and with all her strength twisted, jabbing her elbow up into the side of his neck and then trying to follow through with the kettle, but only managing to throw the cold water over him, the kettle clattering on to the hard floor. He shouted and lifted up his arm. It carved a wide arc in the air, backhanded, and the back of his hand came slamming into the side of her face. She fell against the table, and then on to the floor. He sprang towards her, but the water from the kettle had split all around him, and he slipped, landing on his back. At that moment there was a noise in the hallway and the sound of footsteps running towards the kitchen. From where she was lying on the floor she saw her father arrive and stand still for a second, framed in the doorway of the kitchen.

"What's happening?" he demanded.

As James came into the kitchen, he saw Martin Fielding crouching on the floor, apparently helping Anna up. James heard him saying, "Darling, are you all right?" then watched as he turned round and announced to James sheepishly, "I'm so sorry, we were filling the kettle together and somehow spilled some water and slipped!"

James didn't answer but went over to Anna, "Anna, you're injured. Come and sit down." He pulled out a chair and helped her on to it.

Fielding looked concerned, "Goodness, you're right, we shouldn't have been messing around in the kitchen." He managed to put into his voice a blend of concern mixed with embarrassment, hinting that they had been caught in a moment of passion which had somehow led to them losing balance.

Anna was shaking, holding on to her father. He said to her gently, "I think I should call an ambulance to check what damage has been done. Stay sitting down. Don't try to move."

"No, don't, Daddy. Stay with me. *Please.*"

"I'll only be a minute." He hesitated, noticing she had called him *Daddy* – she hadn't done so for years. He removed her hands from him as she was clinging to him like a small child and went into the hallway to use the phone. He had moved only a few paces when something made him pause and go back to the kitchen. What he saw astounded him. Fielding hurtled across the kitchen towards Anna and put his hands tightly, forcibly, around her head, kissing her on the mouth. He saw her struggle against him, unable to make a sound.

"Fielding! Leave my daughter alone, you idiot."

Fielding spun round, "I'm trying to comfort her. What did you think I was trying to do?"

James, normally mild-mannered, was furious, "If you don't get out of my house by the time I count to three I will have every police officer in this county after you. Get out!"

Fielding's face darkened with rage, and there was a moment's silence as he appeared to weigh up what to do next, then he pushed his way past James into the hallway and out of the front door.

James followed him and bolted it after him with the large iron bolt which they had never used, but now he was pleased to have. He returned to look after Anna.

"I'll call that ambulance now."

"No, Dad— please. Let me just sit down and be quiet for a while. Did you lock the door?"

"Yes, I used the bolt. Anna, the front door was locked when I came home – I thought you weren't home. I respect your wish for some privacy, but..."

"No, no, it wasn't anything like what he said." She was speaking in short breaths, gasping for air, "*He* locked the door, not me... and he took my keys... wouldn't give them back... and, oh no! – he's still got my keys in his pocket! He's got a front and back door key."

James was pacing up and down the kitchen, "So you're telling me he locked you in here with him – against your will? Tell me honestly Anna. If it was some kind of lovers' game, just tell me. I need to know what is going on."

"It was totally, *totally* against my will. I never wanted to see him again. He just came up behind me outside the house and grabbed the keys from me, and got me inside, then locked the door. I came to the kitchen to try to get near the back door. He'd said at first he wanted coffee, so I had started to fill the kettle, but I was trying to work out how to get away from him. He got hold of me – Dad, if you hadn't come home—." Anna put her head in her hands, tears coursing down her face with its painful red mark where Fielding had hit her.

"I'm calling the police."

"But he'll tell them what he told you – that we were in the kitchen messing around – two *lovers* – *ugh!* and they would think you are just an uptight vicar, shocked at his daughter just having some perfectly ordinary fun." Tears rolled down her face and dripped from her chin; she looked totally exhausted, her distress etched deeply on her face. She sighed, her breath shaking, "He's so good at lying."

James stopped pacing and sat down. "It can't just be left, Anna. From what you've told me, he is dangerously obsessed with you. People can get restraining orders against former boyfriends who won't leave them alone."

James made Anna some strong tea with sugar and sat with her while she drank it. His own heart was racing, his imagination working overtime, thinking that this kitchen, the vicarage kitchen, could have been the scene of a horrible violent crime if he hadn't changed his mind and not made the last visit of the day. The thought struck him that his arrival home at that moment was not pure chance – he had been brought back home. God had not abandoned Anna to the evil advances of this violent man, he had sent James home to protect her.

"Anna, before I call the police, we should thank God for protecting you."

They held hands and gave thanks that Anna was safe, even though she was shaken and bruised. They asked for protection, for themselves and all the members of the church. Then James went to the phone and called the local police. He explained there had been an intruder at the vicarage who had... then he had struggled for the right words... had he *attacked* Anna? Or was it more *threatened* to attack? Should he tell them that Fielding had locked the door, trapping Anna in the vicarage with him – he knew Fielding would say he had been helping Anna as her hands were full, and he believed they locked the door for security. Even while he was talking, James realised almost every aspect would be twisted and explained away by Fielding. He would say he had slipped Anna's keys in his pocket absentmindedly. The officer asked, "Do you know the identity of this person?"

James said, "Yes, I do."

"Is anyone injured?"

"No, shaken up, scared, some bruises."

"Is he, I'm assuming it's a 'he', a relation or friend of the family?"

"He is a former friend of my daughter's."

"Former *boyfriend?*" The policeman's tone was unsurprised, accustomed to calls like this. "I see.... Am I right in thinking he has now left, and the young woman is safely at home with you?"

"Yes, that's right."

"That's good. What we do in cases like this is log the name, address, time of the incident, and then get our family liaison officer to call and discuss the situation with the family. Sometimes it's just a one-off, so to speak. The unfortunate aftermath of a break-up between young people. If there's a recurrence, let us know. Clearly, the young woman's safety is paramount. But you've assured me that she is safe now."

James could only reply, "Yes." Somehow the appalling scene in the kitchen had been reduced to a routine occurrence, familiar to the police.

"An officer will be in touch, Reverend Gilchrist."

James came back into the kitchen, saying, "They're going to send someone round."

"Tonight?"

"No, they don't regard it as an emergency."

"Dad, what about him still having my keys?"

"I didn't tell the police about that. I meant to, but it slipped out of my mind among the other details."

"But they're sending someone round?"

"Yes, but I'm not sure when. We'll get the locks changed. I'll find a locksmith now."

James went to the computer in the study and searched for a local locksmith. Within two hours, the locksmith's van pulled on to the vicarage drive.

Chapter Twenty-Four

Netherton Parish Church looked very festive; every window ledge was decorated with boughs of holly and a tall Christmas tree was adorned with twinkling white lights and handmade decorations. It was the final Sunday evening communion service before Christmas. James looked around at the people who had gathered together in the church; the number had increased again. Meg was there with Steven's mother next to her, accompanied this time by Steven; Sam Williams was sitting beside his wife Mary; Jonah was next to Anna, and there was a middle-aged couple James had never seen before. James had to add some chairs to the semicircle at the front to accommodate them all. He thought he had just squeezed them all in when he heard the sound of the door opening again, and Harold Williams came in quietly and walked to the front.

He addressed the congregation, "Welcome, everybody, it's so good to see the number of Christians here in Netherton growing like this."

He saw out of the corner of his eye the same woman lean towards her husband and whisper, "See – good, isn't it!" He must be sure to catch them afterwards.

The service started. Just as before there was a deep sincerity about the way the people joined in. James felt uplifted. This was how church should be – people gathering to worship with eagerness, wanting to communicate with God.

He gave a short address based on the man who had waiting by the pool of Siloam, hoping to be healed. He emphasised that the man had been sick for thirty-eight years. He noticed that Harold Williams shook his head when James said *thirty-eight* years, and then mumbled something. For a fleeting moment James was concerned that he was ill in some way – he did seem very frail, but then he was very old. He continued, "Then one day Jesus came and spoke to the man, and his life changed. It sounds too simple, but that is all it takes, a meeting with Jesus, and your whole life will never be the same."

He finished his short sermon at that point and announced they would now share the bread and wine together in communion. James pronounced the familiar words again, as he lifted up the small loaf of bread and broke it, saying, "This is my body, broken for you."

He looked round the faces in front of him in the semicircle as he held up the broken bread for them to see, and saw that Harold was weeping, his thin old shoulders racked with sobs and his head bowed. The sobs became audible and people turned to see where the sound was coming from. Sam Williams crossed over to him and put his arm around his father, nodding to James to carry on.

The rest of the communion proceeded without any other dramatic events. There was no way of knowing whether the new couple were Christians, but James always had an open view about who should be welcome to the communion table. He felt sure that Jesus would not prevent anyone from taking part who wanted to do so, even if their level of faith was very small indeed. Malcolm and Barbara came forward with the rest, copying what the others did. When they returned to their seats, they closed their eyes as that seemed to be what was expected. Then Barbara got a shock. Beneath her closed eyelids, a frightening scene was revealed to her. She saw the back of a woman who seemed vaguely familiar. The woman was talking in a very unpleasant way to a man. In fact, the talking was almost all by the woman, who hardly stopped for breath, constantly telling him off. The man was shrinking further and further away from her, his face worn and tired. Abruptly, Barbara recognised the clothes the woman was wearing – they were her clothes!

Somewhere inside her, Barbara felt the pain of recognition, of regret, of shame. In that brief moment she had been shown a picture of what she had become until the strange evening at the Mason's Arms. She never wanted to go back to being that miserable person again. She heard the vicar speaking again; he was saying if anyone would like to take a fresh step of faith and have a new start in their life, there was a special opportunity this evening to do so. Perhaps there was someone here tonight who had never offered their life to Jesus Christ before, putting him first as their Lord. Or perhaps someone who wanted to show a fresh level of commitment to him, deeper than ever before, then anyone would be welcome to show that by coming to kneel in front of the altar and he would pray a prayer of blessing over them.

James had surprised himself in suggesting this, as the thought had not even crossed his mind before the service. But as they got near the end, the inspiration hit him forcibly – he felt he really must give this opportunity to the people. He walked over and stood in front of the altar to see if anyone wished to make this sign of commitment. To his surprise he saw an immediate response. Harold Williams got unsteadily to his feet and began to walk towards the altar, followed by other people. The woman whose name he did not know got up with her head bowed and followed the others. Soon most of the people present had gathered near the altar, kneeling on the long stone step which ran along in front of it, or just on the tiled floor of the church. Many were shedding tears. All looked serious and intent. The atmosphere was quiet and charged with what could only be described as the presence of God. James lifted his hands in a gesture of blessing. He opened his mouth and spoke the words which came into his mind, asking the people to repeat the words, line by line, if they wanted to: "Lord I am sorry for everything I have done which has offended you. Please forgive me. Thank you for shedding your blood for me. I open my heart to you and offer you my life." Then he spoke to the people kneeling on the stone step, "Welcome into the Body of Christ Jesus, who died to save you. To all of you who believe in him – your sins are forgiven, and you are set free; through the blood of Jesus you are now a child of God."

He heard murmurs of Amen, or Thank you, Jesus.

Then he blessed them, stretching his hands out towards them – "May God bless you, the Father, the Son and the Holy Spirit and keep you in His Peace."

Again he heard 'Amen' breathed from the lips of the people kneeling humbly on the cold floor, young and old together. He could feel tears running down his own cheeks. He had never known such a heartfelt response.

Gradually the people got on to their feet again, smiling – many of them exchanged a hug with someone near them. There was no tea or coffee or cake to offer them at the end, as in many churches, and no music either, no comforts at all apart from what God seemed to be pouring out on them directly.

There was a buzz of happy conversation as people gradually picked up their belongings. They all spoke to James before they left, some of them hugging or kissing him. He hardly knew what to say – he had never been embraced, much less kissed, at either of his churches in this area. He smiled at them happily as they left.

As they moved towards the church door, Hilda took the opportunity to speak to Harold, "It's so good that you're here, Harold."

Sam and Mary came to join them. Mary put her arm through Hilda's saying, "Why don't you and Harold both come to supper tomorrow? We are all close neighbours after all, and after all your kindness to me, Hilda, it's the least I can do."

*

The following evening, Hilda arrived at Sam and Mary Williams' house a few minutes before half past seven, looking forward to having an evening meal cooked for her. Harold had already arrived. The table was set beautifully with a white cloth and plum-coloured linen napkins, and Mary had lit a row of tea lights in pretty glass dishes in the middle of the table.

"Mary, you've gone to a lot of effort – everything looks lovely – what a treat!"

"You haven't tasted the food yet, Hilda. You may want to change your mind in a few minutes."

But in fact the meal was delicious. They talked about hobbies, the weather and other light topics as they ate. It was only when they were drinking coffee afterwards that the conversation turned to more serious things. Hilda caused this change by saying across the table to Harold, "Wasn't it wonderful at church last night!"

Harold, not given to sharing personal feelings, looked uncomfortable, and said quietly, "Yes, it was a very good service."

But Hilda was not to be put off so easily, "Now Harold, it was much more than that, and we must give the Lord the credit for it. Let's not be begrudging in our praise and thanks."

"Are you telling me off, Hilda?" asked Harold.

"Not exactly, but I'm too old to beat about the bush. Something astonishing is happening among us, and we should make sure we receive it wholeheartedly."

Sam Williams was quick to agree with her, "Certainly something astonishing is happening in the Williams family – first Mary's health being restored, and now—" he looked at his father for affirmation, "something has happened to you and me, Dad."

Harold looked down at the linen napkin spread across his lap, as though some appropriate words may lie there. "I don't know what to say— I find it hard to talk about it."

"But would you agree it's a good thing that's happening?" asked Hilda more gently.

"I feel as though I'm being torn apart," replied Harold. "Everything I thought was secure is being dismantled, and I feel weak as a baby."

Hilda spoke very calmly, "Dear Harold, what's happening is that you've made a decision to step from the kingdom of darkness into the kingdom of Jesus Christ. That's quite a shock to the system, and there's a battle on to make you change your mind and slip back into the old way."

"I'm eighty-one years old, Hilda – I thought I understood what my life was. But recently it's all been unravelling." It was as though, having begun to talk, Harold wanted to get his story out. The words began to pour out of his mouth, but with pain. "It began before coming to the church on Sunday night. At the Guild meetings, which I've been part of for forty years, I've begun to feel an outsider. I feel *uneasy* about it. It's as though something in me started to shift, and then at the service, I couldn't stop crying. I felt broken. When he said come to the altar, I knew I had to go. It was as though something or somebody lifted me out of my chair and propelled me down to the front. I longed to just kneel there, and say, I've got nothing, I'm at the end of myself."

Hilda reached her hand across the table and put it very gently on his, two old hands together on the tablecloth. "My dear friend, what you've described is what can happen when we know it's time to stop depending on ourselves, on our possessions, our connections, and turn to Jesus to depend on him, his love, his forgiveness, his mercy."

Tears ran down Harold's face again and he nodded.

Hilda continued, "You have been born again. For the years you have left you will live as a new person, together with Jesus, your life connected to his life."

He nodded again.

"And the best bit of all is that one day, you will see him face to face."

Harold looked up at her, a smile beginning to break on his face.

"But you've been through a lot, Harold – your life, your *identity* has changed. But there is help at hand; the Bible teaches us that when we become true followers of Jesus we should be filled with God's Holy Spirit. Would you like that?"

During this conversation both Sam and Mary had been riveted to what Hilda was explaining.

"I'm not sure what that means, but if it's from God it must be good, mustn't it? So I say yes, I would like that."

Sam added, "And me too – what about you, Mary?"

Mary thought it sounded like a good idea, "But where would we have to go for it, Hilda?"

Hilda smiled and got up from the table, "No need to go anywhere, I'll just lay my hands on you and ask the Lord to fill you up with his Holy Spirit."

She went to each in turn, moving round the table and standing next to them, laying her hands on their head and praying simply, asking the Holy Spirit of God to come and fill them.

Afterwards, all three looked excited and happy and said they had experienced a deep sensation of peace as Hilda prayed. Harold added, "I could feel rain falling on me, warm rain."

They didn't want to part company yet, there was such a warm feeling of fellowship. Mary made more coffee and brought it to the table.

"Goodness, I do feel different," commented Harold. He laughed. "What shall I do with myself now!" He looked much more vigorous than earlier on in the evening. Then, serious for a moment, "I suspect there'll be changes."

"That's a good sign," said Hilda.

"The Guild."

"What is it exactly, *the Guild*?" asked Hilda.

"It's an old association of men – I've belonged since a young man. We promise to—" he hesitated, trying to find words to express what the promises entailed.

"Yes?" prompted Hilda, wanting Harold to continue.

"Promise to be loyal to one another, and serve one another's interests, and to be obedient."

"Obedient to?" Hilda was on the scent of something she didn't like the sound of.

"Obedient to the Power over us."

Sam said, "So is that God?"

"I suppose it is, it must be, mustn't it? What else could it mean?"

"I'm afraid there are other powers, Harold. We don't like to think so, but there are, the Bible is quite clear about it, and Jesus talked a lot about it."

"So you're saying we could be pledging ourselves to some other power?"

"Yes, it's quite possible."

"I shouldn't even be talking about what goes on inside the Guild."

"It's a secret gathering, then?"

"Yes. Members only, who have taken the oath."

"The oath of obedience to the Power?" Hilda was paying careful attention to what Harold was describing, "What does that involve?"

Harold felt a strange sensation as he opened his mouth to speak. He put his hand up to his throat, pulling at his collar. His face, looking so much healthier a minute ago, turned pale, and he started to gasp for air. "I can't—"

He began to slip from his chair on to the floor, his body convulsing.

"Mary! Call an ambulance!" In a flash, Sam was on the floor beside his father, trying to comfort him. A choking sound was coming from his mouth, then Sam thought he heard something else, not his father's familiar voice. He moved back from him, startled. "Did you hear that, Hilda?" Sam looked round at her, a look of fright on his face.

Mary had run out of the room to ring for an ambulance.

Down at their feet, Harold was still struggling for breath, and Sam and Hilda heard the strange sound again, almost like an animal.

"That's not your father, Sam."

Hilda moved a little closer and said firmly, "Harold belongs to Jesus Christ, you have no right to be here any more!"

There was the low sound of laughter.

"Be quiet! Only the blood of Jesus has power over this man. In the name of Jesus Christ, leave!"

Sam heard a chilling sound as Harold's whole body shook violently and then, just as abruptly, was still. Standing a few feet away he felt his own body trembling with fear. He tried to speak but his mouth had gone dry.

Mary came back into the room as Hilda was praying aloud over Harold, "The peace and healing power of Jesus upon you and in you, Harold, you are a child of God, your life is hidden with Christ in God." She quoted scripture after scripture over Harold as he lay there as though they were doses of healing medicine.

"Is he alive?" asked Sam.

"Yes – I'm sorry, I should have forbidden it to do that as it left. They like to make a show sometimes."

"What happened just then? That was awful."

"I like to think of it as a bit of spring cleaning. Your father will be much better for it."

Harold gradually sat up on the floor and asked what had happened.

Sam said as calmly as he could, "I'm not exactly sure, Dad – can't really explain, but you fell on to the floor, and Hilda has been praying for you. How do you feel?"

"Help me up, Samuel, and I'll tell you."

With Sam's assistance, Harold got back on his feet, rubbing one or two places on his body. "I think I may get a bruise or two, but I actually feel quite good, very good actually."

He smiled around him at the three of them, "It's been a very encouraging evening, it's done me so much good to be here. A wonderful combination – tasty food, prayer and good company. Time to go now though, my bed is calling me!"

His movements were quite sprightly as he kissed his daughter-in-law and shook hands with his son and with Hilda.

Sam Williams was still concerned and shaken by what had happened, "Dad, let me walk with you, to make sure you get home all right."

"No need at all, Samuel, but if you insist, it would be delightful to have your company."

Mary looked at Hilda, astonished – Harold, although normally polite, never enthused like this. What on earth has happened to him, she wondered, as she watched with the two men go through the front door. "I'd better cancel that call for an ambulance."

*

The following morning, Hilda called at Harold's house to check on his welfare. Although she had encountered similar occurrences to what happened last night with Harold before, she knew such events were all different and sometimes needed extended prayer. It was important to check that Harold had stayed free of what had shown itself the previous evening.

When he answered his door to her knock with a broad smile on his face, she immediately felt herself relax – it was obvious that he was in good shape. He asked her if she would like a cup of coffee. She was happy to accept, hoping that he would want to talk about how he was feeling.

Harold was eager to talk. He brought up the subject of the Guild quite willingly.

"I have made a decision Hilda," he said firmly. "I need to get out of the Guild. It's not what I thought it was. I never thought before that it was... in opposition to Christian belief, but it's all becoming clear to me now."

"Do you mind if I remind you what Jesus said about this sort of thing?"

"He said something about the Guild?" asked Harold, amazed.

"Not exactly, but he said something about not being able to serve two masters. He said you had to decide; you could only serve one of them. I think that applies to belonging to something like the Guild. The Guild wants to claim your total loyalty and obedience. A Christian simply can't give that. What you did at the evening service, Harold, was to put your faith and trust in Jesus, absolutely and totally, and to promise you would follow him, that means obey him. The Guild, it seems to me, wants you and the other men to promise to obey someone or something else, very different to Jesus Christ."

"Yes, I swore loyalty, silence and obedience, and invited punishment if I broke my oath. In fact, Hilda," he sounded troubled now, "it was even worse than that. At the time I thought of it as just an elaborate ritual, but –"

"It was more than that Harold. I don't know how much you remember about what happened last night, but when you swore that oath, you invited a nasty influence into your life, into you, and you needed to get free from it. That's why a particular sort of prayer was needed."

"And it worked, didn't it? I feel like a new man!"

"That's wonderful. That's the power of Jesus to set us free. But it's important not to let that *influence* get a grip again. You must stay away from the Guild, from their rituals, worship, whatever it is."

Harold became thoughtful.

"Is something bothering you?" asked Hilda.

"No, I don't think so. I was just thinking about the links I have with the men of the Guild, asking myself if I would miss them. The whole idea is about brotherhood you see, belonging, looking after each other's interests."

"And what is your answer?"

"I don't think I will miss it at all. Recently some of the conversations troubled me – I'm not sure whether the Guild had changed, got more extreme, or if it was me."

"It's fascinating – the Church is designed to be a kind of brotherhood, and sisterhood, where the members of the body belong together, and look after each other. But it's also much more than that. It looks outwards to care for people who don't belong to the church yet, and maybe never will. To just look after the people on the inside wouldn't be Christlike at all. Jesus came to give his life for us while we were sinners, even, like St Paul, against Christ."

Harold nodded, "I feel I am exchanging a cheap imitation for the real thing."

"What a good way of looking at it."

"The Guild was getting quite interested in the church here as a matter of fact."

"Really? How interesting. In what way?"

"The recent growth in numbers was sparking interest, well, more accurately, *annoyance* among some members."

"Oh dear!" Hilda chuckled. "It really does sound like the spiritual battle again."

Harold looked at her quizzically.

She continued brightly, "In this village, no matter how nice it looks, there is a battle going on between good and evil, and the evil forces are trying to get rid of the presence of the Lord Jesus and his people."

Harold raised his white bristly eyebrows in surprise.

She continued, "So both the old church of St Brannock's up on the hill and the parish church down here in the village are under pressure, but I believe God's Holy Spirit is giving us everything we need to overcome these attacks."

"St Brannock's? Up on the land where new houses are going to be built?"

"Yes, there is a purposeful attempt, put into action by the company who are planning to build on the land where the old church is, to get rid of the pilgrims' church. They have, I believe, tricked the remaining members of the landowning family into signing a contract of sale. However, I have written to the descendent of the Haliwells who have for hundreds of years upheld the Christian heritage here, and I am waiting for a reply from her."

*

Hearing a knock, Hilda opened the front door of her cottage to find a group of people standing on the path waiting. She smiled at them, "Welcome, Friends of St Brannock's."

She ushered them into her living room, counting them quietly as they passed her. Nine. What a good turnout at such short notice, she thought. There was another knock. It was Harold, asking, "Have I got the right day?"

When she had spoken to him previously about the Friends' commitment to preserving the old church and its witness to the surrounding area, suggesting he came to the emergency prayer meeting, he had merely looked at her without giving a firm reply. Clearly he had considered it carefully and now here he was.

"It is certainly the right day, and the right time Harold – so glad you have decided to join us. Go straight into my rather crowded living room and join the others."

When Hilda returned to the group a few minutes later with her tea tray there was a pleasing buzz of conversation. The longstanding members of the group had included Harold with warmth, and he looked quite relaxed now, talking with two gentlemen only a little younger than himself.

She delegated the pouring of tea to another lady, and addressed the group – "Welcome dear friends, and thank you for travelling to Netherton. I realise it is a long way for some of you, but you are committed to this task which God has laid on our hearts, so I know you come willingly. I would like to introduce to you my friend Harold, joining us to pray urgently this morning for the saving of the church building and the high cross and beacon, that they will remain a constant witness to this whole area of the lordship of Jesus Christ."

Hilda spent a few more minutes recapping the latest developments for any who had not heard the details about the activities of Bluebird. Then she mentioned, carefully, that there was a group of people in the village who despised the local church and were against its recent growth.

"We must pray for the protection of God's people here, and for the growth of the kingdom of God in this area. That is why St Brannock's was built in the first place."

Hilda decided not to mention The Guild by name. Perhaps that would be very awkward, and even distracting for Harold, she thought. She wondered if he had officially given his resignation yet, although she knew that in his heart it had already been done.

For the next two hours they prayed fervently about every aspect of the situation, including for Elise Haliwell, that she would know the truth of what was really happening. The time flew by; when the hands of Hilda's grandfather clock showed it was noon, they were surprised that so much time had passed. Hilda urged them to keep up their private prayer and to stay in touch by phone.

"So sorry I don't have a computer," she said, "But Morag here is going to start emailing you all – she's very modern, you know."

Morag snorted at this point, "You could do with catching up yourself, Hilda. Give the quill pen a rest and get a keyboard."

Hilda smiled sweetly, "Perhaps I'll get you to teach me dear."

Chapter Twenty-Five

In the Bluebird building, Wheeler was pacing up and down the board room. The others were sitting round the conference table, but he was too charged with anger and impatience to sit down. He shouted at the people sitting at the table while he paced, "We have three projects in progress at the moment, but the biggest potentially is this Netherton one. Everything is set up, I've fixed the local planning department, the labour and materials are organised and now Kirton's telling me there's still a problem. Do I have to do everything myself?" He stopped for a moment, then aimed a final blast at them, "WELL? Has anyone got anything to say?"

Susan Roland pursed her lips petulantly but kept quiet.

Fred cleared his throat and started hesitantly, "Would it be all right, Arnold, for us to know exactly what Alan Kirton said?"

"*He said,*" began Wheeler, with thick sarcasm, "Some old woman has been in contact with him saying we are tricking the Haliwells."

"If it's just one old person, does that matter very much?" threw in Susan, suddenly feeling brave.

Wheeler looked at her, a pitying look on his face, "Had you never thought that one person, if they get to the press, could damage the project? This old bag has implied that we don't intend to adhere to the restrictions on the land."

Susan lowered her head, her brief burst of confidence over. She returned to obsequiousness, "Of course, Arnold, you're right, I should have realised."

Fred rallied to his wife's defence, "Susan was probably thinking that older people don't always think of things like publicity, the press, social media. But I have an idea, Arnold."

"Tell us then." Wheeler swung round to face Fred.

"Now that I am a member of the local men's group in Netherton, I could find out what the extent of objection to the project is, whether it really is an isolated voice, or a larger protest. Would that be helpful?"

Wheeler moved across to Fred and stretched out his hand. Fred flinched, despite himself, but then saw that a brief smile passed over Wheeler's face as he put his hand firmly on Fred's shoulder.

"Fred, you're worth twice as much as anyone else to me. Everyone else seems to have cabbage between their ears at the moment."

Fred felt an enormous sense of relief, but then thought of Susan. "Susan and I do our best, always. You can rely on us, Arnold."

Wheeler glanced at Susan, then away again. She would have to earn his approval, he thought. A bit of competition would do them all good.

"Find out what you can and get back to me quickly. I want to nip this in the bud."

Fielding sat silently through it all. He knew his turn would come soon. Wheeler stepped closer to him, "And you, my 'fixer'. What about you?"

"I'll get on to it." He felt utterly miserable and frustrated. Somehow he needed to push through and start winning again.

Wheeler's outburst was over. He moved towards the door, his short legs stamping hard on the floor as he went, calling over his shoulder, "I'll be hearing from you soon then."

*

The Mason's Arms was adorned with a few cheap Christmas decorations. The previous year the place had looked warm and seasonal with evergreens brought in by Meg. She had searched local hedgerows, looked for branches with plenty of red berries, and the effect had been lovely. This year was very different. Wright had still failed to find a replacement for her.

Soon after opening, Geoff Crawshaw came in. He sat down on a bar stool without speaking. Wright put a pint of ale on the bar, saying, "All right, Geoff? Had a bad day?"

"Quite a few bad days," answered Crawshaw.

The pub was quiet. There were only two other customers, sitting at the other end of the room. Wright hesitated, then said, "What's troubling you then? It's not like you to look so down."

"Family stuff, that's all."

"How are things with your Mark? Has he settled down?"

"Settled down?" answered Crawshaw, "What do you mean?"

"I was thinking about the bit of bother he'd got involved with."

"Bit of bother – is that what you call it?" Crawshaw sounded irritated.

"Don't talk about it if you don't want to."

Crawshaw tapped his fingers on the bar impatiently, "Give me a whisky with this, George."

He started to drink the whisky saying, "How many years have you been in the Guild, George?"

"Twenty-five years – ever since I took on the Mason's Arms. The previous landlord held the meetings here, and I went from just letting the room out to being a member. Why do you ask?"

"Just been thinking, I suppose."

"What's on your mind? There's obviously something bothering you."

"Feeling low, with everything that's happened."

"Everything?"

"My lad— you know."

"Tell me. Has something happened that I don't know about?"

Wright took a bottle of whisky from behind the bar and re-filled Crawshaw's glass, saying, "It's on the house. You look as though you could do with an extra one. Talk to me if it helps. You know what they say, a problem shared is a problem halved."

"I wish it was that simple. I know my lad is not always what he should be. I'm not defending what he did, but what's been done to him now—" He stopped abruptly and looked the other man in the eyes. "Are we talking as friends, or as members of the Guild?"

Wright was silent for a moment, then said slowly, with a touch of resignation, "You know the answer to that, don't you?"

Crawshaw nodded, swigged down the rest of his whisky and stood up. "I'd better go, before I say anything I shouldn't say."

He left quickly, his shoulders down, looking like a man defeated by life's concerns. He would return to a wife with whom he couldn't share his troubles either. At the end of the evening, after more whisky, he would go to bed to lie in the darkness, his eyes open, unable to sleep, thinking about what had happened to his wayward son. Perhaps he should feel satisfied that he had had his comeuppance, that having gone to "give some trouble" to some unfortunate teenager he had received the just punishment ordered by the Guild. But it all seemed so wrong. His son had gone bad, but was the Guild any better? In his mind it was all starting to look the same – bullying, ruthless people having power over weaker ones. He was beginning to despair of it all.

*

Harold walked to the Mason's Arms that Sunday evening with a firm step. His decision had been made; after so many decades, he was about to sever the cord which bound him to the Guild and all that it represented. He just wanted to get it over with now, knowing that he would have to endure objections and criticism. Also, in the future, he would be cold-shouldered by the other members. Cold-shouldered at the very least, he thought, with a slight shiver.

He entered the pub through the same door he had gone through on innumerable occasions, up the stairs for the last time. He paused half-way up to calm himself, then walked down the panelled corridor to the meeting room. He could hear voices inside already, talking together before the meeting. As he went in, some of the men saw him and raised a hand in greeting. Then John Miller, already seated in the Master's chair, banged his gavel to call order, and silence fell on the room. The meeting was about to begin.

Harold had decided to save his announcement until the end, but when the item about new members came up, John Miller addressed him personally, "Harold! What have you got to tell us about your conversations with your son about become a member of the Guild?" Everyone looked at Harold, waiting for him to answer.

"Since you raise this issue..." he was about to say, as was his habit, 'Master' but the word stuck in his mouth – he could no longer address this strange young man as his master, it seemed ridiculous, and wrong.

He started again, "Since you ask me about membership, I have an announcement to make." He stood up. "I resign my membership of this Guild."

There was a moment or two of complete silence while the others took in what he had said, then an outbreak of shock and protest.

Miller banged hard with his gavel. "We demand an explanation for this," his voice threatening and harsh.

"I have recently begun to see that the Guild's way is not compatible with being a Christian."

"Who's told you that? Is it that vicar? He seems to be a disturbing influence in this place."

Now Miller looked at Harold, his head slightly on one side, a smile playing on his lips, speaking as though to a child, "But you seem to have forgotten your oath."

Miller stood up, the insincere smile replaced by a harder look. He picked up the rod and held it upright in his right hand. "As Master, it is my duty to hold all the brotherhood together. Brothers, you have heard one of us express his intention to break his oath. The senior members will meet with me, and I will give my judgement about this." He turned to George Wright and whispered to him. Wright nodded to him and whispered back apparently about some point of the disciplinary code.

Miller turned back and spoke gravely to Harold, "Harold Williams, according to our rules you must leave this meeting immediately and are forbidden to return unless and until summoned by the Guild."

Fred watched as the elderly man, visibly shaking with the stress of facing the hostility which was emanating from John Miller and the other members, bowed his head and walked towards the door. Fred was astonished that a senior member would ever make this decision. Couldn't Harold continue going to church and be a Guild member at the same time?

After Harold's departure the meeting continued with a sense of excitement about it, the members energised by the spectacle of discipline being meted out. They all wanted to know what would happen next. Although in the past they had shown respect and even affection towards Harold, this evaporated once they realised he was breaking ranks with them; they felt a sense of betrayal, even outrage. Harold was now an outsider.

When they got to the 'Any other business' part of the agenda, Fred timidly raised his hand.

"May I ask a question?" he enquired.

All the eyes in the room fixed on him, still the newest and therefore most junior member.

Miller nodded.

"Firstly, may I take the opportunity to thank the brothers here for their interest and support in the building development I represent. My company hopes that even more opportunities for mutual advancement will arise as the work continues." There were murmurs of approval round the room. "But my question is, would any members be able to shine a light on something I have been told about – that someone in Netherton is objecting to the development, and trying to stop it?"

There were looks of surprise, and Mike Small looked very annoyed.

John Miller looked round the large table, "Does any member know anything about this?"

Mike Small spoke up, "As far as I'm concerned, everything is going ahead as planned. I'm involved myself and I believe other members are going be in various ways as the development continues. Even you, Master, have expressed a personal interest."

"Anyone heard of a protest group against it?"

Around the room there was shaking of heads.

"Only Fred Roland has heard then of just one objector?" This time there were nods.

Miller looked thoughtful, "Maybe it's the vicar again."

Fred thanked the meeting. At least he knew now that it was unlikely that a group existed who were going to cause trouble, more likely it was just the one old person the Haliwells' solicitor had told his boss about. Arnold would be pleased to hear this.

*

The inner circle met straight after the meeting ended. As usual, they pulled the armchairs around the fire at the end of the room. George Wright poured more wine for them all, having gone back downstairs to the bar to check that everything was under control – he had reluctantly asked Rob Beccles to watch over the bar while he was upstairs.

Miller got to the point quickly, "Harold Williams. What shall we do about him?" It wasn't a genuine question, more a joking sneer. Ever since the unseemly struggle he'd had with Harold over the leadership of the Guild, Miller had wanted to have some measure of revenge. Even though Miller had won the position of Master, he still resented that Harold had resisted him.

Wright asked, "Shall I read out a case from the past that is similar to this?"

He fetched a leather-bound book from the Guild's box and brought it with a reverential air over to where the others sat, then turned back through the thick pages to a time when another member had wanted to leave the Guild.

"Edward Leighton," he read, "declared to the meeting of the Guild on the night of 29th November 1791 that he no longer wished to attend meetings. His wife, who is a Methodist, objects to him 'belonging to unholy meetings' and has pleaded with him to desist. On account of her poor health, he says he must accord with her request."

George Wright ran his finger down the page and read out a paragraph, "Meeting of the Inner Circle 30th November 1791 to discuss discipline regarding Edward Leighton. Master's judgement: that the full consequence of the breaking of the oath remains." At this point Wright returned to the table, where the large book in which all Guild meetings were recorded lay. He turned back, over two hundred years, to the time of Edward Leighton, skimming through the record of Guild meetings just after November 1791. When he got to the meeting dated 27th December he read again, "It is noted that past member Edward Leighton died on 20th December after falling through the ice formed on the river."

The others listened intently, and nodded, then one after another spoke about the binding nature of the oath, and that to depart from it in any way would be to turn their backs on the nature of the Guild. The safety and sacredness of their bond would be broken unless they adhered to what they had solemnly promised. All would be at risk if the absolute loyalty of the brotherhood was breached.

"We are all of one mind then, gentlemen?" asked Miller, sounding quite calm and civil.

They agreed that they were. Two must be chosen then, to carry out the judgement. They all nodded again. Then Mike Small said quietly, "I am willing. If you want, I am sure Geoff will be the second."

George Wright looked at him, "Are you sure Crawshaw is strong enough for this?"

Small looked taken aback, "Of course, Geoff is solid as houses."

The Master held out his hand to Small and shook it. "Your offer is accepted."

*

Late that night a police car drove into Netherton to check all was quiet following the recent incidents in the area. They were driving down a dark lane when they noticed an orange glare behind a row of houses. What was it? They slowed down and lowered the car window on that side – the smell of burning was unmistakable. One of the officers put a call through to the fire and ambulance services while they sped to find the source of the fire, which was burning more fiercely now, the flames leaping above the level of the rooftops of nearby houses. They turned on their blue light and siren, alerting the neighbourhood to the danger as they neared the burning house, and screeched to a halt outside. Between them they managed to force open the front door, releasing a belch of thick smoke. Ducking down and holding their breath they managed to penetrate a few feet into the little entrance hall as the fire seemed to be at the back of the house. They could just see the outline of a figure lying on the floor near the door, clearly the poor soul had been trying to get out. The two officers each grabbed the man by the shoulders of his dressing-gown and dragged him out, pulling him a safe distance away – there was no time to do it nicely. Then one of them knelt down next to him to see if he was breathing. They rolled him into the recovery position, and then heaved a sigh of relief when they heard an ambulance in the distance. The man seemed to be breathing shallowly – he must have inhaled a lot of smoke.

The neighbours were out on the street now, one of them telling the police that only one old man lived in the burning house, and that his name was Harold Williams.

Chapter Twenty-Six

Although it was only two days before Christmas, the Bluebird building looked no different from the rest of the year. No staff Christmas party was planned, and the workers had been instructed that if they wanted to put decorations up in offices they must stay after working hours to do so. Arnold Wheeler had stipulated that Christmas bonuses would be reserved for a small number of staff who had completed certain special tasks on a very limited timescale. He'd announced that there was no reason to give rewards to people who were only doing what they were paid to do. There were all expected to work until five o'clock on Christmas Eve as though it was any other Friday.

On 23rd December Wheeler sent a cryptic message to Martin Fielding: *Expecting report that desired outcome has been completed within timeframe. Bonus dependent on this. AW.*

Fielding read it sombrely. He knew he had not fulfilled AW's expectations. The success of the Netherton project still depended on him "fixing" the possible obstacle. The previous day he had contacted Alan Kirton to check if all was continuing to move forward on the legal side, bearing in mind the call Kirton had received recently from the old woman in Netherton. Kirton replied that he was glad Fielding had phoned – he had been meaning to contact Mr Wheeler shortly about an unexpected visit he'd had, by two women, one elderly and one rather attractive young woman. They said they wanted to express their concern about the sale of the land on which the old church of St Brannock's stood, and implied that things had not proceeded in the correct way. They wanted him to take note of this and inform the present owner of the land before the sale was complete. The older woman had reminded him of a phone call she had made to him but wanted reassurance that he would act.

Martin Fielding had no doubt as to the identities of the two, and both were major causes of frustration in his life. He hadn't been aware that they knew each other, but it struck him that of course they did, connected through the church. He swore under his breath, then said, "But the sale is complete, isn't it? You haven't taken any notice of them?"

"No, of course not, Mr Fielding – my fee is being paid by Bluebird Design and Construction. I can't afford to get involved in politics – a luxury as far as I'm concerned. I am just waiting to hear a final time from the Americans, and it's signed, sealed and delivered."

"It sounds like it's still not quite in the bag."

"It needs a final signature, which we will do electronically, synchronising both parties."

"So it still could go wrong."

"Highly unlikely at this stage. No, it's more that you may have a possible protestors group forming around the older woman. I did warn Mr Wheeler about this before. But if all proceeds as planned, they'll all simmer down over Christmas, and by New Year it will all be history."

Fielding cursed himself for not acting sooner. He should never have allowed things to drift, he'd wasted time, with his mind on other things, and now things were messy.

*

That same afternoon a feeling of excitement swept over Hilda as she enjoyed her afternoon tea. She was thinking about all the other Friends of St Brannock's, some spread across the world, connected together although separated by so many miles, praying for the saving of the church and the land it stood on. She smiled and then decided to go up the hill to pray. She could imagine herself standing by the high cross up on the hill next to the church, its lichen-covered stone worn by centuries of strong winds and rain, still bearing witness over the area to truth and light and the love of Jesus Christ. The daylight would fade before long, but there would just be enough time.

She hurried to get ready, leaving her tea unfinished. She was eager to get there; soon she was going along the street to the river. When she arrived at the riverbank she walked along it a few yards, looking down at the water. The Ishka is swollen again, she thought, the water level is very high. She looked across into the distance to where the labourers were. They had moved to the far end of the land, she could barely see them, just small smudges. Then she looked up the hill towards the little church. *I must be quick; I can't stand here gazing any longer.* Something in the silver-grey water caught her attention and she leant forward – was it a fish? Engrossed in the moment she was unaware of footsteps behind her until it was too late. She felt a sharp push in the centre of her back, sending her toppling forward, pitching into the cold grey water below. Within seconds the cold gurgling water of the river enveloped her, forcing her frail body under, pulling her downstream, under the bridge and away. She surfaced again, gasping, aware that she was being dragged away. The river was taking her round the wide bend skirting the land where St Brannock's stood, and for a second she caught a glimpse upwards of the high cross, before she was pulled under the cold water again. As the light from the surface above her head became dimmer, she inwardly called out, Jesus— I am coming to you! The swirling grey torrent started to recede from her, and warmth began to embrace her as she was drawn towards another light.

*

Oliver walked along the High Street, thinking about the vicar's last visit to his school. He liked Reverend Gilchrist because he was kind and didn't tell people off. In his years at Netherton Primary School he'd had been told off countless times, which didn't bother him too much but very often mystified him, as most of the time he couldn't make sense of the rules which he was always being accused of breaking. The vicar, however, was never cross and quite often said something interesting, like last time he came into school, when he talked about how God has made beautiful things all around us, and why don't you take a photograph of a beautiful thing, and we'll have a competition. Oliver was heading for the riverbank because trees and water were things which the vicar had said were very beautiful and were good things to take photographs of.

There were no other children with him because they were all in school – he was off sick with a sore throat and should have been watching the television while his mother slipped out to the supermarket, *just for one hour*, she had told him. *Just sit there and watch a programme and I'll be back.* He had done exactly that, sitting there watching a cartoon, until he remembered the photograph competition. Straightaway he took his mobile phone, his very best Christmas present ever, and thought he had just enough time to get some photographs before his mother returned. It was his last chance to enter the competition, as it was meant to be a New Year competition and the children were supposed to have done it over the holiday.

The grass was encrusted with white frost as he slid down the steep side of the river gorge to see if he could get a photograph of the river. He knew he ought to be careful, as they'd been told at the beginning of the term, just two days ago, about the nice old lady who had fallen in the river. They all knew Miss Marshall because she used to come into school and teach the pupils how to sew. The children wrote prayers and messages which were going to be read out at the funeral next week.

The mother of one of the girls in his class had told her that Miss Marshall had been carried away from the village and found further downstream. He thought about it – would it have been exciting to be floating away on the fast river? Perhaps in the summer, he thought, but not when the water was freezing cold. He walked along the side of the river looking around. It was muddy, but over the Christmas holiday it had frozen hard. He wondered where she fell in. It could have been near here, he thought, then felt very sad, perhaps she had slipped and tried to hang on to something, and shouted for help, and nobody came. Perhaps it would be nice to take a beautiful photograph of the last place Miss Marshall had been, a happy memory, not a sad one, and he could write a message on it. He looked for any signs that she had been there, then saw some muddy skid marks in the frozen mud, as though someone's feet had scraped along, and next to them a footprint. It could be hers, he thought, and took a photograph. He looked at it on the screen of his phone, then back again at the footprint. It was a good photograph, but it wasn't really Miss Marshall's footprint, he thought, it was much too big, she had very small feet, he remembered.

The next day Oliver was back at school, eager to give in his photograph for the competition. All of the other entries were in days ago. "Where is it then?" asked his teacher sighed, irritated. He handed her his mobile phone.

"Oliver, you are supposed to hand in an actual photograph. I can't enter your phone into the competition. Anyway, you're not allowed to have phones in school. I should ring your mother up about this."

"No don't!"

The teacher looked at his pale anxious face. He was an unusual boy, often in a world of his own, slightly detached from what the other children were doing. Perhaps it would be good for him to be in this competition, although she doubted whether he had much chance of winning, "Quickly then, show me what you've got, and we'll try to print the best one out."

He showed her the photo gallery on the phone's screen. At first all she could see was some shots of muddy grass.

"It's where Miss Marshall fell into the river," he said earnestly. "Oliver that's far too sad and upsetting to go into our competition. The photos are supposed to be of beautiful things – trees, the sky, things like that."

"But the river is in it, and lots of grass and bushes."

She bent towards him whispered, "Well as long as you don't name it as the place where Miss Marshall slipped into the river. I hope they'll put a fence up now – it's too dangerous to go down there." She paused for a moment, a thought suddenly striking her, "How did you get this photograph? Did you go down to the river on your own?"

He felt trapped – whatever he said he was going to be in trouble.

The teacher put his phone down on her desk, "I don't think we can use this photograph. And I am definitely going to speak to your mother."

Oliver dropped his head, disappointed. "Sorry Miss, I just thought it would be interesting."

She lowered her voice, beginning to lose patience, "I'm not sure we should be too *interested* in how Miss Marshall died. We just need to be sad about it – she was a lovely lady, and I just wish she hadn't been all on her own... perhaps someone could have helped her, and this awful accident would never have happened."

He looked hopeful again, "But she wasn't on her own – someone was with her."

She looked at him thoughtfully thinking again what a strange little boy he was – what on earth was he thinking about now? "What do you mean? You weren't there Oliver – how do you know anything about it?"

He picked up his phone again. "I've got another photograph that proves it!" He sounded pleased – perhaps this would show her the photograph was worth keeping.

She looked at the next photograph on the little screen. "It's a footprint," she said, "That's all it is."

He pointed at the screen, "And skid marks. The footprint is too big for Miss Marshall – she had little feet – I saw them when she was teaching me to sew."

His teacher took the phone out of his hand, "I'll need to keep this for a while. I'll let you have it back soon."

"Am I in trouble Miss?"

"No. I don't know how you got these photographs but you're right, they are very interesting. You're a good boy, you've done well. I shall show these to the headteacher.

Oliver glowed with pride – it was a welcome change from what adults generally said to him.

Chapter Twenty-Seven

The day of Hilda's funeral arrived with a cloudless blue sky. Friends and nephews and nieces gathered in Netherton Parish Church. Only the memorial service was to be held that day – the burial itself was to be delayed as Hilda had written in her will that she would like her body to be buried next to St Brannock's Church. The service was a sweet mixture of gratitude and love for this beautiful soul, shot through with the pain of parting, particularly for Morag, whose life would never be the same without the company of her dearest friend.

James led the service with sensitivity and tenderness, thinking what a privilege it was to lead a memorial service giving thanks for a life so full of faith in the love of Jesus.

The church was full, some people having flown in the previous day from other countries, mainly long-time Friends of St Brannock's. Nobody noticed the figure who slipped in just after the service had started and sat in the furthest corner of the church, wearing a leather jacket over a hooded top, which remained pulled forward obscuring the man's face, preventing anyone from recognizing him if they had turned round during the service. No one did however, and the man sat without moving, listening to the eulogy. At one point he reached into an inside pocket of his jacket and pulled out a piece of paper and looked at it. It was a cheque for a large amount of money. After a while he left as quietly as he had come, unnoticed by the mourners.

*

The following day, Morag was up earlier than usual. She ate her breakfast without putting on the radio to listen to the morning news. She didn't want any distractions, anything that may take her attention off what she was about to do. She put her winter coat on and a felt hat, adjusting it in front of the mirror. She looked at her face as she did so and spoke to herself, "Come on, Morag, don't weaken, this is the right thing, and you're not on your own." At this thought, tears welled up in her eyes as she felt very alone at that moment. As she walked towards the door she prayed, *come with me, Lord, don't let me feel alone as I walk into that place.*

There was no frost or ice that morning, so she got straight into her car and turned on the engine, having a last look at the page of directions which she had with her – she had printed this off from the internet last night – the directions for the offices of Bluebird Design and Construction.

Forty-five minutes later, Morag arrived at the Bluebird building. She drove to the front of the car park, near to the entrance doors and parked her car next to a large sleek Bentley. She said under her breath, I think I can guess who that must belong to. Although her knees were shaking, Morag got out of her car without hesitation and went in through the double doors and up to the reception desk. The girl behind the desk looked at her, surprised to see this elderly lady coming into their building – she must have lost her way, she thought. Morag put her gloved hand on the edge of the desk, partly to steady herself, "Now, dear, tell me where I can find the boss."

The receptionist looked shocked, unsure how to handle this. There was no way Mr Wheeler would agree to see someone like this. He would be very angry if she let her through.

"I'm sorry, Mr Wheeler isn't here this morning."

"Really? Whose car is that then?" demanded Morag sharply.

The girl hesitated, "Not his," she said unconvincingly.

At that moment someone else arrived, coming through the doors looking flustered, carrying an armful of large sheets of paper. He hurried over to the desk, "Morning, Becky, has Mr Wheeler been in the boardroom long? I've been on site and now I'm late." He looked stressed.

"About half an hour, Mr Patterson."

"Oh no," said Ed Patterson, and almost ran towards the lift, clutching his plans, then came back to the desk. "Becky, could you be an angel and run to my office and get Sophie to bring the Netherton plans up."

Paterson rushed to the lift and pressed the button for Floor 2.

The receptionist looked at Morag, "Could you just wait a minute? I'll be back." She left the desk and disappeared down a corridor. Morag walked over to the lift and pressed the button for Floor 2. There were a few moments' delay while the lift returned, but when the receptionist came back to her desk a minute later there was no sign of the old lady, and she presumed she had left the building.

The lift door opened on the second floor and Morag walked out of it and looked at the doors in front of her. She knew now where he was – in the boardroom. It was the last door she came to. She didn't knock, she opened the door and walked in. What she saw on entering the room was a group of six people sitting round a conference table. The man at the top of the table looked up, a look of amusement on his face as he saw the elderly person come in. "What's this?" he shouted in her direction, "This isn't *Help the Aged* in here you know!" The people round the table laughed nervously, looking from their boss to this person who had evidently stumbled into their meeting. Then Wheeler's tone changed, "This place seems to be turning into a shambles – my architect can't be bothered to get to meetings on time and now the reception staff are letting in tramps and strays!"

This was probably the best way Wheeler could have helped Morag – his insult served to give her the adrenaline she needed. She walked up to the conference table and put her handbag squarely down on the table in front of her. "Arnold Wheeler, if you were a gentleman, you would have offered me a seat, but I know that to insult people is your way of dealing with everyone. You are a nasty little man with no principles at all. I have come to give you a message."

"Get security!" shouted Wheeler. "Get this bag lady out of here before she ruins the carpet!" He pressed a button on the phone on the table and yelled into it.

Morag was undaunted. The people round the table stared at her, aghast at her audacity. Wheeler was on his feet, leaning over the table, red-faced.

She said steadily, her eyes fixed on him, "Here's what I've come to say to you: my dear friend Hilda, who is now dead, was not frightened of you, and neither am I. You think you can get away with anything, you think you have won, but I can tell you, you will lose." She gestured around the table, "You think you have all the power, with your swanky cars and big bank accounts and connections, but there are some good people who are standing up for what's right, and God will help us!"

At this point a security guard burst into the room, expecting to tackle a violent intruder. He looked around, seeing only a tall well-dressed elderly lady. He hesitated, unsure what to do. He watched as she said sternly to Arnold Wheeler, "I am not afraid of *you*, Arnold Wheeler!" Then she picked up her handbag and walked out of the door.

When Morag got back into the sanctuary of her own car, she realised she was shaking all over, but also pleased with what she had done. Now she wanted to see what she had just announced come true – this evil plan must be defeated, all of it, all the tangled nastiness of it.

*

James looked at his watch – almost time to go. He must allow plenty of time in the school this morning as he had both the assembly and the photograph competition to judge. A thought suddenly struck him – perhaps Anna would come with him to help with the judging – after all, she was much more artistic than he was. He called upstairs to her.

Ten minutes later they were on their way. When James and Anna went into the school hall, they could see all the children's photographs were already spread out along a line of tables, each photograph numbered and with a title. With a few minutes to spare, Anna lingered over them, studying each one. The one which immediately caught her attention was an unusual one of the riverbank. The title was *For Miss Marshall*. Like all the entries, it had a little prayer of thanks attached, as this was part of the aim of the competition. This prayer was: *Dear God, thank you for Miss Marshall who was very kind and helped us.*

Anna smiled sadly as she read it – how right the sentiment was. But what a strange photograph.... She looked again, noticing the muddy marks on the wet riverbank, then suddenly realised what she was looking at. It was plain to see – skid marks where someone's heels had dragged along the ground as they moved through the mud towards the river, and a clear footprint behind – another person. "Dad!" Anna called out, "look at this!"

Her father hurried across, hearing the alarm in her voice "What is it?"

"I think we're looking at the place where Hilda died, and I don't think it looks like an accident."

James agreed, and asked to speak to the class teacher of the child who had taken the picture. She looked a little embarrassed when James and Anna raised the subject of the photo, "I did ask the headteacher about it, about whether we should call the police, but she thought I was being a bit... over-imaginative."

"Good heavens," James commented, "I think it's your absolute duty to report this, to not withhold information about a possible crime."

The teacher lowered her voice, "Would you mind telling Mrs Morris yourself? She seemed adamant about not wanting to get the school involved in anything *unpleasant*."

James looked extremely irritated and went immediately to tackle Mrs Morris himself, muttering, "More weirdness, this really has to stop – this village has got to start getting straightened out."

James told the school's headteacher that he would speak to the police himself as he was the Chair of the school governors. Two police officers arrived within the hour to interview James, the class teacher, and Oliver, whose mother was also called into school. The photograph was taken away by the police for closer examination and a forensic team dispatched to search the riverbank.

That evening, another of the Friday evening prayer meetings was held. These had continued ever since Hilda had put posters up in the village. It seemed like a very long time since the journey of persistent prayer had begun. Tonight was to be a longer time of prayer than usual. Following the discovery of the photograph, James had felt moved to increase their prayer further. He had asked Morag to contact the Friends of St Brannock's and invite them to come to this Friday's extended prayer – a Prayer Vigil, he called it, a whole night of prayer that things should finally be dealt with – for justice and for rescue and protection. The violence must stop, and only through prayer, he believed, just as Hilda had counselled, would God's power be released.

James was not concerned whether anyone else stayed the whole night to pray, if people could just keep the vigil as much as they were able. He found, however, that as the night progressed, there were always several people in the church praying. Some went home for an hour's sleep, then returned in the early hours to join in with the flow of prayer again. When dawn came, Anna and Meg made everyone breakfast. In fact, there had been cups of tea available throughout the night, partly to stop people freezing in the cold church, despite the heating being turned up as far as it would go. But now, as the sun began to warm the stained-glass windows, the smell of toast filled the church as eggs were boiled in a pan of water on a camping stove set up in the back of the church and Jonah and James set up two long tables for the people to come and sit down to breakfast together. They were all tired, not just through hours of sleep missed, but also, as Hilda would have said, because prayer is work. The atmosphere was of warm fellowship, and boiled eggs with buttered toast had never tasted so good.

Afterwards, they all cleared up together, then went home enriched by the hours spent together in prayer, hopeful that they would see good come of it, and grateful that today was Saturday.

The day was spent peacefully, but when Sunday arrived, the phone started ringing before it was properly light outside. It was the County Police. They had some grim news. A man's body had been found, an apparent suicide, but they believed there was a connection to recent events in Netherton which James had contacted them about in his role of Chair of Governors at the local primary school. They wanted to arrange a time to come to the vicarage. As James finished the call, he decided he would not tell Anna about it until after the morning service. She noticed, however, that her father was much quieter than usual.

"Don't worry about me, Anna, I'm just thinking hard."

"Like to share your deep thoughts?" she teased.

"I just need to concentrate on this morning's service. Other things can wait."

Anna nodded, looking at him curiously, "I guess I can wait until lunchtime," she said.

At lunchtime, the police were on the doorstep before they had had the chance to get some lunch. James showed them into the study and introduced them to his daughter. "My daughter is aware of recent events in Netherton," he said, indicating they could speak in front of her.

"That's all right with us, Reverend Gilchrist. But I must warn you that what I'm about to say is to some extent shocking. As I indicated this morning, we were notified last night of what seems to be a suicide – a man found hanged in Exton."

"I'm sorry to hear that, but you said there was a connection with recent events in Netherton?"

"Yes, our forensics people have conducted initial examinations and have found a match between the deceased and the photographic evidence – the schoolboy's photograph – of what is now regarded as a possible crime scene, that is, the footprint on the riverbank in Netherton. The dead man's shoe, an expensive leather-soled one, is a match."

James and Anna were both silent for a minute, taking it in. Then Anna said shakily, "Do you have a description of the man?"

"Yes indeed, about thirty years old, dark hair, expensive clothes. A strange thing, he had a cheque in his pocket for a very large sum of money. The name on the cheque was Martin Fielding."

Anna was already running from the room, her hand over her mouth.

The police officer apologised for any upset caused to the young lady – did she know the man?

James said yes, they both knew him a little.

Soon the police left, but not before the senior officer remarked, "I notice we had a call-out to this address quite recently, didn't we sir? An intruder. I'm sorry, you seem to be having a difficult time at the moment, don't you?"

"Yes indeed," said James, "But we are hoping things are going to be getting better."

"We may need a statement from you in due course, sir, since you knew the person. Thank you for your help."

Anna was sitting in the kitchen looking pale. She looked up at her father as he came into the room, "Suicide – I can hardly believe it. And his footprint – does that mean...?"

"We'll see. So many awful things have happened, but perhaps things have been coming to a head. We mustn't be frightened." He took her hand in his and patted it. "Martin was a very strange unhappy man – we know that now."

The doorbell rang. Anna jumped, "Oh no, what now?"

It was a surprise visitor – Morag.

Anna heard her bright Scottish voice reverberating down the hallway as she waited in the kitchen to see who had arrived.

"I'm so sorry to disturb you – you probably get little enough time to rest, but I simply had to show you something."

James felt a twist of apprehension – he thought he had already had sufficient revelations over the last couple of days – what on earth was Morag going to say? She held out an envelope to him, "Read this."

He looked at the postage mark. It was from Colorado, USA. He took out the letter and read:

Dear Hilda, and all the Friends of St Brannock's,

First let me thank you for all that you are doing in looking after the lovely old pilgrims' church in Netherton. Despite the fact that we Haliwells have owned the land, and the church, for generations, I am afraid the burden of responsibility rests on your shoulders as we are so many thousands of miles away. Your love and dedication are quite wonderful. In recent times I have wondered how much longer the Friends could be relied on for such selfless work. In relation to this, when I was approached by what seemed to be a community-minded company who wanted to be the protectors of St Brannock's, to safeguard its future, I thought this could be a perfect way forward. How wrong I was - their promises were empty ones; I see that now. I have spoken to my lawyer here, who will stop the sale from being completed. A representative of our family will come shortly to ascertain what damage has been done, and, with your advice, will arrange for it to be put right and discuss how to secure proper provision for the continued witness of the pilgrims' church.

As for your concerns about the workers working illegally on the land, we are in contact with the appropriate authorities to take immediate action against Bluebird Design and Construction.

I will be in touch with you again,
Your sister in Christ,
Elise
Elise Haliwell

James looked up from the letter, "This is wonderful news, Morag.'

"It arrived yesterday at Hilda's cottage. I went in to do the dusting, you know, to look after things for her."

James put his arm round her shoulders for a moment – despite the tough exterior, Morag was only just managing to hold on to the tears which were threatening to burst through the dam of her self-restraint. "You were a wonderful friend to her, still are."

Her voice broke for a moment, "I do expect to see her again you know; I believe that."

"Quite right too, we will see our loved ones again, united together."

Morag sniffed, gathering herself together again. "And another thing, I went to see the boss of Bluebird."

"You did?"

"Yes, and I told him he won't get away with it, no matter how many people he threatens. Sometimes I think that rotten company has been behind a lot of terrible things."

"Now we have this letter, we know their plans will be stopped, thank God. A lot has happened since the Friday night prayer vigil, and all the other times of prayer, and now things are moving in the right direction."

Morag wouldn't stay for a sandwich with them, she said she must let the Friends know, and she was going to send a copy of the letter directly to Arnold Wheeler, she said. They had asked God for justice, and here it was.

Chapter Twenty-Eight

Later in January, on the appointed afternoon, a large number of people in Netherton were walking through the streets. They passed the Mason's Arms, a closure sign displayed on it, alongside a For Sale board. It was the end of an era – the clandestine meetings which had been held there for so long had been brought to an abrupt finish. The police had searched the building following the disappearance of George Wright, discovering written evidence of criminal activity, recorded in the books of the Guild. Despite the coded nature of the records, the police found enough to link members of the Guild to various crimes, including the fire at Harold's house. Arrests of several Guild members followed, the shackles of secrecy and intimidation finally broken. Those who had escaped prosecution now denied all knowledge of the Guild. John Miller was arrested and charged with conspiracy to murder and with ordering various acts of violence. He was not granted bail while awaiting sentencing.

On walked the people, along the High Street, past the row of cottages, heading on towards the river. As James waited by the river watching more people arrive, he felt pleasantly surprised. He had expected the faithful members of the congregation to make every effort to come and hoped that once again many members of the Friends of St Brannock's would travel there. But the fact that the whole village was turning out, having heard by word of mouth that this special service of blessing was to be held, was particularly gratifying. The throng of people gathered on the new bridge and on the far side of the river where they could get a clear view of proceedings.

James was wearing his vestments, not because he felt this was necessary, but because he thought it may add additional solemnity to what they were about to do, especially perhaps for those who were new to the whole notion that the prayers of Christian people should be taken seriously.

When everyone had found somewhere to stand, James spoke with a loud voice so they could all hear him, "Welcome, everybody, to this spot by the River Ishka. Thank you for coming. It's important that we are here to bless this place. As you know, this is where one of our own beloved people spent her last few moments on this earth before going to be with the Lord. Hilda would not have wanted us to continue associating this place with sorrow, or anyone to regard this river as somehow not good. So we are going to dedicate it to God, from this day forward."

There was a murmur of assent from the crowd. Some drops of cold rain started to fall. James was undaunted, refusing to be distracted by how things might be if there was a sudden downpour of freezing rain. He knew what to do – he raised his voice further, thinking of Jesus as he stood up in the boat and calmed the storm. "So, in the holy and powerful name of Jesus Christ we pray—" He stretched out his hand over the side of the bridge, so it extended over the grey water below.

"The blessing of God Almighty, The Father, the Son and the Holy Spirit be upon you and remain with you.

May the Spirit of God bring you healing and peace,

May God drive all darkness from you,

And pour upon you blessing and light."

He looked around at the people present, seeing them watching intently.

"We dedicate this river in the Name of Jesus Christ. Father God, by the power of your Holy Spirit, present here with us now, we pronounce these waters holy. We speak peace to you, river, that you will reflect the peace and beauty of God who created everything that exists."

A sense of peace passed over the crowd – nobody made a sound, not even the toddlers. The January sky lightened, and a patch of blue sky appeared.

James spoke again, "I'd like to invite you to do something which we do in church sometimes – it's called the sign of peace. I say some words about God's peace, and then you, if you would like to, greet somebody, passing on that peace. You could say to them "The Peace of the Lord be with you," and maybe shake their hand."

Then he said the closing words, "Christ is our peace. If anyone is in Christ, they are a new creation.

The old has passed away, the new has come. The Peace of the Lord be always with you. Now let us give each other the sign of peace."

All around him, people repeated, some for the first time, "The Peace of the Lord be with you." James watched with satisfaction as this sizeable portion of Netherton, until recently a place of trouble and violence, expressed peace and blessing. He looked at his daughter, standing near him and noticed how close she was standing to Jonah. As he watched, Jonah put his arm around her. He smiled – what a wonderful day. He saw Harold Williams shaking the hands of other members of the Friends, even receiving hugs from them, and Barbara Morton slip her arm through her husband's affectionately.

James would have liked to exchange the sign of peace with Meg, but she was several feet away from him, so he gave up the idea of reaching her, and waved to Morag who was with a group of friends. He looked again at the river – it really did look calmer and clearer – there was a sparkle in the water that he was sure had not been there before. As he looked, someone put a hand on his arm, "That was lovely, James, and powerful – you can sense that the river really is going to rest in God's peace now." She looked at him steadily, "the Peace of the Lord be with you," and she kissed his cheek. He looked into Meg's eyes, "And with you," he said tenderly.

Discussion Questions for Book Groups / Study Groups
1. In *Vigil*, members of the local church, especially Hilda, recognised there were spiritual forces at the root of the troubles of the village. The church found it had the power to resist and expel those forces. Do Christians today believe their local church could do the same? Ref. Mark 16:17-18, Acts 5:16
2. Hilda believed the pilgrim church of St Brannock was a holy place because of all the years of prayer which had happened there. Do you think physical things can have spiritual power associated with them? Ref. Acts 19:12
3. The Bible has many examples of demonised people – are some people still in that state today? Ref. Acts 16:18. Hilda felt confident about her ability to deal with such people – would you feel as confident? Ref. Luke 10:1-17
4. Before James and Anna went to pray for Mary's healing, James wanted them to pray together, to "clear the decks," he said. What did he mean by that? Ref. James 5:16, James 4:7
5. Harold felt so much better after Hilda had prayed for him. What had happened to him? Can Christians belong to secret societies without compromising their professed faith in Jesus Christ? Ref. Matthew 6:24
6. The Bible speaks of spiritual strongholds – in *Vigil* the Miller family, the Guild, and Bluebird Construction all seem to have become bases for evil spiritual forces – are we willing to think that some institutions and groups known to us may have to be opposed because of what power lies behind them? Ref. Ephesians 6:12, 2 Corinthians 10:4

297

BV - #0011 - 090822 - C0 - 229/152/17 - PB - 9781913181819 - Gloss Lamination